African Folktales

Pantheon Fairy Tale and Folklore Library

Also by Roger D. Abrahams

Afro-American Folktales: Stories from Black Traditions in the New World

African Folktales

Traditional Stories of the Black World

Selected and Retold by
Roger D. Abrahams

PANTHEON BOOKS
NEW YORK

Published in the United States by Pantheon Books, a division of Random House, Inc., New York, and simultaneously in Canada by Random House of Canada Limited, Toronto.

Library of Congress Cataloging in Publication Data
Main entry under title:

African folktales.
(Pantheon Fairy Tale and Folklore Library)
Bibliography: p.
Includes index.
1. Tales—Africa, Sub-Saharan. I. Title.
GR350.A348 1983 398.2'096
83-2474
ISBN 0-394-50236-1
0-394-72117-9 (pbk.)
Permissions Acknowledgments follow Bibliography.

Manufactured in the United States of America

B9876543210

Book Design by Ray Hooper

For Janet

Three storytellers met one day and began to tell stories. Each of them thought that he could excel the others. The first man said, "I will tell you the story of what I saw."

"One day I went into the field and saw two birds fighting. One bird swallowed the other, and then in turn was swallowed by the other bird, so that the two birds swallowed each other."

The next one said, "One day I was going out to the field and I saw a man on the road who had cut off his own head and had it in his mouth eating it."

The third man said, "I was going to a big town and I saw a woman coming from the town with a house, a farm, and all her things on her head. I asked the women where she was going, and she told me she had heard news that she had never heard before. I asked her what it was. The woman said she had heard the news that one man cut off his head and had it in his mouth eating it, so I was afraid and left the town. The woman passed and I went on."

Who told the biggest story?

Table of Contents

Preface

To attempt to put a representative selection of the tales of Black Africa in a single work may seem futile to those who know the subcontinent. Like any such huge geographical region, there is a tremendous range of size, character, and complexity in the societies and cultures of Africa—a range that runs from the elegant and sophisticated ancient city cultures to the forest and desert peoples, who continue to live by the simplest hunting-and-gathering techniques. Immense kingdoms and nations coexist with very small bands, all with their own deep and venerable traditions.

One of the greatest social and cultural achievements of all times came about in the subcontinent, when a great gardening people, within a few thousand years, brought a major portion of it under cultivation. Their accomplishment reflects the high value such an agricultural economy places on land and large expanding families.

But Black Africa includes numerous kinds of wandering peoples: small bands like the forest people of the Ituri and the desert people of the Kalahari, both constantly on the move in search of food; the pastoral nomads, who, along with their people, move huge herds in a progress of watering places; the slash-and-burn agriculturists, who regularly move whole villages as their land plays out; and that widespread contemporary phenomenon, the wage-seeking emigrants, who move to plantation or city, and sometimes even return home. Moreover, there are innumerable peoples who follow the archaic religions of the Spoken Word and equally immense numbers who follow Christ or Muhammad, with all of the cultural implications carried by such religions of the Book. Finally, there are literally thousands of different languages spoken in this area, so many, indeed, that two of the great trade languages, Creole and Swahili, developed specifically as means for the various Africans to understand each other.

In the face of such diversity and the immense geographical areas covered, how could one possibly hope to make any meaningful cultural statement through the putting together of a representative anthology? Fortunately, the question has been answered again and again for us, by Black Africans themselves, and by European and American observers: In spite of the range of culture-types, there are widely observable continuities, especially in the area of aesthetics, to be found in groups throughout the continent. The kinds of materials included in this anthology reveal a powerful tradition. These stories are related through their manner of performance to a number of other kinds of expression for which Black Africa is known to Westerners, especially dancing and drumming. It is a great tradition, one built on the common features of the many little traditions of those who live in the fruitful environment of close communities. As Jacques Maquet phrases it in his overview of historical and ethnographic writings, *Africanity,* a unity can be observed throughout the sub-Saharan region even by the observant traveler, a basically "cultural unity" emerging from a sense of "the totality of knowledge and behavior, ideas and objects, that constitutes [a people's] common heritage . . ." (trans: Joan Rayfield [Oxford: Oxford University Press, 1972], p. 4).

Naturally, this anthology is built on the backs of those who have observed these cultures firsthand and collected these tales in actual performance. And here the record is astonishing, for the oral repertoire of no other area of the world has been as widely reported. There are well over a thousand major collections, most of these made by missionaries and colonial officials around the turn of the century. They often reflect the bias of such reporters, but recently, more "objective" tellings have become available through the reports of anthropologists and folklorists. Of course, it was not until the advent of the tape recorder that such standards for objectivity could be really followed. Recording texts by hand is, obviously, far slower and less accurate than doing it by mechanical means, and the person doing the transcribing does tend to miss the more active details of performance. But even beyond the shortcomings of the method, it must be remembered that the missionary and the colonial administrator set down these stories with other objectives than the understanding of a culture and the place of performance within it.

The tales were first recorded in a form intended to be used either for learning the language of the subject people or for the enjoyment of an audience back home already accustomed to reading folktales. But because the folktales already known were of an especially literary type —the marvelous tales of the Grimms, the more exotic *Thousand Nights and a Night,* other Oriental tales, and later Joel Chandler Harris's collection of jocular trickster tales of the American South—the first collector-translators of African stories may have adopted the literary style already shown to excite the common reader. Or to put it in more positive terms, the great vigor, interest, and readability of these early collections of African stories emerges in some part from the conventions of style used in the existing Western popular folktale collections.

The contemporary anthologizer, facing the question of whether these early efforts reflect the tales most characteristic of the world of Black Africa, must acknowledge that they do so only in part. They represent only the kind of stories that would be told to missionaries and colonial officials or, at best, were heard by them, in the process of living among "their people." They are the most public sort of story, and moreover the kind most easily understood. But with greater study of various cultures by anthropologists—and recently by anthropologically trained Africans—it becomes ever clearer that these tales are only one segment of the African ocean of story.

Recent inventions have made it possible to record actual tale-telling sessions and probe the broad spectrum of types more satisfactorily. Through them we have learned a good deal about the performance of these fictions: who performs for whom, under what conditions, and what the stories reveal about the lives of the people they belong to. However, when tales recorded in this way are transcribed verbatim, the first thing that impresses the reader is that they are often abundantly unreadable, even boring. The text, even when translated with some sense of style, is full of the repetitions and hesitations that are the rule in an oral performance, but hardly to be expected in a written one. Fortunately, a few recent collectors have taken such problems as a challenge, and have given us translations that are not only faithful transcriptions of stories as performed, but have rendered them in a wholly readable and enjoyable style.

I have gravitated to the texts that have the greatest impact in the reading, the tales we can enjoy for themselves. (Our reaction, of course, is not of the same order and character as the involvement with oral performance in the home community.) Sometimes, it seemed that I was drawn to earlier accounts of missionaries precisely because they were not recorded as performed, but slowly dictated, or recalled, and reconstructed after a performance. Often, these are shortened texts that capture the essential plot and the moral or message of the story.

I have also not hesitated to revise, to attempt to enhance the flow of the narrative. In the older texts, revision was necessitated by clumsy language—on the one hand, too literal an attempt at translation, and, on the other, too self-consciously literary in the nineteenth century fashion. Despite my revisions, however, you will immediately detect—and I trust enjoy—the wide variance in style and language, and be able to "feel" the range of flavor in the tales, from the traditional (i.e., Western) narrative to the short pithy fable, with elements of the grotesque, the exotic, the satiric, and the bawdy all finding their proper place.

Though my hand was often hard at work on these texts, I have not tried to make them stylistically consistent. Rather, I have attempted to maintain the distinctive flavor of each, eliminating only those features that made them difficult to read and understand. Thus, the reader will encounter a wide variety of story types, told in many different "voices" and styles, some of which may seem downright strange at first.

It is primarily with texts reported from story-telling performances that wholesale revision has occasionally been called for. In an actual performance, the storyteller takes listener-knowledge of the elements of community life for granted: nearly everyone in the audience already knows the story, knows each other, and has a great deal of common experience to be drawn upon in the telling. The result of this is two-fold: The performance becomes at once overly allusive (narrative detail is decreased) and too concrete (extraneous social detail is increased). Typically, the tale-teller's commentary has little to do with the action, but a great deal to do with how the audience interprets the story and enjoys the performance. If one wishes to read these stories as a way into understanding how the Tiv live, or the Kikuyu, the Bondei, or Kipsigis, then such detail provides extremely important clues to what the group likes to take for granted, what it exclaims over or laughs at. But for the reader who wishes to enjoy these stories *as stories*, such detail is simply a hindrance.

In the introduction, I do, however, give a general explanation of the cultural context of the tales, and against that background, explain how these stories fit into the lives of those who continue to tell and listen to them. In oral cultures, storytelling is a fundamental way of codifying hard-won truths and dramatizing the rationale behind traditions. Thus, the tales will often end with "a message," a point, a truth to remember as one confronts life's problems. Told around the fireside or in the family compound, these stories would be known by everyone—except children and strangers—and are so familiar that they might merely be referred to, rather than fully retold, as a way of making a point in a conversation or an argument. They provide the sources of allusion—allusions drawn upon in orations, in the singing of the praises of a great chief, or in a taunting-song aimed at one judged to be flawed. They might even come into play in interpretating the pattern of cowry shells thrown in a divination session. In other words, they embody the inherited wisdom—social, personal, and moral—of the people whose world we see through the filter of folklore.

In transcribing and revising, I have made no attempt to include texts emerging from all situations in which stories are recounted. For example, there is a rich tradition of stories told in ceremonial settings or in celebration of past events. But, for the reasons noted above, there are not many texts available that satisfactorily illustrate these special occasions. More importantly, even where they do exist, the amount of special knowledge needed to understand the text renders it unusable for the purpose of anthologizing. I have, however, with one type of praise-song, the epic, included a major text, because its collector, Daniel Biebuyck, was able to work with the singing storyteller over a period sufficiently long to elicit the story behind the singing. Through *The Mwindo Epic* one is able to get a glimpse of one way in which stories are used beyond the single storytelling session, in a performance that extends many days.

I have also not drawn upon the legends, the genealogies, and the histories of the various African cultures. Again, histories require too much apparatus to make them understandable to the outsider, understandable in the sense of enabling the reader to recognize what of interest about them makes them memorable—and thus retellable. In the main I have drawn upon stories told as fictions, and told all the way through, not just used allusively. These are stories that are commonly told in the evening, in a public setting, and that are an important medium of entertainment and instruction.

The arrangement of this volume does attempt to base groupings on the uses of the stories rather than on the more usual criteria of form or content. However, because a great many of these stories seem strange to Western tastes, the first section, by way of introduction, is given over to a few wonder tales of the kind that Europeans and Americans are most accustomed to, but that are found here in typically African renderings. The sections that then follow are: shorter stories used to introduce a subject for moral discussions; moral stories specific to the problems of keeping family and community together (and which, therefore, might be called domestic dramas); tales told in praise of great deeds; and finally, a large section of outrageous stories, told primarily to entertain, about the antisocial doings of one or another trickster figure.

An anthology of this sort owes a tremendous debt to the hundreds of collectors and scholars who brought this material together in a meaningful way. I am especially in the debt of Harold Scheub, who brought a bright, enduring, and comprehensive order to the matter of Africa in his *African Oral Narratives, Proverbs, Riddles, Poetry & Song: An Annotated Bibliography* (Boston: G. K. Hall, 1978). An equally useful work in a more descriptive and discursive style is Ruth Finnegan's fine survey, *Oral Literature in Africa* (Oxford: Oxford University Press, 1970). Kofi Awoonor's *The Breast of the Earth* (Garden City, N.Y.: Anchor Press/Doubleday, 1975), is an African poet-anthropologist's evocation of the place of oral and written performance in his Africa. Isadore Okpewho's *The Epic in Africa* (New York: Columbia University Press, 1979), focuses just on the singing of heroic tales on the subcontinent, and he examines closely and analyses clearly a number of epic texts, both oral and written. And William Bascom's *African Dilemma Tales* (The Hague: Mouton, 1976), devoted only to that form of enigma does the job (as always) with superb thoroughness. In the more analytical vein of the tale index, so beloved of comparatist-folklorists, Africa has been well-served, if not yet so comprehensively, as Europe and India. The majority of these have been doctoral dissertations and remain unpublished. Here the documents I found myself calling on most often—all available through University Microfilms International, Ann Arbor, Michigan—were: Kenneth W. Clark's *A Motif-Index of the Folktales of Culture Area V. West Africa* (1958); Mary A Klippie's *African Folktales With the Foreign Analogues* (1938); E. Ojo Arewa's *A Classification of the*

Folktales of the Northern East African Cattle Area by Types (1966); and Winifred Lambrecht's *A Tale Type Index for Central Africa* (1967).

In addition, three review essays were of immense assistance with the forest-for-the-trees problem: Philip M. Peek's "The Power of Words in African Verbal Arts," (*Journal of American Folklore* 94 [1981]: 19–43); Dan Ben-Amos's, "Introduction: Folklore in African Society," (in *Forms of Folklore in Africa*, ed. Bernth Lindfors [Austin: University of Texas Press, 1977: pp. 1–36]); and Richard M. Dorson's "Africa and the Folklorist," (in *African Folklore*, ed. Richard Dorson [Garden City, N.Y.: Anchor Press/Doubleday, 1972: pp. 3–67]).

If this book demonstrates a bias toward the West African Kwa-complex (which includes the Yoruba, Dahomey, Bini, and Ewe peoples), it is because so many of my friends and mentors have worked in these areas: the late Melville Herskovits and William Bascom, Dan Ben-Amos, Kofi Awoonor, E. Ojo Arewa, and Robert Farris Thompson. My deepest thanks to all of these for many favors. In addition, Donald Cosentino, Robert Cancel, Daniel Biebuyck, Elizabeth Tucker, Charles Bird, Lee Haring, and Bernth Lindfors all willingly shared their insights into this vast literature, as did Veronika Görög. Peter Seitel taught me a good deal about how to study one tradition, the Haya, with both sensitivity and depth in understanding the cultural complexities. John Szwed helped me talk through many of these matters, always adding significant perception from his very special point of view. Richard Dorson, by organizing and inviting me to the African Folklore Institute, in a real sense started my thinking in this direction. And Kay Turner was my able and hard-working graduate assistant during the gestation of the work. Ronald Rassner has suggested some useful changes.

Above all, this book owes its existence to André Schiffrin and Wendy Wolf, who dreamed it up, and again and again to Wendy, and her colleague, Nan Graham, for keeping at me, and for perceptive revision and prodding, editorial and otherwise. But in the long run, this is Janet's book—for she not only talked the whole matter through, over and over, but she subtly worried it into being.

African Folktales

Introduction

One of the most common of all stories in Africa describes the encounter of a man and a human skull in the bush. Among the Nupe of Nigeria, for instance, they tell of the hunter who trips over a skull while in pursuit of game and exclaims in wonderment, "What is this? How did you get here?" "Talking brought me here," the skull replies enigmatically. Naturally the hunter is amazed and quickly runs back to his village, exclaiming about what he has found. Eventually, the king hears about this wonder and demands that the hunter take him to see it. They return to the place in the bush where the skull is sitting, and the hunter points it out to his king, who naturally wants to hear the skull's message. The hunter repeats the question: "How did you get here?" but the skull says nothing. The king, angry now, accuses the hunter of deception, and orders his head cut off on the spot. When the royal party departs, the skull speaks out, asking the hunter "What is this? How did you get here?" The head replies "Talking brought me here!"[1]

Others tell the story with an even more pointed punch line, the skull, for instance, saying, "I told you to keep your mouth shut!" To the Nupe and the many other Africans who use this story, the mere mention of the talking skull is enough to deliver its message. The punch line alone has become a proverb and is used to remind someone that uncontrolled speech is a sign of moral laxness.[2]

This strange tale is characteristically African in a variety of ways. Like many of the stories in this volume, it contrasts the village as the place of order with the bush as the locus of mystery, of destructive natural forces, even of death. It also demonstrates another of the most pervasive features of these tales: the use of them to introduce a discussion of how to act correctly. And the device of the separation of body parts is also observable in a number of the stories included here. For instance, the comic enigma tale, "Their Eyes Came Out," deals with separable eyes. In a more serious vein, the three tales in "A Competition of Lies" detail how a spirit achieved human form by borrowing parts of the body from a number of unwitting donors.

But perhaps the most interesting feature of "The Talking Skull" is not the way in which it is characteristic of other tales, but rather that it is a story about storytelling. To the reader who comes to these stories in book form, it is important to recognize that in their African settings (and in oral cultures in general), the spoken word carries great power manifested in several ways. Besides directly addressing deep matters of life, the spoken word can actually create bonds and bring about personal or social transformations—a capacity of words we tend to forget in these duplicitous times (except perhaps when the speaker is wearing robes). This potency of spoken language must be remembered when discussing tales—because tales are, in the ears of their hearers, permissible lies. As Sony Camara's Manding-informants repeatedly told him, their stories are neither a record of reality, nor pure fantasy. Though they are "stories that happened at the beginning of time," they describe things as they happen today. The tale "relates a drama which comes to a head on this side of the reality of the event. It is not a part which is definitely completed: it is an impending drama. It may burst out any time and anywhere."[3]

Stories also have specific meaning in the lives of those who tell them, referring to personal situations and to particular people. As in traditional cultures throughout the world, the performance of certain tales is associated with specific storytellers. And just as each person knows everybody else's "business"—that is, their personal stories—so everyone is presumed to know all the tales of their group's traditional repertoire. The storyteller also will assume such knowledge on the part of the audience except when it is composed exclusively of children, knowing that because the stories are all familiar, listeners will be constantly judging his or her ability to tell the tale. In short, there is continual monitoring of the telling of stories—whether of a tale or just of gossip—in a manner similar to that in which actual behavior is judged all of the time. This is the way of the small community worldwide, for the well-being of the group resides in the sharing of this kind of knowledge, through which family and friendship networks are woven into the web of community.

We tend to think of folktales as the purest of fictions, so self-contained and logical in development that they are lit from within and need no explanation. The fable and its message are one; the ideal book of folktales would need no introduction. But there are numerous reasons why these African stories cannot totally speak for themselves, reasons that exist because of the ways of storymaking and storytelling in this part of the world.

This book is a record of traditions that still live in many places in Black Africa. The stories in it find their fullest vitality in the compounds and villages that remain the living situations of a great many Africans today. There, circumstances demand that actions be fictionalized so that they may be talked about as if human behavior in general, were the subject of the tales rather than what A did to B yesterday. As in small communities throughout the world, stories have become ways in which people who know each other intimately may discuss each other without having to get overly personal. Stories operate, like proverbs, as a means of depersonalizing, of universalizing, by couching the description of how specific people are acting in terms of how people have always acted. This is the element of storytelling that we who read books and live in cities tend to discard and forget—the farther away from the village and the oral world we go, the farther behind us we leave it.

I

The Africa of our storytellers is, to begin with, an immense area, including all of the land south of the Sahara Desert. This encompasses regions of deserts, of mountains, of plateaus, of rain forests, a massive savannah, and as vast an array of coastal environments as one can encounter anyplace in the world. An area over three times the landmass of the continental United States, it is predominantly a vast plateau, with swells and basins, a plain of ancient hard rock on which a wide variety of people have wrested a living from the tropical soil. This they do in the face of the incursions of both desert and rain forest.

In the area from which these stories come, the domestication of animals and crops accounts for the food resources of the great majority of the population. The means and manner of domestication of crops and cattle, and the complexity of social arrangements differ, of course. This focus on domestication is of no little importance to an understanding of these stories, for one theme that informs and energizes them is hunger, indeed the constant threat of starvation. In tropical gardening (compared to temperate agriculture), there is no fallow winter season and no chance to build up humus and its associated nutrients in the soil. As a result, tropical lands tend to play out fairly quickly, and a community may of necessity find itself moving often to secure farmable lands. Scarcity is so dramatically threatening because many of the cultures affected by it subscribe to a world view that places a high value on potency (the Bantu's Muntu, for example); they constantly monitor the relationship between family and community resources—how many hands can be counted upon to help—and responsibilities—how many mouths must be fed. The anxiety is intensified during times of drought, but every year brings a time of want before the harvest comes in.

Nothing strains the web of culture so much as the threat of starvation. We see such matters under constant discussion throughout these tales. Bonds are repeatedly strained or broken because someone steals food, or because children are neglected when crops fail. Therefore, no theme is more important or receives more attention, than the building of families and of friendship ties to provide that strength which, even in the face of natural disaster or perilous human responses to it, ensures a community's survival. Reading these stories, one realizes how great the achievement of family and community is, and how constantly that achievement must be recreated under test.

The intensity of feeling about family and community is reflected in the high value placed on both verbal and behavioral affirmation of traditional practices. Again and again, these stories exemplify the ways in which a parent and child should act in line with past practice, or how husband and wife would treat each other by conforming to long-approved practices.

We have already seen an example of the stress laid on custom in the story about the talking skull, where indirect emphasis on the cautionary decorum of traditional speech provides the moral center of vision. But in a great many stories the argument for maintaining a traditional practice is explicit—often, again, on the cautionary ground of what happens to those who don't keep up the tradition. Consider the grisly story of Hornbill, as told by the Wayao, which details what happens when a community member loses sight of how traditions tie its members together.

Once Hornbill lived in a village but wouldn't conform to the customs "of the people." This was not received well, especially his refusal to attend burial rites (so necessary to consign the dead to their place apart from the living). Again and again, he was asked to pay respect to the dead and accompany the funeral procession of a fellow villager. But he always refused. Then his own child died, and no one came to offer help in preparing the body or in carrying it to the grave site. Not knowing how to do it properly, Hornbill tied the body up, put it on his head, and left the house looking for the burial place. "*Ku notubwe kwas?*" (which, in fact, the Hornbill still cries), "Where are the graves?" he asked the first person he bumped into. "I don't know" was the reply. He wandered on, always asking the same question, "Where is the graveyard, the graveyard?" and always getting the same reply. Eventually, the child's body became so rotten that it began dripping down his back. He has been wandering ever since, forever searching, and asking, "Where is the graveyard, the graveyard?"[4]

The need to maintain tradition has particular resonance for the storyteller. For he is the oral weaver who, through the spell of words and action, must reassert for his audience the flexible strength of the spun threads from which the fabric of life is woven. It is a serious responsibility, one that is carried out not just in the telling and singing of tales, nor just in the other forms of verbal art like divination or speechmaking, but one that spills over even (or especially) into musical and dance performance as well. As in many cultures, these various forms of expressive display draw their energy and purpose from the same basic set of social needs and values. Within the distinctive stylistic features of each category of performance, they all carry the same simple messages about the shared concerns of community.

An African is characteristically unable to resist an opportunity for performatory display of the joys and demands of living, and opportunities for such display present themselves in surprising variety in daily life, even in areas that to a Western mind might seem less than inspiring. Collaborative activity in farming or cattle tending, for example, provides a constant topic to be explored. The work songs associated with Black Africans throughout the world most fully display the prime value of cooperation and of the coordination of energies needed to forge community. Early visitors to Africa (and Afro-America), reported astonishment at the gleaming hoes descending together in the sun, their downward and upward motion coordinated by the singing of the workers. The importance of such hoeing and singing is a central feature in one episode of the tale of "Mandu."

In the village, the question of the role of the individual in the family and community arises constantly, as does the issue of initiative in a world that must stress the subordination of individual will to the good of the group. We meet this subject again and again in story performance, and once more the theme is explained and elaborated upon by another type of performance: the work song. In these, one person does the chanting, the others respond; anyone may seize the role of song leader. Naturally it is the strong-voiced who most commonly will do this leading. But it is a role which is passed around, and one which may be contended for, as the three storytellers in "A Competition of Lies" show us. There are, within the system, then, places in which the competitive use of individual voices is encouraged. A number of the most important traditional forms of stylized activity draw upon this theme of competition; life itself is depicted by high-contrast antagonism, both between individuals and larger principles, such as male and female, age and youth, weak and strong.

We see here an emergent contrast to Western forms, not only in the way work is carried out, but also in the way playing is done. Throughout this culture area, one kind of game predominates: the singing circle-game similar to such playground fare as "The Farmer in the Dell" and "Go In and Out the Window" (but in contrast to these games in Western society, in Africa both adults and children participate in these "ring-plays"). Individuals are placed in the center of the circle and carry on imitational and symbolic acts while the people forming the circle respond. The central figure is constantly replaced. But unlike "The Farmer in the Dell," the African games call not for dramatic action, but for the same kind of response singing that characterizes the work song: one singer leads and the others respond (indeed, the response generally begins before the leader has finished). Many of the tales in this volume have songs embedded in them that are, in fact, in the same pattern as such games. They arise quite naturally in the trickster tales, where the ridiculous (but clever) hero plays at life, getting others to play along by leading games of this type.

This emphatic focus on the community of performance is a central feature of life as well as art in Black Africa. Continuity and culture are a constant achievement, for the destructive forces of nature evidence themselves regularly. Such instability may arise, to some extent, from the characteristics of the African landscape. Once one ascends beyond the coastal escarpment onto the plateau, there are very few actual physical barriers to man or beast (in spite of the impenetrable jungle spoken of by explorers and adventurers). Given the lack of such physical impediments, the weather progresses with an inexorable character that seems to permeate these stories. Boundaries and contrasts must be hewn out of the environment by man. The very smallest geographical units, such as the village and the compound (or kraal), have the quality of man-the-maker written all over them. Because the battle is fierce and endless, the human conquest of nature must constantly be replayed, with vigor, and with respect accorded to both contenders—man and nature. The contrast between the home and the bush, the village and the wilderness, is imposing, the protection of the family fire and the community clearing all the more cherished because of it. Which is not to say that a victory *over* nature is ever celebrated here; on the contrary, it is the descending of nature's vital spirit upon the community, rather than any sense of control over it, that is manifested in performance.

This factor is supremely important in the stylistic development of Black African expressive culture, for their lore speaks constantly of the coordinating of many impulses to one overall effect. This effect, however, does not rely on the carefully realized harmonies, nor on the clear sense of beginning, middle, and end that we are used to expecting in most Western art forms. Rather, we have forms in Africa that highlight the steady thrust of life and art, an effect achieved through the interlocking of voices and the repetition, with variation, of the same basic patterns.

This is one of the distinctive characteristics of African performance pointed out by Alan Lomax in his study of musical styles throughout the world. Lomax recognizes and builds upon the notion that music is commonly an extension and a stylization of the ways people interact. Black African singing, as Lomax evokes it, involves "wide-voiced, superbly cohesive, polyphonic choralizing . . . endlessly rich, rhythmic and orchestral traditions." These involve "a sociable overlapping of parts" in which a "polyrhythmic interaction between voices" underscores the sense of moral community that emerges in the spirit of celebration and argument.[5]

This interactive style relies on getting the greatest variety of timbres and textures into play—even at the expense of ensemble effects. When this is combined with the different meters, imposed one upon another, we have the characteristic African sound and rhythmic effects that have attracted (and been learned and imitated by) Westerners wherever they have encountered them. This aesthetic organization is precisely what is so enthralling about the deep samba of the Brazilian Carnival and the jump-up rhythms of Jamaican reggae that have influenced Western popular music for the last ten years.

But it has entered Western consciousness most fully and forcefully through traditional jazz. Though this form of music uses traditional European instruments and has a strong Western-style sense of beginning and ending, the interlock and overlap of the instrumental voices is the most characteristic dimension of the music—and this is the African contribution. Each instrument underscores the distinctiveness of its "voice" by displaying the melody in the style of that instrument—drawing upon the improvised ornamentations (or "riffs") associated with it—and pushing its possible range of tonal effects as far as possible. Each instrument remains separate, even at the point at which all of them play together. Moreover, as many have pointed out, jazz seems to involve a kind of discussion among the instruments concerning the melody; and, in the "hottest" sessions, the discussion turns into both an argument and a boasting session, a process often called "jamming" or "cutting" by the jazzmen themselves. Such an aggressive display does not undercut the aesthetic effect of the piece, of course; it enhances it.

In the contrast, the contest, even the potential conflict of voices, we can feel the vibrancy of the African creative impulse most fully. Through the powerful coordination of these effects in the face of possible chaos, the African artist achieves his or her sense of mastery; and the manifestations of this achievement across the spectrum of cultural expression are extraordinary.

The master-drummer, for instance, must dominate through his playing, and compel the attentive response of the other drummers joining him. He does this not only through the vigor and subtlety of his playing —"his laying down the beat" (to use another jazz term)—but also by his introduction of variations to which the others must respond, even to the point of altering the basic meter from time to time. I draw upon the example of drumming, not only because here one can perhaps witness the relationship between the individual and the collectivity in its purest form. In African drumming, we not only have to attend to variation in meters and timbres, but we can also feel the meter of the master-drummer pulling against, and away from, that of the others. Indeed, African drumming style, characteristically joins a number of metrical lines. We can actually see the same kind of aesthetic effect occurring in a wide range of African visual traditions, especially in ways of dressing, and in woven ground covers and blankets.

African styles of dress often call for the imposition of high contrast in hue and texture as an indication of rank and dominion. Vivid colors in a variety of cloth types are juxtaposed, setting up a brilliant and arresting image. As in the music, one often finds the widest variety of both textures and pulses superimposed one on the other to establish this vibrant sense of life in the everyday.

Similarly stylized, if in more subdued tonalities, are the great West African woven fabrics, which operate like drum orchestras. By setting up contrasting pulse systems, they instruct the eye to respond multimetrically, much as the ear and body do to polyrhythmic drumming.

As one would expect in such an aestheticized environment, the vivid contrapositions within cloth and costume are paralleled by dramatic contrasts between the ornately decorated and the stripped down, the spare. Many visitors to Africa have noted, for instance, how different one culture is from the next in terms of dress, one having the simplest kind of togalike covering and the other the more complicated overlapping, multilayered style. Similarly, within some of the more stratified groups, one class or caste will be typified by their "hot" style of dressing, dancing, or speaking, while another (usually a dominant group) will be characterized by their restrained style and their owning "the right to silence." Here we can usefully contrast the hot world of the Burundi with the cool environment valued by the Wolof. Among the former, all the men are expected to have developed the power of speech to a high art, and to enter into argument easily and with eloquence. In contrast, the Wolof (along with many other cultures from the Senegambian area), regard the performer-caste *griot* as an overheated half-animal: the more civilized classes manifest themselves through the spare style.[6]

II

I mention these other expressive resources because storytelling itself is part of a large performing complex, one that exists not only to provide entertainments for traditional (oral-aural) peoples, but that is at the center of their moral lives as well. Moreover, storytelling—as pure narration—seldom arises by itself in this part of the world. Stories involve a singing, a dancing, an acting-out of themselves. The audience participates actively in the singing and the dancing songs; the acting-out, through impersonation and masking and comic costuming, imposes a kind of distance through performance mastery. I have outlined this pattern of performance not as an academic exercise in comparative aesthetics—though the pattern is very different from the Western tradition—but as a means of underscoring the relationship between art and life in sub-Saharan Africa.

It would not be overstating the matter to note that in Black Africa, art *is* life and vice-versa, not a mere reflection of humanity and community, but a directly engaged commentary on how things are or should be; rather than just imitation, they heighten and intensify humanity's most important concerns. While we may not be able to define clearly either the Western or the African aesthetic per se, we do know that the difference between the two is great, and due in no small part to the relative importance of performance in each culture. In Africa (traditional Black) art is not set aside from "real life"—it cannot be among a people who do not make such distinctions. It is not just that the Western analytic distinctions between art and life are not meaningful in dealing with African expressive culture, but that the distinction actively threatens the lifeblood of community. Elimo P. Njau, at the first meeting of the Congress of Africanists, eloquently made just that point, which was then echoed by the other participants:

> Before African art was known in its own right, before African music was known as music in its own right, African art and music were the true cement of the African community.
>
> African art and music were so much part and parcel of the daily life of the community that when you talked about art and music you actually talked about the people themselves, their daily activities, their day-to-day aspirations as a community, their joys together, the enemies they fought together and the tears they shed together.[7]

The danger of losing the context of a tale is a small but significant by-product of the fracturing process often associated with Aristotelian thought—a process in which a community and its expressions or its arts are separated out into different piles. The very act of collecting and codifying, as we've seen, invariably distorts the "meaning" of a story. I have made the point already that, even as the subcontintent urbanizes, folktales have been maintained as effective devices for passing on the knowledge and wisdom of the ancestors. Though this is probably true of folktales told throughout the world, too often we forget that as Westerners, we learn these stories through books that underscore their imaginative and imaginary qualities. Equal emphasis should be placed on their effect on and importance to human interaction.

These stories are African; they have African concerns and obey codes and conventions of organization and use. One of the first cultural complications this causes for a Westerner is the fact that in their African setting these tales are called upon not just to deliver a specific message, but to initiate talk about that message. In other words, unlike most of the stories we are accustomed to encountering in books, these come from communities that continue to use stories as ways of pulling apart current subjects and piecing them together again—both through the story itself and, as we'll see soon, through the discussion and argument that story engenders.

It is precisely the way that the storyteller "grabs your shirt" and thrusts you into the tale that isn't there in the folktales we read in literary collections such as those of the Brothers Grimm, where what we find on the whole is a record of stories as remembered by old people who no longer tell them actively. In contrast, the African stories here were recorded while still flourishing in social and cultural environments in which the artful employment of speech in all dimensions of community is encouraged and applauded.

Unfortunately, this quality of immediacy in an African story, including the noise in which it lives, is very hard to capture on paper. Among the attempts to record storytelling as it occurred at a specific time and place, and to record it in such a way that other major situational factors are also conveyed, it is, perhaps, Laura Bohannon's novelistic accounts that come closest to succeeding. In Bohannon's "anthropological novel," *Return to Laughter,*[8] describing her work among the Tiv of Nigeria, she provides us with a description of a tale-telling scene which, though not wholly characteristic of the look and feel of a usual storytelling—the scene occurs after a smallpox epidemic has passed through the village—is nonetheless especially vivid. Her description focuses not on the stories, but rather on the noise out of which the performance emerges, and the performer's mastery of the tumult. She dramatizes the way in which the immediate situation is drawn upon in the stories and wedded to their universal qualities, and how the continuities and the interlayering of voices may be seen to work together in an actual performance context.

> A few nights later we sat under the cold moon of the harmattan in a circle in Kako's homestead yard. My pressure lamp was carefully placed, under Kako's personal direction, to illuminate the storytellers as they passed before us and the assembled elders. Gradually the people gathered from the neighboring homesteads. They brought their wives and children, and they brought wood for the fire and stools to sit on. The homestead was full of preparatory bustle as people borrowed coals to start their fires and jostled each other for a place close to the front. Then, places staked out with fire and stool, people circulated to greet each other, as people do in a theater lobby. The air was filled with happy hum of an audience sure of good entertainment.
>
> Behind Kako's reception hut there was a great deal of coming and going, whispering and giggling, very much like the noise of

people plotting charades. Cholo, who was to tell the first tale, squatted before us in brief, friendly greeting and gave me news of his sister: Atakpa was well; her co-wife had been blinded by smallpox. "It makes more work for Atakpa. They're both after their husband now, to get them a little wife to help."

"Cholo!"

"I'm coming," Cholo shouted toward Kako's reception hut. He glanced at the gathered audience and left. He waved Ihugh to join him. Soon Ihugh was running toward his hut, consulting with his uncles, and then back to join Cholo behind the reception hut. People settled down to wait, with anticipation.

Cholo came out before the lamp, and, with many gestures, began the story of the hare and the elephant.

The hare went hunting one day. He armed himself with a club made of cane grass and, knowing his weapon weak, wore a ferocious mask to petrify his prey with fear.

Here Cholo began to sing, stopping to instruct us all in the chorus of his song: nonsense syllables with a rousing rhythm and a lilting tune. I got interested. This would be far more fun than mere storytelling.

First the hare met a mouse. The mouse screamed with fear when he saw the terrible mask, but instead of standing trembling and ready to the hare's club, the mouse turned to flee.

Again Cholo waved us into the chorus.

As the hare pursued the mouse, his mask slipped down over his eyes. But the hare has long ears, and he was able to follow his prey by the rustling in the dry grass. In his flight, the mouse ran straight into an elephant and the elephant also began to run. The hare, unable to see, now followed the elephant and beat him with his cane club. The elephant, thinking this was the tickle of the mouse's whiskers, ran ever faster.

Again the chorus. Then Cholo disappeared. I had enjoyed the song, and prepared for the next story. But this one was not yet finished. Cholo returned. This time he was the hare. To his head he had tied two waving fronds as ears, over his face a cloth daubed with mud, and in his hands a weak blade of cane grass. He mimed his story, dancing before us, searching for game, finding the mouse, and pursuing it blindly.

Then out came the elephant, roaring: a long bed tied to a man's back—those huge, splay feet could be no one's but Ihugh's—covered with two dark togas that swayed with the elephant's dancing. The youngest children screamed most satisfactorily and had to be comforted by their parents, while the older children told them with great superiority that the elephant was really a man. Cholo now struck the elephant boldly with his grass blade, now used it as a baton to wave us all into his song and chorus. One or two of the young men beat sticks against their chairs, the better to mark the rhythm while the hare and the elephant danced. In a final surge of enthusiastic singing and dancing, the hare and the elephant disappeared.

Immediately one of Ihugh's cousins sprang into the center of the circle and began his tale of the goat who was a blacksmith and how he was tricked by the hare. He too had a song for his story, for the fables themselves are common property, and a storyteller makes his fame with his songs and dancing. Again I found myself laughing wholeheartedly and joining in the singing. I was enjoying myself immensely.

As the evening wore on, other men also rose to tell their stories, pressing brothers and cousins into service in the charades and commandeering props from the women of the homestead. A pot tied snoutlike over the face made a hippopotamus. Sheepskins, leaves, and cloth-covered stools created strange monsters and sprites. There was not a single dull story. The audience wouldn't allow it. They were as loud in their criticism as in their praise, and people will shout down any fable teller who fails to hold their attention: "That's too long." "Your song's no good." "You've got the story wrong." "Learn to dance." Sometimes it needed only the momentary inattention of part of the audience to embolden one of the other storytellers to jump into the center even while another fable was being told. Then for a few moments we heard two tales, two songs at once. Soon people would take up only the one chorus and the other fable teller would sit down.

Mainly it was a contest between Gbodi and Ikpoom, who were the two great storytellers of the country. Gbodi, a short stocky little man with a huge voice, excelled as a dancer and a tumbler. In the tale of the cricket and the praying mantis he danced holding a heavy mahogany mortar in his hands. First, as the praying mantis, he held it over his head; then, placing the mortar on the ground, he continued to dance on it upside down, his hands grasping the edge of the mortar, his feet in the air—and singing all the while.

Ikpoom excelled in mime. His ugly face was extraordinarily expressive, and he was at his best when he could himself act out all parts of the story at once. Now he was telling the tale of a chief's daughter who refused to marry any man, for she knew she was far too good for any suitor who came to court her. Ikpoom's voice was shrilly angry when, as the girl, he warned lovers off the farm and threatened to shoot them with bow and arrow. His voice was eerie and his song uncanny as he portrayed the chief of the underworld sprites, Agundu, who is a head with wild, red eyes and with gouts of blood on the raw cut neck that terminates the creature. He showed us how Agundu borrowed the radiance of the sun and moon and with them dazzled the girl, how she followed this bright illusion away from her own people whom she had scorned, and how at the very gates of the underworld Agundu gave back to the sun his glory and to the moon her beauty. Only then, when it was too late, did the girl see what a monster she had chosen, and then too late and in vain, she longed for a human mate.

I had no need to hear the shouted proverb that marks the end of each story. I knew the moral of this tale. Especially now, in this situation in which our common humanity and pleasure in amusement was so evident, the dangers of parting from one's own to follow beckoning strangeness loomed perilous and sad.

Ikpoom sang the lament of the girl whom blind pride had shut in a strange, dark world away from the sun and familiar light. . . .

Ikpoom sang for Agundu, for the grinning skeleton of the world that underlines all illusion. One can ignore Agundu. But those who follow him can never return, for they have seen and can never forget . . . they knew. All these people laughing around me. They knew how to come back. I had still to learn.

Gbodi was telling a tale now, of the hare's attempt to pass himself off as one of the bush sprites in their own country. Great a trickster as the hare is, infinite as is his ingenuity, he was unable to act and feel as did the bush sprites. At first this enabled him to deceive them the better and to steal the toga that bears one along like the wind, but ultimately this lack of understanding and this difference was his undoing. "This time," sang Gbodi, "the sprites killed the hare and ate him. The fable has killed the hare."

The hare would soon be resurrected in another fable. The trickster is immortal as a type no matter how often any one trickster tricks himself into disaster. But even the greatest trickster cannot transform himself. His personal habits always betray him, as they betray all of us for what we are; we ourselves are the only ones to see ourselves as what we think we ought to be or what we would like to be thought.

Many of my mortal dilemmas had sprung from the very nature of my work which had made me a trickster: one who seems to be what he is not and who professes faith in what he does not believe. But this realization is of little help. It is not enough to be true to oneself. The self may be bad and need to be changed, or it may change unawares into something strange and new. I had changed. Whatever the merits of anthropology to the world or of my work to anthropology, this experience had wrought many changes in me as a human being—and I had thought that what wasn't grist for my notebooks would be adventure. . . .

I had lost track of the fable being told. It was a long one, and I couldn't keep the characters straight. Neither, it seemed, could Accident—energetic as ever and quite unchanged save for a few pockmarks on his nose. Perhaps, though, it was just his sense of mischief that made him bound up from his seat beside his brother and take the stage with the storyteller. "I don't understand. Would you repeat more slowly?"

There was a startled gasp. Then a roar of laughter, even from the interrupted storyteller. "What was his great-great-grandfather's name? And where did he learn to perform that ceremony?" continued Accident, so broadly that I too began to laugh, for it was my own accent and my own questions that Accident was imitating. Aware that he had lost his audience, the fable teller began to play informant to Accident's anthropologist. Accident in turn looked eager to baffled, scribbled in the air as though in a notebook, wiped imaginary glasses, adjusted imaginary skirts, and took off my accent, gestures, errors of grammar, and habits of phrase with such unmerciful accuracy that even as I laughed myself sore I resolved on improvement. Accident finally sat down under a shower of pennies and approving applause. . . .[9]

III

Bohannon's description of an actual performance underscores the fact that the vitality of the storytelling lies in two characteristic elements: first, the seizure of the role of narrator and the maintaining of it in the face of ongoing critical commentary; second, the constant interaction between storyteller and audience, maintained both through audience commentary and the periodic introduction of call-and-response songs. Thus, the occasion of storytelling calls for the same seizing of the center, and the same kind of voice overlap and interlock, as do the many other forms of audience behavior taking place in front of the performer, who, through a sense of personal control, provides a focus for all the noise and random bustle arising on occasions of performance.

Entering into a story often involves a little tension, and getting out of it is often not as definitive a matter as it is in Western storytelling traditions. For, as the Mandingo say at the beginning of a story: "A really unique story has no end." Nearly everyone who gives us an up-close report on African storytelling, emphasizes the importance of beginning dramatically with such a "formulaic opening"—a fixed phrase like the Mandingo's that prepares everyone for what is to come. More than just an opening sentence, the fixed phrase bids for a standard response from the audience that indicates that they are ready and listening.

We see such opening formulas in many of the tales taken from recent reportings (earlier collections exclude them, mainly because of their repetitive character). For instance, "Monkey Steals a Drum" begins with the kind of elaborately playful formula that characterizes the other Yoruba stories included in this volume. "Here is a story," the aspiring narrator shouts out, to which the audience replies, "A story it is," in essence accepting his bid for a hearing. He then responds:

My story breaks sharply, pá,
Don't let it break its arms;
It breaks, whirs, and thuds, wàrà gbì
Don't let it break its neck;
It didn't fall on my *head!*
It didn't fall on my *neck!*
Nor did it fall on the bit of Rat
That I'll eat before I sleep tonight!
Instead, it fell on the heads of the
one hundred and fifty-six animals.

The narrator ingeniously and somewhat whimsically reminds his audience that he is about to launch into an elaborate invention. Just as often, the audience will, in turn, remind the narrator of the ridiculous character of his narrative, especially when the formal part of the story is coming to an end. This is often done, as in the opening, by introducing a first person singular reference, and treating the narrator's speaking persona in a humorous way.

The high energy of the dialogue, then, cannot be neglected in an understanding of how these stories come into being. Just as many of these stories themselves discuss the coming apart of family, friendships, community, the way the stories emerge in contests underscores the enduring nature of the oppositions. Achieving a sense of closure, of strong and definitive conclusion, is a condition regarded as neither possible nor desirable. There are certain parts and relationships which are so central to life itself that their playing out is necessary and never ending: between father and child, man and woman, husband and wife, wife and cowife, humans and witches, life and death. The idea of having a strong sense of resolution then, to which Westerners are so accustomed, seems strange to an African, an anathema.

As we see in most of the stories in Part Three of this book, having storytellers or some other kind of aggressive trickster as a central figure illustrates the motive of competition that informs many of the other tales, too. Sometimes, a kind of mirror effect is added simply by having some kind of performance-in-dialogue as an integral feature of the story. This is most clear in those cases where there is a competitive performance within the story, as in the marvelous Abron "The Contest of Riddles."

Judging from the frequency with which they appear, such open-ended stories, including the dilemma tales of which I'll speak more later, are among the most popular with African audiences. Open-endedness often occurs where a Westerner would least expect it, as in brief tales that make explicit moral commentaries. These can then be explored in conversation, especially among adults and children. Contrary to the closed form of the conventional Western fable, which seems to provide, Aesop-fashion, the "last word" on a subject, these African versions throw the floor open for debate, demonstrating yet again that in the African context the function of storytelling is to initiate as much as to instruct. Even when such a moral "last word" does arise, it commonly is at once so divisive and open-ended in its implications that it calls for further discussion.

Consider, for instance, a story that because it concerns the consequences of talk itself, may be viewed as a companion piece to "The Talking Skull." The Ewe tell of an old man who, by circumstance, was without family and had to board with an old woman in his village. As bad luck would have it, she ran out of food and was forced to suggest to the old man that they eat dog meat. He refused, saying that if word got around that he ate such stuff no one would have anything to do with him. She promised not to tell, so the old man agreed. But when the pet was cooked, he told her to set it aside for the moment and to call her best friend—"the one to whom you can tell anything." When that person came, he gave them the same instruction, and thus a third person joined them. He made the same suggestion to that third person, and so it went until a hundred people had gathered around. Then the old man told the assembled guests what had happened—that the old lady had run out of food and had been forced to serve him dog, promising that she wouldn't tell anyone if he ate it. The moral of the story is obvious enough since each of the guests was one to whom someone else could tell anything.[10]

The picture of life here, as in so many of the tales in this anthology, is deeply informed by the paradoxes of life, especially as they arise among people who live together and discuss things. Such tales argue that wholeness and integrity are but dreams: social division and dissolving of bonds are the expected. This accounts for the great numbers of stories about the betrayal of friendship, usually comic in their style, but deadly serious in their message. In this anthology, we first see such a betrayal in "Cursing the Birds," the story of the dignified blackbird whose view of the appropriate determined how the various other birds, all of whom wanted to change their appearance, should look. We think we understand, until we reach the apparent point of the story: "For the rest of the birds, they are in trouble, they are killed, they are ensnared, they are persecuted . . . all because they were cursed by the blackbird."

The occasion for the curse is unexplained in the story, but details of it are certainly understood by its audience: first, it is vain to wish to change one's coloration simply because of envy; second, the blackbird (like the old man confronting the problem of eating dog), is disgusted by those who do not eat correctly, for it is only through *proper* eating that culture can be manifested. By discussing how physical differences come into being, and are maintained in dramatic opposition, this is, in the deepest sense, an entertainment about the way life *is*. The vibrant performances of tales impart the message that "things" come apart, but never quietly and passively: The dissolution is to be discussed, argued about, entered into knowingly.

This process of engagement, of using moral tales to open rather than close off discussion, is precisely the modus operandi of the group of stories included here in the section called "Stories to Discuss and Even Argue About." Characteristic of Black Africa and seldom encountered elsewhere, they are tales that develop the plot in such a way that the listener is given a choice of endings. Most commonly, the choice is posed as a question, for example, which of the characters has been most valiant or virtuous and thus deserves a reward. The form of the tale, therefore, is designed to lead to discussion or more formal debate. Or, as William Bascom notes in his definitive study of the genre: "Even when they have standard answers, dilemma tales generally evoke spirited discussions, and they train those who participate in the skills of debate and argumentation."[11]

Consider now this principle that stories may be told that have no "proper" conclusion, and are specifically calculated to bring about dispute. "Stories," as *we* define them, should have a strong feeling of completion about them, a wholeness that will seldom call for discussion of motives, much less argument. Consider also a related characteristic: dilemma tales, as well as many of the other types of tales included here, use a tremendous amount of repetition. The narrative may be strung out endlessly through the repetition of the song, begun by the narrator, but taken up by everyone. (A full taste of this technique is given here in "A Competition of Lies" and "The Mwindo Epic.") That such interruptive repetitions are encouraged underlines another aspect of this open-endedness: attention is not on the narrator per se, but on the place of the storyteller as first among many, as in the other forms of performance. Open-endedness and repetition are resolutely connected in the minds of the community with involvement and, indeed, cooperative activity.

Songs set in stories do maintain audience involvement, and as already mentioned, there are often competitive uses of songs (as well as riddles and tests of wit), woven into the fabric of a story. But there are also numerous ways in which the storyteller can use songs simply to move the narrative along. In "The Disobedient Sisters," for instance, the sad account of the separated siblings is revealed in a song-story, a lullaby. In "Tiger Slights the Tortoise," the slow-but-steady turtle gets back at Tiger for refusing to employ him by carrying his harp to Tiger's farm, where he sings a song so compelling that everyone stops working and starts dancing. In "Take Me Carefully, Carefully," the song of the bird not only moves the story along, but becomes the narrator's way of revealing the bird's magical character.

In "Profitable Amends," Yo, the Dahomean trickster figure, is portrayed as a magical singer, one who is capable of employing song as a means of tricking others. Each time he sings, in this amazing myth, he is able to negotiate an unequal exchange of goods, until finally in exchange for just one cowry shell he gets a wife for the king. Unfortunately, the wife turns out to be a voracious sorceress, who is able to sing the king into sending one feast after another into her camp—and this in the midst of a famine!

Another technique for integrating the song into the story is to use it as a recognition device, or signature, which is how it appears in "Demane and Demazana," the very first tale in the book. Here the runaway brother uses a special song to identify himself whenever he wants his sister to unlock her door for him. The story turns on her ability to tell his voice from that of the cannibal intruder.

The most common device for introducing song into the story, however, is to use song as a kind of spotlighting device, a way of amplifying the most important speeches of the antagonists in the drama. We see this technique, for instance, in "The Smart Man and the Fool," where the "foolish" brother uses song as a means of revealing why he let his selfish father choke to death. Similarly, in "He Starved His Own," when the son is old enough to kill game but refuses to give any to his starving father (who has neglected the boy and his mother), he gives his justification for not doing so through song. The importance of the audience involvement that these songs and other techniques create, along with open-ended story structure and communal playing-out of oppositions, cannot be overstressed. For in many African cultures, this is a theological as well as an aesthetic matter. Life is regarded as a pulsating spirit or force, separate from any individual or group, a vital element of the gods that bearing their timeless messages, descends on the group when they engage in a performance. The oppositions given voice and movement at that time are simply temporal representations of the eternal struggles; oppositions are presented, therefore, as complementarities, opposing forces that could not exist without each other.

James Fernandez, who has studied the expressive life of the Fang of Gabon, is describing this central concept when he notes that "what is artistically pleasing to the Fang has a . . . vitality that arises out of a certain relationship of contradictory elements. The Fang will only live easily with such contradictions; they cannot live without them." He goes on to demonstrate that, indeed, aesthetic pleasure (as well as everyday fun), occurs in the dramatizing of some of these basic oppositions, that is, by putting them into a play. This is so because "vitality, arises out of complementary oppositions, . . . what is aesthetically satisfying is the same as what is culturally alive."[12]

Aesthetic canons of pleasure among the Fang, then, dictate the dramatizing of opposition without the attempting of resolution. Specific oppositions often relate to concepts of maleness and femaleness, especially those visible in the interlocking relationships between hot (male), and cold (female), day and sun (male), night and moon (female), sky (male), earth (female), bones, sinews, and brains (male), flesh, blood, and internal organs (female), and so on. Thus a world of reference is created in which the basic stuff of life is constantly available as a means of demonstrating vitality-in-opposition.

The Fang illustrate perfectly my point that in Black Africa, the community celebrates its sense of groupness by coordinating energies in performance, a creative enterprise that embodies binary oppositions in a complexly integrated traditional form, transforming them into complementarities. Group focus is achieved through the practice of group involvement or *interlock;* performer and audience are not separable in the way they are in stage shows, for instance. The energetic demonstration of community will be valued by any group, but especially by those which, like so many in Africa, conceive of life as a reservoir of vital spirit, and of the demonstration of that spirit as the basis of continuity in community life.

Within such a system of presentation and celebration, the individual who sets himself apart from the group does so less to demonstrate his individual talents than to set up a dynamic opposition. The individual and the group thicken the texture of the performance by establishing interlocking voices (whether it be in storytelling, drumming, singing, dancing, or orating). The more interlock, the greater the complexity of the entire event, of course, and the more vitality the community feels is being channeled through them. Thus, there is a high value placed on what Robert Farris Thompson has called "apart playing"; "each [performer] . . . intent upon the production of his own contribution to the polymetric whole." It is in this metrical dimension of performance, the pulses flowing through the group, that "apartness" is most clearly called into play,[13] and we see it to its greatest effect in the displays requiring a special kind of virtuosity; a great performer is judged not only by his ability to control his medium, but also by his ability to engage the participation of the other performers and the audience. Out of the turbulence, the master brings order, teaches value, but also provokes and excites, playing competing rhythms that ultimately convey a message of community of interest and cooperative motives.[14]

A singer-response dialogue establishes a sense of mutual supportiveness between a single performer and the rest of the group. Complementarity is the key to ordering the chaotic; its value becomes clear in those African groups that discuss performances in terms of the importance of "cool"—"an ancient indigenous ideal: patience and collectedness of mind."[15] As one might suppose, from such a perspective both noise and complexity are conceived of as hot, as is any outrageous behavior on the part of the performers or the characters they play or describe. But all these fit the pattern of complementarity. The master singer, dancer, or drummer will draw everyone's attention and channel all the contending voices into a response to his or her forceful initiative. Or to put it in West African aesthetic terminology, he will, through the imposition of a cool elegance and verve, provide a sublime balance to the hot environment by drawing upon the hot element within the performance itself.

IV

Storytelling is of a piece with these other African performance traditions based on the principles of opposition, overlap, apart-playing, and interlock, inasmuch as it shares the aesthetic. But in one important respect, the telling of tales differs from all the others, for its primary medium is the word. It is valuable to understand not only how stories enter into village life, but what such storytelling traditions have in common, albeit in characteristically African fashion, with other oral cultures.

"Traditional," or "oral" culture, refers to the sharing of an expressive body of knowledge and values. Such traditional pieces of knowledge are passed on primarily by observation, common experience, and explicit word-of-mouth transmission. To a certain extent, a group will define itself by the traditional performance forms and the items it shares. When I argue, then, that village Africa has maintained an emphatically oral orientation, I mean that because, ideally, everyone knows all the stories, they may be drawn upon through allusion in any kind of interaction. In the Western world, when we explain a person's behavior as "just sour grapes," or say that someone is "being a dog in a manger," "playing Good Samaritan," or "crying wolf," we may or may not know that there is an ancient fable or parable that lies behind the phrase. If we do, we have probably gotten that information through having encountered the work from which it comes. Nevertheless, our use of allusion is similar to that of an oral culture, for whether or not we know the story in detail, we can still sense its presence behind the saying.

Similarly, such sayings as "fish or cut bait" or "caught between a rock and a hard place" are self-conscious folksy phrases that imply that there is a story even if there isn't. But obviously, these enter our lives much less frequently than correlative expressions in orally oriented cultures, and convey considerably less power to those who use them as clichés and their users as "corny."

Not so the controllers of proverbs and other teaching devices in traditional cultures, for there respect and honor are accorded to those who possess the techniques of conveying wisdom and knowledge. This power is revealed most fully in the ability to be eloquent, and to contend with others in displaying control of the "old words." This adherence to tradition in performance preserves a richness of cultural reference through which a sense of life's continuity is maintained even in the midst of adversity. "The word" endures as a way of keeping order, and maintains its promise of inspiration and illumination. The describing of such oral-aural phenomena has become problematic because of the mystique created around traditional peoples by cultural commentators as diverse as Marshal McLuhan, Carlos Castaneda, Norman O. Brown, Alvin Toffler, and Ivan Illich.[16]

If we clear off this Western cultural baggage, we can make certain valuable observations about oral cultures—in their proper context. For example, there is one respect in which oral recitation does create a promise knitting together all of the diverse elements of life, namely, in the magical system that governs the naming of things. This basic mystery, devised by the gods at the invention of language, is at the center of life—not only social life, but the roots of life. As the Dogon sage, Ogotomêlli, revealed it: Water and words came together at the birth of the world, Nummo the prime mover placed fibers of water and words over his mother's genitalia, thus "clothing" the world by giving it its first way of speaking—a simple but beautiful language. Speech itself is good, for its function was to bring order and agreement.

> . . . Nevertheless from the start it let loose disorder. This was because Jackal, the deluded and deceitful son of God, desired to possess speech, and laid hands on the fibres in which language was embodied, that is, on his mother's skirt. His mother, the earth, resisted this incestuous action . . . [but] in the end she had to admit defeat. . . . The act . . . endowed Jackal with the gift of speech so that ever afterwards he was able to reveal . . . the designs of God.[17]

Thus, speech, from the beginning, is an agency of both order and disorder: a vehicle through which power is expressed and homage is paid; and a way, through curses, spells, lies, and arguments, of causing divisiveness, witchcraft, and death. To be human is to control words and to pursue eloquence. To tell stories is to enter into the constant recreation of the world, of community, of mankind. But as the duplicity of Jackal warns us, speech can reside with the deceivers; indeed, among many African peoples, because stories are lies, they are considered to "belong" to such tricksters. Since the community can't prevent tales from being invented, its attention is shifted to maintaining—or attempting to maintain—control over them, as in the tales of the talking skull and the old man who would not eat dog.

Nowhere is the double character of words more apparent than in the widely told tale of how the message of death came to people in garbled form. Commonly, it is the Moon that attempted to send word to the people that even in apparent death, life will be maintained: "As I die and, dying live, so also shall you die and dying live." But Trickster talked the Moon into letting him carry the word instead, and he told the people, "Like as I die, and dying perish, so shall you die, and come to an end." For this, the moon split Hare, the Trickster's, lip, but the message remains garbled.[18]

The Ikoi of Nigeria tell an elaborate tale in which Trickster actually "owns" all the stories and looses them upon the world. Originally, it was Mouse, it seems, who was the inventor and the holder of all stories, for Mouse is the all-witnessing visitor of human households, looking into the affairs of man whether rich or poor. Tales become her children, and she wove a story-child for each tale, giving each story-child a different colored gown so that she might better tell them from each other. They were hers and hers alone, because to let them be seen was to reveal the doings of humans to each other, and we all know to what condition such information leads.

Unfortunately, the protection it was assumed the ownership of stories provided, was built on the belief that within the village friendship and cooperation ruled. Sheep and Leopard were special friends and each had a child. Sad to report, famine fell on the land, and they were forced to make a pact to kill their children and feed them to each other in order to get by. Sheep contrived a trick, however, and arranged things so that her child was spared. In fact, by dint of her cleverness, she was able to do this year after year, always finding a substitute food to serve up to Leopard. Of course, eventually, Leopard discovered Sheep's duplicity, and she had to run away from the village. During her flight she met up with many people, whom she was also able to gull. But in time, thugs caught up with her, and she was cornered in the house of a woman of another place. In a frenzy, she got too close to Mouse's dwelling and fell against the door, at which point all of Mouse's children escaped into the world.[19]

Throughout Africa, there are stories that "belong to" animals like Mouse, some creature who intrudes into the human community, but continues to live in a wild state. It is Hare and Spider and Jackal and the many other small and clever creatures living near man in the nooks and crannies and on the borders, who are the carriers of such tales. Living in the in-between places, they share in both the power of nature and the products of culture, but they obey neither the rules of man nor the laws of nature. Thus, these animals thrive not only on upsetting rules and boundaries, but also on attacking the family, friendships, and all the ways in which people have learned to live in harmony. The stories in the fourth chapter of this work are about the doings of such creatures, and are especially characteristic of African tales. To understand them, one must remember that the strangely chaotic motives that drive these tricksters are the ones that elicit gales of laughter when they are dramatized.

Trickster is the figure who most fully illustrates how not to act within society. But whereas his activities comment implicitly on improper behavior and do it within a fictional form, gossip comments more explicitly and is based on stories purported to be true. In the village environment, gossip is needed to provide everyone with a kind of social map of the terrain. Moreover, it is a way—important in such small communities—for people to keep a check on each other's activities as part of a self-protection system. At the same time, however, gossip can be very dangerous, because it judges character and makes personal references, which can easily lead to upset and misunderstanding. Therefore, the more impersonal kinds of stories assume great importance in defusing possible contention, because they comment on human behavior in the less personal, the more universal manner.

Tales within an oral world, then, are ways of "going round for long," using speech for purposes of making indirect personal arguments in socially restricted situations. They are more powerful for this indirectness. They argue by analogy, not only with regard to how people should and should not act to be useful members of society, community, and family, but also in regard to how such actions give meaning and power to the very being of all within the community. This indirect approach brings together the African love of proverbs and stories—both forms, though succinct, take the long way around problems. Both suggest in an open-ended manner how people should behave in certain situations. Each of these suggestions partakes of the argumentative nature of talk, for each proverb or story is not only itself open to discussion, but may, at any time, be countered by another proverb or story with a contrary message.

Because proverbs and stories are indirect and impersonal means of engaging in deep discussion, their use is considered good manners. When Americans say, "You know what they say," before using an old adage, we are employing the same kind of indirection, for "they" are the forefathers, the wise ones of the past whose accumulated experience has been embodied in memorable sayings. If we don't use such proverbs much anymore, it is not just that nowadays we don't look to our ancestors to solve our problems. Much more relevant is the fact that, for the most part, we no longer live in the kind of close communities in which our manners constantly have to be minded. In addition, because we have come to value peer friendships more than family relationships, and it is with friends that we most want to discuss ourselves and our feelings, we now prefer a more direct approach to one another. Among traditional peoples, feelings are guarded more closely. The asking of direct questions, especially of a personal sort, is likely to be misconstrued, because that which is not immediately apparent is meant to be hidden. Discretion is highly valued, not only as a way to keep down the talk, but also as a way to maintain the essential power of words. For as "The Talking Skull" reminds us, ill-considered talk can often lead to trouble and can even dissipate the vitality of the group. A Mandingo saying, commenting on this situation and the importance of verbal economy, puts it this way: "One contributes to the power of the fetish by leaving it in the bag." The curative powers of a fetish are enhanced by keeping it hidden; so, too, with words and their power.

Interestingly, such concealed power may also be associated with storytelling, for stories are often told only at night, the guarded and secret time. The Mandingo peoples possess a category of words with special powers, *kuma,* those words uttered only at night in the telling of myths, legends, and tales. They are embodiments of disguised knowledge, enabling individuals within the group to reveal their feelings by virtue of indirection, without risking dissipation of vital spirit.[20]

To mention *kuma* is to begin to recognize not only the relationship between word power and mystery, but to understand the power often contained within the expressive system of a culture. Here the African record is an especially rich one. Many investigators have pointed to native systems of exegesis—that is, open and subtle analysis of the kinds of talk available in a speech-community. This is what Griaule documents, in fact, in his *Conversations with Ogôtomelli,* referred to above. Though this book is unique for the depth and intensity of its reporting on a single tribal philosopher, a number of other workers in the field have explored such native systems more generally, especially the categories of tale.

Of these systems, none is more complex, nor more fascinating, than that reported by Deirdre LaPin of the Yoruba. This populous and culturally important group is actually a nation within a nation, with important "colonies" in Haiti, Brazil, Cuba, and Trinidad. An ancient city society, it has one of the most fully documented expressive cultures in the Old World. A true ceremonial state, it constantly celebrates its vision of life through an elaborate set of performance forms and events. In Yoruba culture, distinctions are made between a number of different kinds of storytelling: *ìtàn,* a straightforward and direct story; *àlọ́,* stories told in indirect terms, replete with analogy and metaphor; *òwe,* stories told to explain the force of a proverb; and *arọ̀,* formulaic tales (like "The House that Jack Built"), or one of many other tightly structured narrative techniques. But none of these names is used to mean the stories alone. *Arọ̀* may refer to any of a number of tightly structured poetic forms, *òwe* to the proverbs, as well as the stories that explain them, *àlọ́* to a song that alludes to a story. *Itàn* is also a term referring to the recounting of any past event performed without singing, such as the deeds of great men, stories of families and lineages, battles, even personal anecdotes. Each story type is performed for a different kind of audience. Yet, virtually the same story told in the form of *ìtàn,* may emerge as *àlọ́,* or *arọ̀.* Moreover, it may be alluded to in riddle or proverb form, in an *ijálá,* (hunter's praise-poem to an *orisha* god), or in *odù Ifá,* or cowryshell divination, as people's fortunes are being read.[21]

V

I have given Yoruba terms in detail here, not only to show one kind of classification system, but also because this is an especially subtle tradition. However, the Yoruba differ from many of the other cultures in which these stories live because they are not only a village people, but have built large urban centers as well. Even in the city environment, they maintain their range of oral tradition, including the various kinds of storytelling.

This brings up the very important question of what happens to expressive performance as Africans become urbanized and "modernized"? The written record is inconclusive, but extremely suggestive. Storytelling (and traditions of performance in general), evidently does not disappear under such conditions, but is changed, turned into an evening's entertainment away from job and domicile.

Many of the same stories are still told, it would seem, but are now performed by professional or semiprofessional entertainers, and in situations in which the performers do not know the members of the audience in the same intimate way. Thus, the local references used in the village context, and immediately understood by all, are lost. Likewise, a specific person's style can no longer be parodied and must be replaced by a stock character, a more generalized "type," whose traits are immediately recognizable ("the government official," "the priest," and so on). The greatest change arises in the techniques the performer uses to assert and maintain mastery. For in these urban contexts, he must not only have the loudest voice and the broadest imitational abilities, he must also be able to dazzle the audience with his control of language. This leads to the development of what Donald Cosentino calls the "Baroque Style of Narration"[22]—one in which elaboration and ornamentation come to the center of the storytelling art. The teller justifies the attentions paid him by spinning out the stories at ever greater length, introducing constantly more elaborate detail, and using increasingly more sophisticated instrumental accompaniment.

Though Consentino—and Dan Ben-Amos[23]—describe a recent development, there is little doubt that such a professionalizing process has been going on for some time, whenever large market towns arise. Take, for example, the case of the *griot* entertainer in the Senegambian region, paralleled by the *maroki* (beggars), among the Hausa of Nigeria. Both are reknowned for their abilities to praise-sing and to curse, to carry stories about, and to perform them exquisitely. For this, however, they are made outcasts, people of the road and the marketplace, using their art as a way of getting by. These, as it were, African meistersingers and troubadours, thus reproduce a cultural process that has been observed several other places throughout the world—a process of professionalization of performers and performances, and of distancing between performer and audience.

But while in performances at the marketplace, singing and dancing and instrumental music-making prevail, storytelling, in the main, slowly, but inexorably, falls by the way. Perhaps it is too personal a form to maintain itself very long away from the fireside and the family compound. Its decline, however, takes considerable time. With the development of larger cities, the marketplace changes its character, balloons, and becomes more specialized, and, therefore, more threatening to large segments of the populace. At that point, the storyteller seems to find his way to the drinking hall and even the theater, where he performs as one type of entertainer at Concert Parties. These public entertainments, found in many urban areas, often involve people of many languages and cultures coming together in the expectation that everyone will understand everything. Naturally, the style of performance and even the range of stories that can be told is altered for these events, and the emphasis on individual performing virtuosity becomes even greater. Undoubtedly, popular new ways of telling stories will emerge from this, in the same way that "high life" music and numerous new trans-African dance styles have developed offshoots. But such developments are far removed from the kind of village artistry that has kept the stories in this volume afire for such a long time.

The history of the African aesthetic impulse suggests only one development that can be comfortably predicted—new styles and new forms will constantly evolve out of the old. We will get new heroes and even new gods using modern means of power to perform; but their connection with the old gods and the old ways will remain profound, for Trickster, cutting up, still living at the crossroads and in nooks and crannies, will always be with us. Not that he will continue in the form of rabbit or spider, or hyena or hare, for he changes his shape to suit the situation. The aesthetic pulse that runs through African art maintains, in this way, its connection with vital spirit, with life itself. As long as art and life are one, beauty and endurance will remain sisters.

To the stories, then, with the hope that in this collection I have successfully captured the distinctive blend of traditional vision and adaptive vitality that marks the narrative spirit of Africa. As to their essential and representative humanity, the stories will speak for themselves, even when they "go round for long."

NOTES TO INTRODUCTION

1 Cf. Leo Frobenius and Douglas C. Fox, *African Genesis* (Stackpole Sons, 1937), p. 236.

2 William Bascom surveys its appearance in "The Talking Skull Refuses to Talk," *Research in African Literatures* 8 (1977): 226–91.

3 Sony Camara, "Tales in the Night: Toward an Anthropology of the Imaginary," in *Varia Folklorica*, ed. Alan Dundes (The Hague: Mouton and Co., 1978), p. 95.

4 Found in Stannus.

5 Alan Lomax, *Cantometrics: An Approach to an Anthropology of Music: Handbook* (Berkeley: University of California Extension Media Center, 1976), p. 42.

6 Ethel Albert describes the Burundi approach in "Cultural Patterning of Speech Behavior in Burundi," *Directions in Sociolinguistics*, ed. John Gumperz and Dell Hymes (New York: Holt, Rinehart and Winston, 1972), pp. 72–105. The Wolof situation is surveyed by Judith Irvine. Her insights are usefully summarized in her "Formality and Informality in Communicative Events," *American Anthropologist* 81 (1979): 778, 790.

The richest study of the relationship between hot noise and cool, restrained, weighty speech is Karl Reisman's "Noise and Order," in *Language in its Social Setting*, ed. William W. Gage (Washington, D.C.: The Anthropological Society of Washington, 1974), pp. 56–73.

7 Elimo P. Njau, "African Art," in *Proceedings of the First International Congress of Africanists*, ed. Lolage Bowa and Michael Crowden (Paris: *Cahiers Etudes Africaine*, 1964), pp. 237–38.

8 Written under the name of Elinore Smith Bowen (Garden City, N.Y.: Anchor Press/Doubleday, 1964), p. 293.

9 Ibid., pp. 285–93.

10 From George W. Ellis, *Negro Culture in West Africa* (New York: Neale Publishing Co., 1914), p. 228.

11 William Bascom, *African Dilemma Tales* (The Hague: Mouton and Co., 1975), pp. 1–3.

12 "Principles of Opposition and Vitality of Fang Esthetics," in *Art and Aesthetics in Primitive Societies*, ed. Carol Jopling (New York: E. P. Dutton Co., 1971), p. 358.

13 This and the other terms and concepts for the Black African aesthetics emerge from my reading of the work of Thompson, as well as Lomax, *Cantometrics*. The quotation comes from Thompson, "An Aesthetic of the Cool: West African Dance," in *African Forum II* (1972): 87.

14 Robert Farris Thompson, "An Introduction to Trans-Atlantic Black Art History: Remarks in Anticipation of a Coming Golden Age of Afro-America," in *Discovering Afro-America*, ed. Roger D. Abrahams and John F. Szwed (Leyden: E. J. Brill, 1975), pp. 64, 67.

15 Thompson, *Aesthetic*.

16 What these professional innocents and seekers-after-wholeness project upon reality is the ability of mystic words to help us recapture earlier experiences —a kind of "creative regression" operating upon the individual and on society in general. All seem to promulgate the small-is-beautiful view of humanity, which elevates the agricultural, pastoral, sometimes even the hunting-and-gathering community to a place of honor because of their simplicity and their relative naturalness! I'll refrain from commenting on this Rousseauvian and Utopian vision, except by implication—the lives of the "simple" villagers who have created and maintained these stories hardly conforms to anyone's idyllic vision of anything.

17 Marcel Griaule, *Conversations with Ogotomêlli* (Oxford: Oxford University Press, 1965): p. 21.

18 Cf. Sammi Metelerkamp, *Outa Karel's Stories* (London: Macmillan & Co., 1914), pp. 70–77.

19 Cf. Susan Feldman, *African Myths and Tales* (New York: Dell Publishing Co., 1963), pp. 170–73.

20 Camara, *Tales*.

21 This information comes from Deirdre LaPin, *Story, Medium and Masque: the Idea and Art of Yoruba Storytelling* (Ann Arbor, Mich.: University Microfilms International, 1977).

22 Donald Cosentino, *African Arts* 13, no. 3 (May 1980): 54–57.

23 Ben-Amos's monograph, *Sweet Words: Storytelling Events in Bini* (Philadelphia: ISHI, 1975), details this changeover in roles and styles between village and town contexts.

Part I

Tales of Wonder from the Great Ocean of Story

Introduction

The emphasis in the introduction on the unique features of Black African performance may have created the impression that the subcontinent is a cultural entity with few connections to other areas of the Old World. But as the stories throughout this book will attest, that is far from the case. In many areas, the connection is a direct one: native cultures have been strongly influenced by Mediterranean and Middle Eastern forms brought in with Islam. And in a number of other ways, too, Black African traditional practices can be seen as part-and-parcel of an Old World cultural complex.

In addition, as many of the stories in this section testify, the folk or fairy tale as Westerners are accustomed to think of it is also widely found here—although Africanized both in form and content. It seems useful, then, to introduce the reader to African tales through a few of the familiar ones that are in international circulation. Included are stories in the general mold of "The Race of the Tortoise and the Hare," "Hansel and Gretel," and "Ali Baba and the Forty Thieves," as well as some of the Br'er Rabbit stories, such as "Tar Baby."

Here, then, you will find the familiar wonder-tale patterns of the passing of the multiple tests, the progression of magical helpers, the winning of the king's beautiful daughter. In "The Three Tests," for instance, we see the youngest son perform a set of marvelous tasks in order to free his older brothers from a spell and win in marriage the lovely princess. In "Rubiya," the tests are devised by the sultan chief protecting his daughters. In a very complicated development of the pattern, the hero conquers, and adopts as brothers, various helping figures; then he wins the hands of a series of beautiful princesses and gives them, magnanimously, to one or another of the helpers. Obviously, he has larger things in mind. In "Profitable Amends," we begin to see other more African patterns emerge. Here, the trickster, Yo, wins the beautiful girl through his powers of trading; but in this case, he does so for the benefit of Dada Segbo, his king, who needs a queen with whom to found the royal house. Unfortunately, as in so many of the African tales, the new mate turns out to be a sorceress and has to be sent back to "the bush," from which she emerged.

Yo "trades up" for this sorceress through a series of clever exchanges, each of which brings about a recounting of his trading abilities in a song composed of cumulative verses that will remind the reader of "For Want of a Nail the Horse Was Lost" or "The House That Jack Built." A similar technique, chronicling progressive disasters, but driving toward a more positive end—the hero's attainment of the chieftancy—is to be found in "The Hare's Hoe." In a fanciful retelling of the tale of the tortoise and the hare, "The Tortoise and the Falcon," we see the racing sequence combined with that of the hero's quest for the chief's lovely daughter. Here, Hare goes into a partnership with Tortoise in competition with Falcon.

This section begins with two stories that turn on the use of a password. In the first, reminiscent of Hansel and Gretel, it is employed as a defense against the cannibal-ogre who (naturally) wants to eat the young girl. Demazana in the latter, a version of "Ali Baba and the Forty Thieves" (but with a twist), the boy who discovers the cave has a brother who unsuccessfully tries to use the password to repeat the deception.

The section ends with another tale of a familiar type, one related to "Jack and the Beanstalk," but taking a wonderful turn, the fight at the center of the narrative is given a cosmological explanation that provides insight into how such stories may be made to signify in a traditional culture.

1

Demane and Demazana

Once upon a time, a brother and sister who were twins and orphans, being poorly treated at home, were obliged to run away from their relatives. The boy's name was *Demane,* the girl's *Demazana.*

They went to live in a cave that had two holes to let in air and light, the entrance to which was protected by a very strong door with a fastening inside. *Demane* went out hunting by day, and told his sister that she was not to roast any meat while he was absent, lest the cannibals should discover their retreat by the smell. Whenever he returned, he would sing this song and his sister would let him in:

Demazana, Demazana,
Child of my mother,
Open this cave to me.
The swallows can enter it.
It has two openings.

But then it happened that a cannibal overheard it.

The girl would have been quite safe if she had done as her brother commanded. But she was strongheaded, and one day she took some buffalo meat and put it on a fire to roast. The cannibal smelled the flesh cooking, and went to the cave, but found the door fastened. So he tried to imitate *Demane*'s voice, and asked to be let in by singing the song:

Demazana, Demazana,
Child of my mother,
Open this cave to me.
The swallows can enter it.
It has two openings.

Demazana said: "No. You are not my brother, for your voice is not like his at all."

The cannibal went away, but after a little time came back again and spoke in another tone of voice: "Do let me in, my sister."

Demazana, Demazana,
Child of my mother,
Open this cave to me.
The swallows can enter it.
It has two openings.

The girl answered: "Go away, you cannibal; your voice is hoarse, you are not my brother."

So he went away and consulted with another cannibal. He said: "What must I do to obtain what I desire?" He was afraid to tell what his desire was, lest the other cannibal should want a share of the girl. His friend said: "You must burn your throat with a hot iron."

He did so, and then no longer spoke hoarsely. Again he presented himself before the door of the cave, and sang:

Demazana, Demazana,
Child of my mother,
Open this cave to me.
The swallows can enter it.
It has two openings.

The girl was deceived, and believing her brother had come back from hunting, she opened the door. The cannibal went in and seized her, but as she was being carried away, she dropped some ashes here and there along the path. Soon after this, *Demane,* who had found nothing to eat that day but a swarm of bees and their honey, returned and found his sister gone. He guessed what had happened, and by means of the ashes followed the path until he came to where the cannibal, *Zim,* lived. The cannibal's family was out gathering firewood, but he was at home and had just put *Demazana* in a big bag, where he intended to keep her till the fire was made.

Entering the room, *Demane* said: "Give me water to drink, father." *Zim* replied: "I will if you will promise not to touch my bag." *Demane* promised. Then *Zim* went to get some water, and while he was away, *Demane* took his sister out of the bag and put the bees in it, after which they both hid.

When *Zim* came with the water, his wife and son and daughter came also with firewood. He said to his daughter: "There is something nice in the bag; go bring it." She went and put her hand in the bag, but the bees stung her hand, and she called out: "It is biting." He sent his son, and afterwards, his wife, but always the same thing happened. He got angry at them and kicked them out of his house. He put a block of wood in the doorway so *Damazana* couldn't run away. Then he opened the bag himself. The bees swarmed out and stung his head; his eyes swelled up so that he couldn't see.

There was a little hole in the thatch and through this he forced his way. He jumped about howling with pain. Then he ran and fell headlong into a pond, where his head stuck fast in the mud and he became a block of wood, like the stump of a tree. The bees made their home in the stump, but no one could get their honey because when any one tried, his hand stuck fast.

Demane and *Demazana* then took all *Zim*'s possessions, which were numerous and great, and they became wealthy people.

—*Kaffir**

2
The Password

Good! There were six thieves. They were the chiefs of all thieves. Their name was *Adjotogan.* Good. There was a mountain full of gold. No one knew that gold was inside it. Only these six thieves knew. They slept there. Good. Whatever they stole, they put inside this mountain. The mountain was their house.

There was a father who had eight sons. He called them one day and asked each of them what he wanted to become. "I am an old man. Tell me what you want to be."

The first son said he wanted to become a mason.

The second said, "I want to become a carpenter."

The third said he wanted to be a farmer.

The fourth said, "I want to become a great thief."

The fifth said, "I want to become a trader." The sixth said, "I want to become a liar."

The seventh said, "I am going to the forest to cut down wood, and I will sell it in the market."

The eighth said, "I will also get wood and sell it."

The elder of the two youngest sons was called Jean, the younger, Joseph. They began to go to the forest for firewood, and they sold the firewood for a franc a bundle. When Jean sold a bundle of wood, he spent the money he got for it. Joseph saved his earnings. This went on.

* *Complete bibliographic information for the tales will be found in the Bibliography, p. 343.*

Once, Joseph, the richer of the two went to the forest, and climbed up a tree. Some distance from there was a mountain. He could see clearly from where he was for the mountain was only two kilometers away. It was all swept and clean. Now, Joseph was curious, and he watched to see what would come out of this mountain. He no longer looked for firewood, but remained hidden in the branches of the tree and watched. He remained there all day.

This was towards two o'clock. If the thieves went out at five in the morning, they came back at two o'clock in the afternoon. At two o'clock, then, they arrived. The thieves did not know that there was someone up the tree spying on them. Now, the thieves have a charm with which to open the mountain. To open the mountain, they put the charm on the ground. It was a pea, which was hammered into the mountain with the foot. Then they would say, "Open." The mountain opened.

Now, Joseph was there near the mountain and he could look right inside. When the door opened, he saw gold, animals, everything. He said, "Oh, do such things exist!"

Now, the thieves stayed inside the mountain. They ate, and then they put away what they had brought with them—the things stolen that day.

Then, when the thieves went out they said to the mountain, "We are coming back in two days, or three days." They always fixed the day for their return. To close the mountain, they took out the pea and put it in at the side of the mountain for safekeeping. They went away.

And Joseph also went away. He went back home. Now, Joseph no longer wanted to bother with gathering wood. Joseph had a little education—he knew how to write—and on the third day he went and posted himself in the same place in order to write down what the thieves said to open the mountain. Again the thieves came back at two o'clock. They pounded in the pea, and said, "Open," and the mountain opened. Now, Joseph wrote all this down on a paper. After having eaten, the thieves went out again towards dark. They told the mountain that they would be away three days. Good. Now, they told the mountain to close.

When the thieves were eight kilometers distant, Joseph climbed down from the tree. He approached the mountain and took up the charm that he had seen hidden at the side of the mountain. He did just as the thieves had done. He commanded the mountain, he said, "Open." The mountain opened.

Then Joseph entered. He began to gather up the gold so that he might carry it away with him. He worked from morning till night. The next day also he labored from morning till night. He no longer looked for firewood. Now, during the day, he slept.

He went to put eighty sacks in the bank vault. He asked the king for land to build a great compound. The king gave him the land. They called one hundred workmen together for him. After three days, he again returned to the mountain, and again he gathered up money.

Now, all the people were very astonished to see Joseph become so rich. They said, "A man who sells only firewood cannot become so rich." The workers began to build. They raised a house of several stories, one story higher than the king's house. Now, all the people admired this house.

On the third day, he returned to the mountain again. He did once more as he had done before. He gathered up all the money he could carry away. Good. Now he was very, very rich. He went to marry a girl.

His brother Jean was very, very poor. He came to see him one day. Joseph greeted him and gave him a good place. He told his wife to prepare a meal for him. The two ate together. He gave him money—a whole sackful.

Jean refused it. He said, "I do not want money. I ask only to know what you did to become so rich. We both gathered firewood, and you got rich. Show me the way to do it." Jean took a knife and said, "If you do not tell me, I will kill you."

Joseph said, "If I tell you now, you won't know how to act. You'll only be killed yourself."

Jean said to him, "Why do you say I will die?"

Joseph said, "If you go, you will die. You cannot read. You won't know how to manage."

Jean said, "Good. Tell me just the same."

Joseph showed him the road. Jean went to the place and climbed up a tree. The thieves arrived. They said the words. They commanded the mountain, they said, "Open." The mountain opened.

Jean heard this. Now, towards five o'clock, the thieves again went out. Jean did not want to return home and come in the morning. He went at once to the mountain and commanded it to open. He entered and gathered up all he could carry away. He piled up the sacks. Now, he wanted to come out, but he forgot the right words. Instead of saying "Open," he said, "Close." Instead of asking the mountain to open, he kept telling it to close. Now, the mountain was shut tight. He was there inside. He was there till the thieves came.

The thieves commanded the mountain to open. The mountain did not want to open, for it was tightly closed.

One of the thieves said, "Surely, we have a man inside."

They opened the mountain and saw the man seated on the sacks. They came inside. They asked him, "Where do you come from?"

"I am the brother of Joseph, who has been gathering money here. That is why he is so rich. It is he who showed me the way here."

One thief asked him, "Is it the young one who lives in the house of several stories, near the king's house?"

Jean said, "Yes."

The thieves now killed Jean. They dismembered him, limb from limb, and nailed him to the wall of the mountain. Now, they went out again.

The next day his brother Joseph came, for he had not seen Jean for three days. He came with his notebook and a sack. He put his brother's flesh inside the sack, and put with it some money that he took.

At the house, he had all the leather workers of the village come. He said, "Who is the one who knows how to sew best? If I killed a goat and I cut it into several pieces, who could resew it?" There was a young leather worker there who said he could. So there and then they killed a goat and cut it into several pieces. Then this leather worker resewed it.

Joseph had this leather worker come at night. He showed him Jean's dead body and asked him to sew it together so that he could bury it. The leather worker did this, and at night they buried Jean.

The next day, when the thieves came back, they did not find Jean's flesh there. They said, "Joseph has courage. He came to get his brother's body, which we cut up. It must be Jean's burial that was held yesterday. We heard the noise."

Now, they began to plot how to kill Joseph. The next day, an important thief came to town to see the leather worker. He asked the leather workers of the village, "Who among you knows how to sew well?"

There was one leather worker there who said, "I know how to sew well." He said, "The other night at Joseph's house I sewed up a dead body."

"Whose dead body?"

"Jean's dead body." The thief knew then that it was Joseph who had taken his brother's body.

The thief went back to the mountain. Toward noon he gathered a hundred men. Good. One thief went to see Joseph and said he had one hundred sacks of salt. He would bring these about midnight. The thief went to find a hundred empty sacks.

At night, towards eight o'clock, Joseph went for a walk, leaving his wife behind. The thief then came to Joseph's house, for he had promised to bring one hundred sacks of salt. He entered with one hundred men and one hundred empty sacks, and Joseph's wife looked on through the windows but did nothing.

The chief of these thieves told each man to get into a sack, so that it seemed to be full of salt. Then he closed each sack and put it against a wall. When he had finished putting the men in the sacks, all the sacks were full, each with a man in it. The chief said, "At midnight,

I shall whistle. You are to come out of the sacks and we will all rob the man."

As his wife had seen this, she sent her boy to look for his master. When her husband arrived, she told him that these were not sacks of salt, but that there were men in them.

Joseph and his wife prepared a charm with water; if but a drop of this water touched your head, you would die. During the night, before midnight, they prepared the potion, and at the hour for eating, they asked the two chief thieves to come up to eat with them. Joseph and his wife sat down on the same stool, and on the opposite side of the room, the two thieves sat also on one stool. Before they climbed the stairs, Joseph had given a revolver to his wife, and he had a loaded one, too. He had said to his wife, "Madam, when we start eating, if I put my foot on yours, it will be the signal to shoot the two thieves."

When the two brigands had climbed up, they said to Joseph, "We will not eat with you. We have left our sacks of salt below and someone might steal them." Joseph told them that there were no thieves there and offered them the chair he had placed for them. He put his foot on the foot of his wife, and they shot the two thieves.

There were those in the sacks who said to the others, "Who is that shooting up there?"

And the others said, "Joseph is killing his pigeons."

After having killed the two thieves, Joseph came down accompanied by his two boys, and he brought with him the potion. As he came to each sack, he told the man in it, who believed that this was his master and not Joseph, "Here is some medicine, so that you will not be too tired." He gave it to the first, and the sack, which had stood upright, fell to the ground. The second, the same thing, and the same until he had finished ninety-nine sacks. The last man escaped.

Now, Joseph had put in nails on top of his walls in order that people could not climb over them, and so the one hundredth thief was stuck on one of these nails. He said, "Why have you killed my comrades?" Joseph went to sleep, leaving the bodies where they fell.

The next day he went to see the king of the country and the king sent men to see the dead bodies of the thieves. So the king of that country gave the order to make a road all the way to the mountain. And all the gold there belonged to Joseph.

—Dahomey

3
The Three Tests

A certain sultan had seven sons. And the eldest of them went to his father and said that he wished to travel. His father agreed and provided him with a sailing boat and food and money. So he set out and sailed until he came to an island where there were many beautiful fruits growing. He landed on this island and walked among the fruit trees. And as he walked he plucked the fruits and ate them. But when he spat out the seeds of the fruits, as soon as they touched the ground, they became new plants and bore fruit immediately. And the young man, wondering about this, gathered baskets of the fruit and took them on board his ship.

He left the island and sailed night and day until he came to another island, ruled by a sultan. Here the young man, wishing to inform the sultan of the marvelous fruit that he carried, went into his presence, and said—"Oh my Lord Sultan! I have here a marvelous fruit, the seeds of which spring up and bear fruit as soon as they touch the ground, and I would show this wonder to you." But the sultan would not believe his story, and said, "If what you say is true I will reward you, but if you are lying, then I will cast you into prison." So the young man brought the fruit and ate it and cast the seeds upon the ground, but the seeds lay there and nothing happened. Then the sultan cast him into prison and kept him there.

In the meantime, the brothers of the young man became anxious as to his fate, and the eldest of those that remained went to his father, the sultan, and asked him for a vessel and food and money that he might look for his brother. The sultan gave him all he asked for, and he set sail. He, too, arrived at the island that contained the wonderful fruit, and when he had eaten of it and found that the seeds sprang to life and bore fruit as soon as they touched the ground, he gathered baskets of it as his brother had done, placed them on board his boat, and set sail. When he came to the island on which his brother was imprisoned, he, too, proclaimed the virtue of the fruit that he had brought, and even entered the presence of the sultan to boast of it. Wishing to show this miracle to the sultan, he ate of the fruit and cast the seeds upon the ground. But they failed to spring up, and the sultan, in anger, cast him also into prison.

One by one, all the brothers, with the exception of the youngest, set sail to search for the others. Each landed on the island and gathered the magic fruit, each failed to show the miracle to the sultan who lived on the second island, and each was cast into prison.

At last there remained but the youngest son, whose name was *Sadaka,* and he went to his father and asked for a boat. When he had obtained it, he loaded it with millet and rice and cattle, and then he set sail. After several days, he reached an island that was full of birds, and these birds had no food and were starving. So *Sadaka* landed his millet upon the island, and scattered it for the birds to eat. The sultan of the birds, in return for this kindness, gave *Sadaka* a piece of incense, and said, "Burn this if at any time you need us, and we shall smell it and come to help you." So *Sadaka* took the incense and set sail. After a further journey he came to another island. And this island was full of flies who were starving and could find no food. Then *Sadaka,* filled with compassion, slew his cattle and threw them on the island for the flies to eat. When the flies were satisfied, the sultan of the flies thanked *Sadaka* and gave him a piece of incense, and said, "If at any time you need us, burn this incense and we will come to help you." So *Sadaka* took the incense and continued his journey. After a time, he came to a third island, and this island was filled with jinns, who were also without food, and hungry. So *Sadaka* took a great pot and filled it with rice, and he lit a fire underneath the pot, and said to the jinns, "Wait a little and I will cook you rice." So the jinns thanked him, and said, "Take care that you put no salt in the pot." And *Sadaka* replied, "Have no fear, there is not salt in it." So when the rice was cooked, the jinns gathered round and ate. When they were satisfied, the sultan of the jinns came to *Sadaka* and gave him a piece of incense, saying, "If at any time you need us, burn this and we will come to you." So *Sadaka* took the incense and sailed away.

In due course, he came to the island where grew the magic fruit that his brothers had found. When he, too, found that the seeds sprang to life and bore fruit as soon as they touched the ground, he gathered the fruit, and returned to the island of the jinns to show it to them. But the sultan of the jinns told him, "This miracle will only happen when the seeds fall on special soil. Therefore, if you want to show this wonder to strangers, take the soil of this island and when the seeds fall upon it they will spring up and bear fruit." So *Sadaka* filled his vessel with the soil and sailed away. Eventually he arrived at the island on which his brothers were imprisoned. He presented himself before the sultan, and said, "Oh my Lord Sultan! I have here a magic fruit, the seeds of which grow and bear fruit as soon as they touch the ground." But the sultan said, "There are now six men in prison for having failed to show me this miracle, and, if you also fail, you shall join them." *Sadaka* said, "Tomorrow, I will show this wonder." The sultan replied, "So be it, but remember if you fail, you, too, shall be cast into prison." That night *Sadaka* spread everywhere the soil that he had brought from the island of the jinns. The next morning, he ate the fruit in the presence of the sultan and his wise men and nobles. When he had eaten, he strew the seeds upon the ground and they sprang up and bore fruit. The sultan and his retinue, and all the people of the island, wondered greatly, and ate the fruit and cast the seeds upon the ground, and, speedily, the whole island blossomed with the magic fruit.

Now the sultan possessed a daughter of extraordinary beauty. When *Sadaka* heard of her charms, he desired her greatly, and asked the sultan to give her to him that he might marry her. Then the sultan gathered together sacks containing all kinds of grain, and mixed the contents of the sacks together in a room. In the evening, he locked *Sadaka* in the room with the grain saying, "If you can separate all these different kinds of grain, each into its own sack, then you can marry the princess, but if you fail, you will die." So *Sadaka* slept in the room that night, and the next morning, he burnt the incense that the sultan of the birds had given him. Immediately, the air was filled with birds and the sultan of the birds asked *Sadaka* what he wanted. When the birds heard what the sultan had ordered *Sadaka* to do, they flew into the room and, picking up the grain in their beaks, separated each kind into its own sack. But when the sultan came to *Sadaka* in the evening, and saw that all the grain was separated as he had ordered, he said to *Sadaka,* "You must prove yourself once more if you want to marry my daughter. If you can cut through the trunk of a baobab tree at one stroke of your sword, then you can take her. But if you fail, then you will die." Then he showed *Sadaka* the baobab tree, which was of enormous size.

Sadaka went back to his room, and burnt the incense that the sultan of the jinns had given him. When the jinns appeared, he told them what the sultan wanted him to do. Then the jinns brought white ants in great numbers and instructed them to gnaw at the trunk of the baobab tree. And the ants ate away the trunk of the tree, leaving only the bark. And two jinns, making themselves invisible, held the branches of the tree for fear that a wind might arise and blow it to the ground. But there was no wind, and *Sadaka* approached the tree with the sultan and his retinue. In their presence, he drew his sword and smote the tree and cut it in half. And the jinns, who were holding it, guided its fall that it might kill no one.

Then the sultan said, "Tomorrow all the maidens of the city, including the princess, my daughter, will pass in front of you, one by one, and you must pick the princess from among them. If you choose right, you shall have her in marriage; but if you fail to discover which is the princess, then you will die." Then *Sadaka* retired once more to his chamber, and burnt the incense that the sultan of the flies had given him. Immediately, the sultan of the flies appeared, and *Sadaka* told him what the sultan had decreed. Then the sultan of the flies said, "When the maidens of the city pass before you, I will stand in front of you, and you will watch me. When the princess is drawing near, I will drum my wings as if I am about to fly. Then, when she passes in front of you, I will alight on her shoulder and you shall take her." So the next day all the maidens of the city passed before *Sadaka,* and the sultan of the flies stood in front of *Sadaka,* and *Sadaka* watched him. Suddenly, he began to drum the air with his wings, and *soon* flew around and landed on the shoulder of the princess as she walked past. Then *Sadaka* took her by the arm and led her away, and *Sadaka* married the princess and released his brothers from prison. The story is finished.

—Swahili

4 Monkey Steals a Drum

This text comes from a performance by Mr. Adégbóyègún Fáàdójútìmí. It was collected by Deirdre LaPin and translated by Deirdre LaPin and Túndé Ayándòkun.

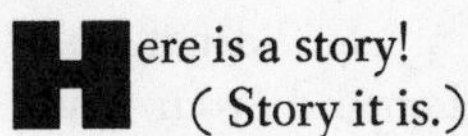

Here is a story!
(Story it is.)

Everyone be still and listen carefully to our story. Anybody who can sing the chorus needn't make any extra noise.

> *My story breaks sharply,* pá,
> *Don't let it break its arms;*
> *It breaks, whirs, and thuds,* wàrà gbì
> *Don't let it break its neck;*
> *It didn't fall on* my *head!*
> *It didn't fall on* my *neck!*
> *Nor did it fall on the bit of Rat*
> *That I'll eat before I sleep tonight!*
> *Instead, it fell on the heads of the*
> *one hundred and fifty-six animals.*

Now, one day a meeting was held and all the animals were told to come, every last one. Each was greeted, "Hello," and asked about its affairs. Then all of them were instructed to peel off a piece of skin from their bodies, so that they could make drums for dancing and having a good time. Up to now, nobody had ever thought of such a thing, and they all agreed that their omission was most unfortunate. So each started to peel off its skin and make it into a drum, they made drums every last one.

Eventually, market day came—the day when their meeting was always held—and every one of them brought his drum. Well! Friends, were they happy! They beat out a dance rhythm and danced into the afternoon; they danced and danced and danced and danced.

You know, greed is a bad thing. Yes, sir. Leopard had never known anything like it before. He finished eating and friends, he had eaten so much that he threw everything up, *gọ̀ọ̀rọ̀gọ̀*. While he slept, excreta was flowing from his bowels. The like had never been known before, friends, he ate to his fill and went to sleep, stuffed.

Now, Colobus Monkey said that he couldn't really peel off a piece of his skin for a drum; he was such a tiny little thing that if he took any skin from his body, what would there be left? Friends, Leopard was sleeping away there, and Monkey said to himself that here was a sure chance to have a drum of his own to beat. He stretched out his hand toward Leopard's drum, picked it up, and set off down the road. He headed for home.

Well! Leopard woke up. "Where is it! I put my drum down right here, this is where I left it." After searching all round for it, some people said, "Ha! We saw Monkey carrying a drum. He did not bring any of his own when he came to the meeting. Leopard, your drum must be with Monkey." So he said, "Okay, I see," and went home. He was so furious that his bowels rumbled and his heart was on fire. How was he going to catch Monkey? "Ha! I've never experienced a thing like this before, what's the best way to go about this?" Market day came again, the day when they would hold their meeting. Well, just a little before cockcrow, Leopard got up and went to the three-way intersection in the town of *Ajaloko* and he swept the roadway absolutely clean. *Àjànàkú* sat down: His two eyes were blazing brightly. When day broke, all one-hundred-and-fifty-six animals came along to go to the meeting. Giant Rat woke up earliest, and was the first to come hopping along with his tail flying behind him, *gọ́ọ́lọ gọ́ọ́lọ gọ́ọ́lọ*. As soon as his eyes lit on The Warrior of Lagos—"Oh! Oh! Well! My goodness!" He prostrated himself before him and stretched out his hand, palm upward—"*Àjànàkú,* the One Who Wakes Up and Washes His Hands and Face Like a Muslim." Friends, he beseeched him; "*Kábiyèsí,* my Protecting God, I am innocent," he said. Then he took up a song that went like this:

What's your trouble, Warrior?
Yẹ́ẹ́yẹ Irànmatẹ́kọ̀n
What's your trouble, Warrior?
Yẹ́ẹ́yẹ Irànmatẹ́kọ̀n
What's your trouble, Warrior?
Yẹ́ẹ́yẹ Irànmatẹ́kọ̀n
He said, "Everybody made a drum,
Yẹ́ẹ́yẹ Irànmatẹ́kọ̀n
And Monkey took my drum away;
Yẹ́ẹ́yẹ Irànmatẹ́kọ̀n
We'll set our eyes on him today,
Yẹ́ẹ́yẹ Irànmatẹ́kọ̀n
'Cause the dust here is still unstirred;
Yẹ́ẹ́yẹ Irànmatẹ́kọ̀n
We'll offer meat to an expectant mother,
Yẹ́ẹ́yẹ Irànmatẹ́kọ̀n
We'll give meat to everyone!
Yẹ́ẹ́yẹ Irànmatẹ́kọ̀n
You'll come and eat and eat and eat.
Yẹ́ẹ́yẹ Irànmatẹ́kọ̀n
Hey, don't you *want to eat?*
Yẹ́ẹ́yẹ Irànmatẹ́kọ̀n
Hey, don't you *want to eat?*
Yẹ́ẹ́yẹ Irànmatẹ́kọ̀n
They'll eat meat, eat meat, more meat."
Yẹ́ẹ́yẹ Irànmatẹ́kọ̀n
What's your trouble, Warrior?
Yẹ́ẹ́yẹ Irànmatẹ́kọ̀n

Well, Rat said he didn't want to get mixed up in any trouble. He had gotten up early and ran straight into trouble. He turned around and scampered off.

Àjànàkú sat back down on his haunches and waited. You see, he cleared the ground where they would fight. Ha! Yes, sir. I congratulate myself, He Who Tells Stories without Muffing the Job, Son of He with a Slender Neck. It's not easy to work for a living. If somebody's peeled some skin off his own body, he's not going to let someone else get away with doing nothing, is he? Cutting Grass scampered by, *yúghú yúghú yúghú yúghú*. *Àjànàkú* was really terrifying. You know, his front teeth are red in color. Even if *Olódùmarè* himself passed by this *Àjànàkú,* his eyes would turn a deep, deep red. Ha! So he said, "*Kábiyèsí,* my Protecting God, I'm innocent." You see, his anus had receded into his bowels—the anus he shit from—and he was anxiously rubbing his palms together. "Hey, what's your trouble, Warrior?"

What's your trouble, Warrior?
Yẹ́ẹ̀yẹ Iràǹmatẹ́kọ̀n
What's your trouble, Warrior?
Yẹ́ẹ̀yẹ Iràǹmatẹ́kọ̀n
He said, "Everybody made a drum,
Yẹ́ẹ̀yẹ Iràǹmatẹ́kọ̀n
And Monkey took my drum away;
Yẹ́ẹ̀yẹ Iràǹmatẹ́kọ̀n
We'll set our eyes on him today,
Yẹ́ẹ̀yẹ Iràǹmatẹ́kọ̀n
'Cause the dust here is still unstirred;
Yẹ́ẹ̀yẹ Iràǹmatẹ́kọ̀n
We'll offer meat to an expectant mother,
Yẹ́ẹ̀yẹ Iràǹmatẹ́kọ̀n
We'll offer meat to a big-assed gal,
Yẹ́ẹ̀yẹ Iràǹmatẹ́kọ̀n
We'll give meat to everyone!
Yẹ́ẹ̀yẹ Iràǹmatẹ́kọ̀n
You'll come and eat and eat and eat.
Yẹ́ẹ̀yẹ Iràǹmatẹ́kọ̀n
Hey, don't you *want to eat?*
Yẹ́ẹ̀yẹ Iràǹmatẹ́kọ̀n
Hey, don't you *want to eat?*
Yẹ́ẹ̀yẹ Iràǹmatẹ́kọ̀n
They'll eat meat, eat meat, more meat."
Yẹ́ẹ̀yẹ Iràǹmatẹ́kọ̀n
What's your trouble, Warrior?
Yẹ́ẹ̀yẹ Iràǹmatẹ́kọ̀n

Nobody had the nerve to pass by that spot where he was cutting grass. He turned right around and bolted off. Well! He caused quite an uproar as he turned around and scampered off, *fù*, in a flash!

Now *Duiker* had waked up and was trotting, *béléké béléké,* along to the meeting. He was going to eat himself silly just as he had done eight days before. Whew! You see now he was bounding along at a fast clip, *ṣobgá ṣobgá ṣobgá,* his tail flying in the air behind him, when suddenly, right there in the middle of the road was *Àjànàkú*. Duiker spied him, Owner of the Black Locust Bean Farm, the One Who Drove the Household Head Up the Ọdán Tree and Chased the Elder into a Hole, the One Who Tore a Woman's Child to Pieces. As soon as he looked into his face, he said, "What's your trouble, Warrior?"

What's your trouble, Warrior?
Yẹ́ẹ̀yẹ Iràǹmatẹ́kọ̀n

What's your trouble, Warrior?
Yẹ́ẹ́yẹ Irànmatẹ́kọ̀n
He said, "Everybody made a drum,
Yẹ́ẹ́yẹ Irànmatẹ́kọ̀n
And Monkey took my drum away;
Yẹ́ẹ́yẹ Irànmatẹ́kọ̀n
We'll set our eyes on him today,
Yẹ́ẹ́yẹ Irànmatẹ́kọ̀n
'Cause the dust here is still unstirred;
Yẹ́ẹ́yẹ Irànmatẹ́kọ̀n
We'll offer meat to an expectant mother,
Yẹ́ẹ́yẹ Irànmatẹ́kọ̀n
We'll offer meat to a big-assed gal,
Yẹ́ẹ́yẹ Irànmatẹ́kọ̀n
We'll give meat to everyone!
Yẹ́ẹ́yẹ Irànmatẹ́kọ̀n
You'll come and eat and eat and eat.
Yẹ́ẹ́yẹ Irànmatẹ́kọ̀n
Hey, don't you *want to eat?*
Yẹ́ẹ́yẹ Irànmatẹ́kọ̀n
Hey, don't you *want to eat?*
Yẹ́ẹ́yẹ Irànmatẹ́kọ̀n
Which of them will have a chance to eat?
Yẹ́ẹ́yẹ Irànmatẹ́kọ̀n
They'll eat meat, eat meat, more meat."
Yẹ́ẹ́yẹ Irànmatẹ́kọ̀n
All of them will eat meat, eat meat."
Yẹ́ẹ́yẹ Irànmatẹ́kọ̀n
What's your trouble, Warrior?
Yẹ́ẹ́yẹ Irànmatẹ́kọ̀n

As soon as Duiker took a look at him, he said to himself, "Today is not the day for a yamfest and this is not a place where one should pass." Duiker turned tail and dashed away so fast that he went nearly a mile in three bounds!

Deer was prancing along, *jìgọlọ jìgọlọ jìgọlọ*, carrying a load of yam on top of his big horns. He was passing by in his swift and determined stride, *ghàn ghàn ghàn*, when suddenly he saw Owner of the Black Locust Bean Farm, and stopped instantly. "*Kábiyèsí*, my Protecting God, what's your trouble, Warrior?"

What's your trouble, Warrior?
Yẹ́ẹ́yẹ Irànmatẹ́kọ̀n

What's your trouble, Warrior?
Yẹ́ẹ́yẹ Irà̀nmatẹ́kọ̀n
He said, "Everybody made a drum,
Yẹ́ẹ́yẹ Iràǹmatẹ́kọ̀n
And Monkey took my drum away;
Yẹ́ẹ́yẹ Iràǹmatẹ́kọ̀n
We'll set our eyes on him today,
Yẹ́ẹ́yẹ Iràǹmatẹ́kọ̀n
'Cause the dust here is still unstirred;
Yẹ́ẹ́yẹ Iràǹmatẹ́kọ̀n
We'll offer meat to an expectant mother,
Yẹ́ẹ́yẹ Iràǹmatẹ́kọ̀n
We'll offer meat to a big-assed gal,
Yẹ́ẹ́yẹ Iràǹmatẹ́kọ̀n
We'll give meat to everyone!
Yẹ́ẹ́yẹ Iràǹmatẹ́kọ̀n
You'll come and eat and eat and eat.
Yẹ́ẹ́yẹ Iràǹmatẹ́kọ̀n
Hey, don't you *want to eat?*
Yẹ́ẹ́yẹ Iràǹmatẹ́kọ̀n
Hey, don't you *want to eat?*
Yẹ́ẹ́yẹ Iràǹmatẹ́kọ̀n
They'll eat meat, eat meat, more meat."
Yẹ́ẹ́yẹ Iràǹmatẹ́kọ̀n
What's your trouble, Warrior?
Yẹ́ẹ́yẹ Iràǹmatẹ́kọ̀n

You know, as soon as he finished his reply, Deer looked ahead, looked behind—and clattered away fast, *ayà yà yà!* As he was running, *"Yay! Hai! Horror, horror, horror," gìdì gìdì gìdì,* whoosh, *ṣọ̀ ṣọ̀*. Ha! He knocked over an *akika* tree. He nearly fainted with hunger—he hadn't really eaten for eight days. The situation was not good.

Buck came along, belly hanging from his belly. Poor Devil Who Swallows His Fruits Whole, he could be killed by a mouse. *Olódùmarè,* don't let me be killed by a mouse! Now, when he looked into the face of Owner of the Black Locust Bean Farm—*aiye!* He stopped dead in his tracks, his legs splayed. He asked, "What's your trouble, Warrior?"

What's your trouble, Warrior?
Yẹ́ẹ́yẹ Iràǹmatẹ́kọ̀n
What's your trouble, Warrior?
Yẹ́ẹ́yẹ Iràǹmatẹ́kọ̀n
He said, "Everybody made a drum,
Yẹ́ẹ́yẹ Iràǹmatẹ́kọ̀n

And Monkey took my drum away;
Yẹ́ẹ̀yẹ Irà̀nmatẹ́kọ̀n
We'll set our eyes on him today,
Yẹ́ẹ̀yẹ Iràǹmatẹ́kọ̀n
'Cause the dust here is still unstirred;
Yẹ́ẹ̀yẹ Iràǹmatẹ́kọ̀n
We'll offer meat to an expectant mother,
Yẹ́ẹ̀yẹ Iràǹmatẹ́kọ̀n
We'll offer meat to a big-assed gal,
Yẹ́ẹ̀yẹ Iràǹmatẹ́kọ̀n
We'll give meat to everyone!
Yẹ́ẹ̀yẹ Iràǹmatẹ́kọ̀n
You'll come and eat and eat and eat.
Yẹ́ẹ̀yẹ Iràǹmatẹ́kọ̀n
Hey, don't you *want to eat?*
Yẹ́ẹ̀yẹ Iràǹmatẹ́kọ̀n
Hey, don't you *want to eat?*
Yẹ́ẹ̀yẹ Iràǹmatẹ́kọ̀n
The European will eat meat, eat meat."
Yẹ́ẹ̀yẹ Iràǹmatẹ́kọ̀n
What's your trouble, Warrior?
Yẹ́ẹ̀yẹ Iràǹmatẹ́kọ̀n

When Buck took off he was like a grasshopper, ready to burst open in the fire. His head knocked against a tree and pulled the bark clean off, he was running so fast. *Àjànàkú* kept his eyes shut as Buck ran.

He next saw Bush Cow coming along with his ponderous gait, *gìrágwo gìrágwo gìrágwo. Olódùmarè,* his great horns swung from side to side. When he got there, and saw Owner of the Black Locust Bean Farm, the One Who Chased the Elder into a Hole, the One Who Drove the Household Head Up the Ọdán Tree, *Àjànàkú*'s two eyes were glowing. You know what a palm fruit is, that we use to make soup with on the farm, the thing we cut down and make oil from that is bright, bright red? Well, Owner of Black Locust Bean Farm had eyes like that—it was Leopard, mind you, not *this* Leopard. As soon as Bush Cow looked at him, "Horrors!" he said, "Ha! I'm innocent, innocent, *Kábiyèsí,* my Protecting God. What's your trouble, Warrior?"

What's your trouble, Warrior?
Yẹ́ẹ̀yẹ Iràǹmatẹ́kọ̀n
What's your trouble, Warrior?
Yẹ́ẹ̀yẹ Iràǹmatẹ́kọ̀n
He said, "Everybody made a drum,
Yẹ́ẹ̀yẹ Iràǹmatẹ́kọ̀n

And Monkey took my drum away;
Yẹ́ẹ̀yẹ Iràǹmatẹ́kọ̀n
We'll set our eyes on him today,
Yẹ́ẹ̀yẹ Iràǹmatẹ́kọ̀n
We'll offer meat to an expectant mother,
Yẹ́ẹ̀yẹ Iràǹmatẹ́kọ̀n
We'll offer meat to a big-assed gal,
Yẹ́ẹ̀yẹ Iràǹmatẹ́kọ̀n
We'll give meat to everyone!
Yẹ́ẹ̀yẹ Iràǹmatẹ́kọ̀n
You'll come and eat and eat and eat.
Yẹ́ẹ̀yẹ Iràǹmatẹ́kọ̀n
Hey, don't you *want to eat?*
Yẹ́ẹ̀yẹ Iràǹmatẹ́kọ̀n
Hey, don't you *want to eat?*
Yẹ́ẹ̀yẹ Iràǹmatẹ́kọ̀n
They'll eat meat, eat meat, more meat."
Yẹ́ẹ̀yẹ Iràǹmatẹ́kọ̀n
What's your trouble, Warrior?
Yẹ́ẹ̀yẹ Iràǹmatẹ́kọ̀n

Oh, *Olódùmarè,* protect us from trouble as we are walking along. I Who Tell Stories without Muffing the Job, Son of He with a Slender Neck. Bush Cow started to run away. My Father! If he met a tree along the way, it would never be met again. He brewed up a storm! *Olódùmarè* keep us from trouble like that. He hightailed it away; he had expected a feast like the one eight days earlier—food like that could kill a person!

Just then, Elephant appeared, *Laaye,* Spirit of the Forest, *Orìṣà* with One Arm, Who Wakes and Bathes Himself in Dew. He trundled along, his ears flapping. As soon as he noticed Owner of the Black Locust Bean Farm—*Ai!* Well, now, he stopped in his tracks. He said, "What's your trouble, Warrior?"

What's your trouble, Warrior?
Yẹ́ẹ̀yẹ Iràǹmatẹ́kọ̀n
What's your trouble, Warrior?
Yẹ́ẹ̀yẹ Iràǹmatẹ́kọ̀n
He said, "Everybody made a drum,
Yẹ́ẹ̀yẹ Iràǹmatẹ́kọ̀n
And Monkey took my drum away;
Yẹ́ẹ̀yẹ Iràǹmatẹ́kọ̀n
We'll set our eyes on him today,
Yẹ́ẹ̀yẹ Iràǹmatẹ́kọ̀n

'Cause the dust here is still unstirred;
Yẹ́ẹ̀yẹ Irànmatẹ́kọ̀n
We'll offer meat to an expectant mother,
Yẹ́ẹ̀yẹ Irànmatẹ́kọ̀n
We'll offer meat to a big-assed gal,
Yẹ́ẹ̀yẹ Irànmatẹ́kọ̀n
We'll give meat to everyone!
Yẹ́ẹ̀yẹ Irànmatẹ́kọ̀n
You'll come and eat and eat and eat.
Yẹ́ẹ̀yẹ Irànmatẹ́kọ̀n
Hey, don't you *want to eat?*
Yẹ́ẹ̀yẹ Irànmatẹ́kọ̀n
Hey, don't you *want to eat?*
Yẹ́ẹ̀yẹ Irànmatẹ́kọ̀n
They'll eat meat, eat meat, more meat."
Yẹ́ẹ̀yẹ Irànmatẹ́kọ̀n
What's your trouble, Warrior?
Yẹ́ẹ̀yẹ Irànmatẹ́kọ̀n

Laaye turned round, saying he hoped he would never see anything like that again in his life! It didn't matter whether he ate or not. So he walked off, and his path made a roadway that is used up until today. It has become the model for all roads ever since—big wide streets of today. But his was more shiny and bare than any highway. Yes sir! *Olódùmarè!* May no one hear a false tale from my mouth. Since when have I been telling lies? I'm telling the truth today. You know, the mouse I put in the hearth yesterday was eaten up by a melon!

Just then, Monkey came scampering along, *gọọlọ gọọlọ gọọlọ,* his tail flying behind him and his drum slung around his neck. He got to the same spot and saw the Warrior of Lagos. *Ai!* May I not be confronted by problems early in the morning.

Didn't he jump into the trees? He didn't climb into the trees because monkeys in those days walked on the ground. As soon as he set eyes on Owner of the Black Locust Bean Farm, the One Who Drove the Household Head Up to the Top of the Ọdán Tree, Who Chased the Elder into a Hole, the One Who Tears a Woman's Child to Pieces, my father! His two eyes—the jig was up. As soon as he spied Monkey things really got hot. *Olódùmarè,* don't let me experience a thing like that! Have you ever seen a cat's tail when he's chasing a lizard outdoors? His tail was twitching from side to side, *pọn pọn pọn. Olódùmarè,* his tail was stuck straight out. He said, "*Kábiyèsí, Kábiyèsí,* my Protecting God." You know that in the past Monkey's hands were just like a human's. He rubbed them together anxiously, "*Kábiyèsí.* What's your trouble, Warrior?"

What's your trouble, Warrior?
Yẹ́ẹ́yẹ Iràǹmatẹ́kọ̀n
What's your trouble, Warrior?
Yẹ́ẹ́yẹ Iràǹmatẹ́kọ̀n
He said, "Everybody made a drum,
Yẹ́ẹ́yẹ Iràǹmatẹ́kọ̀n
And Monkey took my drum away;
Yẹ́ẹ́yẹ Iràǹmatẹ́kọ̀n
We'll set our eyes on him today,
Yẹ́ẹ́yẹ Iràǹmatẹ́kọ̀n
'Cause the dust here is still unstirred;
Yẹ́ẹ́yẹ Iràǹmatẹ́kọ̀n
We'll offer meat to an expectant mother,
Yẹ́ẹ́yẹ Iràǹmatẹ́kọ̀n
We'll offer meat to a big-assed gal,
Yẹ́ẹ́yẹ Iràǹmatẹ́kọ̀n
We'll give meat to everyone!
Yẹ́ẹ́yẹ Iràǹmatẹ́kọ̀n
You'll come and eat and eat and eat.
Yẹ́ẹ́yẹ Iràǹmatẹ́kọ̀n
Hey, don't you *want to eat?*
Yẹ́ẹ́yẹ Iràǹmatẹ́kọ̀n
Hey, don't you *want to eat?*
Yẹ́ẹ́yẹ Iràǹmatẹ́kọ̀n
They'll eat meat, eat meat, more meat."
Yẹ́ẹ́yẹ Iràǹmatẹ́kọ̀n
What's your trouble, Warrior?
Yẹ́ẹ́yẹ Iràǹmatẹ́kọ̀n

Olódùmarè, protect me, don't let anyone say they've heard an evil tale from my lips—you see, just then *Gbùàgàdà* summoned all his strength and shot out after Monkey. As soon as he grabbed hold of him, he raised his arm and landed sprawled on the ground! He was so strong that he lost his balance as soon as he made his catch. He used only a hand to catch him. "Rats! You mean I've been wasting my energy on *this?*" Monkey scoffed, "Ha-ha-ha, for a little thing like me? You've geared yourself all up as if you were going to a fight to the death, ha-ha-ha, when it was only me, whom you could just pick up and put in your pocket, I, who am so small that if you put me in your mouth there'd be enough room left to whistle through? Ha-ha! You really shouldn't have taken such pains!"

Well, Leopard breathed a sigh of satisfaction and said, "Thanks be to *Ọlọ́'run,*" and pinned Monkey to the ground. "Oh, no! Don't press me like that! You know I've never been very fat! There won't be anything left! Do you know how I can fatten up so I'll be better eating? You can see, can't you, how very thin I am?" "Yes, so what can we do to make you fatter?" said Leopard. "No, listen, Monkey told him. You should cut a piece of rope from one of the slippery creepers that grows on the ground, and tie my hands together with it. Then you should throw me up high; when I've fallen through the air and landed on the ground, I'll grow a little fatter. More fat, the second time—seven times in all. You know, when I've been thrown like that seven times, I'll be fatter than you are! Leopard, that way you'll have plenty of meat to share with whomever you want. They told me you would have meat to divide all around." Leopard was surprised, "Oh, yeah?" "And as you know," Monkey went on, "there's no hole around here where I can hide, it's true. You've got me. You know only too well that you've got me."

So, Leopard went off and got a smooth vine—poor guy—the kind of vine called *yẹnghẹ́n*. He pulled it up and broke a piece off. Then he tied it round Monkey's hands. "Ouch! Ouch! Are you trying to kill me for no good reason? Loosen the rope a little!" So, he loosened it slightly. Then he rewound it round Monkey's hands and tied it in a knot. He threw him into the air; Monkey swelled himself up a bit. "Well, you've grown, it's true!" Poor guy. Outdone because he wants to eat.

Then it was the second time. "Throw me again." "Okay." He threw him up and he fell on the ground again. He swelled up a little more. "Now, don't you see I'm getting even fatter?" "Yep! It's true, you're getting bigger!"

The third time came around. He threw him up a third time. Monkey fell to the ground and inflated himself a bit more. "Look," he said, "you ought to throw me higher—that way I'll get even fatter." Friends, he summoned all his force and threw him up. You know the tree known as *ẹkú* in those days, a thick tall tree. Monkey tried to grab hold of its leaves, but his hands slipped and he fell back to the ground. He puffed himself up and puffed himself up even more. "Ha!" said Leopard. "So, you see it's working. This thing is getting even bigger, it's true!" Monkey replied, "Well, you haven't been doing a very good job of it. I haven't landed with the wind knocked out of me yet. If you throw me higher, I'll get even fatter, as fat as Leopard himself!" Then Leopard summoned all his strength and threw him with a whoosh! Monkey stretched out his arms and caught hold of a branch of the *ẹkú* tree.

Father, he clambered through the branches, *gẹ́tẹ gẹ́tẹ gẹ́tẹ,* using both his legs and arms to grip the tree. He declared he would shake the dew off onto the head of an elder. Leopard stared at him in surprise. All the dew on the tree rained down on Leopard's head. Leopard said, "I've really been defeated." *Olódùmarè,* don't let us suffer.

Leopard suffered a second defeat on top of the first. That was as far as I went before I came home.

—*Yoruba*

5 A Man Who Could Transform Himself

There was a man called *Mbokothe,* and he had a brother. The two were orphans and they lived together. Their parents had left them two cows when they died, and one day, *Mbokothe* said to his brother, "Let me take these two cows and go to a medicine man, so that he can give me some treatment, the giving of magical powers." And his elder brother told him to take them.

Mbokothe led the two cows out of their home, and drove them to a famous medicine man in another part of the country. The medicine man treated him, and gave him magical powers, so that he could transform himself into any kind of animal that he wanted. He returned to his home, told his brother about it, and said, "If I change into an animal, don't tell anyone my secret."

One day *Mbokothe* transformed himself into a huge bull, and his brother drove him to the market to sell him. All the people that saw them stopped and stared, wondering where such a big bull had come from. One man came looking to buy and he asked how much that big bull cost. The brother told him that he would exchange it for two cows and five goats. So the man bought the bull, intending to slaughter it to impress the man whose daughter he wanted to marry.

The buyer drove the bull towards his home, but before they got there, the bull escaped and ran away. The man chased after it, with no luck, until he was exhausted. The bull transformed itself so that one half of it looked like a lion, and then disappeared into the forest. The man followed its trail and saw on the ground the prints of a lion's paw, and he exclaimed, "It has already been eaten by a lion!" So he went back home, upset at having wasted so much time and energy. The bull went on, and when it was far from where people lived, it transformed itself back into a man, and *Mbokothe* returned home and saw the cows and goats that his brother had obtained from the market that day.

On another market day, these two brothers did the same thing, and again *Mbokothe* transformed himself into a bull. His brother sold him for ten goats, and drove the goats back to their home while *Mbokothe* was being driven to the home of the man who bought him. But to their misfortune, the man who bought the bull had also been to the medicine man, and had himself gotten a powerful charm. When they came near the house of the man, the bull ran off, as on the previous occasion, and the owner chased it towards the forest. He came very near to catching it, and *Mbokothe* decided to transform himself into a lion, thinking that the man would be scared if he saw a lion, but the other man was also able to change into a lion, and continued to chase *Mbokothe*. When *Mbokothe* saw that he was about to be caught, he transformed himself into a bird and flew away. But the other man changed into a kite, and then both of them flew in the sky, chasing each other.

Again, *Mbokothe* saw that he was on the point of being caught, so he came down to the ground, changed himself into an antelope, and continued to run. His pursuer changed into a wolf, and the two ran on till at last *Mbokothe* yielded, and said to the other man, after they had both changed back into human beings, "Okay, let's go to my home and I'll give you back your goats." They went to his home and *Mbokothe* gave the man his ten goats. For he knew that he had met his match in making magic.

—*Akamba*

Tale of an Old Woman

There was once an old woman who had no husband and no relations, no money and no food. One day she took her axe and went to the forest to cut a little firewood to sell, so that she could buy something to eat. She went very far, right into the heart of the bush, and she came to a large tree covered with flowers, and the tree was called *Musiwa*. The woman took her axe and began to fell the tree. The tree said to her, "Why are you cutting me? What have I done to you?" The woman said to the tree, "I am cutting you down to make some firewood to sell, so that I can get some money, so that I can buy food to keep from starving, for I am very poor and have no husband or relations." The tree said to her, "Let me give you some children to be your own children to help you in your work, but you must not beat them, nor are you to scold them. If you scold them you will see the consequences." The woman said, "All right, I won't scold them." Then the flowers of that tree turned into many boys and girls. The woman took them and brought them home.

Each child had its own work—some tilled, others hunted elephants, and still others fished. There were girls who had the work of cutting firewood, and girls who had the work of collecting vegetables, and girls who pounded flour and cooked it. The old woman didn't have to work any more, for now she was blessed.

Among the girls, there was one smaller than all the rest. The others said to the woman, "This little girl must not work. When she is hungry and cries for food, give it to her and don't be angry at her for all of this." The woman said to them, "All right, my children, whatever you tell me I will do."

In this way, they lived together for some time. The woman didn't have to work except to feed the littlest child when it wanted to eat. One day the child said to the woman, "I am very hungry. Give me some food to eat." The woman scolded the child, saying, "How you pester me, you children of the bush! Get it out of the pot yourself." The child cried and cried because it had been scolded by the woman. Some of her brothers and sisters came, and asked her what was the matter. She told them, "When I said I was hungry and asked for food, our mother said to me, 'How I am worried by these bush children.' " Then the boys and girls waited until those who had gone hunting returned, and they told them how the matter stood. So they said to the woman, "So you said we are children of the bush. We'll just go back to our mother, *Musiwa,* and you can dwell alone." The woman pleaded with them every way, but they wouldn't stay. They all returned to the tree and became flowers again, as it was before, and all the people laughed at her. She dwelt in poverty till she died, because she did not heed the instruction given to her by the tree.

—*Bondei*

7

The King's Daughter Who Lost Her Hair

A long, long time ago, there was a king who had one daughter. All the people in his kingdom said that she was the most beautiful girl on the face of the earth. Her face was like glass—it glittered like precious stones of great price—and her eyes were like the sun. But it was her hair that dazzled people, for it was very, very beautiful, and in color it was neither black nor golden, but between the two. The hair was so long that it touched the ground when she walked.

The king loved his daughter very much, and used to give her pearls and diamonds because she adored them. She also loved flowers, and every morning fresh ones were brought to her room. Some she put in her hair, and the others she put in a vase on the table. All who went to the king's palace used to exclaim, "What a pity it would be if she ever lost her hair!"

Now, one morning, while the girl was standing near the window in her room doing little tasks, a bird came flying by. It was a very big, ugly, greenish bird, and had red and terrifying eyes. After a little while, it flew back, passing to and fro in front of her window. Finally, it landed on a nearby tree and stared in at the beautiful girl. She didn't see it until the bird spoke to her, and then she was very surprised. The bird said, "Good afternoon, lovely girl! You have very, very beautiful hair, which I have heard about everywhere. Now I believe the report!" The girl smiled and felt warm satisfaction at hearing a bird comment on her hair. Then she said, "How wonderful it is that I have the most lovely hair in all my father's kingdom! I have more exquisite hair than all the women in the world!"

The bird said to the princess, "Now, you have enough hair for yourself, so you can certainly afford to spare some for me. I have nothing to build a nest out of. I need something as fine and soft as this to lay my eggs on. Since you have so much hair, if you were to give me only a small lock, I would be very happy." The girl answered, "My hair? My beautiful hair? Such lovely hair to be put in your nest and wasted! I am a king's daughter, and I love my hair more than anything else on earth!" The bird said, "I would pay you to give me some of your hair." She replied, "I won't give you even one hair. I have never heard such foolishness before. Go away or I will call the soldiers to come and shoot you."

Then the bird smiled and said, "They can't shoot me! You better not call them for they couldn't do it if they wanted to. Now, for the last time, princess, will you give me some of your hair?" The king's daughter got angry and cried, "I will not!" Just as she was about to weep, the bird remarked, "Well, never mind then," and flew round and round the tree, singing:

As leaves fall in the dry season,
So let this girl's hair fall off.
Leaves return in the rainy season,
But when will she get back her hair?

When the bird had finished singing, he spoke once to the girl and flew away, leaving her bewildered and frightened.

Now, the rains stopped and the dry season came. A strong wind began to blow, and the tree outside the princess's room began to lose its leaves, until soon they were all on the ground. In the same way that these leaves had fallen, the hair of the king's daughter began to fall. As you can imagine, she was furious and then inconsolable. She threw herself about in great sorrow. Then she went to tell her father. On hearing her story, the king shook with laughter and said, "How can a bird cause you this great loss of your hair!" The girl was certainly not very pleased with her father's response, and she continued to cry. And her hair continued to fall out. She was very unhappy, and the other girls who came to wash and comb her hair tried to comfort her, but she did not stop crying. All her hair came out, and she looked exceedingly ugly.

The king called together all the wisemen and magicians in his kingdom, and said to them, "Whoever will put back the hair on the head of my daughter, I will give him many pieces of gold." But every one of those wisemen and magicians failed to put it back.

One night, as the king's daughter was sleeping, she dreamt a dream. In her dream she saw a tree that produced hair, and saw a young man who danced very well and sang this song:

Where there is no grass,
Plant seeds in the soil,
That there may grow some grass.

In the dream she saw that when the young man had sung that song, he took a seed out of his bag and cast it on the ground, and where the seed fell a tree grew up immediately. When the tree had become big, it produced fruits, and when those fruits ripened, they produced much hair, and the hair covered the tree completely. When the girl woke up in the morning, she thought hard about the dream and the tree that produced hair. She could think of nothing else that whole day.

She went and called her father, the king, and said, "In a dream I saw a tree that was growing hair. Now, you should get your wise men and magicians, and ask them to look for the seeds of this tree." So the king called his wise men and magicians again, and said that he would give many more pieces of gold to whoever would bring the seeds of the hair-producing tree. All the people looked for that tree, but no one was able to find it or any of its seeds. Indeed, no one had ever seen or heard of it.

In that country, there was one young man who was very poor and lonely. His name was *Muoma,* and he had a small infection on his leg. When he heard that the king had requested the people to look for the hair-producing tree, he decided he would try to find it because such a vast amount of gold would make him rich. He had neither father nor mother, brother nor sister—no relatives at all. He said to himself, "I don't see why I shouldn't go to find this tree." So he took a trip to look for it; but it turned out to be a very foolish journey!

As the man traveled, he got to one place where birds talked like men, and another where the animals talked like men, too. He saw trees with fingers and eyes like men, and he felt that it was very likely he would find the tree he wanted. Of course, wherever he went he asked all the birds, the animals, the trees about the tree which grew hair. He went on for many months in this manner. He thought he was going to reach the right place quickly, but he came to the sea without success. He made himself a boat and started sailing. All the time he was traveling eastwards.

Muoma sailed on and on, until he came to an island. From his boat he could see it was a very small and barren island and there were only three trees there. One tree had red beans; the second had a gray-green hue that showed it was a tree of silver; and the third was golden, and very wonderful. This third tree was very tall, and the top of it was like a golden dome. He guided his boat to the shores of the island, got out, and went and stood under the golden dome. Suddenly, with a very loud explosion, the dome split into twelve pieces. They all fell to the ground at the same time, and immediately the whole tree caught fire and burned to the ground.

Muoma was exceedingly frightened, and he shook his head and looked at the ground while all this went on. When the sound had died away and the fire had gone out, he picked up one red bean from the ground and put it into his bag; then he picked up other beans, too, and carried them to his boat. He set off again, now assured he was on the right track and that soon he would see the tree he wanted.

After sailing a little while, he heard a thundering sound in the sky. He looked up and saw a huge bird, which alighted on his boat and stared him in the face. The bird asked if he had gotten the red beans from that little island, and he replied that he had. Then the bird said, "Take one bean pod, open it, and give me one of the beans." When the bird had eaten the bean, it said to the young man, "Where are you going?" He told the bird what had happened to the king's daughter, how she had lost her hair and was very anxious to get it back.

When the bird had heard the story, it said, "I remember coming to your country and talking to the king's daughter about her hair. It was I who told her that she would lose it because she refused to give me a little of it to make my nest." The bird asked *Muoma* for another red bean, and he went on feeding it while he told it how the king's daughter had had a dream about a tree that grew hair, and how the king had promised to give a big reward to the person who could find that tree. The bird said to him, "You will search for that tree for a long time. If the girl is waiting for that tree, I am sure she will wait for a much longer time still! She would have been wiser if she had been generous to me!" Then the bird gave him instructions for finding the tree.

Muoma sailed on and on for many more days till he came to a new land. The trees that he saw there were moving around like human beings, but he found no people living there, nor any animals. As he walked in that strange country, he came across one flower that stretched forth its hands as if to seize him, and he got ready to shoot it with his bow and arrows, but the flower said to him, "Do not shoot me! I will not do you any harm!" *Muoma* stopped short. Then the flower continued, "Where do you come from? I have never seen human beings in this country before. You are the first one to visit this land." *Muoma* replied, "I came in my little canoe looking for the tree that produces hair. My name is *Muoma*." The flower said, "What do you want to do with that tree? Tell me, for since you have managed to get here alive, I will help you." So *Muoma* told the flower about the king's daughter and about his journey to this new country. The flower said, "The red beans that you were carrying from the small island are the ones that saved you. If you had not had them, the bird that alighted on your boat would have eaten you. Keep the ones that are left, for they will help you with the many more dangers to come." Then the flower started to cry, and *Muoma* was amazed, and asked it, "What can I do to help you?" The flower replied, "Give me one of your red beans, for I am very hungry, but keep the rest, for they will save you from danger. Then go on, the same way, and you will find the tree that bears human hair." *Muoma* gave the flower one of his red beans, and then went on.

Now, as he traveled, the road began to get narrower; and the rocks that had hitherto seemed far away came nearer. He traveled on and on, until he reached an area with only barren rocks. The wind began to blow hard and to rage as if with great wrath, and there was a fearful loud noise all around him, as if it were coming from a waterfall. He went on until he came to a huge boulder that blocked his path. He stopped and looked carefully; he saw a little door, and on the door there this was written, in golden letters:

Only he who knows can get in,
Nobody else, save he who fears not.

When he saw that writing, *Muoma* remembered the bird's instructions concerning this rock and the door, so he whispered the words that the big bird taught him:

I am he who knows, knows,
That the wind blows, blows,
That the water flows, flows;
Here the tree of hair grows, grows,
I am he who knows, knows.

As soon as he finished saying those words, the little door opened by itself and he climbed into the rock. There, inside it, he saw the tree that bears human hair, and when he saw it, he felt great joy, for he knew that he had reached the end of his long journey. He went near and picked as much as he needed to take with him, and he took some of its fruits and seeds as well. Then he started the journey back to his country.

When he arrived, he went straight to the king and gave him the hair for his daughter. They put it back on her head, and it grew there, and looked as beautiful as ever before. The king, his daughter, and all the people of the kingdom rejoiced for many days, and the king gave *Muoma* much gold, and also his daughter. She became his wife. So *Muoma* and the king's daughter lived happily together for many days.

That is the end of my story.

—*Akamba*

8
Profitable Amends

When people first came into the world, the king, *Dada Segbo,* had no wife. He called all the people together. He took out a cowry shell, for that is what they used for money in those days. He told his people to take that cowry and find a wife for him.

The people said to themselves, "What does the king mean? Can one get a wife with only one cowry? It is impossible." All agreed: "We cannot do it. A man can never find a wife for one cowry."

But one man, *Yo,* came forward, and said he *could* get a girl for one cowry. *Dada Segbo* said, "All right."

First *Yo* sent someone to buy flint and bamboo tinder with the cowry. Then he went and found dry straw and set it on fire with the flint and tinder. The grasshoppers hiding in the straw began to jump, and *Yo* took the sack he had ready, and collected them inside it.

So *Yo* went on his way with this sack of grasshoppers, until he came to the house of an old woman. Now, this woman was trying to dry beans in front of her house, but the chickens would come and eat them all up before they were ready.

Yo said, "Haven't you corn to give your chickens?" But this was the time of famine, and there was nothing to eat. *Yo* then told the woman, "All right. I have grasshoppers here. If I throw these to your chickens, they will let your beans alone." The woman agreed, and he gave the grasshoppers to the chickens, but when they had finished eating them, he took the beans.

The old woman cried out, "But, *Yo,* why are you taking away my beans?"

He said, "Didn't you tell me to throw my grasshoppers to your chickens? I bought the beans with a cowry."

The grasshoppers came from the straw,
The money for the straw came from Dada Segbo.

So *Yo* went on. Now he came to a river where fishermen were fishing. He saw that the people from the village of *Tofi* were trying to fish, but that the fish had nothing to eat. So he said, "If you like, I will throw my beans in the river. The fish will come to eat and you will have a good catch."

The people said, "True, true," and they told him to throw in the beans. Soon the fishermen caught many, many fish.

Yo picked out the largest fish for himself. The fishermen cried out after him, "*Yo*, why are you taking away our fish?"

Yo said, "Did you forget that you took my beans?"

> *The beans came from the old woman,*
> *The old woman took my grasshoppers;*
> *The grasshoppers came from the straw,*
> *The money for the straw came from* Dada Segbo.

"I do nothing without getting my reward."

Yo continued on his way till he came to a place where blacksmiths were working. There were hoes all over the ground, but when he saw the blacksmiths, they were very tired.

Yo said, "Why are you tired, blacksmiths? Have you had nothing to eat? You cannot even lift your hammers. If you like, I will leave you my fish, so you can eat."

The blacksmiths said, "True, true."

They took the fish, and ate. When they had finished eating the fish, *Yo* took hoes and bush knives, and filled up his sack with them.

The blacksmiths cried out, "Where are you going, *Yo*? Where are you going with our hoes and bush knives?"

But *Yo* said to the blacksmiths, "Didn't you know, before you took my fish?"

> *The fish came from the fishermen,*
> *The fishermen took my beans;*
> *The beans came from the old woman,*
> *The old woman took my grasshoppers;*
> *The grasshoppers came from the straw,*
> *The straw came from the money I got from* Dada Segbo.

Then *Yo* came to a field where men were working. Now, these men had neither knives nor hoes. They worked with their hands. He asked them, "Don't you want bush knives and hoes to work with?"

The men answered, "Yes," so he gave them the tools, and with them they worked fast.

Yo stood and watched. Now, the men had with them a dish of beans and cassava flour called *abla*. *Yo* went and gathered it all up.

They cried out, "*Yo*, *Yo*, what are you doing with our food."

Yo said, "Don't you know?"

The hoes and knives came from the blacksmiths,
The blacksmiths took my fish;
The fish came from the river,
The fishermen took my beans;
The beans came from the old woman,
The old woman took my grasshoppers;
The grasshoppers came from the straw,
The straw took my cowry;
The cowry came from Dada Segbo.

"I do nothing without getting my reward."

So again he went on his way. He walked for a long time, until he came to a house beside the road. In this house there was a dead girl. All the people were wailing. They had nothing to eat, and could not bury the body.

Yo went inside and said, "I see you have nothing to eat. I have *abla* with me. Divide it among you and drink water with it. Then you will be refreshed, and you will find a way to bury your dead."

So they made *Yo* sit down next to the dead, even though he was a stranger. Then at night, while the others were digging the grave, he took the body.

The people ran after him and cried, "*Yo, Yo,* why are you taking the body?"

Yo answered, "Don't you know?"

Abla *came from the farmers,*
The farmers took my hoes;
The hoes came from the blacksmiths,
The blacksmiths ate my fish;
The fish came from the river,
The fishermen took my beans;
The beans came from the old woman,
The old woman took my grasshoppers;
The grasshoppers came from the straw,
The straw came from one cowry;
And the cowry came from Dada Segbo.

So he left with the dead body. That day *Yo* traveled from early morning till night. He went to see the king of the country, and said to him that *Dada Segbo* had told him to go and look for a wife for him. And now, as he had found her, he wanted a place to spend the night with this girl who belonged to *Dada Segbo.*

He put the dead body in the house that they gave him, and went inside with it. At cockcrow he left the body there, and went away. When he returned at six o'clock, he went into the house and began to wail.

"The people here killed *Dada Segbo*'s wife! They killed *Dada Segbo*'s wife! What shall I do? What am I going to tell *Dada Segbo?*"

The head of the family now called together all the people. The people said, "*Yo* is lying. This woman was dead when she came here. No one saw her. No one went near her. *Yo* is deceiving us."

Yo said, "I dare not take this dead body to *Dada Segbo.* I must have another girl, as fine looking as she."

So all the old people came together and talked this over. They said, "We cannot anger *Dada Segbo. Yo* says he brought this woman here alive. Now she is dead. She died in our village. We must find another woman." And since the king of that country had a fine young daughter, they said he must give that one to *Yo* for *Dada Segbo.*

Yo began to wail again. "What shall I do? What will I tell *Dada Segbo?*"

So they gave him the girl, and he went on his way. They came to a village called *Bodenu-Mawu-Bode.* From there *Yo* sent a message to *Dada Segbo* that with only one cowry, he had found a wife for him.

The girl began to sing:

Hunger comes from afar,
Hunger has followed the road here;
The intestines come from afar,
The intestines have followed the road here.

Now, *Dada Segbo* sent many men to meet *Yo* on the way. He also had many, many dishes cooked which he sent along with the men. The girl and *Yo* were given much to eat. When the food came, the girl said, "Swallow it fast." And when she had said this, the food disappeared. *Yo* was astonished.

So the girl and *Yo* arrived at a place called *Todogba. Yo* sent another message to *Dada Segbo* asking for food, and *Dada Segbo* sent him more than before. There were six hundred and forty calabashes of food. There was water. There were bottles of strong drink. When the girl saw the food coming, she began to sing the same song again:

Hunger comes from afar,
Hunger has followed the road here;
The intestines come from afar,
The intestines have followed the road here.

And when the men and women came near with all the food, the girl called out, "Swallow fast." The food vanished.

Yo said to *Dada Segbo*'s people, "This woman astonishes me. She never eats with her hand, but when she says, 'Swallow fast!' the food disappears." He sent a message to *Dada Segbo* saying he wanted forty guns, and powder, and eight hundred calabashes of food.

When the girl saw the new food approaching, she began to sing the same song:

Hunger comes from afar,
Hunger has followed the road here;
The intestines come from afar,
The intestines have followed the road here.

Then, the people went back to tell *Dada Segbo* that the girl was too much for them. The moment she saw food come, she had but to exclaim, "Swallow fast!" and everything vanished.

But *Yo* sent still another request for food to *Dada Segbo*. This time he asked for three thousand calabashes. The food came, and the girl did the same thing again, but this time, when she had made the food disappear, she began to eat the men. The moment she saw a man approaching, she called out "Swallow fast!" and the man was no longer to be seen.

A man hurried to tell *Dada Segbo* that the girl was evil. She had finished the three thousand calabashes and now was doing away with the men. *Dada Segbo* called together all his elders. They said, "It is terrible to have a beautiful woman like this, who eats people. It is very strange."

They brought the girl to *Dada Segbo*. All the people of the country were gathered before the king's door to see her. But the moment this girl fixed a man with her eyes and said, "Swallow fast!" the man disappeared.

Dada Segbo asked the chief minister, Minga, "What shall we do now? Here is a girl who eats much, and is not satisfied unless she eats men, too. What shall we do?"

The chief minister said, "This woman knows only to kill. Let us kill her. *Yo* has no family, so he is no man to send to find a wife."

Today, in order to marry, a man must have much money. In former times, one needed only to have a cowry to marry, but all a man was likely to get with it was a sorceress.

—*Dahomey*

9 The Man and the Muskrat

There was a certain hunter who used to go out with his dog searching for game to bring back to his wife and children. One day he said: "I'm going deep into the bush because game has become very scarce these days." He set off with his bow, arrows, spear, and dog.

When he had gone some way, he heard a voice saying, "Oh, you, hunter, help me over the crossroads, and I will help you another day."

He looked round without seeing who had spoken to him, then stopped, and said, "Who is it who's talking? Speak again, so that I can see what you are?"

Then he heard again: "Oh, sir, help me over the crossroads and I'll help you some other time—I, a muskrat."

The man looked down and saw the animal, and said, "I would help you across the road only you stink so and will make me smell likewise."

The muskrat replied, "Oh no, sir, just help me across the road, because if I don't get over I shall die. If you do help me, I will save you one day."

The man said, "What! You who are so small will save me who am so big? Whatever could beat me that you would be able to cope with? You're lying, you little animal!"

The muskrat replied, "Oh, no sir, just lift me with your bow if you're afraid I will make you stink, and throw me so that I fall on the other side of the path, and one day I will rescue you from a great trouble!"

The gentleman took his bow and lifted the muskrat over the path, dropping him on the other side.

"Thank you very much for having pity on me," said the muskrat. Then both went their separate ways. That was all that happened on that day.

In the evening, the man returned home and told his wife about his encounter with the muskrat and what it had told him. His wife said scornfully, "What nonsense! How could a rat help you!" The husband replied, "Well, I thought that, too, when he said he would save me one day, but that's what he promised." And the father slept until morning. That day he stayed in the village, saying that the next day he would go hunting in the bush. When darkness returned, he slept again.

Came the morning, he said to his wife, "Oh, wife, prepare some food so that I can eat, because today I am going farther than I have ever gone before."

His wife heated some relish, grilled some flour, and prepared millet porridge. Her husband ate and was satisfied. Then he took his customary hunting equipment, called his dog, and set out.

He kept going until he had covered a great distance. It was the wet season, at that time, and the sky was heavy with rain, with vast clouds obscuring the view. He said to himself, "Yes, today I'm going to get soaked, but what can I do?"

He thought, "Just let me find somewhere to shelter"—the man would have died for sure, if he hadn't exerted himself—and after that he killed three guinea fowl.

He kept going and then, luckily, he noticed a cave and got inside with his dog just as the rain began pelting down. Well, there hidden in the darkness was the muskrat, too.

Now, it happened that a certain lion, who had also been hunting, was himself seeking shelter from the rain, and he came to that very cave. The man glanced up and saw the lion had come in. Fear gripped him, and his dog began to bark, but the man silenced him by holding his muzzle. Then he said, "Yes, O Lion, you may eat me, but I want to say that I am not a thief, I have not stolen people's goods, nor taken from their granaries, neither have I ever killed anyone. I am just a man of the bush, a poor man with wife and children, and like you, I was looking for food, and the rain has brought you here, so now you can eat me."

Then the lion began to roar, until the tears fell from the man's eyes, plop, plop, plop. He gripped his weapons with manly courage, but the lion set to roaring even more, until the cave shook and seemed about to collapse.

Then the lion said to the man, "Oh, sir, give your dog those guinea fowl there, and when he has eaten, you can eat the dog, and finally I'll eat you. What do you say?" The gentleman, whose insides had by this time turned to water, said, "Yes, today I'm going to die because of this hunting business of mine!"

The lion told him again, "You sir, give your dog the guinea fowl, and when he has eaten, then you eat the dog, and then I'll eat you. How about it?"

At that moment, they heard a voice coming from somewhere in the cave, saying, "Yes, sir, give the dog those guinea fowl, and when he has eaten, you can eat the dog, and Mr. Lion can eat you, and when he has eaten, I'll eat *him*." When the muskrat had finished saying this, he added, "Well, my boys of the royal bodyguard, what do you say?"

And the termites in the cave wall replied, *"Mmmmmmm."*

At this, the lion and the man were amazed, wondering who was speaking in there. Then they heard again, "You sir, give the dog the guinea fowl, and you eat the dog, and the lion will eat you, and then I will eat the lion. All right, men of the royal bodyguard?" The termites replied, "*Mmmmmmmm.*"

Now, the lion was thinking more about being eaten than about eating anyone else, and the man said to him, "Hold up the cave so it doesn't collapse, and I'll go and cut some timber so we can shore it up." The lion agreed. The man then left, with the lion still holding up the cave, thinking it would fall. The man hurried off as fast as he could go, and his dog likewise, and they didn't stop until they reached home.

One day, he met the muskrat again, and the rat said, "Did you know who it was speaking in the cave, saying, 'Oh, sir, give the dog the guinea fowl and you eat the dog and the lion can eat you, then I'll eat the lion?' Did I not say I would save you when you helped me across the path? And indeed I scared the lion and rescued you."

The man thanked him very much, then went home and told his wife, and they were all happy.

—*Fipa*

The Hare's Hoe

One day Hare said to Gray Antelope, "Let us go and sow peas," but Antelope said, "I don't like peas, I prefer wild beans," so Hare went by himself. When the peas began to sprout, he noticed that they were disappearing, so he hid himself in the field, and caught Antelope digging up his peas. "Aha!" said he, "you are a thief. Pay the fine!" Antelope gave him a hoe and off he went.

He met some women who were digging clay with sticks. He said to them, "Haven't you got any hoes?" "No," they said, "we haven't a single one." "Then take this one," he said. "You can give it back to me later on." When they had finished, the last one who used the hoe broke it. Then Hare sang the following song:

Clay diggers, give back my hoe, my friends,
My hoe that Antelope gave me,
Antelope who paid the fine for my peas.

The women took one of their pots, and gave it to him.

He left, and met some men who were harvesting honey; they were putting it in a piece of tree bark. "Haven't you got any pot to put your honey into?" he asked. "No," said the men, "we haven't got any." So he gave them his pot. The last one who handled it, broke it. When it was broken Hare sang:

Honey harvesters, give me back my pot.
My pot that the clay diggers gave me;
The clay diggers paid for my hoe,
My hoe that antelope gave me,
Antelope who paid the fine for my peas.

So they took some of their honey and gave it to him.

He came to a village, and there he saw women pounding maize flour. He said to them, "Haven't you any honey to mix with your flour?" "No," they said, "we have none." So he gave them his honey, saying, "Take it, but be careful to leave me some of it." But the last one finished it all. Then he sang:

Pestle pounders, give me back my honey,
The honey that the honey harvesters gave me;
The honey harvesters paid for my pot,
The pot that the clay diggers gave me;
The clay diggers paid for my hoe,
The hoe that antelope gave me,
Antelope who paid the fine for my peas.

They took some of their dough, and gave it to him.

He went on, and met some boys herding goats. "Haven't you anything to eat?" he said, "your lips look very dry." "No," they replied, "we have no food at all." So he gave them the dough, saying, "Eat away! but leave some for me." The last one ate the last bite. Then sang Hare:

Goatherds, give me back my dough,
The dough that the pestle pounders gave me;
The pestle pounders paid for my honey,
The honey that the honey harvesters gave me;
The honey harvesters paid for my pot,
The pot that the clay diggers gave me;
The clay diggers paid for my hoe,
The hoe that antelope gave me,
Antelope who paid the fine for my peas.

They took a goat, and gave it to him.

He met some young men tending oxen. He said to them, "Your lips seem very dry; haven't you anything to eat?" "No," they said, "we have nothing." So he said, "Take this goat, but be sure to leave some for me." The last one devoured the last bite. Then Hare sang:

Cattle men, give me back my goat
My dough that the pestle pounders gave me;
The pestle pounders paid for my honey,
My honey that the honey harvesters gave me;
The honey harvesters paid for my pot,
My pot that the clay diggers gave me;
The clay diggers paid for my hoe,
My hoe that antelope gave me,
Antelope who paid the fine for my peas.

They seized him and beat him, and when he was quite unconscious, they took him out of the village, thinking he was dead. But he regained his senses and climbed up a tree, which was in the middle of the village, just on the spot where they were all drinking beer; no one noticed him and, when he reached the top of the tree, he attracted in his direction all the light beer and the water in the wells, in such a way that it all ran away into the ground, and folks soon found that there was nothing to drink. The little ones cried for water and there was none! The men and the women started to fetch water, but they could not find any; the rivers even were all dried up! The little ones died, and so did both women and men! Just a few survived. These went to Hare, and said to him, "My Lord, we ask for water, as we are dying of thirst." "Pull up this reed by the roots," said he. All the men, even the strongest, tried hard to pull up the reed, but could not succeed. "Now," said Hare, and with one finger, he pulled it out of the ground, and forth flowed water and beer, light and strong. Then said he, "Give me five old women." He plunged them in the pond, and drowned them. After this, they allotted him a small province, where he reigned as chief.

—*Thanga*

Why the Hare Runs Away

This is a story of the hare and the other animals.

The dry weather was drying up the earth into hardness. There was no dew. Even the creatures of the water suffered from thirst. Famine soon followed, and the animals, having nothing to eat, assembled in council.

"What shall we do," said they, "to keep ourselves from dying of hunger and thirst?" And they deliberated a long time.

At last it was decided that each animal should cut off the tips of its ears, and extract the fat from them. Then all the fat would be collected and sold, and with the money they would get for it, they would buy a hoe and dig a well, so as to get some water.

And all cried, "It is well. Let us cut off the tips of our ears."

They did so, but when it came the hare's turn he refused.

The other animals were astonished, but they said nothing. They took up the ears, extracted the fat, went and sold all, and bought a hoe with the money.

They brought back the hoe and began to dig a well in the dry bed of a lagoon, until at last they found water. They said, "Ha! At last we can slake our thirst a little."

The hare was not there, but when the sun was in the middle of the sky, he took a calabash and went towards the well.

As he walked along, the calabash dragged on the ground and made a great noise. It said, *"Chan-gañ-gañ-gañ, Chan-gañ-gañ-gañ."*

The animals, who were watching by the lagoon, heard this terrible noise and were frightened. They asked each other, "What is it?" then, as the noise kept coming nearer, they ran away. Reaching home, they said something terrible at the lagoon had put them to flight.

When all the animals were gone, the hare could draw up water from the lagoon without interference. Then he went down into the well and bathed, so that the water was muddied.

When the next day came, all the animals ran to get water, and they found it muddied.

"Oh," they cried, "who has spoiled our well?"

Saying this, they went and took a dummy-image. They made bird-lime and spread it over the image.

Then, when the sun was again in the middle of the sky, all the animals went and hid in the bush near the well.

Soon the hare came, his calabash crying, "*Chan-gañ-gañ-gañ, Chan-gañ-gañ-gañ.*" He approached the image. He never suspected that all the animals were hidden in the bush.

The hare saluted the image. The image said nothing. He saluted again, and still the image said nothing.

"Take care," said the hare, "or I will give you a slap."

He gave it a slap, and his right hand was stuck fast in the birdlime. He slapped with his left hand, and that was held fast, too.

"Oh! oh!" cried he, "I'll kick with my feet," and he did, but his feet became fixed, and he could not get away.

Then the animals ran out of the bush and came to see the hare and his calabash.

"Shame, shame, oh, hare!" they cried together. "Did you not agree with us to cut off the tips of your ears, and, when it came to your turn, did you not refuse? What! You refused, and yet you come to muddy our water?"

They took whips, they fell upon the hare, and they beat him. They beat him so that they nearly killed him.

"We ought to kill you, accursed hare," they said. "But no—run."

They let him go, and the hare fled. Since then, he does not leave the grass.

—*Ewe*

12
The Tortoise and the Falcon

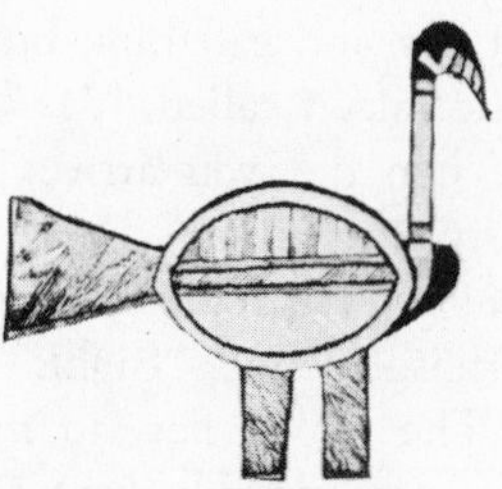

A chief at *Vugha,* named *Kimweli,* once had a beautiful daughter, and he told the people that no one should have her unless they competed for her. The one who surpassed his fellows would be his son-in-law. So there came forward a falcon and a tortoise who told the chief they wanted to compete. He said to them, "Go to *Pangani* and wait a day, and another day, and on the third day start in the morning, and in five days be at *Vugha.*"

And off they went. Now the tortoise knew he could not travel that far that fast, and so he sought his companions, and said to them, "Help me in this business, for if I am beaten it will be as if you were beaten."

They consented and said, "We will help, but what can we do? None of us can travel that swiftly." One of them said, "Let us make friends with the hare, and he will help us." So they came to the hare, who was sitting at home, and greeted him, and explained the problem. The hare asked how he could help. They said, "We have ten halting places in the five days, two for each day. Now you go to *Pangani* and place one of us there, and then one at each halting place as you come to it; but each one is to be called *Madalamba,* because the name of the one who is at *Vugha* is *Madalamba."* So the hare went to *Pangani,* and he placed the first and told him his name was to be *Madalamba.* Then he went on and placed the rest, telling the same to each.

Now it was the third day, the morning they were to leave *Pangani.* There, the tortoise set out with the falcon, himself on foot, the bird flying. When they had proceeded a little way, the tortoise hid himself. The falcon flew to the first halting place and settled on a tree, thinking, "Now I have left the tortoise a long way behind, but still I will just call him and see if he replies." So he called, *"Madalamba, Madalamba,"* and he heard below, *"Yoo,"* and peeping down, he saw that the tortoise was there. The falcon said to *Madalamba,* "Let us go," and he replied, "All right." The falcon flew off and the tortoise waddled along slowly, and then hid himself. The falcon did not rest, "I shall have the chief's daughter," he said. He went on to the next stage.

It was now evening, and the falcon peered about. He saw a creature jogging along below, looking for firewood to make a fire. The falcon kept silent till he saw the wood was burning, and then he said, "Let me try and call him, but I know it certainly cannot be *Madalamba."* The falcon called, *"Madalamba."* The tortoise replied, *"Yoo."* He said, "When did you arrive?" He answered, "Did you not know that we arrived together?" They slept. In the morning the falcon called, *"Madalamba."* He replied, *"Yoo."* And the falcon said, "Let us go," and the tortoise replied, "Right." So they set out.

The falcon flew to the third halting place, and looked down but saw nothing. He kept silent awhile, and saw *Madalamba* appear; he asked him, "Where were you?" *Madalamba* said, "You left me a little way behind." They rested, and having rested they went a little way, and the tortoise hid himself. In the evening, the falcon flew on to the fourth stage, and he saw the tortoise was there. So it was at every stage, until the fifth, near to *Vugha.* There, he met his companion on the ground. The tortoise said to the falcon, "Tomorrow we shall enter *Vugha* early," and the falcon agreed.

Now, where they were, if a drum sounded, you could hear it. The falcon thought—"This person is with me everywhere. So tomorrow I will run off very early."

Now the real *Madalamba*—the tortoise who had entered the competition—was in *Vugha* already, hiding in the chief's court, though no one knew it; everyone supposed he was at *Pangani*. In the very early morning of the fifth day, the falcon did not ask the tortoise to start with him, so, when the tortoise awoke from sleep, his companion had gone. *Madalamba,* there in the chief's court, came out early and entered the forest, and when it was light the falcon was seen coming in the distance, and all the people in the town of *Yugha* cried out, "The falcon will beat the tortoise." Now, when the falcon was getting near, the tortoise came out of the forest, into the inner end of *Vugha,* while all the people were at the entrance, looking at the falcon. The tortoise proceeded to the chief's door, where there was a pile of firewood, and hid himself in that wood. The falcon came crying, as he flew round the town, "I have beaten him." The chief's daughter laughed, saying, "The falcon has beaten the tortoise." The falcon came to the chief's house and settled on the central point, and said to the people, "You see I have passed the tortoise. However, even though I have passed him, I will call him, so that everyone may know that I have beaten *Madalamba*." So the falcon called, "You, *Madalamba,* You, *Madalamba!*" Immediately, the people saw the tortoise come out from the firewood. The falcon was still calling him, "You *Madalamba,*" when he replied, "*Yoooo.*" The falcon was startled. "When did you get here?" He said, "I came some time before you." The face of the chief's daughter grew dark quickly, for her father said, "This is your husband. I do not know the other one." The marriage was celebrated.

Now *Madalamba,* though a tortoise, was really a fine young man who had taken on the tortoise shell on purpose. But his wife didn't know this yet, and so they sat. But each night, at midnight, *Madalamba* came out of his shell while his wife slept, warmed himself at the fire, and then entered his shell again. One night, by chance, the girl awoke and saw a bright fire, and looking at her husband, she saw what a fine fellow he really was. It dazzled her to look at him. She searched for the shell and saw it there behind him. She remained quite quiet until the next evening. Then, she did not go to sleep, but only pretended to, and at midnight she saw him come out of the shell and warm himself. Then the girl arose from the bed and took the shell and put it on the fire. Then *Madalamba* said, "You have killed me." She said, "No, I have not killed you; you are a fine person and you have done this purposely." So they slept, and in the morning, the chief's daughter said to her father, *Kimweli,* "Behold, father, my husband is a man, and a fine one. Now we shall not come out of this house until you have killed an ox, and we will step over it when we pass out." *Kimweli* brought an ox, it was slaughtered there at the door, and his son-in-law and his daughter stepped over it as they came out. And all the people noted that *Madalamba* was a stranger.

Now when you first see a person, let him not be despised in your eyes, for you do not know where he comes from, what he is, or where he is going.

—Bondei

13 Rubiya

A certain sultan gave orders that all the male children born in his kingdom should be put to death, and that only the female infants should be preserved. Shortly after this order came into force, a son was born to a man and his wife who lived in the capital of that land. Since the child was huge and strong, his parents said, "It is a pity that he should die. We'll keep him within the house, and when he is grown we will send him out into the forest to fend for himself." The child grew exceedingly quickly, and as soon as he could speak, he said to his parents, "My name is *Rubiya.*"

Now, every day *Rubiya* used to leave his parents' house just to play with the female children of the neighbors. But one day as he was playing, he hit one of his friends on the head with his finger, and so great was his strength that he split open her forehead and drew blood. When her parents saw the wound they went straightaway to the sultan to complain that there was a male child named *Rubiya,* who had been hidden by his parents in defiance of the law that the sultan had made. When *Rubiya*'s parents heard of what had happened, they were afraid, and said, "If we keep him here, the sultan will put him to death, and us, as well, for having hidden him." Now, on the farm that belonged to this man and his wife, there lived a jinn who killed all who approached, and for this reason no one could tend the land. "It is better that we should send him to the country farm for the jinn to devour," said *Rubiya*'s parents. So his father, giving *Rubiya* a great sword that he had in the house, led him from the town. After they had walked for some time along the high road, they came to a narrow footpath all filled with grass and overgrown, and the man said to *Rubiya,* "Follow this footpath and it will lead you to the farm in the bush. So *Rubiya* followed the footpath, and in due course arrived at the farm, which he found to be full of ripe pineapples, bananas, and other fruits. There were palm trees with coconuts just lying on the ground beneath them, for men were afraid to come and gather them because of the jinn.

Rubiya entered the house at the farm. There, in an inner room, he found a female jinn, whose head he cut off with his sword. Leaving her lying there, he hid himself in the outer room of the house. Presently her husband, the jinn who occupied the farm, returned, saying, "I smell the blood of a human being." He called to his wife, but received no answer. Presently, he went into the inner room and found her body. Then, *Rubiya* came from his hiding place and, seizing the jinn, drew his sword to kill him. But the jinn cried, "If you will spare me, I will reward you." *Rubiya* asked what he would give him, and the jinn replied, "I will give you a bowl of magic water, and if you wish to know if any friend of yours is in trouble, you have but to look therein. If the water remains clear, no trouble has befallen him, but if the water becomes black, then he is in need of assistance." *Rubiya* said, "Give me this magic water, and I will spare you." So the jinn brought the water, and gave it to *Rubiya,* who took it and drove the jinn from the farm.

Then *Rubiya* gathered together a great bundle of coconuts and, slinging them over his shoulder, set out to return to his parents. But on the road he met men who asked if he had seen *Rubiya,* for they had been sent by the sultan to arrest him. *Rubiya* said to them, "You are not capable of arresting *Rubiya,* for he is very strong." But they replied that should they meet him, they were ready to try. Then *Rubiya* said, "I am a friend of *Rubiya,* and if you can seize me, you can seize him." He drew his sword and slew all of those men except two. One of these he bound, and he cut off the ears of the other, and told him to return to the sultan and inform him of what had happened.

When the sultan heard that *Rubiya* had overcome the men whom he had sent to seize him, he was very angry, and sent forces to seize *Rubiya.* But *Rubiya* slew them also, all except two. Of these two, one he bound, and he cut off the hand of the other, and told him, "Go to the sultan, and tell him that if he sends men to seize me a third time, I will enter his palace and kill him." Then *Rubiya* set free the two men whom he had bound, and said, "Will you go with me and be my brothers?" The men agreed to this, so the three of them set out.

One day, as they were traveling in the bush, they heard voices. *Rubiya* crept up quietly, and looking through the branches, saw two jinns talking together. Now one of them was that jinn who had formerly dwelt on the farm that belonged to *Rubiya*'s father, and he was telling the other jinn how he had been seized by *Rubiya* and had only escaped with his life by presenting him with the magic water. When *Rubiya* heard this, he rushed out and seized the jinn whom he had not seen before. But the jinn cried out, saying, "If you will spare my life,

I will give you certain seeds that I have. If you want to know whether any one of your friends is in trouble, you have but to pour water upon one of these seeds and a tree will spring up. If the leaves of this tree are fresh, then your friend is safe, but if the leaves are dried and dead, then your friend has need of your assistance." So *Rubiya* took the seeds, and allowed the jinns to depart.

Rubiya and his brothers traveled until they reached a land ruled by another sultan. Entering the chief city of that land, they found lodging in an upper floor, and lay down to sleep. At daybreak, *Rubiya* wanted to walk in the streets, and coming down from his room, he went to open the door of the house. But the woman who owned the house said to him, "Don't go out so early, for there is a great lion that goes about the city from sunset until dawn, forcing everyone to stay in their homes." But *Rubiya* said to her, "I don't fear the lion." So he went out, and the woman shut and bolted the door behind him. As he was wandering, he met the lion. He drew his sword, and, as the lion sprang at him, he slashed at its head and killed it. He cut off the lion's claws and tail, took them, and went away. Though he didn't know it, the daughter of the sultan was looking from the window of the palace nearby, and saw all that had happened.

Soon one of the sultan's soldiers passed, and saw the body of the lion. He took his spear and stabbed the lion many times with it, and, after bathing his arms in its blood, he ran to the sultan and told him that he had killed the beast. The sultan was overjoyed when he heard this, and said, "As a reward for your bravery, I give you my daughter, the princess, in marriage." But the princess said, "I will not marry this man. Let me first see the body of the lion that he has killed." Then the body of the lion was brought in, and the princess said, "Where are the claws?" The soldier replied, "It has killed so many men that it has lost its claws." Then the princess said, "Where is the tail?" The soldier replied, "It has no tail." Then the princess said, "Who has ever heard of a tailless lion? You didn't kill it, but another great man did, one I saw from the window of my palace." Then the princess described *Rubiya* to her father, and he sent men to search for him. They soon found him, and brought him to the palace. When he showed the sultan the claws and tail that he had cut from the lion, the sultan ordered the soldier who had pretended to have killed the lion to be put to death. He offered his daughter to *Rubiya* in marriage, but *Rubiya* said, "I am but a youth, and these, my brothers, are older than I am. Therefore, it is only fair that they should marry before I do." So one of *Rubiya*'s brothers married the daughter of the sultan, and *Rubiya* gave to him the magic water, and said to him, "Look in this water every morning, and if it remains clear you will know that I am safe, but if it becomes black that is a sign that I am in trouble." So the man took the water, and *Rubiya* went away with the brother who remained with him.

At length they reached a land ruled over by another sultan. Now this sultan had previously possessed seven daughters, but now only one remained and she was a maiden of extraordinary beauty. About this city, there was only one place where water might be obtained, and this was a great lake situated nearby. This lake was inhabited by a great seven-headed serpent who each morning had to be given one of the sultan's daughters to devour, before the people of the city might draw water. On the night of *Rubiya*'s arrival, the youngest daughter was placed on her bed at the edge of the lake, so that in the morning, when the serpent emerged, he might devour her. *Rubiya,* when he heard the story of the serpent, remained near the princess so that he could save her.

When the dawn broke, the waters of the lake turned blood red, then drained away until only mud remained. After the water boiled and bubbled and rose again, the serpent emerged from the lake to devour the princess. *Rubiya* drew his sword, cut off the seven heads of the serpent, and killed it. Then he went to the princess and placed on her finger a silver ring that had his name engraved upon the inside of it. When he had done this, he returned to the city.

Presently, one of the sultan's servants came down to the lake. When he saw the dead body of the serpent, he ran to the sultan and told him that he had slain it and saved the princess. The sultan was overjoyed, and promised to give the princess in marriage to the servant. But when the princess heard of his intention, she said to the sultan, "I do not want to marry this man." Then the sultan said, "Though he is a slave, he has saved you from the serpent, and therefore you should gladly reward him." Then the princess said to the servant, "Do you know this ring and what is written on the inside of it?" The servant said, "I don't know it." Then the princess said, "The one who slew the serpent placed this ring upon my finger, and he knows what is written there." That morning *Rubiya* came into the presence of the sultan, and said, "Your daughter has a silver ring upon her finger, and on the inside is written my name— *Rubiya.*" The princess answered, "It is true. This is the one who slew the serpent." When the sultan heard this, he was overjoyed, and offered his daughter to *Rubiya* in marriage. But *Rubiya* replied, "I am but a youth, and this man, my brother, is older than I am. Let him, therefore, take the princess and marry her." So *Rubiya*'s brother married the daughter of the sultan, and *Rubiya* gave to his brother the magic seeds, saying, "Pour water upon one of these every morning, and a tree shall spring up. If the leaves of the tree be fresh, then you shall know that I am well; but if they be dried and withered, I am in need of you." Then, after showing his brother the road he was about to take, he set out.

After many days, he came to the land of the jinns and, entering one of their cities, he hid himself in a house. Presently, the jinns came into the city, bearing loads of ivory and silver and rich merchandise. *Rubiya* came forth from his hiding place, drew his sword, and slashed at them, right and left. Amongst them were those two jinns who had given him the magic water and seeds, and when they saw who he was, they fled, spreading the report of his coming on all sides. When *Rubiya* had slain all the jinns in that city, he continued his journey till he came to another of their cities, and here also he hid himself in one of the houses. Again, the jinns arrived bearing merchandise and silver and ivory, and again *Rubiya* drew his sword and killed them one by one, until none remained. When he had completely cleared the city of jinns, he traveled on until he came to the chief city of that land, where the sultana of the jinns lived, there being no sultan. Though she was an old woman, she appeared as a young girl of great beauty, with firm outstanding breasts. When *Rubiya* saw her, she came towards him and said, "I have been waiting for you, and now you shall take me to be your wife." To this *Rubiya* agreed, and the maiden continued, "But first, you shall wash these dirty clothes for me." *Rubiya* agreed to this, as well. And leaving his sword in the house, he went out with the clothes to wash them. When he had gone, the maiden took his sword and hid it.

When *Rubiya* returned with the clothes the maiden said to him, "Now, I will kill you, for you have destroyed everyone in two of my towns." On the walls of that room hung many swords, all cunningly manufactured out of clay. When *Rubiya* heard the maiden's words, he seized one of these swords and struck her with it. And when that sword broke, he seized another and struck with it, but it, too, broke into pieces. Then the maiden took up a black rod and struck *Rubiya* with it, and he immediately turned into a stone.

Now, every day, to see if he was well and safe, *Rubiya*'s brothers faithfully examined the magic water and the leaves of the tree that sprang from the magic seeds. One morning, the one with the magic water found that it turned black when he looked into it, and he who had the magic seeds found that when he poured water on them, up sprang a tree whose leaves were dried and withered. So each started out to search for *Rubiya,* and they met upon the road. They said to each other, "*Rubiya* has treated us as his brothers, and has married each of us to a sultan's daughter. Therefore, we must do our best to help him." So they traveled on, searching for *Rubiya,* and passed through the two towns of the jinns where the inhabitants had been slain. In due course, they arrived at the principal city of the jinns, and came to the palace of the sultana. When she saw them, she said, "I have been waiting for you, and now one of you must marry me and the other will be my brother-in-law." The two brothers agreed to this, and they remained in the house conversing with the sultana. After a time she said to them, "Observe this stone. Some days ago, a youth named *Rubiya* came this way, and I struck him with this black stick and he became a stone." One of the brothers said to the maiden, "Will he always remain a stone?" and the maiden replied, "No. For when the stone is struck with this white stick, then it will vanish and *Rubiya* will remain in its place." When the brothers heard this, they drew their swords and killed the queen of the jinns. And then they took the white stick that she had shown them, and struck the stone with it, and the stone disappeared and *Rubiya* stood in its place.

Rubiya gave each of his brothers one of the conquered cities of the jinns, and the third city, in which the sultana of the jinns had dwelt, he kept for himself. *Rubiya* returned to his own land, to the house of his father and mother, and his brothers returned to their wives. The story is finished.

—*Swahili*

14
The Flying Lion

Once upon a time, *Oom Leeuw* used to fly, and nothing could escape him. His wings were not covered with feathers: they were like the wings of Brother Bat, all skin and ribs. But they were very big, and very thick, and very strong, and when he wasn't flying, they were folded flat against his sides. When he was angry he let the points down to the ground, *tr-r-r,* like *Oubaas* Turkey when he gobbles and struts before his wives, *tr-r-r,* and when he wanted to rise from the ground, he spread them out and flapped them up and down slowly at first, then faster and faster—so, so, so—till he made a big wind with them and sailed away into the air.

Oh, but it was a terrible sight! Then, when he was high above the earth, he looked down for something to kill. If he saw a herd of springbok, he would fly along till he was just over them, and pick out a nice fat one; then he would stretch out his iron claws, fold his wings and—whoosh!—down he would fall on the poor bokkie before it had time to jump away. Yes, that was the way *Oom Leeuw* hunted in the olden times.

There was only one thing he was afraid of, and that was that the bones of the animals he caught and ate would be broken to pieces. No one knew why, and everyone was too frightened of *Oom Leeum* to try and find out. He used to keep them all at his home and he had crows to look after them, two at a time—not like the ugly black crows that build in the willow trees near the dam, but white crows, the kind that come only once in many years. As soon as a white crow baby was found, it was taken to *Oom Leeuw*—that was his order. Then he kept it in the mountains and let it grow big; and when the old white crows died, the next eldest became watchmen, and so there were always white crows to watch the bones when *Oom Leeuw* went hunting.

But one day, while he was away, Big Bullfrog came along, hop-hop-hoppity-hop, hop-hop-hoppity-hop, and said: "Why do you sit here all day, you whitehead crows?" And the white crows said: "We sit here to look after the bones for *Oom Leeuw*." "But you must be tired of sitting!" said Big Bullfrog. "Fly away for a while and stretch your wings. I'll sit here and look after the bones." The white crows looked this way and that way, up and down and all round, but no! They couldn't see *Oom Leeuw,* and they thought: "Now is our chance to get away for a fly." So they said, "Cr-r-raw, cr-r-raw," and stretched out their wings and flew away. Big Bullfrog called out after them: "Don't hurry back. Stay as long as you like. I will take care of the bones."

But as soon as they were gone, he said: "Now I shall find out why *Oom Leeuw* keeps the bones from being broken. And he went from one end to the other of *Oom Leeuw*'s house, breaking all the bones he could find. He worked quickly! Crack! crack, crack, crack! Wherever he went, he broke bones. Then when he had finished, he hopped away, as fast as he could. When he had nearly reached his dam, the white crows overtook him. They had been to the mountain, and when they returned and saw all the broken bones, they were frightened.

"Craw, craw" they said, "Brother Big Bullfrog, why are you so wicked? *Oom Leeuw* will be so angry, he'll bite off our nice white heads. Without a head, who can live?"

But Big Bullfrog pretended he didn't hear. He just hopped as fast as he could, and the white crows went after him.

"It's no good hopping away, Bullfrog," they said. "*Oom Leeuw* will find you wherever you are, and with one blow of his iron claws, he will kill you."

But old Big Bullfrog didn't take any notice. He just hopped on, and when he came to his dam he sat back at the edge of the water and blinked the beautiful eyes in his ugly old head, and said: "When *Oom Leeuw* comes, tell him I am the one who broke the bones. Tell him I live in this dam, and if he wants to see me, he must come here."

The white crows were very cross. They flew down quickly to peck Big Bullfrog, but they only dug their beaks into the soft mud, because Big Bullfrog wasn't sitting there any longer. He had dived into the dam, and the white crows could only see the rings round the place where he had made a hole in the water.

Oom Leeuw was far away, waiting for food, waiting for food. At last he saw a herd of zebras, and he tried to fly up so that he could fall on one of them, but he couldn't. He tried again, but no, he couldn't. He spread out his wings and flapped them, but they were quite weak.

Then *Oom Leeuw* knew there must be something wrong at his house, and he was angry. He struck his iron claws into the ground and roared and roared. Softly he began, like thunder far away rolling through the kloofs, then louder and louder, till—*"hoor-rr-rr-rr, hoor-rr-rr-rr"*—the earth beneath him seemed to shake. It was a terrible noise.

But all his roaring did not help him, and at last he had to get up and walk home. He found the poor white crows nearly dead with fright, but they soon found out that he could no longer fly, so they were not afraid of him.

"Hoor-rr-rr-rr, hoor-rr-rr-rr!" he roared. "What have you done to make my wings so weak?" And they said: "While *Oom* was away, someone came and broke all the bones." And *Oom Leeuw* said: "You were put here to watch them. It is your fault that they are broken, and to punish you I am going to bite your stupid white heads off. *Hoor-rr-rr-rr!*"

He sprang towards them, but now they were not afraid of him. They flew away and sailed round in the air over his head, just too high for him to reach, and they called out: "Ha-ha! *Oom* cannot catch us! The bones are broken, and his wings are useless. Now men and animals can live again. We will fly away and tell them the good news."

Oom Leeuw sprang into the air, first to one side and then to the other, striking at them, but he couldn't reach them, and when he found all his efforts were in vain, he rolled on the ground and roared louder than ever. The white crows flew round him in rings, and called out: "Ha-ha! He can no longer fly! He only rolls and roars! The one who broke the bones said: 'If *Oom Leeuw* wants me, he can come and look for me at the dam.' Craw, craw," and away they flew.

Then *Oom Leeuw* thought: "Wait, I'll get hold of the one who broke the bones. I'll get him." So he went to the dam, and there was old Bullfrog sitting in the sun at the water's edge. *Oom Leeuw* crept up slowly, quietly, behind Bullfrog.

"Ha! Now I've got him," he thought, and made a spring, but Bullfrog said, "Ho!" and dived into the dam and came up on the other side, and sat there blinking in the sun. *Oom Leeuw* ran round as hard as he could, and was just going to spring, when Bullfrog dived in again and came up at the other side. And so it went on. Each time, just when *Oom Leeuw* had nearly caught him, Bullfrog dived in and called out, "Ho!" from the other side of the dam.

Then, at last, *Oom Leeuw* saw it was no use trying to catch Bullfrog, so he went home to see if he could mend the broken bones. But he couldn't, and from that day he could no longer fly, only walk upon his iron claws. From that day, too, he learned to creep quietly after his game, and though he still catches them and eats them, he is not as dangerous as he was when he could fly.

And the white crows can no longer speak. They can only say, "Craw, craw."

But old Big Bullfrog still goes hop-hop-hoppity-hop round the dam, and whenever he sees *Oom Leeuw*, he just says, "Ho!" and dives into the water as fast as he can, and sits there laughing when he hears *Oom Leeuw* roar.

—*South Africa*

15 A-Man-Among-Men

This story is about a forest giant, and about a man called, A-Man-Among-Men. A story, a story. Let it go, let it come.

There was a certain man by the name of A-Man-Among-Men. Always when he came from the bush, he would uproot a tree and throw it to earth, saying, "I am A-Man-Among-Men." His wife said, "Come now, stop saying you are a-man-among-men; if you saw a-man-among-men you would run." But he said, "That is a lie." Now, it was always so—whenever he brought in wood, he would say the same thing, and his wife would answer the same.

Now, one day his wife went to the stream. She came to a certain well; the bucket there was so heavy that it took ten men to draw it up. She went there, but had to do without water, so she turned back. She was going home when she met another woman, who said, "Where are you going with a calabash with no water?" She said, "I have come and seen a bucket there that I could not draw, so I had to turn back home." This other woman, who had a son, said, "Let us go back, so that you may get your water." The first woman said, "All right." So they returned together to the well. The woman who had the son, told the boy to lift the bucket and draw water. Now the boy was small, not past the age when he was carried on his mother's back. But he lifted the bucket then and there, put it in the well, and drew up the water. They filled their large water pots, they bathed, they washed their clothes, they lifted up the water to go home. The first woman was astonished. Then she saw that the one who had the boy had turned off the path and was entering the bush. The wife of the one who called himself A-Man-Among-Men said, "Where are you going?" The other answered, "I am going home, where else?" "Is that the way to your home?" "Yes." "Whose home is it?" "The home of A-Man-Among-Men." The wife was silent till she got home. Then she told her husband what had happened, that she had met a child, the son of a man who was really called A-Man-Among-Men, and deserved the name because he was so strong. He replied that tomorrow she must take him there. She replied, "May Allah give us a tomorrow."

Next morning he was the first to get up from sleep. He took his weapons and slung them over his shoulder. He put his axe on his shoulder and woke up his wife. He said, "Get up, let us go. Take me that I may see, that I may really see the one you say is really A-Man-Among-Men." She got up, lifted her large water pot, and passed on in front. He followed her until they got to the edge of the well. Now they found what they sought indeed. As they were coming, the wife of A-Man-Among-Men came up, both she and her son. They greeted her, and the wife of the boaster showed him the bucket, and said, "Lift it up and draw water for me." So he lifted up the bucket in a rage, and when he let it down the well, the bucket pulled him so hard that he would have fallen after it; but the little boy grabbed hold of him, both the man and the bucket, and pulled him out and threw him to the side, for he was indeed a weakling. Then the boy lifted up the bucket, put it in the well, drew water, and filled their water pots. The man's wife said, "You have said you are going to see him called A-Man-Among-Men. You have seen this is his wife and son. If you still want to go, you can follow them. As for me, I am not going." The boy's mother said, "I'm warning you, you had better not come, for my husband is truly named A-Man-Among-Men." But he insisted, and she said, "Let us be off." They set out. When they arrived at the house, she showed him a place for storing meat so that he could hide in it and see this man, and he got inside. Now, the master of the house was not at home; he had gone to the bush. His wife said, "You have seen he has gone to the bush; but you must not stir when he comes back." He sat inside till evening. The master of the house came. When he came, he said, "I smell the smell of a man." His wife said, "Is there another person here? Is it not I?" Thus, if he said he smelled the smell of a man, then she would say, "Is there another person here? Is it not I? If you want to eat me up, well and good, for there is no one else but I."

Now he was a huge man, his words like a tornado; ten elephants he would eat. When dawn came, he made his morning meal of one elephant, then he went to the bush, and if he should see a person there, he would kill him. Now, the boaster stayed hidden in the storehouse. The man's wife told him, "You must not move till he is asleep. If you have seen the place dark, he is not asleep; if you have seen the place light, that is a sign he is asleep. You better run away then." Shortly after, he saw the place had become light as day, and he came out. He ran and ran, until dawn, he was running, till the sun rose he was running, he did not stand.

Then A-Man-Among-Men woke up from sleep, and he said, "I smell the smell of a man, I smell the smell of a man." He rose up, he followed where the man had gone, he ran after. The boaster kept running until he met up with some people who were clearing the ground for a farm. They asked what had happened, and he said, "Someone is chasing me." They said, "Stand here till he comes." A short time passed, and the wind caused by the giant, A-Man-Among-Men, came; it lifted them and cast them down. And he said, "Yes, that is it, the wind he makes running; he himself has not yet come. If you are able to withstand him, tell me. If you are not able, say so." And they said, "Pass on." So he ran off.

Soon he came to some people hoeing. They asked, "What is chasing you?" He replied, "Someone is pursuing me." They said, "What kind of man is chasing one such as you." He answered, "Someone who says he is A-Man-Among-Men." They said, "Not a-man-among-men, a-man-among-women. Stand till he comes." He stayed there, and he was there when the wind began. It was pushing the men who were hoeing. So he said, "You have seen that is the wind A-Man-Among-Men makes even before he comes. If you are a match for him, tell me; if not say so." They said, "Pass on," and off he ran.

He was running when he came across some people sowing. They said, "What are you running for?" He said, "Someone is chasing me." And they said, "What kind of a man is it who is chasing the likes of you?" He said, "His name is A-Man-Among-Men." They said, "Sit here till he comes." He sat down. In a short time, the wind came and it lifted them and threw them down on the earth. And they said, "What kind of wind is that?" The man who was being pursued, said, "It is his wind." And they said, "Pass on." They threw away their sowing implements, and went into the bush and hid, but the one who had boasted ran on.

Now he went on until he ran into a huge man sitting alone at the foot of a baobab tree. This man had killed elephants and was roasting them. He could eat twenty elephants all at once, but in the morning he breakfasted on only five. His name was the Giant of the Forest. The giant asked him, "Where are you going in all this haste?" And he said, "A-Man-Among-Men is chasing me." And the Giant of the Forest said, "Come here, sit down till he comes." He sat down, and they waited a little while. Then the wind made by A-Man-Among-Men came, and lifted the man, and was about to carry him off, when the Giant of the

Forest shouted to him to come back. He said, "I am not running away. The wind caused by A-Man-Among-Men is carrying me away." At that, the Giant of the Forest flew into a rage, he got up and caught the man's hand, and placed it under his thigh.

He was sitting there when A-Man-Among-Men came up, and said, "You sitting there, are you of the living or of the dead?" And the Giant of the Forest answered, "Don't interfere." And A-Man-Among-Men said, "If you want to stay healthy, give me the one you are keeping there." And the Giant of the Forest said, "Why don't you come and take him?" And, at that, he flew into a rage and jumped and seized him. They began wrestling with each other. When they had twisted their legs round one another, they leaped into the heavens. Up to this day, they are wrestling there. When they get tired, they sit down and rest; and when they rise up to struggle, that is the thunder in the sky—it is their struggling.

The man, all this while, was watching, and suddenly found himself free. He went home and told the tale. And his wife said, "That is why I was always telling you, whatever you do, make little of it. Whether it be you are great in strength, or in power, or riches, or poverty, and are puffed up with pride, it is all the same; someone is always better than you. You said it was wrong to believe so, but now, your own eyes have seen."

—*Hausa*

16
A Competition of Lies

To understand how stories such as these are told in African style, I have included here a group of them that were recently recorded by Donald Cosentino, and that are incorporated in his study of the storytelling traditions, or *domeisia*, of the Mende of Sierra Leone. These three texts were created by Hannah Samba (identified here as Storyteller I), Mariatu Sandi (Storyteller II), and Manungo (Storyteller III). They are rival storytellers in active competition, playing around with the narrative possibilities of one dramatic situation. The focus is on the situation that arises when a female protagonist acts in a most unmannerly way because of her uncontrollable sex drive. (This behavior is especially unclean, because it flies directly in the face of the rules of the Mende women's initiation group, the *Sande* society.) Her excesses lead to her being willingly carried away to the bush by a supermasculine figure who, it appears, is a spirit, *Kpana*, who has borrowed his handsome features from a number of individuals to whom he must return them. The plot turns on the woman's situation, her discovery of the true character of her captor, the conditions of her having a child, and her dying on returning to the village.

As Cosentino explains it, these stories emerged in the course of a normal evening's entertainment in the village. The gathering consisted of three women who are regularly antagonistic to each other. Such antagonism is not antithetical to creativity. Rather, because it likely engages the interest of everyone in the listening group to see the women go at each other, the public face-off sharpens the skill of the storytellers. As Cosentino puts it: "Despite their antipathy, or perhaps because of it, such a gathering was not unusual. The women were used to their oppositions, to the tensions that arose when they conversed, and to the polarities in their lives. The performance of *domeisia* was another dimension of their rivalry, a transformation of their hostility into works of art whose final shapes were dictated not only by the [tales' conventions] but by the nature of the human relationships which bound the narrators to a lifelong competition."

All three of these narratives tell essentially the same story, one which is not terribly different in construction from some of our most familiar fairy tales, such as *Jack the Giant Killer*. All turn on the spirit falling asleep for an extended period of time. But the performers here play with this basic plot to demonstrate their individual storytelling abilities —especially through the command of ideophonic sound effects, the elaborating of the scenes with contemporary references, and the use of the story to point up a unique moral. In this report, an exact translation, we can see the importance of the various vocal techniques for establishing and maintaining fluency and dramatic interest. The first storyteller begins, as always, by saying, "I have a story, *Domei oo Domeisia*," to which the onlookers respond, "*Sa Konde*." She then leaps into it.

Storyteller I [Hannah Samba]: Behold this girl from long ago, she was a great fornicator. She continued fornicating for a long time, then they initiated the *Sande* society in that town. Spirits came from the big forest; they came to this dancing place. One of the spirits was named *Kpana*. When that spirit came he spoke words of love to her. She accepted these loving words spoken to her, but she said nothing of it to her parents. The spirits slept the night, then at daybreak, they begged leave to go.

They said, "We're going tomorrow."

She and her companions (they were five) went with these fellows, they accompanied them. Now they went accompanying them.

Then their lovers said to them, "My dears, go back, our destination is not pleasant." For that reason they said, "Go back!"

Then they returned, those four, and she alone remained.

So her lover said to her, "*Yombo*. Return!"

She replied, "Let's go there."

He said, "My destination is not pleasant, for that reason, return!"

"*Koo*," she said. "*Kpana*, your dying place is my sleeping place. No matter where you go, I must go!"

She begged him a long time. He gave her £100.

"Oh," she said, "I'll go for sure now." She said, "Even if you gave me £300, I'd follow you wherever you go."

So he said, "All right."

As they were going, this *Kpana* . . . all these things he had, these handsome features . . . behold, he was a Big Thing! His human features, all those features he borrowed, they were finished. As they reached a place, he would go to visit that person and return his own handsome feature. As they reached another place, he would go to visit that person and return his own handsome feature. So he changed back into a spirit. Then they reached deep into his own forest.

Before they arrived at his own place, while that fellow was changing himself, a great fear came over her, but there was nothing to be done about it because they had gone so very far. There was nothing to be done now for her return. So she showed her *womanness*, her *heart* was *strengthened* now. They traveled far now to that Big Thing's own place.

At daybreak, this *Thing* would go to the *bush*, the *hunting place*. He'd go there and catch this person, then he'd go back and catch an animal, a bush animal, and he'd come with it.

He would say, "*He he*," he would say, "*Yombo, Yombo*, the smooth one or the hairy one, which do you prefer?"

"*Koo*," she said, "Father, we have always eaten the hairy one over there."

He said, "Then here it is."

Then she took the hairy one and the Big Thing took the smooth one and ate it. He ate it all.

They stayed there. They sat together, and so they knew each other now. She stayed there and then she bore a child.

That Big Thing, long ago he'd sleep for a year. When he was sleepy he would lie down and he would sleep for one full year, and then he would wake up. (Ah, this stubbornness she had, she would show it again in the same way.) So this Big Thing packed up plenty of things, plenty of food, enough for her for one year; he gathered it all, and he came with it. He packed it all in one house till it was full, because he slept one year before he would wake. Then that Big Thing informed her about that.

"Kwo," she said, "I don't agree to stay out alone. We two, let's go into that house together."

"Ee," the Big Thing said to her, *"Yombo,* this thing I said to you, listen to me." He said, "I will sleep for one year."

She said, "Let's go into that house together, I'll make that sleep too." She thought it was a joke he was playing on her.

So they entered that house. She and that Big Thing, they entered that big story-house. It was made of iron, even the window sills. So that Big Thing entered: *gbugbuNG gbugbuNG gbugbuNG.*

Then all that house was locked, it was finished *seNG.* Then he went and lay on his bed. When he went and lay on his bed, the Big Thing made this snore: I WILL SLEEP A YEAR, I WILL SLEEP A YEAR, I WILL SLEEP A YEAR. He made that snoring sound. He stayed making this snoring sound a long time. He did so for two months, then for three months. In the fourth month the child in *Yombo*'s hands became sick. Even though the child was sick in her hands, oh friends, the whole house was locked with iron! Thus, she could do nothing at all to open it. When this child was sick now in her hands, she thought it was a joke this Big Thing was playing on her. Oh *yaa.* She sang a song to this Big Thing lying there in sleep.

Don't sleep lekemo, *don't sleep* lekemo,
You deceiving in-laws, you deceiving in-laws,
Your child, look at him dying in my hands.
Look at me dying like this. . . .
I WILL SLEEP A YEAR, I WILL SLEEP A YEAR.

She stayed singing that song. She stayed singing that song. Then that child died in her hands. When that child died in her hands, she herself fell down. She too fell and died.

For a long time that Big Thing was lying down. The year completely passed and he awoke. When he awoke, he discovered their bones there. He discovered them scattered there, she and her child. When that Big Thing got up, he took a straw broom and an empty dustpan and he gathered those bones *we we we.* He went and threw them away.

Therefore stubbornness isn't good. Whatever you do, whenever a person says, "Don't do this," listen to him.

My story passes to . . .

Storyteller II [Mariatu Sandi]: *Domei oo Domeisia.*
Audience: Sa konde.
Storyteller II: Behold these spirits long ago, there were twelve of

them in their forest. Then a dance was held in the town; it was a big *Sande* initiation dance, a dance for getting married. There were two dances being held in one town. Then all these spirits, they all changed into young men. Oh! the beauty of these young men! When all the women saw them, they wanted them, without even getting a present! So they were all dressed up and coming to the dance; then they came and they all made love in the town—these twelve, all of them. They got twelve girls at this dance, and they danced for ten months—there remained only two months for completing one year.

Then they begged leave, they said, "We are leaving tomorrow."

All those small things which they had, they gave to their lovers. Then at daybreak they caught the road. Their pals went along as guides. There was one girl among them who was very stubborn; moreover, she was really seeking a man. (This story I'm telling, I tell it for us fornicators; I'm not telling it for any other people than we who truly commit adultery. It's our story I'm telling. Also, we whose ears are closed, we who don't agree to any truthful talk, we closed eared people, and we insatiable fornicators, this is our story.) Then these companions of hers, the eleven girls, they went back. So of these twelve spirits also, eleven spirits all came out from their places one-by-one. They came to their meeting place on the big road; then those eleven went back.

So he remained alone, he and his girlfriend. So he said to her (this spirit is named *Kpana,* the girl's name is *Yombo*), he said to her, "Yombo—Return! There where we're going, there it is bad." He said, "You see all your comrades have returned; you too, I beg you, go back."

On his finger there is a beautiful gold ring. When he went like this [turning gesture], it glittered. Really, long ago white people took it and turned it into electricity which shines so today . . .

Audience: Kwo!

Storyteller II: Then he gave it to her and said, "Go back!" She said, "I won't go back." She said, "Wherever you go, I will reach there. Your dying place is my sleeping place."

This spirit then took out a kola from his trousers (from the small place where we put something—we call it *boi,* the white people call it pocket—it was on his trousers); then he took out the kola from the inside of the *boi* and he split it and gave part of it to her. So this girl took it in her hand, and the spirit also took part of it in his hand.

They went far, they passed one bush; then he said to her, "*Yombo,* wait for me." He said, "Let me go into the bush." He entered the bush but it wasn't shit he was shooting. The first person he reached was the hairy person. (As you white people there, your hair is now, so too was his hair which he had lent to the spirit.) The spirit's own hair was really only one strand on his head. Then he took this hair and he went with it.

He said, "*Ee,* Hairy *Fetingo* my dear, I have your hair. Give me my one hair back."

So Hairy *Fetingo* then grabbed his own hair and returned the spirit's one hair to his head.

Audience: Kwo!

Storyteller II: As he was coming out then this *Yombo* said, "What the hell?" She said, "What's coming?"

He said, "Don't fear me, it's me *Kpana,*" He said, "*He he he . . . Yombo, Yombo,* your own kola, my own kola—isn't this it?"

Then he pulled this kola from his *boi,* his pocket; it's really the one. He said, "Your own kola, my own kola, isn't this it?" He said, "Let's go!"

This now caused a great fright. They went on and they reached *Hakawama.* Then he entered with two legs. He went and he returned them. Only one leg is under the spirit. He had returned them to him. I say it was like elephantiasis. Then he returned and *Yombo* feared him.

She said, "Why is it as we traveled today my father's legs were two, and now he has one leg?"

He said, "*He he he . . .* your own kola, my own kola, isn't this it?"

She said, "Father, let's go then!"

This created a great fear in *Yombo,* All those things God made for mortal men—his fingers, his hair, his neck, everything—this *Kpana* returned them.

Then they went and they reached a river. At this water crossing place long ago there sat this fellow at the water's edge. He crossed the river with people in his boat. His name was *Sherbro* Man. As they were going then, this spirit told the *Sherbro* Man that he should cross the water with them. *Yombo* herself, as she walks beside men she is happy; she sucked her teeth at this fellow, *Sherbro* Man. Then she sang this song:

Sherbro *Man*—Sherbro *Man*—Sher . . .

You all say it.

Audience:

Sherbro *Man*—Sherbro *Man*—Sher . . .

Storyteller II:

Cross the river with me-o
I can't cross the river with you,
You big fat lip.
You go about eating dirty broom straws.

They continued like that, then they went and they reached his hometown. So this *Sherbro* Man remained sitting at the riverside.

Thus they reached this spirit's cement-block houses which long ago this spirit had built. It's only in America that there is this type of house. In the whole of Freetown, all Freetown, there isn't a block house of this kind. (If you tell lies, it's like this you should do it, you should arrange it so): the mirrors of these block houses, it is those which long ago the white people worked over and fastened to their car fronts which go about today on the roads helping people.

At daybreak this spirit would go to the hunting place. He'd go hunting and catch animals; sometimes he'd catch nine-hundred animals. Of living people, sometimes he'd catch seven people. Then he'd come with them and pile them *bushu,* he'd pile them *bushu,* then he'd fall down. He lay there, he was exhausted. He remained lying a long time; the sun would set over there in the sea.

Now hunger wasn't troubling *Yombo,* simply because as soon as they arrived, he gave food to her which would suffice for two days. So *Yombo* was experiencing fullness.

He said, "*He he, Yombo, Yombo,* the smooth or the hairy one, which do you prefer?" (It's the devil's voice which is heavy like this.)

Yombo replied, "As for us, Father, we usually eat the hairy one."

Then he said, "Take whatever you like." (The spirit spoke like that.)

So *Yombo* remained taking care of this meat. While she was preparing this one, that one would be spoiling; that one would be drying; that one would be frying; that one would be steaming; that one would be salted. This fellow also put those human beings, all those seven people he had caught, in a place where he would eat them for seven months.

They stayed like this for a long time, then *Yombo* became pregnant. She bore a child. The child's name is *Bobo* (his father's name is *Kpana,* his name is *Bobo Kpana*). That child stayed there long, then he grew and he became truly handsome. He reached the age of a grown man, this *Bobo Kpana.*

So one year passed. Then *Kpana* went again to the animal hunting place. When *Kpana* went to this hunting place, he would stay there for up to nine years hunting for these animals. He stayed in this hunting place because *Yombo* hadn't done anything to these nine hundred animals; some had maggots in them.

Then one man came and said, "I've come, let's stay together in this place."

She said, "Hm-m-m, I agree to this proposal to stay together which you've brought, because I'm here alone, the only living person, I and this my small child. She said, "This person who long ago came with me is a spirit. Any kind of food I want, he hunts for it; he puts it in this house; he fills it *kooboNG.* When it's there we'll be eating it, we'll be playing in it, whatever we want with it, we do. But as you've come here, whether from Jericho or from in back of Freetown or from the stone-growing place, from wherever, father's nose will discover your smell. He'll come and when he comes, he will eat you yourself!"

He asked "Why?"

She said, "He eats people. The only people he doesn't eat are me and my child. He doesn't eat only us two. Despite all that," she said, "we'll stay here."

Then this girl cooked food quickly and she gave it to this fellow, to this guest. The guest's name is *Majia*. Then she gave it to *Majia* and he ate it. Oh *ya*. Then this spirit's coming-back time arrived.

A big storm was brewing. It was that very storm that God shared out between the land and the sea. When you are sitting by the sea and you hear it *daa daa,* it was such a storm; it does that in the sea. That storm would do that long ago, whenever the spirit returned. That very storm by the seaside which you hear *daa daa*. Oh *ya*. It started from over there and it reached nearly to the end of the world.

She said, "*Koo,* young man, this living together we've been doing, my husband's arrival time (*wati*) is now approaching." (White people, you call it *taimi,* we call it *wati*.)

She said, "The time is now approaching. This is what he said he'd do, and he's coming."

Then shit came out of the girl. That very shit, it was none other than pig shit; it came out of her. Oo!

Then he came. So she picked up the youth and carried him there, to the tenth story of this skyscraper, this many-storied house that he'd laid—so far, *poloNG!*

Actually, when this spirit would come, he'd drop down from seven years before he woke up. Just as he arrived, the spirit came and assembled those things. He said, "*He, he, he, Yombo, Yombo,* the hairy one or the smooth one, which do you prefer?

She said, "Father, it's the hairy one we eat, we in our own country."

He said, "Well then, take it."

This spirit then lay down. His nostrils started doing this, so he said, "Hm-hm, a fresh-fresh person is smelling." (That one was a spirit.) He wanted to know what the girl had done for those seven years he had been to the flesh-hunting place.

"*Ee,*" she said, "I say Father, you know *Kpana Bobo* is a human being; myself, I'm a human being. You say a fresh-fresh person is smelling; what about these people you came with, aren't they fresh-fresh people?"

He said, "*He, he, he, he, he, Yombo, Yombo,* I don't know what you're thinking of. Don't make a fool of me. I say a fresh-fresh person is smelling."

They kept on [arguing] like that for a long time. Then that spirit forgot [about it]. So he arranged all those affairs.

So this person who had come today, whom *Yombo* had lifted to the sky, he had a *kpafei*. This *kpafei* was the kind twins also have. It was long and thin and small like this; it was inside his hair. All this wealth passing in the world, you white people, that wealth [of yours], it is *Yombo* who long ago came with that wealth which you white people came with. You who are giving us money, who are partial to our affairs, it is *Yombo* who brought it. Well, then *Yombo* gathered up all that wealth and the lover brought out his *kpafei* for the sake of that one meal she had given him.

He said, "I have struck the *kpafei gba!*"

The spirit was lying asleep because he used to sleep for even more than seven years. He was lying in this sleep.

He said, "I have struck the *kpafei* here *gba!*"

He said, "The block house, the skyscraper, the zinc roof, anything whatsoever a person needs, bags of rice, a thousand bags of hard rice," he said they should all enter in his *kpafei*. He said that a thousand goats should enter into his *kpafei*. He said a thousand sheep; he said anything whatsoever, a thousand of them—cows, ducks, chickens, all—should enter [the *kpafei*].

Then this lover said he would strike his *kpafei* here and *Kpana Bobo* should then enter this *kpafei*. He said his mother also should enter and she entered in. So one year passed *tuNG*. This spirit was in sleep; he slept, he slept, he slept *pu*. This fellow hit the road with them. As they were going *taki taki taki,* they stepped *tele* and they fell. Ah, then this spirit who had slept for five years awoke from his sleep and he hit the road. There he is hitting the road. Oh, the town is far. When you would be returning, you'd forget the road you had gone on, you would take another road. But this fellow, he knew the road which went to town.

They continued going, then this spirit said, "Aa, Great God, if you took a person and you came with her to your town, and you gave [gifts] to her, and you did everything for her, and then she went and she didn't even say goodbye to you—oh, oh! It's me *Kpana,*" he said. Whatever she wanted I did for her. She stole all my wealth—my cows, my sheep, horses, chickens, ducks, pigs, everything—she went with them. She didn't even say goodbye to me! Oh Maker, that's the truth, I don't see her anymore, she's not here. Oh let me reach her now."

I say, when this spirit arose the distance between them was from this verandah pillar here to the door of that house over there.

Then that fellow turned and from the inside of the *kpafei Yombo* said, "*Kpo!* Buddy, turn around, the spirit over there is coming up behind us." Then she too said, "Great God, suppose a person comes with somebody's child and to his own town and doesn't return with her to her own sleeping place, doesn't return her to her own sleeping place? This spirit came long ago with me. He met me long ago on love business, he loved me; he said, 'Come with me,' but he wants to eat me! Maker, help me so that I might reach my own family."

I say, a wind it is that set upon them. They remained going a long time, *haaNG*, then that spirit slipped and fell. He was to remain four hundred hours in that fall. He was paralyzed, he couldn't get up.

They remained going *haaNG*. At last they reached the outskirts of the town. The spirit had truly failed now, for when he saw the people in the town, then he became afraid. He didn't go on any further, but he returned. When he returned, there was nothing there, merely an empty farmhouse. He discovered that termites had eaten and finished off everything. All is broken and scattered *wojoNG*. Food too he couldn't get; that spirit himself, he could get nothing.

So that fellow arrived beside that town with these people. Look at the house. Look at the town.

Then he set them down and said, "We have reached there."

Kpana Bobo and his mother, *Yombo,* got down then, and they greeted all the townspeople. All the people had missed them, but they didn't recognize them, for she had been just in her youth. She was a lovely, lovely youth when she got up long ago and followed that spirit.

Her real mother who had given birth to her, she had dried out. They had ground her up and put her in a jar. When her child came back, just then they turned it upside down and they shook her out. So that woman returned, she changed into a living person in God's Chiefdom. Then she went and saw her child, and they went about greeting people.

The people agreed when she said, "Hey, give me a place to build on."

I say, no sooner was that said, then all of a sudden there was a town like *SaloNG* over there (like Freetown, where you were recently). So it was that town was like that. At once they were all joined together and cement was smoothed on there and tar was rubbed on and streets were laid everywhere reaching to all the forests, completely finished, *seNG*.

It was *Yombo* who brought the cement houses. It was she who came long ago with riches. She it was who came long ago with cow stables. She it was who came long ago with pig taming. That stubbornness that *Yombo* one practiced, her own suited her. Ah, *Yombo* has done this for us today. We who now stay in shiny places that they call "zinc roofed," we used to put elephant grass on top of our houses. *Yombo* it was whom that spirit enriched with his wealth. It's thanks to that food she gave that lover, that is what made wealth come into the world, all that wealth of old.

I've heard that and I've said it.

Storyteller III [Manungo]: *Domei oo Domeisia.*

Audience: Sa konde. [Don't tell a long story, Storyteller.]

Storyteller III: It's the ending of jealousy I'm going to explain to you.

Audience: The story you told yesterday, don't tell it again!

Storyteller III: That's not what I'll tell. I'll tell about jealousy; that's what I'll show you.

There was a dance long ago; they initiated a great *Sande* society in a town. So a great dance took place. *Jenge jenge jenge,* then the ancestors came out; ancestors, they were spirits, I'll call them ancestors. Then they came to that dance. They were two only.

A girl is named *Yombo.* The bush person who came long ago is named *Kpana.* He proposed love to her. His mate, his name is *Jinabemba,* he proposed love to another. So they made love for three days at this dance; then they said, "We're going."

So they accompanied them. Then his mate told his own girl to go back. He said, "Go back!" So she went back.

Yombo said, "No matter what, you and I will go together."

Her lover replied, "Over there where we're going is far. Therefore, don't follow me!"

"Koo," she said, "my dear, since you've already loved me, I love you. Over there where you really stay, where you come from . . ."

He said, *"Ee?"*

She said, "You and I are going there."

Then they went. While they were going, they came to a small stream and they crossed it. He had a kola nut; he split it and gave part to her and kept part himself. So they went a while longer . . .

Audience: Don't tell lies

Storyteller III: If I'm lying, when frogs make their croaking . . . I'll stop there, I'll say no more.

Then they crossed a small stream, and he split the kola *va,* and he gave his girl her own, and he kept his own. Then he said, "Don't go back!"

She said, "I won't go back." So they went on. They went on a long way, then *va,* a chain came down from the sky. *Yoyoyoyo,* it came down.

He said, "Girl . . ."

She said, *"Ee?"*

He said, "With this chain, you and I will go to that town."

She said, *"Ee."*

He said, "Hold this chain well."

She said, *"Ee."*

He said, "Hold on to my waist tightly. I'll hold this chain, and you hold me tightly, hold on to my waist tightly. If one lets go of this chain, he'll fall and die."

So he held that chain and said:

JeNG jeNG jeNG jeNG jeNG
Ma jeNG ki jeNG
JeNG jeNG jeNG jeNG jeNG
Ma jeNG ki jeNG
Let's hold the rope well, let's go.
I told you long ago
My destination is Bugbalee.
JeNG jeNG jeNG
Ma jeNG ki jeNG.
Let's hold the rope well, let's go.

He would say, "Let me say to you . . ."

She said, *"Ee?"*

He said, "When you joined me, as we were going, I explained to you that when we reach that town, if you see a frog, or an earthworm, or a person with sores, or a sick person, or a leper, and if they come up to you with joy, you must greet them. You must not back away; do you understand?"

She said, *"Ee."*

He said, "You must not back away, do you understand?"

She said, *"Ee."*

He said, "Do you understand?"

She said, *"Ee."*

JeNG jeNG jeNG
Ma jeNG ki jeNG
Let's hold the rope well; let's go.

They continued going; they continued going; they continued going; they reached a town like Mattru is now. They reached there and he said, "You see that town there?"

She said, *"Ee."*

He said, "Love . . ."

She said, *"Ee."*

He said, "I told you we love each other. For three days I stayed in your town, you said you and I should come; I said, 'don't come,' I said, 'my sleeping place is far:' you came closer, *KoniiiNG*. Now, as we're going [to the town], if you see a person with a sore, or a frog, or a worm, if it comes to you *jogba jogba* [saying] 'my wife has come! Mother has come! Something has come!,' don't back away! If you back away from them, you'll be severely punished."

JeNG jeNG jeNG
Ma jeNG ki jeNG
Let's hold the rope well; let's go.

KpuNGame, they arrived in the town. People rushed to them: *Kpi*, you'll see that one coming, *tiNG*, big balls is coming *diNGde*, all sorts are coming [shouting]: "Our wife! Our brother has come with our wife. Our brother is coming . . ."

Then that one came and she hugged him, *vigba,* they embraced. Then that one came, *vigba,* they embraced. Then that one came, *vigba* . . .

They entered the house, *kote*. He said to her, " I said to you . . ."

She said, *"Ee?"*

He said, "If my real mother who bore me, if you see her and if she has a sore, if she has a sore on her and there is nowhere that pus doesn't come out of her, and blood comes out of her, don't back away from it, okay? Whatever sort of person comes, even a leper, remain seated. If she cooks food and gives it to you, don't back away from it, okay? Whatever sort of person comes, even a leper, remain seated. If she cooks food and gives it to you, don't back away from it, okay?"

She said, "Yes."

When she went, they all did [as he has said] with her. One month finished there, *kpoNGjoNG*. Behold—all those people were good people!

So at daybreak her husband's mother said to her, "Young lady, boil a little water so I might wash, okay?"

Then she boiled that water and she gave it to her. She washed with it. She showed her woman's strength for three days. Twice she brought the boiled water. On the third day she said, "Girl . . ."

She replied, *"Ee?"*

She said, "This water you've boiled for me so I could wash. Go in that forest now. You'll really see a wood which is very hard, like this *nikii* whip; it's really tough *klekle*.

She replied, *"Ee."*

She said, "You break it. Shake the leaves off, tie it tightly and come with it. Then you wash this sore, treat it *seNG,* and then strike it *voli*. When you see something jump out at you, that will be yours."

Then that girl left her washing and cut that thing—that *nikii* whip—quickly. She came with it. She cleaned the leaves off, *poli;* she tied it like the *koogba* bundle which *Wunde* Society people had long ago. When she came to that sore, she whipped it; she whipped it, *toNG-joNG*. A gold ring which was the first on a chain jumped out. *ToNG-joNG:* iron boxes, three iron boxes which were huge jumped out; all the iron boxes were her own. She went back and she whipped it again. She got that thing, that leopard's tooth, which if you had long ago, you were rich. So they lifted that big box, and the girl got up then, and she went with it to her house.

Then he said to her, *"Yombo . . ."*

She said, *"Ee?"*

He said, "When you take leave of me (your leaving-time is approaching), let me tell you: don't spoil things! When you take leave of me (your leave-time approaching), I'll report it to my family. When you go . . ."

She said, *"Ee?"*

He said, "That box in that house, that iron box, if you see a very, very dirty one . . . are you listening?—don't pick out the shiny one! Okay?"

She said, *"Ee."*

He said, "Don't pick out the shiny one! Okay?"

(Cowives' jealousy is what I'm getting to now.)

She said she agreed. They slept two nights. On the third she was going. So he went and arranged her leave-taking with his family.

He said, "This girl who came accompanying me says she is leaving now."

They said, *"Koo—Kpana,* let's sleep on this. At daybreak we'll discuss it."

In the morning the girl washed herself completely. She brought her own mother-in-law's water and she washed. They said, "Let's go there."

Behold this they had built, a round house. It was a round house they had built. There is a center pole, one hundred people could sit on that seat around that pole. People of olden times used wood like that over there to circle a pillar with a seat.

So they crowded about *venjeNG*. They said to her, "Come and sit." Then they gave her a chair. They said, "My dear . . ."

She said, *"Ee?"*

"Our brother has come with you, but you say you are bidding us goodbye, you are going. Therefore, of those boxes standing there, which ones do you want to go back with?"

Then she pointed at one dirty one. So they took that one and set it over there. Then she pointed at another, and they took it and set it over there. Then she pointed at another, and they took it and set it over there. All three boxes, they are really boxes. Those who don't lie say that box—those three boxes—which that person pointed at stretched from here to that bridge over there. As for me, who am a liar . . . well, I'll stop there.

Then she went. The road they had gone on long ago was very far; her journey wasn't short. One mile—that second one—then *chachala* she jumped out there. Her family cried out; they were very happy; they were very happy; they were very happy.

Her cowife and her own child are there. (This fornicating we're doing, we and these women are doing it . . . the ending of jealousy is what I'm getting at now . . .) That girl handed over those gifts to her family—goats . . . all sorts of things—my father, that family was now rich! That woman nagged her child all the time, "Look at your mate. You're forever looking to get laid, but you get nothing for it. Look at your mate, she and you from one house! Those fellows came long ago, you hung around with them, but now she comes back with all that wealth for her family!"

God Almighty said, "This [affair]—yes, I'll also see the end of this!"

After a short time, another dance was held again. *Wujugu*, a lot of people came again to that dance. When they came *feNG*, her child hung around with that fellow. Her own now, he too slept for two nights. On the third . . .

Audience: Was it the same fellow?

Storyteller III: No, it was another. They slept for two nights. She said, "Let's you and I go."

"Let's you and I go."

"*Koo*," he said, "girl, don't go!"

"Sweetie, my dear," she said, "let's you and I go there."

He said, "Don't go!"

"My dear," she said, "as I've said, let's go there!"

They went far. As they were going he said:

> *Swing me gently* vio, *swing me gently-o.*

A chain was entwined around her. I'll sing this song:

> *Swing me gently* vio, *swing me gently-o.*

It was a chain. You know how quick tricks are!

> *Swing me gently* vio, *swing me gently-o.*

Kunje, they jumped down and landed in the town. Behold the town over there.

He said, "Girl . . ."

She said, "*Ee?*"

He said, "When we go there, you and I, you will see sick people. You will see a worm, you will see a millipede, you will see all sorts of things. Don't back away from them! Do you understand?"

She said, "*Ee.*"

He said, "Now that we're reaching the town, have you understood me?"

She said, "*Ee.*"

He said, "You've seen the town, have you understood me?"

She said, "*Ee.*"

He said, "This instruction I'm giving you, don't disregard it!"

> *Swing me gently* vio, *swing me gently-o.*
> *Swing me gently* vio, *swing me gently-o.*

Kunje, they landed in the town—"Our brother's come with our wife!"

"*Koo,*" she said, "what the hell is this? Good heavens, my dear family, look at these nasty things—the filth I've entered into—ah, this screwing around will really throw someone's head off! God Almighty, don't let such filth get on me here."

While she sits there then a person comes, his balls swinging *tiNGbeNG*. "*Koo,*" she says, "what kind of dangerous thing is coming?"

Since she came as a guest they cooked food that night. They cooked food and gave it to her. She ate it, "*haaaa*" (she was vomiting). On the third day she still hadn't eaten. The fellow said, "This marriage is bothersome to me."

"*Koo,*" she said, "my dear, my dear, if it's like this here, since you brought me here, then try to help me for I'm going. I'm returning tomorrow."

The fellow said, "Is that right?"

She said, "*Ee!*"

He said, "Let me report this tomorrow to my family since you're going back."

That night he reported to his family, he did everything *seNG*. He said, "This girl I came with wants to return; therefore, I'm reporting to you."

The people again said, "We agree."

At daybreak the following day, as the dawn was breaking, they filled their huge round house full to the top: *kpa*. Then they said to her, "Girl, you came with our brother, you and he came and we loved you boundlessly, yet, nonetheless, you're going back. From among all these boxes . . ."

She said, "*Ee?*"

They said, ". . . take your heart's choice. The one you choose you may take and go with."

Then her head went like this, she showed her choice like this: "That's it. I want that very shiny one with gold rubbed all over it, the one with gold rubbed all over it!" (Really, if you didn't squint your eyes, or when you open them, if you didn't squeeze them hard, you wouldn't be able to set your eyes on it.)

So he took that one and he set it aside. Then she looked at another and he set it aside. Her mate had taken three but she took four! They set them on her head . . .

> *Swing me gently* vio, *swing me gently-o.*
> *Swing me gently* vio, *swing me gently-o.*

She's gone. Behold—she's gone.

Kule: suddenly she reached the town. Her mother said, "*Oyaya*, my child . . ." That huge box, *ngwungwungwungwungwu* (they struggled to pick it up).

Audience: Will they be rich soon?

Storyteller III: Ah, my family, those boxes, none of the people could set their eyes on them unless they hung a cloth before their eyes. Then they could set their eyes on them.

Audience 1: Manungo, why didn't he, her husband or lover, explain about those boxes to her?

Audience 2: She didn't listen to his words so he didn't explain to her . . . don't make her go backwards!

Storyteller III: They went and spent the day; then they slept the night *gbu.* At dawn then she assembled her family like a wife who has returned from her husband's place laden with gifts her man had given her.

Audience: Just her family?

Storyteller III: Mm-m. Just her family. Then that girl said, "My family, let's lock our house up tightly." So they locked up the house tightly. They closed their bedroom doors tightly *kpaNG kpaNG kpaNG.* Like our house is right now closed *kpaNG,* so it was the same with their own. Then that person opened the big boxes and all those Things' teeth were like this. They killed them all! They cut their heads off!

Ah, therefore, to have your eyes set on a thing is not good. I've heard that little story and I've told it. My story now reaches to you . . .

—*Mende*

Part II
Stories to Discuss and Even Argue About

Introduction

These are short stories about the moral aspect of behaving, told to initiate deep discussion on important topics, for example, how to live within the family and the community. They focus closely on the fundamental and recurrent problems of social relations: the qualities of love, the nature of obedience, the ethics of choice under stress conditions.

But, in spite of the fact that they deal with everyday problems, these are among the most fanciful and even ridiculous tales in this book. They epitomize the central paradox of hearing, reading, and dealing with stories, because they are fictions about truths—a contradiction that does not go unrecognized by their critical African audiences. These tales are subject to the same criteria of judgment as the wonder tales and the heroic stories. If any narrative is badly told, this will seem to the audience to compromise the continuity of group tradition. The community will respond with judgments that impugn the veracity, as well as the fluency of the storyteller. From the perspective of the listeners, truth will out, as much from an eloquent and lively recounting, as from an appeal to experience.

This chapter brings together two types of short narrative that appear to be diametrically opposed. The first eighteen are dilemma tales, tales without an end; the rest are profound moral examples, stories that explicate a lesson, or answer a central question. The two types are discussed in different contexts, the latter, in those situations in which a purportedly wiser person speaks to those less knowledgeable in the ways of the world; the former among cohorts of equal experience and power.

Because dilemma or enigma tales are, as I have argued, both characteristically Black African and atypical of the stories usually found in tale collections, it seems useful to briefly describe the situations in which these stories arise.

Virtue, in the context of African storytelling, resides both in the ability to argue eloquently and in the ability to demonstrate a command of tradition. In arguments over the problems set by the stories, it cannot be stressed too strongly that it is the flow of the discussion that counts, not the finding of a solution. Through argument, the customary practices of the community are rehearsed and celebrated. When the Kpelle of Sierra Leone, for instance, gather together to tell tales like this, the argument that follows the story is pursued by extended analogies with everyday activities.

Each person tries to put his interpretation of the situation "in the best possible light. There is no argument over the facts of the case, but over the interpretation." Decision-making becomes "something of a corporate process." Finally, this discussion comes to a halt, not because a definitive response is given by someone, but rather because "an influential town elder . . . expresses the concerns of the group," to which everybody assents because of his eloquent summation.[1]

These "folk problems" are reported in a range of styles, from that of the wonder tale, as in "An Eye for an Eye," or "The Contest of Riddles," to the typical dilemma tale, as in "Leopard, Goat, and Yam" (an African version of a classic logical puzzle).

Because most of the stories have claims for superior virtue or power embedded within them, in a sense they reflect the argumentative context of their telling. The moral tales, like the dilemma tales, are short and sharp. Their message, however, is usually clear, and often epigrammatic. Most of these are domestic dramas, focusing on questions arising from the mishandling of relationships or problems brought about through misfortune.

Many of the moral stories reflect upon the condition of the community and family under stress: how people act when they don't have enough to eat. Perhaps most important here is the emphasis placed on the sharing of food, usually illustrated by the selfishness of one character or another. Thus, in "Rich Man, Poor Man," the disparity between the two is illustrated by their approach to sharing; and in "Finders Keepers" the action is instigated by a theft of food (the monitor lizard claims to have "found" it).

A related theme is that of a "do-unto-others" form of reciprocity—or the lack of it. Here, the African record is a strange one, for as often as not selfish behavior is shown to be the norm, as in "Killed for a Horse." Bad may be the return for good; in "The Nature of the Beast," the kind wife is rewarded for releasing the heron, by having it gouge her eye out—an all-too-obvious illustration of how the beneficiary of a good deed may answer his benefactor with scorn or even harm. But, on balance, a kindly act and a long-suffering approach to life lead to eventual repayment and the ultimate triumph of virtue.

Many of the moral stories and dilemma tales alike focus on aspects of living "correctly" within the family. Thus, in "He Starved His Own Father," the father dies of hunger because he provided for a lover instead of his wife and son. "The Smart Man and the Fool" has a similar outcome but offers an interesting variation on the subject.

Another important theme in these tales is that of keeping one's own counsel. In "Fembar's Curiosity," the protagonist dies for having told a secret, and in "A Father's Advice," the dying father admonishes his son not to tell his "private affairs" to his wife.

[1] John Gay and Michael Cole, *The New Math in an Old Culture* (New York, Chicago, and San Francisco: Holt, Rinehart and Winston, 1967), p. 25.

17
The Contest of Riddles

There was once a king who had only one child, a daughter. When she was still a little girl, she told her father that she wanted to marry a man who was wise in the knowledge of riddles. When she became old enough to choose a husband, her father called the chiefs of all the *Abron* cantons before him to find the man who would pass her test. Before they went to court, each chief called the men of his village together and had them teach him all the riddles they knew. But when the chiefs arrived at the house of the king, and each recited all his riddles for the princess, she wouldn't accept any of them.

Some months later, two young men of a distant village decided to try their luck with the king's daughter. The journey to the court was long, so they took a youth with them to carry their belongings. When they arrived at court, the daughter of the king said that they must wait three days, and then on the fourth day, she would accept one of them in marriage. The first day, she made *futu* for them, the bread dough that is the staple of life. In the center of the ball of dough, she put a red kola nut. When the two men found the kola, they threw it away, but their serving youth recovered and kept it. On the second day and the third, she again put a red kola nut in the center of the dough ball, and, each time, the two men threw the kola away, and the youth recovered it. On the fourth day, the king's daughter once more prepared *futu* for the men, but this time she put a small cotton ball in the center of it. When the two men found the cotton ball, they discarded it, as they had the kola, but the youth saved it, as he had saved the kola.

When the men finally came before the girl, the first of them recounted all the riddles he knew, but when he had finished, the king's daughter said, "I cannot marry you." Then the second man recounted all the riddles he knew, but when he had finished, the girl said, "I cannot marry you." The youth, who had stood silent all this time, then asked to speak. The two men refused to give him permission, but the king's daughter commanded that he have his chance, too. The youth stepped forward, and said, "I have very little to say and so I will not take much of your time. The first day of our arrival, the King's daughter put a red kola nut in the middle of the *futu*. On the second and third days, she did the same thing, but on the fourth day, she put in a cotton ball. Now I say that on the first three days she was menstruating, but that on the fourth day she had finished." The king's daughter responded that the youth was indeed wise and that she would marry him. The other men were jealous, and announced they were going to leave, and the youth must come with them to carry their things. The king's daughter replied that they must all stay one more day, so that she and the young man could get married, and they agreed.

As soon as the marriage was completed, the three men set out for their own village. Along the way, the first man said, "We must kill the youth." The second said, "No, we cannot, but let us take him back to the village and give him to his parents." After some argument, they finally agreed to tie the youth to a tree and abandon him, and so they did. Bound up though he was, the boy did not cry, but waited. After some time, a vendor of kola came by. The youth said to him, "Go to the daughter of the king, my wife, and say to her, 'Untie this kola and guard it or it will surely rot.' " When the vendor had done so, the girl, without saying a word, ran to her father and asked him to give her two horses. "My husband is tied to a tree, and if I do not go and free him, he will surely die." And so she rode off and rescued him. From then, they lived happily. Now, my children, which of the two, the youth or the king's daughter, was wiser in the knowledge of riddles?

—Abron

18

Leopard, Goat, and Yam

A certain man was running away from his village, and he was taking with him all his property. This consisted of a leopard, a goat, and a yam. Now in time he came to a river where there was only one canoe. It was so small that it was impossible for him to take more than one part of his property with him at a time. Now how did he succeed in getting it all to the other side, for if he left the yam with the goat or the leopard with the goat, the goat would eat the yam or the leopard devour the goat.

The answer is: He took the goat over first and then the yam. He then recrossed the goat and ferried over the leopard, returning a fourth time for the goat.

—Hausa

19

An Eye for an Eye?

The son of a chief once heard tell of the beautiful daughter of another chief and set off to visit her. And as he traveled, he met a young fellow. He said, "Young man, I'd like you to come with me, for I'm off to seek a wife." "Oh, no," said the other, "for I have a father who has nothing, neither gown nor trousers nor loincloth; and this leather loincloth that you see me wearing is all that we have between us, my father and I. If my father is going out from our hole in the baobab tree, then he takes it and puts it on; and I do the same when I'm going out." "Where is your father?" asked the chief's son. "Over there, in the hole in the baobab tree." And the chief's son asked to be taken to him.

And off they went. When the boy got to the hole in the baobab tree, he said "Daddy, look! I was out walking, I met the son of a chief who said he wanted me to go with him to seek a wife. But I answered that I must come and tell you first and hear whatever you had to say about it." "By all means go along with him," answered his father. And the chief's son said, "Take the leather loincloth off and give it to your father." And the chief's son had a traveling bag opened and a gown taken out, and trousers, and a turban, and a cap, and a sword, and a sword sling, and all these together were given to the other. And he had him shaved and bathed, too.

And so they took the road and traveled till they reached the other town. When word was brought to the chief's daughter that she had visitors, they were taken to lodgings. She had food prepared for them—three rams were slaughtered, and chickens, too.

Soon the chief's daughter rose and came to them. But when she got there, her heart went out to the servant of the chief's son, he whose father lived in the hole of the tree. And she spoke and said that he was the one she loved. "No, no!" he said, "I wouldn't dare. See, here's my master." "No," she answered, "You're the one I love." But again he protested that he and his father had nothing, but lived in a hole in a baobab tree, and added, "Even the clothes that I'm wearing were given my be the chief's son here." "Oh," she replied, "is that all?"

She sent home to her father's compound, asking for two carrying bags, one with a gown, and one with trousers; and she sent for a turban, as well. All her wishes were conveyed to her father, who got together everything she had asked for, and handed it over to her. Then she said, "Take those things off, and return them to him. Take these and put them on." "Very well," he answered, and did as she had said. He collected the chief's son's clothes, and returned them to him.

So the chief's son set off home alone, leaving the son of the man with the leather loincloth. For the chief's daughter had decided it was he that she loved. Then she went and told her father, saying, "Father, today I want to be married." "Very well," he said, and so they were married.

Time passed and her father died. His large estate was duly divided and she inherited it all as he had no sons or other daughters. Her mother left the chief's compound and had a separate compound built for herself. Then the girl said to her husband, "Where is your father? Let someone go and fetch him, and let him and my mother be married." And he answered, "He's back there in the hole in the baobab tree."

They went and fetched him, and when they returned, the marriage duly took place. And so they lived for some time.

But after a while there came a time when the elder couple had a quarrel and the father of the girl's husband knocked his wife down, striking out one of her eyes. The girl then said, angrily, "Your father has quarreled with my mother and knocked her eye out. If you value our marriage, you'll go and put out one of your father's eyes. If you don't, take your leather loincloth, and you and your father can go back to your hole in the baobab tree. But if you do, then let our marriage continue." Well, here was a nice problem! He had been quite destitute. If he put out his own father's eye, he might continue to live with his wife; but if he didn't, then he must go back with his father to the hole in the baobab tree, whence they had come!

—*Hausa*

20 Wondrous Powers: Mirror, Sandals, and a Medicine Bag

An old man had three children, all boys. When they had grown up to manhood, he called them together and told them that now he was very old and no longer able to provide, even for himself. He ordered them to go out and bring him food and clothing.

The three brothers set out, and after a very long while they came to a large river. As they had gone on together for such a time, they decided that once they got across they would separate. The eldest told the youngest to take the middle road, and the second to go to the right, while he himself would go to the left. Then, in a year's time, they would come back to the same spot.

So they parted, and at the end of a year, as agreed, they found their way back to the riverside. The eldest asked the youngest what he had gotten during his travels, and the boy replied: "I have nothing but a mirror, but it has wonderful power. If you look into it, you can see all over the country, no matter how far away." When asked, in turn, what he had gotten, the second brother replied: "Only a pair of sandals that are so full of power, that if one puts them on one can walk at once to any place in the country in one step." Then, the eldest himself, said: "I, too, have obtained but little, a small calabash of medicine, that is all. But let us look into the mirror and see how father fares."

The youngest produced his mirror, and they all looked into it and saw that their father was already dead and that even the funeral custom was finished. Then the elder said: "Let us hasten home and see what we can do." So the second brought out his sandals, and all three placed their feet inside them and, immediately, they were borne to their father's grave. Then the eldest shook the medicine out of his bag, and poured it over the grave. At once their father arose, as if nothing had been the matter with him. Now which of these three sons has performed the best?

—*Togo*

21

The Devil Comes Between Them

A youth once saw a maiden and told her that he loved her; she saw him and told him the same. So the young fellow went and picked up his sleeping mat, took the girl by the hand, and went off with her into the bush. There the boy spread out the mat and invited the girl to sit. The two sat and chatted. *Iblis* the devil came by that way, seized the boy, killed him, and then cut off his head. The girl could do nothing but sit on the mat and lament.

Meanwhile both mothers and both fathers were searching for their son and daughter. An old woman told them where they should look for them. Thanking her, they went quickly off down the road, where, the boy's parents found their son killed, with his head taken off. At this, they began to lament, as well.

Suddenly, up came *Iblis* again. He made a river of fire, and a river of water, and a river of black-hooded cobras, and in this last he placed a land monitor. Then he went up to the group—the girl's mother and her father, and the boy's mother and his father, and the girl herself—and said to them, "Would you like me to help you recover your son and bring him back to life?" "Of course!" they answered. "Very well," he said, "You, the boy's mother, must go into the river of fire, and then into the river of water, and then into the river of cobras, where you must seize the land monitor and bring it out." But the boy's mother answered, "No! I'm not going into a river of fire to be burnt up, nor am I going into the river of cobras, to be thoroughly bitten." *Iblis* said, "Had you gone and captured the land monitor, I'd have helped you with your son."

Whereupon the girl said, "Is that so? If that land monitor is captured and brought here, will the boy come to life?" "Yes," said *Iblis.* Up jumped the girl and swam across the river of fire. Then she plunged into the river of water and swam till she was through it. Then into the river of cobras, where pushing aside the slithering snakes, she seized the land monitor. Back she came through the rivers, and handed the lizard to *Iblis.*

Then, said *Iblis,* "So! So you've got the land monitor for me?" And the boy came to life and stood up. Then *Iblis* spoke again, saying, "Now, if this land monitor is slaughtered, the boy's mother will die, but if it isn't slaughtered, the girl's mother will die."

Well then—is the boy going to slaughter the land monitor, so that his own mother dies, or will he spare it, so that the girl's mother dies? Which of the two will he choose do you think?

—*Hausa*

22

The Quality of Friendship

Two young men, each named *Kamo,* knew of each other, but had never seen each other; one lived in the East and one in the West. The young man from the West went to the man who told fortunes by cutting sand, and said, "I want to go over and see my friend whom I have never seen, and I want you to cut sand, so that I will know whether I will meet good or bad luck." The man cut sand and told him that if he went to see his friend, he would not find him home, but would meet him on the path, and that when he reached the country of his friend, he must not go out at night, no matter who called, because if he did, he would surely die and never be able to return home.

Not satisfied with what the fortune-teller had said, the young man went to another, who also cut sand, and then told him the same thing that the first fortune-teller had told him. Hearing the same words from two different fortune-tellers, he finally believed them, and said, "I will now go to see my friend, but I will keep in mind what I have been told."

He walked three days and met his friend, but, of course, he did not recognize him, and he asked the other where he was going. The young man from the East answered: "My name is *Kamo*. I am going to see my friend in the West, who is also named *Kamo*." The young man from the West replied, "That's me! I was going to see you." So *Kamo* from the East said: "You have walked three days and I have only walked one. Come back with me to my place."

Whereupon both *Kamos* went East together. On the night they arrived, a big snake swallowed *Kamo* of the East. That *Kamo* cried and cried from within the belly of the big snake until *Kamo* of the West heard him and woke up. He wanted to help his friend, but he remembered that the fortune-tellers had told him that he must not go out at night. He sat down, but thought to himself, "I know I'll meet trouble if I go out, but how can I stay when my friend is in distress?" And so he went outside and found that the snake had swallowed all but the head of his friend. Taking his knife, then, *Kamo* from the West killed the snake by ripping his mouth open. In doing so, some of the blood from the snake flew into his eyes and he at once became blind.

Now *Kamo* from the East was free, but he was sorry for his friend who had done so much for him and had been blinded in doing it. So *Kamo* from the East went to find a fortune-teller. The man cut sand, and told him, "You have one son; go and cut his throat, and take his blood for your friend to wash his face, and then his sight will be restored." *Kamo* from the East went home and killed his son. *Kamo* from the West washed his face in the blood of his friend's son, and immediately his sight was restored and his trouble was at an end.

Who was the greater friend, *Kamo* of the East or *Kamo* of the West?

—*Vai*

23
The Four Champions

The Horny Head champion, the Penis champion, the Farting champion, and the Testicles champion set off on a journey together. They came to a town, where they lodged in the compound of the chief. Bundles of corn were sent to feed them from the chief's storehouse—but the town had nowhere to thresh it!

Then the Horny Head said, "May the chief's life be prolonged! Here we are and yet they're looking for a place to thresh. Let them come and do it on my head!" So they came and undid the bundles on Horny Head's noggin.

But then they had to find a piece of wood with which to thresh the corn so Penis said. "May the chief's life be prolonged! Here we are now, and yet they're looking for something to thresh with! Just give me a bit of room and you'll see!" And pulling out his penis, he began threshing, and presently the corn was threshed.

But there was no wind, and word was brought to the chief that, though the corn was threshed, there was no wind and so could be no winnowing. Then said the Wind Breaker, "May the chief's life be prolonged! Here are we, and in spite of that they're still looking for wind!" And he unveiled his anus, and let rip. And all the chaff was blown away, leaving just the grain.

But they had no bag to put the grain in. So Testicles said, "May the chief's life be prolonged! Here are we, and in spite of what we've done, they're still looking for a sack to catch the grain!" And opening his scrotum, he said, "Bring me the grain and pour in in here." And they did it, and he carried the corn home.

All right, among the four of them that exercised his special gift, who was the champion?

—*Hausa*

24
Who Should He Kill?

There was once a man who did no other job but digging out pesky ground squirrels. Taking his son to work with him one day, he said, "You stop up the back entrances, and I'll dig." But when the father set about digging in the ground squirrel's hole, the ground squirrel came out where the son was, and made off. Then the father hit his son and with the handle of his hoe and knocked him senseless.

A little later in the evening, up came an Arab taking a stroll, and he saw the son of the squirrel digger, who was just coming to his senses. Now this Arab had never had any children, so he picked up the boy and took him home. His nose was dirty and full of ants, and the Arab wiped them away and had him bathed in hot water. When the boy recovered completely, the Arab dressed him in a black and white gown, embroidered trousers, and a heavily indigoed gown, as well, with a turban twenty cubits long and twenty strips wide.

Now in this area, the rich merchants' sons used to ride and compete at the racetrack. The Arab brought out a saddle ornamented in gold and silver, with brass stirrups from Tripoli, and all the other trappings for a horse. Then he told the boy to mount up, and said to him, "When you get to the track, whatever you see the other riders do—you do it, too!" So the boy joined the rich merchants' sons and went along with them. Some great arguments arose among the people over whose son he was, but no one knew the truth.

When the merchants' sons got home, each one said to his father, "There's an Arab who has a son who has more finery than we have." And their fathers answered, "No, it's not really his son. That's false." But they added, "All the same, we will test him. Tomorrow when you go riding with him, let each one give away his horse and equipment before he comes home. Then we'll see! For generosity is the way to demonstrate true wealth."

So the sons went out the next day, and afterwards they gave away their horses. And watching carefully, the Arab's boy, too, gave away his horse.

After this, the merchants gave their sons other horses, each worth a million cowries, and told them, "When you go riding, before you come home, cut down your horses!" And the Arab's boy was given a horse worth ten million. When they had had their gallop, each one took his sword and cut down his horse. Then the Arab's boy, without even troubling to take the saddle off, cut down his horse and went off home.

And they said, "Did you see? He cut down his horse," and again, "Well! The Arab's boy didn't even take off the horse's equipment; he left it there." Then people said, "So it seems he is his son after all!"

Time passed and the Muslim festival was at hand. In the morning, the usual mounted procession took place, and in all the town, there wasn't a youth whose horse was fitted out to touch the Arab's. And as they were coming back from the mosque, they passed among the common people who had come from the country into the town for prayers.

Well, it happened that the squirrel digger, the real father of the boy, had come to town for the festival and had joined the crowd. When he saw his son, he exclaimed, "Hey! Get down from that horse—you know it's not your own father's, you rascal! Look at your brothers there—one of them has killed nine ground squirrels, one of them ten, and you—here are you in dissipation and idleness!" And the Arab said to him, "Please, please keep it to yourself! Here—take your son!"

And in the evening, the Arab chose two horses and saddled them up, picked out two gowns, a black one and a white one, and gave them to the boy's father. And the Arab gave him twenty thousand cowry shells and provisions for the journey. Then all three mounted up and rode out.

They left the town and came into the bush. Suddenly, the Arab produced a sword and gave it to the boy, saying, "Now! Either me or your father—cut down one of us!"

Well that's the question—the Arab, who had given him so many things? Or his own father, who had struck him unconscious because of the ground squirrel? Which should he kill?

—*Hausa*

25 Killing Virtue

In the olden time, a man went hunting in the far bush. He took with him his wife. But one day he left her by a shea-butter tree and did not return, and the woman could not find her way home to their village. She therefore built herself a shelter near the tree, where not long after she gave birth to a boy child.

Now, a lioness lived quite close to the tree, and she gave birth to a male cub at the same time as the woman too bore her child; but she was unaware that the woman was nearby. Every day the lioness went into the bush to look for meat, and the woman also wandered away in search of roots and fruits. While they were absent, the two children, the man-child and the lion cub, met and played together, and became the fastest of friends, without either parent's knowledge.

One day, however, the lioness lay in wait near the shea-butter tree, sprang on the woman as she was returning home, killed her, and brought the body back to share with her cub. The man-child missed his mother at midday, but even so went out in the evening to play with the lion cub. The cub, however, would not play, and kept looking at his friend, who at last, said: "Lion, what is the matter?" And the lion replied: "Man, I have had no food today; I have bad trouble for you. Follow me."

So the man-child went with the lion cub back to the latter's home, and there he saw his mother lying dead on the ground. He began to cry, but the lion cub said: "Stop! I have sworn a big oath today that as my mother has killed your mother, I shall be your faithful friend until I die. I will avenge you, and until then I shall care for you." Having said this, he took the man-child back home.

Each day, for many months after that, the lion cub brought a large share of the meat his mother gave him to the man-child. They grew up together, playing and becoming more and more friendly, and every morning the lion cub called the man-child, and, placing his paw in the paw-mark of his mother, said: "Soon, very soon, I shall be strong enough."

At last, there came the day when the two fitted exactly, the footprints of the cub and of its mother. Then the cub went out with its mother, and said: "Teach me how to catch meat."

After a few lessons, the cub thought he was strong enough, and he told the man-child that the next day he would avenge the slaying of his mother. The following morning, the cub killed the lioness, his mother, and showed the corpse to his friend, saying: "Now, I have kept the first part of my oath."

Then for a long time the two lived quite happily together, but one evening the lion cub said to his friend, "It is time for you to return to your brothers, marry, and live in the village. I have seen a very fine girl, the daughter of a chief; she must be your wife. Now listen to my plan. Go to the village. I will hide myself near the watering place and, when I see this girl, I will catch her, but I won't harm her. Everyone else will run away scared, so if you go to the chief and ask him for his daughter, he will agree if you can save her. Then follow me and I will give her up to you. Build your house on the outskirts of the village. I will come to see you every Friday evening, and you must meet me here in the bush alone. But remember this, never take a second wife or trouble will surely come."

The man-child followed the lion's instructions, and rescued and married the chief's daughter. The people built him a house outside the village, but every Friday he sent his wife to spend the night with her family, while he and the lion played together and exchanged their news.

A long time passed in this way, when one day there came to the village a woman of great wealth and power. She had refused every man's offer of marriage and having decided to choose for herself, was traveling everywhere throughout the land in search of a suitable husband. She saw the man-child, fell in love, and asked him to marry her. But he, mindful of the lion cub's words, refused her. She insisted, so he compromised, and took her into his household.

Every Friday, however, he sent her to the village with his wife. The lion foretold trouble, but the man-child said that there would be no problem because he had not married the woman; she was merely his.

But unlike his wife, this woman had a curiosity which she couldn't contain—and one Friday, instead of leaving, she hid herself and saw the lion coming to meet his friend. She went to tell a hunter and that night, while the two friends had their usual fun, he hid himself in the lion's path. When the lion left in the morning, the hunter shot him—and then immediately went back to tell the people. On hearing the news, the man-child ran to his friend's corpse and, seizing the arrow that had killed him, he stabbed himself with it and died. When his wife arrived and saw the body of her husband and his friend, she went straight back to the house, found a rope, and hanged herself.

"Now which of the three, lion, man, or wife, do you think was the most virtuous?"

—*Ashanti*

26 A Spirited Contending

There were once two young men who were courting the same girl, and each man had two spears. One day, on their way home with her, they passed through the bush, and a lion waylaid them. The girl fell down saying that her stomach was paining her. The lion leapt at them, and the first youth threw his spear, but the lion dodged and the spear fell to the ground. The youth threw his second spear also, and that, too, fell to the ground.

In his turn, the other young fellow stepped forward and he, too, threw a spear, but like the rest it just fell to the ground. Then he threw his second spear, but again he missed the lion. So all their spears were used up and still the beast hadn't been hit.

Then one of the two youths said to the other, "Hurry, and run home. In my mother's hut, at the head of the bed, you'll find some spears. Bring them, and some water in a calabash, and some potash, too." At once, the boy ran off to do these things.

Meanwhile, the other young fellow leapt at the lion, and after a struggle, threw him, and taking his knife cut his throat. Then he lifted the lion into a squatting position, and the girl came over and lay down beside the lion. The youth got behind the mane and hid.

Soon the one who had left returned with the spears, the water, and the potash, but he couldn't find the other youth and the girl. A little further on, he bumped into the lion crouching there, with the girl lying in front of him, but he didn't recognize her. He said to himself, "So that was the trick was it? The two went off and ran away, and left the lion to kill someone else's child! Well, then, I can't let the lion live to do that again." And tossing away his spears and his little calabash of water and the potash, he threw himself at the lion. He grappled with it, and the lion, of course, fell right over. The girl and the other boy got up laughing.

Well then—which of the two, the boy who killed the lion, or the other boy who went and fetched the spears and the little calabash of water and the potash—which of the two of them showed greater spirit?

—*Hausa*

27

Love Caused It All

A chief married a wife, but they could not seem to produce children, so he called a magician. "Wise man," he said, "I love my wife, but we have no child. That is it. You are to help me, so that we may have a child." The wise man agreed and went into his room. He sat there for a long time, perhaps a month. When he came out, he said,

“You will get a child, you with your wife. But no one is to see him except you and your wife and the one who cooks for him—only these three.”

Sure enough, the wife became pregnant, and when her time came, she gave birth. The child was brought into the house, and a room made ready for him in the attic. There the child remained for a long time, and there he grew. The child even learned to walk on his own, for he was alone in the attic, high up. He became a young man, but still he stayed in the attic, looking down at the people below, wondering at the life outside.

One day a girl walked out in the village, so that he could see her from his perch. They let their eyes meet, she and the boy (he forgot that he had been told that he should not be seen by any other person). They stood looking at each other for a long time. The girl decided she must find this strange boy’s room. She searched for a long ladder, and when she found one, she leaned it against the house.

Evening came. The girl climbed up into the attic and told the boy, “Since I saw you yesterday, my heart has not stood still. That is why I have come, I love you.” The boy explained why he was hidden away. Then they lay down together.

When the sun had risen, the woman who cooked for the boy brought water for him to wash himself, and she found the girl sitting there, and the child, the boy, he was dead! She called the chief and his mother. “Come here! Come here! I have seen something amazing. The boy has died, and a woman is in the room, just sitting there!” The chief went with the mother and saw the boy’s body, and saw the girl sitting. He asked if she had killed his son, and she replied, “Yes. Our love caused it.”

The distraught parents called the wise man again. “Ha! the child you struggled for us to get, that child has died.” The wise man said, “Well, all right. Let us burn the body. Let me have men now to go and cut wood and bring it to the village.” The men went out then to cut some wood. They brought it to the village, where they put it down, and the wise man asked if they had a can of kerosene. They did, and he said, “Well, fetch it.” Then he poured it all over the wood, and made a big fire of it. When it was blazing, he turned to the father. “Aha. Chief, do you love your son?” “Yes.” “Well, then, go into the fire.” The chief went up to the fire, but it was so hot that he turned back. He went up to it again, and then he sat down and wept. The wise man said, “Ah! chief, I suppose you don’t love your son.”

He called the mother, “Well, do you love your son?” “Yes.” “Well, you go into the fire, so that you may be burnt with him.” His mother went up as well, but it was too hot. She retreated. She came near it again, but then said, “All right. I will not be burnt, too. I will leave it as it is.” “Well, all right.”

The girl was called, the one who found the boy and caused him to die. "Girl, do you love the man?" "Yes." "Well then, go into the fire, so you may both be burnt." The girl leaped into the fire. Then they were burnt together, the two of them.

When the fire died down, the wise man took the ashes, and went back to his room again. Once more he stayed for a whole month. There he made a complete woman and man. He made them just like *Limba* people, they were alive. He said, "Aha, chief. The work you called me for, I have finished it. Here is the man and the woman." The chief said, "Thank you, thank you, thank you." He paid the magician. The wise man went off, and the boy came out with his wife. He said, "Father, I cannot live here. I must go upcountry, far away." "All right, my son, all right. Go, with your wife."

They spent the whole day traveling. Then hunger seized the man so badly that he was weak all over and could not go any further. There was nearby a woman who had hired some men to clear out a swamp for her. She had cooked some rice with meat and putting it on her head, had set out to take it to her workers. On the way, she came upon the place where the traveler had collapsed with hunger, the man and his wife. The woman, when she saw them said, "Hey, this man is fine, isn't he! I want to marry him." The wife said, "No! No! No! No! I won't allow it." The woman replied, "If you agree to let me marry him, I will take this rice and give it to him, he can eat it—this rice I have cooked for my workers." The girl said, "All right." So she gave them the rice and they ate it up.

Then the two women and their husband set out together. They soon met another woman, a mother of a young child, washing at the water. She said, "Hey, that man is fine! I must marry him." The other woman said, "I can't allow it. No! No! No! No! I took my rice, the rice for my workers, and gave it all to the man, so that my workers were left with none at all. Now you come to say just like that that you want the man. I can't allow it." The girl said, "Do you see this water here, this big river? There are many crocodiles in it, and no one can cross here without first throwing someone in the water, so that the crocodiles may have something to eat. All right. If you let me marry this man, I will take my child and throw him to the crocodiles, and you may cross safely in the boat." The other agreed, so the mother took and threw her child into the water. Then the three wives and their man got into the boat and they quickly crossed the river. The crocodiles did not catch them.

Well, a stranger could not safely enter the village to which they went, unless he could show where the chief's afterbirth was buried. When they reached the village, the chief's daughter, his firstborn, she said, "Hey, I love the man who is come to our village. I will go there to marry him." Then said the woman, "No! No! No! No! I can't agree.

I took my child whom I bore, I threw him to the crocodiles in the river so we could cross. Now we have gotten this far and you say you are coming to our husband to take him away and marry him. I can't allow it." The chief's daughter said, "Oh! If you allow me to come in marriage to your husband, I will show you the secret of the village, and your husband will not be killed." And so they all agreed. The chief's daughter said, "Tomorrow morning when your husband gets up, have him walk out on the veranda and look around. I will be sweeping the compound. Where I beat out the broom, that is the place where the chief's afterbirth is buried." And thus the man was shown the secret.

Later that day, the old people of the village came to challenge him with their test, ending with, "If you do not know the place, we must kill you." The man said, "Oh, well, all right. Everything there is, as the greatest god wills it." He went and showed the place, "Is it not here? It is there."

The chief of the village was an old man and soon died. When this happened, the stranger was taken as chief. He remained for a long time in this chieftainship, and he bore children by all of these wives he had married on his travels. He lived long.

Then one day when he was very old, he died. His wives were left with the children, all of those whom the chief had fathered. The one who had gone into the fire for the man said, "My child owns the inheritance and must become the new chief." But the next one said, "It is not your child who should be the next in line, for I took the rice I had cooked for my workers and gave that to the man when he could not go on. My rice saved him." The next said, "No, that is not just, for I took my own child and threw him to the crocodiles. If I had not done that, our husband would not ever have been able to cross the river. The crocodiles would have eaten him." Then said the last, "Hey, what about me? I came and showed the place of my father's afterbirth, so that our man would not be killed. It was because of this, that when my father died he was made chief."

Well, of all these women, the wives, whose child alone should get the inheritance?

—Limba

28

Killed for a Horse

The son of a certain chief was married to the daughter of a former chief, and he had a horse, a light gray one. They had been married for some time, and the husband, before entering the hut, was in the habit of saying, "Gray horse, gray horse, you're worth more than the women of today, these modern women." Then, when he got into the hut, his wife would say to him, "You must kill that gray horse, before you come near me." "Don't stir yourself," he said, "for I'm not killing the gray."

This went on for some time, until one day another chief's son heard about it. Now he also had a gray horse. He put some clothes into his traveling bag, and mounting his gray, set off. When he got to the town he put up at the compound of an old woman. And he asked her, "Old woman, what's the news?" "News about what?" says she. "About the chief's son and the old chief's daughter," he said. "Oh, that," said she. "Yes, they were married, but he hasn't yet slept with her. For she says to have her he must kill his gray horse; but he, without fail, sings his gray horse's praises every night." "Isn't that amazing?" he said. "Tell me, what sort of clothes does he wear, this chief's son?" "He wears a black- and blue-checked robe, embroidered trousers, a dark blue turban."

Well, that day the young husband went to visit the compound of a friend of his, and they sat there, chatting, until late. And while the husband was away, this other chief's son, having put on a black and blue-gown, embroidered trousers, and a dark blue turban went into his compound. And as he went to the wife's hut, he said, "Gray horse, you're worth more than the women of today, these modern women." And as usual, the chief's daughter answered, "You must kill that gray horse, if you want to come to me." "Is that all?" he said, "Yes," she said. And he went and drew his sword and slew the gray.

Later that night, the chief's son returned home, and when he entered the compound he found his dead horse. He said, "Someone had a grudge against the gray and has killed him." And his wife said to him, "You've lost both ways—you've lost your horse and you've lost what was yours by rights." "H'm. I see," said he. "But don't say a word," she said, "just keep quiet about it. I'll take revenge for you. Don't get upset." Then she got herself a razor, and put it into a basket, and collected some cloths and put them in the basket, and in went a little leather box of antimony, and a mirror, and her cola nuts, and her tobacco flowers. Then she took the basket and gave it to one of her girls to carry for her.

And she set off along the road, inquiring the way, till she reached the town where the other chief's son was. And there she found him, together with his courtiers. They exclaimed, "Well! *There's* a girl! Is she married?" "No," said one, and they all agreed with him that she couldn't possibly be married and be alone like that. Then another of them said, "But she must have been married before." The chief's son said, "I want her. Take her to my compound." And away they went with her and took her there.

The sun set, and the chief's son returned to his compound, and when night fell, he threw himself on the girl. When they had finished, he was overcome by sleep, whereupon the girl got up quietly, and taking her razor, seized his penis and cut it off. The young fellow started awake, and leaping up, tried to stand, but he fell back. A second time he tried, but again he fell back, and so died. The girl put the penis into her basket, and gave it to her servant to carry for her. Once again they took to the road, and made their way home.

Meanwhile, the young men who were friends of the chief's son, entered his compound and found him dead. So they went and told the chief. And the chief summoned his horsemen, saying, "As there is no horse in the whole town as fast as the one this boy rode, go quickly and tell his younger brother to saddle up the gray. Let him go after his murderer before any reinforcements come. And when he catches up with her, let him take his sword and kill her."

"Very well," said the younger son, on hearing this, and he got on the gray and galloped until he caught up with her—close to where there was a large palm tree. He drew his sword to kill her, but said to himself, "Surely a girl as beautiful as this ought not to be killed." "Look girl, let us lie together, you and I, and then I'll let you go another way before my friends catch up with us." But the girl answered with spirit, "What? Right here? Out in the open? No, I certainly won't lie with you! I'm afraid you'll just have to kill me. But, if you climb that palm tree and cut down some of its large leaves and then come down, why we can spread them out, and then you can lie with me." "My—is that all?" said he, and proceeded to take off his gowns, his trousers, his turban, until he was wearing only a loincloth, and carrying his sword with which to cut off the leaves. Then he climbed the palm tree. But when the girl saw him make his first slash, she and her slave girl got on the horse, and spurring it, escaped. All the young man could do was say, "Come back, please, please come back, for God's sake and the Prophet's. I won't kill you. Only let me have my horse back!"

So there he was, squatting up in the tree when the other horsemen came up looking for him, right where the horse had stood. "Perhaps he has killed the girl," one said. But another replied, "Not likely! For if he had killed her, we would see blood here—and there isn't any." Whereupon one of them lifted his head and saw him, squatting there up in the tree, and he said to the others, "Well, look, there he is, up in the palm tree!" "Well!" said the others in surprise. "How did you get up there dressed like that?" "Well—you see—she took my horse," he answered. Then the others all said, "We better not trifle around with her." So there they stopped, and suggested to him that he get down from the tree. Then they made one of his brother's servants dismount from his horse, and gave it to him to ride. And so they returned home.

The girl continued on and returned to her husband. "There you are," she said, "I told I would take revenge for you, didn't I? Look—I've done so, I've cut off his penis, and I've brought you his horse, which no one could distinguish from yours. They're like twins."

Well now, which of the three of them would you say got most harmed—the girl, her husband, the chief's son, or the other chief's son?

—*Hausa*

29 Three Wives

There was once a man who had three wives. It happened that they were all about to bear him children, and they asked him for permission to return to their homes. He agreed to this, and on the appointed day set out with them to lead them on their way.

Presently, they came to a place where the road branched in three directions. The man turned to his women, and said: "Here I will leave you, as here it is that you will each take your different roads." As he said this, he fell dead.

Then the women began to make a great ado. The first woman said that she would not leave her husband like that, but would follow him, and then she went and hanged herself. The second woman said she could not leave her husband's body for the vultures and hyenas to devour, and she sat down by the corpse and kept everything away from it. The third ran into the bush bewailing her man's death, and there she saw a man who asked her what was the matter. When he heard, he said that he would help, and went back with the woman to the crossroads. There he took his magic cow's tail, and tapping the dead woman and man, raised them both from the dead and gave them back their life.

Now which of those women is best?

—Dagomba

30 The Five Helpers

There was once a beautiful girl, the daughter of a chief. She was finer to look upon than any other girl that men could see. But there was no one whom she would agree to marry.

Men came from all countries, but she would not have them. And all the land heard the news of this girl, that though she was of marriageable age, she would take no one.

There was also a snake, a large python who dwelt in a vast lake nearby the river. When he heard about this girl, he decided that he would marry her. So he changed himself into a man and came to the village.

As soon as the maiden saw the young man she was delighted, and said she would marry him at once. Everyone was pleased, and that night they took the young man and the girl on to the roof of the house, for the houses in that village had flat roofs, and there they left them.

Now during the night, the snake licked the girl all over and swallowed her, and changing again into his snake form, he made off to the great lake.

Next morning people came to the house and called to the girl and her man to come down. There was no answer, and the chief told the people to climb up and see what was the matter. This they did, and reported that both the girl and the man were missing.

The chief was very angry, and at once ordered all the people to follow the girl and her lover. But they could find no tracks. So they called for a man who could smell everything. He at once smelled the trail of the girl and followed it down to the great water. There he could go no further. The people, urged on by the anger of the chief, then called on a man famous through all the country for his thirst. They told him to drink up the lake. This he did. But still there was no sign of the man or the girl. Then the people called a man famous for his capacity for work and told him to take out all the mud from the lake. This he did, and thereby revealed a hole. But it was so deep that no one could reach the bottom. Then they remembered that there was a man with an arm that could stretch over all the Dagomba Island. They told him to put his arm in the hole and pull. Out came the great python, which was immediately killed. And when they had cut open its stomach, they found the girl inside, but she was dead. Then the people remembered a man who had the power of medicine, and was able to raise the dead. He came at once and restored the girl to life. Now which of those five men did best?

—*Grumshi*

31

Many Miracles

A holy teacher of Islam wanted to leave his city and go for a while to another one. He met a man with a club, who knew how to fight very well, and who asked to go with him. "If you wish, please do!" the *Mallem* replied. Then a hunter came, and said, "I know how to shoot very well; would you like me to accompany you?" "If you like, please do!" The hunter took his bow and arrow and the three set off.

In front of the city was a big river, but since it was the dry season, they didn't need a canoe for they were able to wade across. And so they came to the other city, where they stayed for a month. Then the holy teacher, the *Mallem,* said they must depart, so that they could cross the river before the rainy season. But before they reached it, the first rain had fallen, and the river was in flood. Because there was no canoe there, the *Mallem* advised that they wait a day for the waters to subside. During the wait, they had nothing to eat.

The king of their home city appeared on the other bank, having come to view the swollen river. He saw the holy teacher and called across to him: "Hello, *Mallem,* what are you doing over there?" "We came early this morning, but couldn't get across." "I don't believe," shouted the king, "that the river is going to fall soon, and we don't have any canoes." "Then I'll try it without a canoe," answered the *Mallem,* who took out his papers, lay them on the water, stepped on them, lay more paper in front of him, stepped on it, picked up the paper behind him and put it in front of him, stepped on it, and so on, until he reached the other bank safely. Neither man nor paper had a drop of water on them.

When the hunter saw this, he followed the example of the *Mallem,* shot an arrow into the water, stepped on it, shot another arrow into the water, stepped on it, picked up the first arrow, shot it into the water again, and so on, until he also reached the far shore safely. Then the man with the club thought: "What those two can do, so can I." With his club he struck the water, which immediately divided itself. He crossed the riverbed with dry feet, and the water closed again behind him.

The three joined the train of the king. Along the way, they passed an old woman, and the *Mallem* asked if she had something for him to eat, since he had not eaten since that morning. The woman answered, "I have nothing. When I heard that the king was coming, in my excitement, I poured cold water into the boiling water. Now I've shaken it all out onto the mat in order to separate the boiling water from the cold water once more." The three continued on their way. Near the city, they met a man who was digging a well. "Don't you have some food to sell?" asked the *Mallem.* "No," answered the man, "but here it is very hot, so much so that I'm just getting ready to move my well to the shadows of that tree there. When the sun sets, I'll move it back again." The three went on, and came home.

Who now, asks the storyteller, is the most miraculous of the five? *The Mallem,* who crossed the river on his papers, the hunter who went across the river on his arrows, the man who divided the river with his club, the woman who separated boiling water from cold water, or the man who moved his well under a tree and back again?

—*Karekare*

32

Their Eyes Came Out

A man was once on a trading journey with his mother, his younger sister, his wife, and his wife's mother. They had traveled some way and the heat of the sun made them very thirsty. Reaching the foot of a tree, they sat down.

The husband looked out and saw what seemed to be a well, and said to his sister, "Go and see if there is any water in that well. If so, draw some and bring it." She went and peered over the edge of the well, and one of her eyes fell out, down into the well. She quickly clasped a hand over the other one and kneeled down there in no little distress.

A little time went by, and when she didn't return, the wife said, "Let me go and see what's happening to that girl." She went over and found her sitting by the well. Says she, "What's made you sit there without drawing any drinking water for us? Isn't there any?" And she went up and peered into the well—and one of her eyes fell into it, too. Then she also sat down wondering what to do.

Next, the man's mother said, "What's taking them so long?" and she went after them. When she got there, she asked why they were just sitting. "Isn't there any water?" she asked. And she peered down into the well—and one of her eyes also dropped down into it. Then she quickly covered her other one. And she, too, sat there.

More time passed, and the man said, "Well, what is going on here? I guess I'll have to go after them and see what's happening." He did, and when he got near the well, he said, "What's the matter with all of you, just sitting there like that?" His wife tried to make him turn away by signaling him, but he took no notice and peered into the well, and one of his eyes fell down into it, too. Holding on to the other one, he sat down. And there the five of them were, moaning, with one eye each.

Eventually, a soldier came upon them out of the bush, and the man saw him. The soldier saw them as well, and came towards them. "Stop there, my friend, till I come to get you," said the man. He obeyed, and the man came up to him, still holding his eye. Says he, "I stopped you to keep you from coming to this well. I, my mother, my mother-in-law, my wife, and my younger sister, all of us now have only one eye each from peering into the well." "Really?" said the soldier. "Then you couldn't have heard about this well. There is a jinn in it." "I didn't know," said the man. The soldier asked, "If I go into the well and fetch out your eyes, may I take one of them?" "Yes," answered the man.

The soldier went down into the well, which was more than a hundred cubits deep. He quickly came back up with all five eyes. He handed the man four, and put one in his pocket, and went off. The husband took one and replaced his own. That left three. Well, who would you give those three to? Who would you *not* give them to?

—*Hausa*

33 He Starved His Own

Once there was a man who had a wife, heavy with child, but he neglected her and fell in love with another woman. He used to go out fishing, but instead of giving his wife the catch, he gave it to his lover. When he killed an antelope, he gave his wife none. If he trapped a rabbit, it, too, went to the wicked woman.

The poor starved wife
Brought forth a son,
She gave it life,
Poor weakly one!

When his son was born, he grew up and complained to his mother that while he had eaten the produce of her farm, he had never gotten any of the food killed by his father, nor even worn a cloth given by him.

One day a friend gave him a knife, and unknown to his mother, he went to the woods and hills. He tried to kill some game by throwing his knife at it, but it didn't work. He grieved at his bad luck. So before he left for home, he cut vines, out of which he made string, and set a trap to try to catch some bird or other.

Next morning he went out again, and was delighted to find a guinea fowl in his trap. He ran away home with his prize, and, while yet afar off, shouted to his mother: "Mother, get the tapioca ready!" "Tapioca! my son. How is this? You return too early for mealtime and call for tapioca? Your father has brought me no food. What are you saying, then, my son, do you have real food for me to cook?" "Never mind all that mother, get the tapioca ready."

The mother prepared the tapioca, and the son laid the bird at her feet. When she saw that her son could bring her food, she no longer thought of her troubles or her husband.

About this time, the husband had grown tired of his lover and sent her away; now with no one to cook for him, he remained in his house hungering.

When he heard that his son now went out hunting, and had plenty of food, he sneaked out of his house, and begged his son to give him food.

My son, can it be true
That you me food deny?
Upon my knees I sue,
My son, let me not die.

Then the mother replied:

You first denied us food;
We starved and nearly died;
We will not give him food
Who kept that girl supplied.

Another day, when the son had been lucky and caught a bird, after killing and cleaning it, he said: "Mother, time was when we nearly died of hunger, but now we have plenty, and now that I am a man, you won't need for either cloth or food." And as they were feeding, the father, very thin and weak crawled out of his house, and cried:

Oh, Zinga, *my son,* Zinga,
Will you let your father die?
Oh, Kengi, *my wife,* Kengi,
Here starving I do lie.

When the son heard his father crying so bitterly, he was greatly moved, and asked his mother to put some food on a plate and send it to him. But the mother refused, saying that he deserved none. Then the son wept and sang:

Mother, father wronged us
When he starved us;

Let us feed him now he asks us,
Or God may kill us.

And then he put some food upon a plate and was about to give it to his father, when his father dropped down dead from starvation.

An inquiry was held to find out how the father had died, and when the people had heard all, they gave judgment. "He died by the avenging hand of the Great Spirit."

—*Fjort*

34
The Smart Man and the Fool

Let us tell another story; let us be off!

"Pull away!"

Let us be off!

"Pull away!"

There were two brothers, the Smart Man and the Fool. And it was their habit to go out shooting to keep their parents supplied with food. Thus, one day, they went together into the mangrove swamp, just as the tide was going down, to watch for the fish as they nibbled at the roots of the trees. The Fool saw a fish, fired at it, and killed it. The Smart Man fired also, but got nothing. He then ran up to the Fool, and said: "Fool, have you killed anything?" "Yes, Smart Man, I am a fool—but I killed a fish."

"Yes, you are a fool," answered the Smart Man, "for when I fired I hit the fish that went your way; so the fish you think you killed is mine. Here, give it to me." The Fool gave the Smart Man the fish.

Then they went to their town, and the Smart Man, addressing his father, said: "Father, here is a fish that your son shot, but the Fool got nothing." The mother prepared and cooked the fish, and the father and the Smart Man ate it, giving none to the Fool.

Then they went to the mangrove swamp again, and the Fool fired, and with his first shot killed a big fish. "Did you hear me fire?" asked the Smart Man. "No," answered the Fool. "No?" returned the Smart

Man. "Don't you see the fish I killed?" "All right then," said the Fool, "take the fish."

When they got home, they gave the fish to their mother; and when she had cooked it, the Smart Man and his father ate it, but gave none to the Fool. But as they were enjoying the fish, a bone stuck in the father's throat. Then the Smart Man called to the Fool and told him to go for a doctor.

"No," said the Fool, "I can't. I'm afraid something will happen." And he sang:

Everyday you eat my fish, you call me Fool,
And would let me starve.

"How can you sing," said the Smart Man, "when you see that our father is suffering?"

But the Fool went on singing:

You eat and eat until you're sick;
A bone sticks in your throat;
And now your life is nearly over,
The bone still in your throat.

So you, smart brother, killed the fish,
And gave the fool to eat?
Nay! but now he's dead, do you wish
You'd given the Fool to eat.

While the Fool was yet singing, the father died. Then the neighbors came and joined the family circle, and asked the Fool how it was that he could go on singing now that his father was dead.

The Fool answered: "Our Father made us both, one a smart man, the other a fool. The Fool kills the food and they eat it, giving none to the Fool. They must not curse him, therefore, if he sings while they suffer. He suffered hunger while they had plenty."

And when the people had thought about it for a while, they decided the Fool was right, and they left.

The father had died, and so been justly punished for not having given the Fool food.

"He who eats fish with much oil must suffer from indigestion."

And now I have finished my story.

"Just so!"

—*Fjort*

35

Fembar's Curiosity

A man named *Jarbar* had come from a foreign county to marry *Fembar,* and settled in his wife's country. One day, when he was working on his farm, he saw a very strange serpent; it was immense and had large and small parts alternating, and everywhere he went on the farm, he met some part of that serpent.

Soon *Jarbar* noticed that he understood the language of the animals, reptiles, and birds—for all have their own tongue—but, in a vision, the gods warned him not to impart to anyone knowledge gained in this way, but to keep inviolate the secret of everything he heard. This gift of understanding was the result of having seen the serpent. The reptile would appear and talk to him at anytime. *Jarbar* came to be used to his gift and to these strange visits, too, but still he kept them a secret.

For a long period of time, *Jarbar* obeyed this injunction to silence, and greatly enjoyed the novelty of hearing what all the animal kingdom had to say, for they are often very wise. But one day, as he was eating dinner with *Fembar,* they received news of the death of her father. The next day she put her house in order and prepared to go to her home village to join the mourners.

In the morning, when she had everything arranged and was ready to start, her husband heard a voice say, "Since you are putting everything away, what about us whom you are leaving here?" and he laughed.

His wife became angry and declared that he was laughing at her bereavement, and though he denied it, she remained suspicious. Finally, in desperation, he told her that if he explained the cause of his laughter, it would result in his death. She insisted, however, and at last he gave in and revealed the secret. Shortly after, he died for having disobeyed the command of the reptile.

This sad event taught the wife that one should never be so curious as to insist upon knowing something that it is better for one not to know.

—*Liberia*

36

A Father's Advice

An old man called his son to him, and said, "I am dying, but before I go, there are three things I wish you to beware of doing: First, do not tell your wife your private affairs; second, do not make friends with a policeman; third, do not borrow money from a poor man, but from a rich man." Having uttered these warnings, the old man died.

No sooner was the burial over, than the son thought over his father's words and decided to try and see whether there was wisdom in them. So he went along to a poor man and borrowed sixpence and to a rich man and borrowed a sovereign, and thence home.

Saying nothing about the money, he left his house the following morning and bought a goat. Waiting in the bush till dark, he killed it, and then bound up the carcass in some grass and carried it to his hut. There, he excitedly told his wife that he had killed a man and wanted to bury the corpse, which he had brought with him, under the floor of the hut. So the woman brought a hoe, and together they dug a hole in the middle of the floor and deposited the body in it. The earth was filled in, and the woman replastered the floor with mud and made her cooking fire over the spot.

"Now," said the young man to himself, "my father told me not to tell my wife any of my private affairs and not to borrow money from a poor man. Both these I have done. One thing remains—I must find a policeman to make friends with." Going out, he met two policemen, so he said to one of them, "I should like to be friends with you, come to my house." And the policeman agreed and went with him. He introduced the policeman to his wife, and she started cooking porridge. When it was ready, she brought it, and water to wash their hands, to the two men who were sitting on the veranda. The men commenced eating. Then the man called his wife back, saying the porridge was not well cooked—"It is only fit for dogs!"—and struck his wife a blow. The woman immediately appealed to the policeman to protect her, saying her husband would kill her as he had just killed a man a short time before.

So the policeman arrested the man and took him away. Then the magistrate sent the police back with the man to find his victim. Its resting place was pointed out by the woman, and after digging, they found the body tied up in the grass. All said, "It is just as the woman stated!" and they began striking the man and made him carry the corpse back to the magistrate.

On the way, they met the poor man, who on seeing his debtor cried out, "Where are you going, where is my sixpence?" "I am going to the magistrate. I am supposed to have murdered a man," he replied. "Where is my sixpence? You will get hanged and I shall be the loser!" yelled the poor man. "Wait a bit, I may not be killed," said the man, "I may be able to pay you back presently." "No you won't, you will be hanged," was the reply, and the poor man hit him as he passed.

Later, the party met the rich man and the accused called out to him, "I am in trouble and don't know when I may be able to repay you your loan." And the rich man answered, saying, "Never mind about that now. I am sorry you are in trouble." When at last they came before the magistrate and the man put down his load, it was unbound and the body of the goat disclosed. The man explained to the magistrate that he had been testing his father's advice—and it all proved to be sound indeed.

—*Wayao*

37

Is It Right That He Should Bite Me?

One time a large stone fell upon Snake and covered her so that she could not rise. A white man, it is said, came upon her and lifted at the stone, but when he had done so, she wanted to bite him. The White Man said, "Stop! Let us first go to someone wise." They went to Hyena, and the White Man asked him, "Is it right that Snake should want to bite me, even though I helped her so much?"

Hyena (who was looking for his own share of the White Man's body) said, "If you were bitten, what would it matter?"

So Snake thought that settled it, but the White Man said again, "Wait a little, and let us go to other wise people, that I may hear whether this is right."

They went and met Jackal, and the White Man put the same question to him.

Jackal replied, "I don't believe that Snake could ever be so covered by a stone that she could not rise. Unless I saw it with my two eyes, I wouldn't believe it. Take me to the place where you say it happened so I can see for myself whether it can possibly be true."

They went together to that place, and Jackal said, "Snake, lie down, and let yourself be covered."

Snake did so, and the White Man covered her with the stone; and although she tried with all her strength Snake couldn't get up. Then the White Man wanted to let Snake go again, but Jackal stopped him, saying, "Don't lift the stone. She wanted to bite you, therefore, let her get up and lift it herself."

Then they both went away and left Snake there, just as before.

—*Amalouw* or *Amakosa*

38

Take Me Carefully, Carefully

Long ago there was a man, that man had a wife, together they had five children, and all were sons. The man's garden was large, but when it was planted, a bird kept eating the seeds. The eldest boy made a trap for the bird, but for a long time he could not catch it.

Then one day, when the boy went to check his trap, he found the bird inside. Very carefully, the boy freed it and then the bird spoke, saying:

Take me carefully, carefully!
Next year
You will mention the bird,
Child of the bush!

The boy took the bird home. He did not want to kill it because it was very nice, so he kept it instead.

It happened after a while that his mother and father wanted the bird to eat with their porridge, but when the boy went to kill it, again it sang:

Kill me carefully, carefully!
Next year
You will mention the bird,
Child of the bush!

The boy killed the bird, and while its flesh was being cooked, it sang again:

Cook me carefully, carefully!
Next year
You will mention the bird,
Child of the bush!

When the meat was ready, it was divided so that they all might eat it with the porridge, and then it sang again:

Eat me carefully, carefully!
Next year
You will mention the bird,
Child of the bush!

One of the smaller children refused to eat the talking meat, but all his brothers and his father and his mother ate. When they had finished, their stomachs started to swell. The father and his wife and their children burst, and then died. When they burst, the meat they each had eaten came back together, and then the bird was again just as it had been before, and it flew off into the bush.

—*Kaguru*

39

Tiger Slights the Tortoise

Tiger once invited all the animals in his town—except Tortoise—to work for him on his farm. Tortoise was not only insulted, but embarrassed at having been ignored, and he decided to look into the matter. He found out that Tiger had not invited him, because he thought he was too weak to do farm work. Tortoise felt this slight deeply, and made up his mind to seek revenge on Tiger. On the morning of the next day, all the animals assembled on Tiger's farm, and set to work. As it approached noon, Tiger sent his eldest son home to remind his wives to bring food and palm wine for everyone.

Meanwhile, Tortoise had employed Rabbit, who came from a neighboring town, to dig a tunnel to a place alongside of Tiger's farm. When it was dug, Tortoise took his harp and went underground through the hole and started playing.

Poor animals working for Tiger
Kiri bamba kiri
Foolish animals working for Tiger
Kiri bamba kiri
Drop your hoes, foolish beasts
Kiri bamba kiri
Drop your knives, foolish beasts
Kiri bamba kiri
For you will break your back on another man's farm
Kiri bamba kiri
For you will die working for another man
Kiri bamba kiri
Save your strength for your own farm
Kiri bamba kiri
Poor animals, foolish beasts
Kiri bamba kiri.

Tortoise's song had a beautiful melody, unlike any that the animals had heard before.

On his way home, Tiger's son heard the music, stopped, and looked around for the singer and player. Although he could not find anyone, he was so enchanted by the sound that he completely forgot the errand he was running, and instead began to dance.

Meanwhile, Tiger had been anxiously waiting for his wives or son to arrive from home, for all the workers were very hungry and wanted to eat. When no one came, Tiger became so worried that he set out himself to find out why the food and wine had not been brought to the farm.

By then his wives had also arrived at the place where singing and dancing were going on. They put down the food and wine they were carrying, and they, too, began to dance. Tiger saw them from a considerable distance. He became enraged and cut off long sticks from a tree, with which to beat them. However, as he approached, the music caught his ears, too, and he started nodding his head in time to it. When he arrived there, without even knowing it, he dropped the sticks, and began to dance himself.

By now, the workers were completely exhausted. They stopped their labor and were waiting impatiently for food and drink. When no one arrived, they took up their hoes and machetes and set out for home.

They grumbled and muttered as they left: "Tiger does not seem to realize that the horse can run only on what is in his stomach."

On their way home, they came upon the dancers and, as if their hunger had suddenly vanished, they, too, started dancing with gusto. Realizing that the group was fully assembled, Tortoise put more zest into his music and added all sorts of ornate embellishments. The words of the song became more distinct, and as each of the workers danced, he silently blamed himself for having gone to work for Tiger. Tortoise continued playing his music until the revelers became weary with dancing.

The music then stopped abruptly, and Tortoise emerged from his hole. To Tiger he said, "Since you did not invite me to work for you, I had to invite myself. If I have not enough strength to work with my hoe, I have enough strength to distract the workers with my harp. I hope that from now on you will not forget the needs of any of your fellow animals."

And to the others, the Tortoise said, "Goodbye, his workers, goodbye, my dancers."

—Igbo

40
The Nature of the Beast

A farmer was once working on his land, when a snake came up to him and said he was being chased by a lot of men.

"You must hide me," said the snake.

"Where can I hide you?" asked the farmer.

"Just save my life," said the snake, "that's all I ask."

The farmer couldn't think of anywhere to hide the snake, so he crouched down and allowed it to creep into his belly. When the pursuers came up, they said, "Hey you, where's the snake we were after—it came your way."

"I haven't seen it," said the farmer.

When the men had gone, the farmer said to the snake, "The coast's clear—you can come out now."

"Not likely," said the snake, "I've found myself a home."

The farmer's belly was now so puffed out that you would have thought that he was a woman with child. He was about to set off for home when he saw a heron. He beckoned to it and told it in a whisper what had happened.

"Go and squat," said the heron, "and when you've done, don't get up—keep straining until I come."

The farmer did as he was told and, after a time, the snake put its head out and began snapping at flies. As it did so, the heron darted forward and caught its head in his bill. Then he gradually pulled the rest of the snake out of the farmer's belly, and killed it.

The farmer got up and said to the heron, "You have rid me of the snake, but now I want a potion to drink because he may have left some of his poison behind." "You must go and find six white fowls," said the heron, "and cook and eat them—that's the remedy." "Come to think of it," said the farmer, "you're a white fowl, so you'll do for a start."

So saying, he seized the heron, tied it up, and carried it off home. There he hung it up in his hut while he told his wife what had happened. "I'm surprised at you," said his wife. "The bird does you a kindness, rids you of the evil in your belly, saves your life, in fact, and yet you catch it and talk of killing it." With that she released the heron and it flew away. But as it went, it gouged out one of her eyes.

That is all. When you see water flowing uphill, it means that someone is repaying a kindness.

—*Hausa*

41
The Disobedient Sisters

A very long time ago, the people of a certain village lived in terror of the beasts of the land and of the sea, for these beasts occasionally invaded them and carried many of their children away.

Omelumma and *Omelukpagham*, two sisters, were very young children during this period of great fear. Their parents, like all others in the village, were worried about the safety of their children. Whenever they had to go away on a trip, they would leave the children plenty of food, and tell them to stay inside the house.

One day, the parents had to go to a distant market. Before they set out on their journey, they warned the two sisters to be very careful. They said, "Children, while we are away, don't let the smoke of the cooking fire escape into the air. When you pound the grain into meal, don't hit the mortar too hard with the pestle. And above all girls, don't join the other children at play in the open field."

But *Omelumma* and *Omelukpagham* were irresponsible and they did not listen to their parents' warnings. As soon as they were alone, they started to do exactly those things they had been instructed not to do. They made a huge fire and let plenty of smoke escape into the air. They pounded heavily in the mortar as they crushed the grain. Worse still, as soon as they heard the shouting and laughter of the other children in the field, they ran out and joined them.

They had not played long when—just as the adults had feared—the beasts of the sea and the land invaded the field. The children ran for dear life, each in a different direction. The beasts of the sea caught *Omelumma,* while the beasts of the land carried away her younger sister. And so they were separated and placed in bondage.

Omelumma was later sold to a youth who loved her so well that he married her. *Omelukpagham* did not have the same luck. She was sold to one wicked person after another, and used for all sorts of odd jobs.

Years after their capture, when the girls had become women, *Omelumma* gave birth to a baby boy. Her husband went to the market to buy a servant for her and—as luck would have it—he bought *Omelukpagham*. Neither sister recognized the other.

Omelumma treated *Omelukpagham* most harshly. Before *Omelumma* went to market, she would draw up a long list of the jobs for her sister to complete while she was away. She also warned her to keep the baby comfortable so he would not cry. But if *Omelukpagham* put the baby on a mat so that she could do her work, it would cry bitterly, and *Omelumma,* furious, would beat her when she returned. If, on the other hand, she carried the baby around so he would not cry, *Omelumma* would beat her for failing to complete her tasks. And to make matters worse, it seemed that the baby often cried no matter what she did, and the neighbors always reported it to *Omelumma. Omelukpagham* had a real problem.

One day, as *Omelukpagham* tried to work, the baby cried very, very loudly. She placed it on her lap and sang to it. Just then one of the neighbors came by and asked her why she was not working. *Omelukpagham* jumped up, and then, in desperation, sat back down with the baby on her lap, and sang him a lullaby.

Child, stop, stop, stop crying
Zemililize
Stop crying, Omelukpagham's *child*
Zemililize

Our mother warned us not to allow smoke to escape
Zemililize
But we allowed smoke to escape
Zemililize
Our father warned us not to pound hard in the mortar
Zemililize
But we pounded hard in the mortar
Zemililize

The lullaby went on to tell the rest of the story of that fateful day when *Omelukpagham* was separated from her sister.

An old woman in the next compound heard *Omelukpagham* singing this sad tale. And because she had once heard the same story from *Omelumma* it came to her that the servant must be *Omelumma*'s lost sister. The old woman went out to find *Omelumma* before she could return home and beat her sister again, and she told her the story of the lullaby. On the following day, after the usual threats and instructions, *Omelumma* made as if to leave for the market, but actually she hid behind the house.

When the baby began crying and would not stop, *Omelukpagham* sang the lullaby, resigning herself to whatever ill-treatment she might receive for not working. Suddenly, *Omelumma,* weeping bitterly, rushed out from her hiding place and warmly embraced her. Startled and afraid, *Omelukpagham* tried to explain why she hadn't done her work, but her sister interrupted her with, "*Omelukpagham,* I am your sister *Omelumma.*" Both of them fell into each other's arms and wept, while *Omelumma* went on and on apologizing for her past brutality.

From that day on, they both lived happily as tender sisters. And *Omelumma* resolved never to mistreat a servant again.

—*Igbo*

42

Rich Man, Poor Man

It happened one time, long, long ago, that in one of the villages of the *Akamba,* there were two men who lived as neighbors. One was rich, and the other was poor, but they were friends. The poor man worked for the rich man, helping him. Now a famine came to the land. And when the suffering became very severe, the rich man forgot the poor man, and the poor man who used to eat at his friend's house now had to beg from him. Finally, the rich man chased him away altogether, because a rich man cannot remain a friend of a poor person for too long, and he felt that even the scraps he now gave his poor neighbor were just too much.

One day, this poor man was scrounging about in the village for something to eat. He was given maize by a man who took pity on him, and he took it home to his wife, and she cooked it. But they had no meat with which to make it into soup; nor did they have salt with which to season it. So the man said, "I will go to see if my rich friend is having a good soup tonight." He went and found that the meal cooking there gave out a nice sweet smell. So he returned back to his house, got the cooked maize, and brought it back to the rich man's house, where he sat against the wall and ate it, breathing in the smell that came from the rich man's meal. When he had eaten, he returned to his own home.

Another day, the poor man saw the rich man and went up to him and said, "I came a few days ago, while you were eating your food, and I sat by the wall, and ate my food together with the delicious smell that came from your food."

The rich man was furious, and he said, "So that's why my food was completely tasteless that day! It was you who ate the good taste from my food, and you must pay me for it! I'm taking you to the judge to file a case against you." And he did that, and the poor man was told to pay one goat to the rich man for eating the sweet smell from his food. But the poor man could not afford even one goat, and he broke down and cried as he went back to his house.

On his way home, he met a wise man and speechmaker, and he told him what had happened. The wise man gave him a goat, and told him to keep that goat until he came back. Now, the judge had appointed a certain day when the poor man was to pay the rich man; and on that day, many people came together to witness the payment. The wise man came also, and when he saw the people talking, he asked, "Why are you making so much fuss here?" The judge said, "This poor man is supposed to pay this rich man a goat, for the smell he breathed from the rich man's food." The wise man asked his first question again, and he was given the same answer. So the wise man said, "Will you let me give another judgment on this case?" The people said, "Yes, if you are a good judge!" So he went on to say, "A man who steals must give back only as much as he has taken, no more, no less."

When the people asked him how he could pay back just the smell of good food, the wise man replied, "I will show you!" Then he turned to the rich man, and said to him, "Rich man, I am going to hit this goat, and when it bleats, I want you to take its bleating sound! You are not to touch this poor man's goat, unless he touched your food." Then he said again to the people, "Listen now, while I pay back the rich man." So he beat the goat, and it bleated, and he said to the rich man, "Take that sound as payment for the smell of your good food!"

—Akamba

43
Finders Keepers

There was once a time of great famine, and Tortoise, like everyone else, was busy seeking food for his children. He bought much maize and made up a good load. On his way home he came to a fallen tree lying across the road, and he could not get over it. He walked up and down along the trunk of the tree, and at last his load slipped off and fell down on the other side. Just then a monitor lizard happened to pass, and, seeing the load, exclaimed—"Well look what I have found." Tortoise (having by this time finally made his way around the tree) said to him, "That's mine—it just slipped off my head and fell on this side." Monitor Lizard replied, "I don't know about that; all I know is that I picked it up. Finders keepers, losers weepers." Tortoise said, "Let us go to the elders and have them judge what to do."

When they came to the elders, Tortoise explained what happened: "I came from gathering food and there was a fallen tree blocking the road. My load of food slipped off and fell on the other side of the tree. Then Monitor Lizard saw it and claimed it." The elders said to Tortoise, "You know that the finder of such things is permitted to keep them. That is our rule." So Tortoise went his way, and Monitor took up what he had "found" and carried it to his children.

Now, it happened one day that Tortoise and his companions went hunting, and they made a fire to lure prey into their trap. In the grass that they had set on fire, Monitor was sleeping. He woke up and ran here and there, and found a small hole in which to hide, but his tail stuck out of it. Tortoise, seeing Monitor's tail exposed, put out his hand and seized it, saying, "Finders keepers, losers weepers."

Monitor said, "You have got hold of my tail, my friend, let me alone." Tortoise said, "I did not touch your tail, I have found something to which I am entitled, a beautiful sword." Monitor begged, "My friend this is my tail, you cannot claim it as spoil." Tortoise said to him, "Let us go to the elders." When they arrived, Monitor said, "I was running away from a fire and I entered a small hole, but my tail was outside; then this person came along and said, 'It is a sword,' and I said, 'It is my tail,' but he would not listen." Tortoise said, "Today you are surprised. Lately you took my food-gathering, and you thought nothing of it." The elders said, "Remember what you recently did to your friend." Monitor said, "It was only food I took that day. Wait my friend, and I will fetch what I took." Tortoise said, "Today is today." The elders said to Monitor, "Give your companion his sword." Monitor said, "But it is not a sword, it is my tail." They said, "Give it to him," and the tail was cut off. Tortoise said, "Cut it high up, that I may have a good handle." So Monitor's tail was cut off, and given to Tortoise, and halfway home he threw it away, saying, "I only wanted to be even with him." Monitor wriggled and died. If a person does harm to another, he should remember what may happen to him another day.

—*Bondei*

44

The Leopard Woman

A man and a woman were once making a hard journey through the bush. The woman had her baby strapped upon her back as she walked along the rough path overgrown with vines and shrubbery. They had nothing to eat with them, and as they traveled on they became very hungry.

Suddenly, emerging from the heavily wooded forest into a grassy plain, they came upon a herd of bush cows grazing quietly.

The man said to the woman, "You have the power of transforming yourself into whatever you like; change now to a leopard and capture one of the bush cows, that I may have something to eat and not perish." The woman looked at the man significantly, and said, "Do you really mean what you ask, or are you joking?" "I mean it," said the man, for he was very hungry.

The woman untied the baby from her back, and put it upon the ground. Hair began growing upon her neck and body. She dropped her loincloth; a change came over her face. Her hands and feet turned into claws. And, in a few moments, a wild leopard was standing before the man, staring at him with fiery eyes. The poor man was frightened nearly to death and clambered up a tree for protection. When he was nearly to the top, he saw that the poor little baby was almost within the leopard's jaws, but he was so afraid, that he couldn't make himself come down to rescue it.

When the leopard saw that she already had the man good and frightened, and full of terror, she ran away to the flock of cattle to do for him as he had asked her to. Capturing a large young heifer, she dragged it back to the foot of the tree. The man, who was still as far up in its top as he could go, cried out, and piteously begged the leopard to transform herself back into a woman.

Slowly, the hair receded, and the claws disappeared, until finally, the woman stood before the man once more. But so frightened was he still, that he would not come down until he saw her take up her clothes and tie her baby to her back. Then she said to him, "Never ask a woman to do a man's work again."

Women must care for the farms, raise breadstuffs, fish, etc., but it is man's work to do the hunting and bring in the meat for the family.

—Liberia

Part III

Tales of Trickster and Other Ridiculous Creatures: Tales to Entertain

Introduction

The stories in this section are perhaps the most common type of tale in the African repertoire. They also may be the strangest to Western readers if only because they depict such chaotic motives and unprincipled actions. These are the tales of the doings and undoings of Trickster, a figure who, at one and the same time, represents primal creativity and pathological destructiveness, childish innocence and self-absorption. We witness a great deal of scheming, but with little thought of the consequences, even to the schemer. Most important for an understanding of the place of these tales in African village life, whenever Trickster emerges, everyone begins to laugh, for the very idea of his existence is ridiculous. His antics represent just what sane and mature people do not do. Sometimes the scheming is fairly harmless, as in "How Squirrel Robbed Rabbit of His Tail," but more often, death and destruction become ends in themselves, it seems, as in the string of horrors of "Hlakanyana" or the outright brutality of "Stuffing the Hyena."

Trickster is always a marked creature, an anomaly among animals or humans. His physical character and qualities, as well as his outrageous actions, remind the audience to laugh at his ridiculous antics. He is always a pest, vermin, one who lives in the wilds, but makes regular incursions into the human community bringing filth and contagion. When he appears in actual human form, as in "The Great Dikithi," he is described as being one-eyed, one-armed, one-legged; his lack of physiological balance makes a moral as well as a physical statement. And like Dikithi, he is often capable of changing shape because he is a witch or controls some other kind of transforming magical power. He openly competes with everyone, human and animal, for food resources, but he eats badly; he eats meat uncooked, is a cannibal, a carrion eater. He is also a murderer, even of members of his own family; moreover, he is sexually voracious, again even within his own family.

As a matter of convention, the scene is set for Trickster by reminding the audience at the start of a narrative that at the beginning of time everything in nature was harmonious, everyone was friend and family to everyone else. This state is referred to only for dramatic contrast to the chaos that is about to be described, and the tellers do not dwell on the tranquility of such an Edenic condition.

Of course, these kinds of stories are not totally out of the realm of experience of the Westerner. Most of the Uncle Remus tales subscribe to this pattern of action, and focus on the doings of Trickster—Br'er Rabbit. But his antics are not quite so badly destructive and to be feared as those of the African Trickster. In a sense, as these are hilarious stories, they might best be understood as jokes without punchlines—jokes not unlike our "sick jokes" or "moron" stories, but in which the same kind of wildly destructive and self-destructive acts are succinctly described and glibly resolved in a punchline. ("Why did the moron jump off the Empire State Building? To make a hit on Broadway.") The African equivalent of the punchline may be the explanatory statement found at the end of some of these tales; for example, "And that is why, to this day, the monkey lives in the trees and all the other animals chase him."

Alan Dundes has noticed the characteristically African patterning of tales of this sort, discussing them in terms of a progression from *contract* (friendship or family) to a *deception*, a *violation* of the contract, and the dissolution of the bond and everything it stands for.[1] Lee Haring, in a parallel study of narrative, independently notices that both in Black Africa and among Afro-Americans, one can see a pattern of false friendship that leads to a contract, the violation of the contract, a series of deceptions, and finally escape.[2] Perhaps it is this last factor, the failure to punish the transgressor, which most strongly departs from our notions of story. But it is the vitality and the protean abilities of Trickster that are continually fascinating, and which carry, in yet one more way, the characteristic African message that life is celebrated most fully through the dramatizing of oppositions.

We feel the open-endedness of such actions especially strongly when these stories are strung together as they commonly are in actual storytelling sessions. In one tale given here, "The Story of Hlakanyana," the stringing actually occurs within the single narrative, and is much like the Trickster tales of New World Indians in its cumulative power.

In another kind of spun-out telling, "All the Little Animals," we have a particularly attractive and well-rounded rendition of a tale translated from an actual performance (the story includes the same kinds of ideophonic sound effects we saw in Laura Bohannon's portrayal of Tiv storytelling). Here Rabbit explicitly represents all of the other little marginal animals, the sharp-toothed vermin, as they contend for food with the larger predators. It describes how Rabbit scares them away by hiding in a bag and surprising them, a device used again and

[1] Alan Dundes, "The Making and Breaking of Friendship as a Structural Frame in African Folk Tales," in *Structural Analysis of Oral Tradition*, eds. Pierre Miranda and Elli Kongas Miranda (Philadelphia: University of Pennsylvania Press, 1971), pp. 171–180.

[2] Lee Haring, "A Characteristic African Folktale Pattern," in *African Folklore*, ed. by Richard M. Dorson (Garden City, N.Y.: Doubleday and Co., 1972), pp. 165–82. See also Jay Edwards's exploratory essay, in *Afro-American Trickster Tales: A Structural Analysis*, Folklore Monograph 3 (Bloomington, Ind.: Indiana University).

again in these tales. Indeed, deception most commonly occurs through hiding (or sometimes through the ability of Trickster to sing or drum so compellingly that others are lulled into complacency or placed in thrall). These undercover deceptions of Trickster's can have quite grave consequences, as, for example, in "The Shundi and the Cock," when the shundi dies trying to imitate an outrageous hiding trick.[3]

The final story, "Talking Drums Discovered," demonstrates one further feature of these stories—that to be funny, they need not be about the actions of Trickster or the failure of friendship. Here the protagonist, Guinea Fowl, is more a fool or clown than a Trickster. But his misunderstandings lead to the same result—the creation of distrust among the animals, a distrust which continues to the present day.

[3] This pattern has been pointed out as characteristic of the African repertoire by Denise Paulme in "The Impossible Imitation in African Trickster Tales," in *Forms of Folklore in Africa*, ed. Bernth Lindfors (Austin, Texas: University of Texas Press, 1977), pp. 64–103.

45
Why Monkeys Live in Trees

Listen to the story of the bush cat.

The bush cat had been hunting all day, and had got nothing. She was tired. She went to sit down and rest, but the fleas wouldn't give her any peace.

She saw a monkey passing. She called to him, "Monkey, please come and flea me," (for that is what friends do for each other). The monkey agreed, and while he was picking out the fleas, the bush cat fell asleep. Then the monkey took the tail of the bush cat, tied it to a tree, and ran away.

The bush cat awoke. She wanted to get up and leave, but she found her tail tied to the tree. She struggled to get free, but she could not do it, so she remained there panting.

A snail came along. "Please unfasten my tail," cried the bush cat when she saw him. "You will not kill me if I untie you?" asked the snail. "No, I will do nothing to you," answered the bush cat. So the snail untied her.

The bush cat went home. Then she said to all her animals friends, "On the fifth day from now, announce that I am dead, and that you are going to bury me." The animals said, "Very well."

On the fifth day, the bush cat lay down flat, pretending to be dead. And all the animals came, and all danced round her. They danced.

The bush cat sprang up all at once. She leaped to catch the monkey. But the monkey had already jumped into a tree. He escaped.

So this is why the monkey lives in the trees, and will not stay on the ground. He is too much afraid of the bush cat.

—*Ewe*

46
All the Little Animals

It was the little animals, all the little sharp-toothed animals, all the fierce animals—they lived in a certain valley, and their town, no one visited it. So they lived there a long time, always killing the larger animals and bringing them back, just killing animals and bringing them back, killing animals and bringing them back.

Then one day Rabbit was out wandering and decided to go to the valley because it is a very good place for rabbits to find food. But the other animals, all the peaceful animals, told Rabbit, "Rabbit, don't go there! That's where the clan of dangerous, sharp-toothed animals live." Rabbit thought about it, and didn't go. After that, when Rabbit went out, he would go sneaking around the valley, avoiding the valley, always avoiding the valley.

Rabbit thought, "But what is this? This land belongs to all of us, and they say there is a ruler, there is a chief. Now, if you are a ruler, won't your subjects go to visit you? Won't strangers come to greet you?" But the others said, no, he shouldn't go there, because the chief kills animals. "Since you are a larger animal, if you go there, he will kill you," they said.

Rabbit thought, Rabbit said, "Okay, now that I have heard that the powerful ones hate us, what we will do is this: We will seem to chase each other and thus appear to be each other's enemies. The enemies will chase each other out of this valley."

Rabbit waited a while, son of a gun! Now Rabbit had a large flock of chickens and the chickens laid many eggs, so many that if you were to come to the place, wow-wee! The eggs filled all the storage places around the house! So Rabbit went back and forged a great big bell, just the mouth of the bell alone was this wide! Its clapper was so big that if you struck it, wow-wee! So Rabbit took a big basket of eggs, Rabbit took the bell and then went to the edge of the river that belonged to Lion and his people, there where the dangerous animals lived. He climbed into a stand of reeds, *Mek Mek Mek Mek Mek Mek,* and squatted down.

He waited there and suddenly he heard, son of a gun! the chief of the village. It was he, Lion, who sent them to come and draw water. The chief was Lion. When he sent them to do something, they would come and do it. If he didn't send them, they wouldn't come.

So, Lion sent Fox, he said that Fox should come and draw water so that they could prepare food for him, Lion, to eat, so that when the sun was up, *ser,* they could scatter to hunt for animals. When Rabbit heard the feet of Fox bounding, *kirik kirik,* he readied the basket of eggs that he had, setting it down beside himself, he readied the bell, untying its cover, putting it close at hand. Then when Fox arrived, just as he took his pot and began to rinse it out, *hokoro hokoro,* to wash it out before filling it with water, Rabbit began with his great bell, singing his hunting song which boasts to the animals:

Gbevevevevevevе!
My dogs don't hunt with bells, sic 'em, Big Lion!
The little animals are all dead, tendee vem
　　It will get in my eyes, tendee
Hyena, it will get in your eyes, tendee vem
　　It will get in your eyes, tendee
Fox, it will get in your eyes, tendee vem,
　　Vem tendee
The little animals are all dead, tendee vem,
　　Vem tendee
Hyena, it will get in my eyes, tendee vem
　　It will get in my eyes, tendee
The little animals are all dead, tendee vem,
　　Vem tendee

Son of a gun! Fox listened. "Now, what kind of a bell is this that makes the earth shake all around? Since we moved to this place with our fathers, nothing like this has ever come to the edge of our stream. What is it?" He stopped a moment to listen before tearing off for town, and Rabbit let loose with a rotten egg! The egg flew, *tqqq*. As Fox cocked his head to listen, *lop!* The egg landed on the top of his head, and Rabbit shouted, "Touch it with your hand! Touch it! Touch it!" And when he touched it and then smelled it, by God—

My head is open, to fe, fe ye
The world is ruined, to fe, fe ye
Scatter, scatter, to fe
　　Die, it is Rabbit's water, to fe
　　See, it is Rabbit's water, to fe
See, it is Rabbit's water, to fe
My head is open, to fe, *Chief,*
The world is ruined, to fe
　　See something has come to the water's edge,
　　　　to fe, fe ye
　　Rabbit's water....

And Fox ran, *kiliwili!* And, *bakatak bakatak bakatak,* he burst into the compound, saying, "Chief! The world is ruined! Since we built our town here nothing like this has happened!" And the chief said, "What is this?" He asked what had happened, and Fox replied, "Something has come to the edge of the water and I am terribly scared! Since we began living together here with you, I have heard of nothing like this." That's what Fox went back and told the chief, who responded, "No, sir! Are you such a coward? You just always eat things raw, you just eat things raw without even putting them on the fire and cooking them before you eat them. You're too much of a glutton!"

Then he sent Hyena. Hyena was a very strong animal, Hyena was a strong person, Hyena could run down and draw water quickly and come back and prepare cassava to eat so that Lion could leave. And so Hyena rushed down, *hoVoVovo.* When he arrived at the stream he rinsed, rinsed, and rinsed, and as he washed out the pot quickly, son of a gun! Rabbit heard and put his hand to the bell!

Gbeveveveveveveve!
My dogs don't hunt with bells, sic 'em, Big Lion!
The little animals are all dead, tendee vem
  It will get in my eyes, tendee
Hyena, it will get in your eyes, tendee vem
  It will get in your eyes, tendee
The little animals are all dead, tendee vem
  All dead, tendee
The little animals are all dead, tendee vem,
  Vem tendee
The little animals are all dead, tendee vem,
  Vem tendee
The little animals are all dead, tendee vem
  It will get in my eyes, tendee
It will get in your eyes, tendee vem
  It will get in your eyes, tendee
The little animals are all dead, tendee vem,
  Vem tendee
The little animals are all dead, tendee vem
  It will get in your eyes, tendee
It will get in your eyes, tendee vem

Wow! Hyena heard that, Hyena heard that and said to himself, "No, sir! The kind of song that is being sung here in the reeds, see, it's bad!" Then as Hyena turned to run, *zak vakdilak,* to escape up to the top of the hill to listen from there, *lop!* As he leaped to flee, Rabbit let loose with a rotten egg, and as Hyena turned his head like this, *lop!* the egg hit him on the top of the head! And Rabbit shouted, "Touch it! Touch it!" And when he touched it and smelled it, mm mmm!

My head is open, to fe, fe ye
The world is ruined, to fe, fe ye
Scatter, scatter, to fe
Die, it is Rabbit's water, to fe
See, it is Rabbit's water, to fe
See, it is Rabbit's water, to fe, fe ye

BaDambang daDambang baDambang baDambang baDambang baDambang purup! he burst into the compound after the chief! And he said that since he had begun living in that town he had never seen anything like that! So he should send some other really strong person to draw the water. As for himself, he wouldn't go near the place!

So all the little sharp-toothed animals came and tried to draw water. But they couldn't. Rabbit closed off the way. Finally Lion said, "No, sir! Now, you are all great followers and when I looked at you, I felt proud. But I have sent you into battle and you have each run away. Okay, who else is there that I should send? As for you all, you're just running from nothing! I am the chief here! There is nothing that will defeat me!" And so he set out, he came closer, ever closer to the water's edge, and, son of a gun! he shook.

Pufufuk kpinggim!
I take and throw the buffalo, ringgim!
I take the buffalo, I throw it, ringgim! *throw it,*
ringgim! rim! rim!

He stretched his neck, *nge nge nge.* He came forward.

Tukpik kpinggim!
Tiktik kpinggim!

Rabbit sat over in the stand of reeds listening, "What kind of noise is that? My bell makes more noise than that! Okay, so you make such a big fuss because you don't think that I, a rabbit, am very big?" Lion moved forward and then said that his buddy, whoever it was, his friend, the man that was making noise in the reeds there, should come out and take a look. At that, Rabbit set his hand to his bell!

Gbeveveveveveveve!
My dogs don't hunt with bells, sic 'em, Big Lion!
The little animals are all dead, tendee vem
It will get in my eyes, tendee
Lion, it will get in my eyes, tendee vem
It will get in my eyes, tendee
The little animals are all dead, tendee vem
It will get in my eyes, tendee
Hyena, it will get in my eyes, tendee vem,
Vem tendee
The little animals are all dead, tendee vem
It will get in my eyes, tendee vem
Hyena, it will get in my eyes, tendee vem

When Lion heard that, he said, "No, this place, the place, the children really did find something bad here!" And then, as Lion was going to turn, *ngaldak,* and escape, Rabbit let loose with the rotten eggs, he let loose with the rotten eggs, *lop lop!* They hit the big man's head twice, "Chief, touch it! Touch it!" When he touched it and smelled it, *mm mmm!*

Children, my head is open, to fe, fe ye
The world is ruined, to fe, fe ye
Let's scatter, scatter, to fe
See, it is Rabbit's water, to fe
See, it is Rabbit's water, to fe
See, it is Rabbit's water, to fe, fe ye
My head is open, to fe, fe ye
The world is ruined, to fe, fe ye

BaDambang baDambang baDambang baDambang baDambang baDambang purup! into the compound, and they—all the women—had already prepared everything, and it was just headlong flight, *pamdal!* All the animals fled, and they ran on and on and on and on and on and on.

As they came to the middle of the barren plain, he said, "Children, stop a bit!" And they stopped, *rip,* all his sharp-toothed followers, all his young men stopped, and he asked, "Now, our big bag that we put our powders for killing animals in and our charms, where did we leave it?" And they answered, "Oh, Chief! We left it in the *kofia* tree in your compound, where we put it!"

"*Wow-wee!* What are we going to do? See, what will we kill animals with to eat— See, if your town falls into ruin around you, you will take your knowledge and move on and kill other things to eat. But now that we have forgotten our most important thing, what are we, you and I, going to do? Young men, stand still a bit. The strong one who will run here, *hoVoVovo,* to go and hit that thing quickly to bring us the bag, who is he?"

One said, "No, as for me, I won't go. That place that I have heard is so dangerous, should I go for the same thing to happen to me?"

Now, as it turned out, when they ran away like that, Rabbit climbed up, *harr,* with his bell and got inside the bag and pulled the strings, closing it, and then he sat still, *sem,* and they didn't know what had happened.

So the chief was quiet a while, *sem,* and then said, "No, children, let's not leave the bag like that. Send someone to go and get the bag." (That was someone else talking to him.) So he said, "Okay, now the person who is going to run there is Hyena. Hyena is a powerful person. If the same thing happens, Hyena will escape." (A powerful person never dies, does he?)

Hyena ran, *hoVoVovo.* When he came to the place, he threw something and hit the bag that Rabbit was inside, *kpikirik kpikirik,* he knocked the bag down. The bell was still, *sem,* Rabbit was inside it. And so he swung the bag over his shoulder, Rabbit and all! He didn't know that Rabbit was inside it. He went along until he came to where the chief and the others were, and he said, "Sir, I have gotten the bag, our fortunes have changed now. Even though we have deserted our town, we will take this bag and move on and eat from it." And the chief agreed, and took the bag and said, "You have acted like a man!" And then, just as he said that, just as he said, "You have acted like a man!" he, Rabbit, started, with the bell under his arm:

Gbeveveveveveveve!
My dogs don't hunt with bells, sic 'em. Big Lion!
Hyena, it will get in my eyes, tendee vem
    It will get in my eyes, tendee
It will get in my eyes, tendee vem
    It will get in my eyes, tendee
The little animals have all died, tendee vem

When the Lion heard that, he was surprised and frightened. He said, "No sir-ee! He has arrived!" and he fell, hitting his neck on the ground, and he moaned, *Hmmm'm!,* thinking that his neck was broken and that he was already dead! And as he came, he fell into a great gully, and as he fell—

My head is open, to fe, fe ye
The world is ruined, to fe, fe ye
Let's scatter, scatter, to fe
    See, it's Rabbit's town, to fe
    See, it's Rabbit's town, to fe
The world is ruined, to fe, fe ye
Scatter, scatter, to fe, fe ye
The world is ruined, to fe, fe ye
    Rabbit's water. . . .

He ran on and on and on, and as he ran under a thorny vine to escape, a thorn pierced the string of the bag and, *mgbot,* the string broke and the bag fell—with Rabbit inside—to the ground. He came back, *horrr,* took all their plants and brought them back to the town that they had deserted. He gathered his family in the place that before had been forbidden, he gathered them and came and settled there, *Deteng.* And so all the strangers who came, just found him there, and they settled and made a great town. But the people who had been jealous, saying no one should come to their place, no one should come to their place, all of them have left that place, they no longer rule there.

This story is told to you by me, Daniel Ndanga, taking off my anklet-rings, *ray ras,* the story is over.*

—Gbaya

*This ending is Mr. Ndanga's personal formula, used by no one else. He alludes, humorously, to the removal of anklets which marks the end of traditional dances by women.

47
Why the Dog Always Chases Other Animals

In the olden days, there was once a dog. He was lying fast asleep in the ashes of a fire, in the middle of the forest. He was very warm, and very comfortable.

A monkey came by and saw the dog, and said: "Now what kind of a person is that, lying there so peacefully?"

He couldn't decide, so he called the other animals of the forest. They came running in from all sides to see the strange thing the monkey had found.

The monkey turned first of all to the elephant. "What kind of a person is that?" he asked, pointing to the dog, "and what does he do?" "I'm sure I don't know!" grumbled the elephant, flapping his big ears.

Then the monkey asked the okapi: "What kind of a person is that?" The okapi looked hard at the dog, shook his head, and blinked his velvety brown eyes. "I'm sorry, I don't know," he said.

Next, the pangolin came to have a look. He sharpened his claws and ruffled his scales and put out his long, thin tongue. He looked so wise that everyone thought that he must surely know. But the pangolin just curled himself up and went to sleep without saying a word.

The monkey called all the animals of the forest in turn, but none of them could say what manner of person the dog was.

The dog slept peacefully on.

Finally, when all the animals had come together, but no one could answer the monkey's question, they heard a voice from way up in a tree. It was the old turtle.

"Are you finished?" he asked.

"Yes!" said the monkey, "But we can't tell what it is or what it does."

"That is a dog," said the turtle, and he woke the dog up. "Dog!" he said, "Chase all these animals away!"

The dog, angry at being awakened from his sleep, leapt up and chased all the animals of the forest—the monkey, the wild pig, the elephant, the buffalo, and the chimpanzee—every one of them he chased right away. Then he came back and said: "And now, where is that animal that woke me up! I'm going to kill him—kill him completely!"

But the sly old turtle had crawled back into his house, and replied: "You can't find me, dog, but from now on you will have to chase every animal you see."

And so it is, even today.

—*Ituri*

48

The Story of Hlakanyana

Once upon a time there was a village with many women in it. All the women had children, except the wife of the chief. The children grew, and all the women gave birth to others; but the wife of the chief still had no child. So the people decided they would kill an ox to see if that would break the curse.

While they were sacrificing it, the chief's wife heard a voice saying, "Bear me, mother, before the meat of my father is all finished." It was the voice of *Hlakanyana,* the great one.

The woman did not pay any attention, thinking it was a ringing in her ears. The voice said again: "Bear me mother, before the meat of my father is all finished."

The woman took a small piece of wood and cleaned her ears. She heard the voice again. Then she became excited. She said, "I have just now cleaned my ears, but still there is something in them; I would like to know what it is." The voice said again: "Make haste and bear me, mother, before the meat of my father is all finished."

The woman said: "What is this? there was never a child that could speak before it was born."

The voice said again: "Bear me mother, as all my father's cattle are being finished, and I have not yet eaten anything of them." Then the woman gave birth to that child.

When she saw that to which she had given birth, she was very much astonished; it was a boy, but tiny in size and with the face of an old man.

He said to his mother: "Mother, give me a skin robe," and she did. Then he went at once to the corral where the ox was being killed. He said to the chief, "Father, father, give me a piece of meat."

The chief was astonished to hear this newborn child calling him father. He said: "Oh men, what thing is this that calls me father?" So he continued with the skinning of the ox. But *Hlakanyana* also continued to ask for meat. Finally, the chief became very angry, and pushed him, and ordered him away.

Hlakanyana said, "I am your child, give me meat." The chief picked up a stick, and said: "If you trouble me again, I will strike you with this." *Hlakanyana* replied: "Give me meat first, and I will go away," but because he was very angry, the chief would not answer.

Hlakanyana continued asking. Then the chief threw him out of the corral, and went on with his work. After a little time, the child returned, still asking.

So the chief said to the men that were with him: "What strange thing is this?" The men replied: "We don't know him at all." When the chief asked them their advice, they replied: "Give him a piece of meat."

So the chief cut off a piece of meat and gave it to him. *Hlakanyana* ran to his mother and gave the meat to her to be cooked.

Then he returned to his father, and said again: "Father, give me some meat."

The chief took him and trampled upon him, and left him there, thinking he was dead. But he rose again, and returned to his father, still saying, "Father, give me some meat."

Then the chief, thinking to get rid of him by giving him meat again, gave him a piece of liver. *Hlakanyana* threw it away. Fat was then given to him. He put it down on one side. Flesh was then given to him, and a bone with much marrow in it.

Hlakanyana said: "I am a man today." He said: "This is the beginning of my father's cattle."

At this time, the men were saying to each other: "Who will carry the meat to our huts?" *Hlakanyana* answered: "I will do it." They said: "How can such a thing as you are carry meat?" *Hlakanyana* replied: "I am stronger then you—just see if you can lift this piece of meat."

The men tried, but they could not lift it. Then *Hlakanyana* took the piece of meat and carried it out of the corral. The men said: "That will do. Now carry our meat for us."

Hlakanyana took the meat and brought it to the house of his mother. He took blood and put it on the eating mats at the houses of the men. When the men went to their houses, and saw this, they called *Hlakanyana,* and asked him what he had done with the meat. He replied: "Surely, I put it here where the blood is. It must have been taken by the dogs. Surely the dogs have eaten it."

Then those men beat the women and children because they did not guard the meat from the dogs. As for *Hlakanyana,* he was only delighted with this trick of his. He was more cunning than any of the old men.

Hlakanyana said to his mother that she must put the meat in the pot to cook, but that it must not be eaten before the next morning. Then, in the night, this cunning little fellow rose and went to the pot. Hearing the noise he made, his mother struck out with a stick. *Hlakanyana* cried like a dog. His mother said: "Surely a dog is eating the meat." Later, when she had left, *Hlakanyana* returned to the pot and ate everything but the bones. In the morning, he asked his mother for meat. His mother went to the pot, and found nothing but bones. The cunning little fellow pretended to be astonished, and his mother told him that the meat had been eaten by a dog.

Hlakanyana said: "As that is so, give me the bones, for you who are the wife of the chief, should not eat from the same pot as a dog." And his mother gave him the bones.

Hlakanyana went to sleep in the same house with the rest of the village boys, but they were unwilling to let him stay. Laughing, they said: "Who are you? You are just a child of a few days." *Hlakanyana* answered: "I am older than you."

He slept there that night. When the boys were asleep, he got up and went to the cattle corral. He killed two cows and ate all their insides. Then, he took blood and smeared it on one of the boys who was sleeping. In the morning, the men found the cows' carcasses and went looking for the thief. When they found the boy with blood upon him, they killed him, thinking he was the robber.

Hlakanyana said to himself: "Today it has been seen who is a child and who is a man."

Another day, the father of *Hlakanyana* killed an ox. The head was put in a pot to be cooked. *Hlakanyana* thought long about how he could get that meat. Finally, he drove all the cattle of the village into a forest, a very thick forest, and tied them by their tails to the trees. After that he cut his arms, and legs, and breast, with a sharp stone, and stood on a hill, and cried out with a loud voice: "The enemy has taken our cattle. The cattle are being driven away. Come up, come up, there is an army going away with the cattle."

The men ran quickly to him. He said to them: "Why are you eating meat while the enemy is going away with the cattle? I was fighting with them; just look at my body."

They saw he was covered with blood, and they believed it was as he said. So the men took their spears and ran after the cattle, but they took the wrong way. Only one old man, *Hlakanyana*, and the children were left behind, and the children were nowhere to be seen.

Then *Hlakanyana* said to the old man: "I am very tired with fighting; just go to the river, grandfather, and get some water."

The old man went; and as soon as he was alone, *Hlakanyana* ate the meat that was in the pot and he filled the pot with dung. When the old man returned with the water, he was very tired, for the river was far for an old man to go, and therefore, he fell asleep. While he was sleeping, *Hlakanyana* took a bone and put it beside the old man. He also took some fat and put it on the mouth of the old man. Then he ran to the forest and let loose the cattle that he had tied by their tails.

At this time, the men were returning from seeking the enemy. *Hlakanyana,* coming from the other side with the cattle, shouted: "I have conquered the enemy." He also said: "The meat must be eaten now."

When they opened the pot they found no meat, only dung.

Then the men said: "Who has done this?"

Hlakanyana answered: "It must be the old man who is sleeping there."

They looked, and saw the bone by the side of the old man, and the fat on his mouth. They decided then to kill him because he had stolen the meat of the chief.

When the children saw that the old man was to be killed, they told the men that he did not eat the meat of the chief.

The men said: "We saw fat on his mouth and a bone beside him."

The children replied: "He didn't do it. *Hlakanyana* did it. He ate the meat and put dung in the pot. We were hidden, and saw him."

Hlakanyana denied it, of course. He said: "Let me go and ask the women; perhaps they saw who ate the meat of the chief."

The men sent a young man with him to the women, but when they were a short distance away, *Hlakanyana* escaped.

The chief sent an army after him. The army pursued, and saw *Hlakanyana* sitting by a bush. They ran to catch him. When they came to the bush only an old woman was sitting there.

They said to her: "Where is *Hlakanyana?*"

The old woman replied: "He just went across the river. See you make haste to follow him, for the river is rising."

The army crossed the river quickly. Then the old woman turned into *Hlakanyana* again. He said to himself: "I will now go on a journey, for I am wiser than the counselors of my father, since I am really older than they."

The cunning little fellow went to a village where he saw an old woman sitting beside her house.

He said to her: "Would you like to be made young, grandmother?"

The old woman replied: "Yes, my grandchild, if you could make me young, I would be very glad."

Hlakanyana said: "Take that pot, grandmother, and go for some water."

The old woman replied: "I cannot walk."

Hlakanyana said: "Just try, grandmother. The river is near, and may be you can reach it." The old woman limped along and got the water.

Then *Hlakanyana* took a large pot, set it on the fire, and poured the water into it.

He said to the old woman: "You must cook me a little first, and then I will cook you a little."

The old woman agreed to that. *Hlakanyana* was the first to be put in the pot. When the water began to get hot, he said: "Take me out, grandmother; I am in long enough."

The old woman took him out, and got into the pot for her turn. Soon she said: "Take me out now, my grandchild; I am in long enough."

Hlakanyana replied: "Not yet, grandmother; it is not yet time."

So the old woman died in the pot.

Hlakanyana took all the bones of the old woman and threw them away. He left only the toes and the fingers. Then he took the clothing of the old woman and put it on. The two sons of this old woman came from hunting.

They went into the hut, and said: "Whose meat is this in the pot?"

Hlakanyana was lying down. He said in a voice like that of their mother: "It is yours, my sons."

Then, while they were eating, the younger one said: "Look at this, it is like the toe of mother."

The elder one said: "How can you say such a thing? Did not mother give us this meat to eat?"

Again the younger one said: "Look at this, it is like the finger of mother."

Hlakanyana said: "You are speaking evil of me, my son."

Hlakanyana thought to himself: "I am going to be discovered, I guess it is time for me to get away." So he slipped quietly out of the house. When he got a little way off, he called out: "You are eating your mother. Did anyone ever see people eating their mother before?"

The two young men took their spears and ran after him with their dogs. Just as they reached the river the cunning fellow changed himself into a little round stone on its banks. One of the young men picked it up, saying: "If I could see him, I would throw this stone at him." The young man hurled the stone over the river, and it turned into *Hlakanyana* again. He just laughed and went on his way.

He was singing this song:

I met with Nonothloya.
We cooked each other,
I was half cooked,
She was well cooked.

Hlakanyana met a boy tending some goats. The boy had a digging stick with him. *Hlakanyana* proposed that they should hunt birds, and the boy agreed. They ran after birds the whole day.

In the evening, when the sun set, *Hlakanyana* said: "It is time now to roast our birds."

The place was on the bank of a river, so they decided to swim before they ate.

Hlakanyana said: "Let's dive in and see who can stay under longest."

Hlakanyana came up last. Then the cunning fellow said: "Let us try once more."

The boy agreed and they dove into the water again. This time *Hlakanyana* came up quickly and climbed out, and ate all the birds. He only left the heads. Then he dove back into the water. While he was still under, the boy came out.

When *Hlakanyana* had also emerged, he said: "Let us go now and eat our birds." But they found only the heads.

Hlakanyana said: "You have eaten them, because you came out of the water first, and you have left me the heads only."

The boy denied having done so, but *Hlakanyana* said: "You must pay for my birds with that digging stick."

So the boy gave him the digging stick, and *Hlakanyana* went on his way.

He saw some people making pots of clay, and he said to them: "Why don't you ask me to lend you this digging stick, instead of digging with your hands?"

They said: "Well, lend it to us."

Hlakanyana lent them the digging stick, and the first time they stuck it in the clay it broke.

He said: "You have broken my digging stick, the digging stick that I received from my companion, my companion who ate my birds and left me with the heads."

So they gave him a pot.

Hlakanyana carried the pot till he came to some boys who were herding goats. He said to them: "You foolish boys, you only watch the goats, but you don't milk them. Why don't you ask me to lend you this pot to milk them into?"

The boys said: "Well, lend it to us."

Hlakanyana lent them the pot. While the boys were milking, the pot broke.

Hlakanyana said: "You have broken my pot, the pot that I received from the people who make pots, the people who broke my digging stick, the digging stick that I received from my companion, my companion who ate my birds and left me with the heads."

The boys gave him a goat.

Hlakanyana came to the keepers of calves.

He said to them: "You foolish fellows, you sit here and drink nothing. Why don't you ask me to let you milk this goat and then you can drink?"

The keepers of the calves said: "Well, let us milk this goat."

Hlakanyana gave them the goat. While they were milking it, the goat died.

Hlakanyana said: "You have killed my goat, the goat that I received from the boys that were tending goats, the boys that broke my pot, the pot that I received from the people who make pots, the people who broke my digging stick, the digging stick that I received from my companion, my companion who ate my birds and left me with the heads."

They gave him a calf.

Hlakanyana came to the keepers of cows.

He said to them: "You milk the cows without letting the calf suck first. Why don't you ask me to lend you this calf, and then the cows will give their milk more freely?"

They said: "Well, lend us the calf."

Hlakanyana permitted them to take the calf. While they had the calf, it died.

Hlakanyana said: "You have killed my calf, the calf that I received from the keepers of calves, the keepers of calves that killed my goat, the goat that I received from the boys that were tending goats, the boys that broke my pot, the pot that I received from the people who make pots, the people who broke my digging stick, the digging stick that I received from my companion, my companion who ate my birds and left me with the heads."

They gave him a cow.

Hlakanyana continued on his journey. He saw a young man going the same way.

Hlakanyana said: "Let us be companions and travel together." The young man agreed.

They came to a place, and *Hlakanyana* said: "This is a magic place. We must protect ourselves by throwing our spoons into it."

The foolish boy threw his spoon away, but the cunning little fellow only pretended to throw his. They went on.

They came to another place, and *Hlakanyana* said: "This is a place we must throw our knives away." Again it happened as with the spoons. *Hlakanyana* concealed his knife, while his companion threw his away.

Pretty soon, they came to a village. The people said to them: "Tell us the news."

Hlakanyana replied: "Give us something to eat first. Just look at the wrinkles in our stomachs and see how hungry we are!"

The people of that village brought meat.

Hlakanyana said to his companion: "Well let's eat."

The youth answered: "I have no knife."

Hlakanyana said: "You are just a child; I'm not going to lend you my knife."

The people of that village brought millet and put it before them.

Hlakanyana said to his companion: "Why aren't you eating?"

He answered: "I don't have a spoon."

Hlakanyana said: "You are just a child; I'm not going to lend you my spoon."

So *Hlakanyana* had all the meat and the millet to himself.

Hlakanyana met a girl herding some goats.

He said: "Where are the boys of your village, that the goats are herded by a girl?"

She answered: "There are no boys in my village."

He went to the father of the girl and said: "You must give me your daughter to live with, and I will herd the goats." The father of the girl agreed.

Then *Hlakanyana* went with the goats, and every day he killed one and ate it, until all were gone. Then, he scratched his body with thorns.

The father of the girl came and saw that there were no goats. He said: "Where are the goats?"

Hlakanyana replied: "Can't you see how I have been fighting with the wild dogs? The wild dogs have eaten the goats. I'm not going to stay around here."

So he went on his way.

As he was walking, he saw a trap for catching birds. There were some birds in it. *Hlakanyana* took the birds out and ate them. The owners of the trap were cannibals. They saw the footprints of *Hlakanyana,* and said: "This is a little boy that is stealing our birds." They watched for him. *Hlakanyana* came again to the trap, and again saw a bird caught in it. He was just going to take it out, when the cannibals caught him. They made a big fire and put a pot on for the purpose of cooking him. *Hlakanyana* produced two oxen. One was white, the other was red.

He said to the cannibals: "You can take whichever of these oxen you like instead of me."

The cannibals said: "We will take the white one because it is white inside also."

Then *Hlakanyana* went away with the red ox. When the cannibals had eaten the white ox, they ran after *Hlakanyana.* They caught up to him near a big stone. He jumped on the stone, and sang this song:

I went to hear the news,
About rain from the girls.

The cannibals couldn't resist dancing when they heard the song, so he was able to run away while the stone continued to sing the song for him.

As he was going along, he saw a hyena building a house. The hyena had just cooked some meat, and *Hlakanyana* asked it to give him some.

The hyena said: "No, I will not give you any; there is not enough even for me."

Hlakanyana said: "Don't you want me to help you with your house?"

The hyena replied: "All right, if you want to, but do it quickly."

While they were thatching the roof, *Hlakanyana* wove the tail of the hyena into the thatch. Then he took the pot and sat down.

The hyena said: "Leave that pot alone, *Hlakanyana.*"

Hlakanyana replied: "I am going to eat now."

The hyena tried to come down, but he found his tail was fast.

Hlakanyana ate all the meat, and threw the bones at the hyena. The hyena tried to frighten him by saying that there were many hyenas coming to devour him. He answered: "You're lying," and kept on eating until the meat was all gone. Then he went on his way.

Soon, *Hlakanyana* came to the house of a leopardess. He offered to take care of her children while she went out to hunt, and the leopardess agreed. There were four cubs. After the leopardess had gone, *Hlakanyana* took one of the cubs and ate it.

At the time for nursing, the leopardess came back and said: "Give me my children for it is time for me to feed them."

Hlakanyana gave one.

The mother said: "Give me all of them."

Hlakanyana replied: "It is better that one should drink and then another."

The leopardess agreed. After three had drunk, he gave her the first one back again.

Then the leopardess went to hunt again.

Hlakanyana took another of the cubs and ate it. He also made the door of the house very small so that the mother of the cubs could not come in, and then he made a little hole in the ground at the back of the house, so that he could go out. The next day the leopardess came to nurse her children. There were only two left now. *Hlakanyana* gave each of them to her twice. After that, the leopardess went away as before.

Now, *Hlakanyana* ate another of the cubs, so that only one was left. When the mother came, he gave this one to her four times. When he gave it the last time, it was already full. The leopardess said: "Why won't my child drink more today?"

Hlakanyana replied: "I think this one is sick."

The mother said: "You must take good care of it."

Hlakanyana promised to do so, but when the leopardess was gone he ate that one also.

The next day, when the leopardess came, there was no cub left to give her. She tried to get into the house, but the door was too small. She sat down in front to watch. Then *Hlakanyana* went out the back, through the hole he had made in the ground. The leopardess saw him and ran after him. He went under a big rock, and cried out loudly for help, saying the rock was falling.

The leopardess said: "What is that you are saying?"

Hlakanyana replied: "Can't you see that this rock is falling? Just hold it up while I get a prop to put under it."

The leopardess went to hold the rock up, and *Hlakanyana* did not return. He just ran away.

Hlakanyana came to the house of a jackal. He asked for food, but the jackal said there was none. Then *Hlakanyana* made a plan.

He said to the jackal: "You must climb up on the house and cry out with a loud voice, 'We are going to be fat today, because *Hlakanyana* is dead.' "

The foolish jackal did this. All the animals came running to hear the news. Because the door was open, they went inside the house. Then *Hlakanyana* locked the door, and the animals were caught. He killed them and ate his fill.

Now, *Hlakanyana* returned to the home of his father. He was told that his sister had gone to get some red clay. When he saw her returning, he shouted: "Let all the black cattle that have white teeth be killed. The daughter of my father has white teeth."

The chief said: "What is the matter with you *Hlakanyana?*"

He just repeated the same thing.

Finally, the chief said: "Let a black ox be killed." So *Hlakanyana* got fat meat to eat that day.

Another time, *Hlakanyana* went to tend his father's calves. On his way, he met a tortoise.

He said: "Where are you going tortoise?"

The tortoise answered: "To that big stone."

Hlakanyana said: "Aren't you tired?"

The tortoise replied: "No, I am not tired." But *Hlakanyana* took the tortoise and put it on his back. Then he went to the house of his mother.

His mother said: "What have you got there, my son?"

Hlakanyana answered: "Just take it off my back, mother."

But the tortoise held fast and couldn't be pulled off. The mother then heated some fat and poured it on him, which made the tortoise let go so quickly, that the fat fell on *Hlakanyana*. It burnt him, and he died. That was the end of this cunning little fellow.

—*Kaffir*

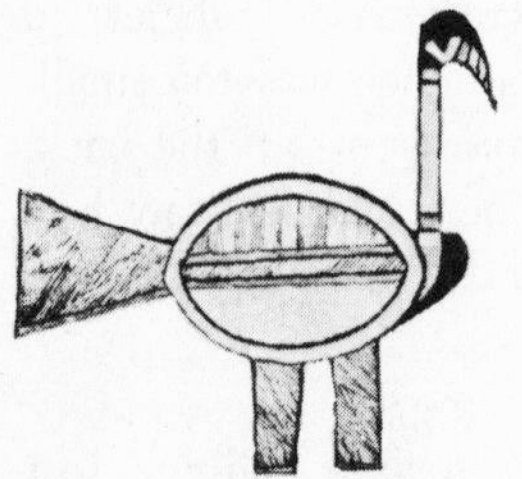

49
Cursing the Birds

Blackbird, Ringdove, and many of the other birds once met together. Ringdove opened the conversation by asking, "Here, where we are all together, who is the most beautiful?" The birds answered: "Blackbird is the only beautiful one. How very black he is!"

Then Ringdove said to himself: "I am going to ask Blackbird for a potion for medicine that will make me as beautiful as he is." He implored Blackbird, saying, "Change me, so that we may be alike." Blackbird promised to give him a potion the next day. "When we are all together, and Lapwing is there, and Kestrel and Eagle and Francolin and Tomtit and Guinea Fowl, when the birds of all species are together, I will give you the potion." Ringdove was very grateful, and said: "I shall be very thankful to be like you."

The next day, all the birds were gathered together, feeding in the cool of the morning. Blackbird came to where they were assembled, and said: "Ringdove, you are wanting a potion?" "Yes," he replied. Blackbird said: "Come here," and putting his finger around Ringdove's neck, he made the black ring which Ringdove still wears today. All the birds were astounded. Then another bird asked for the same, and Blackbird said: "What will you give me in return?" All the birds answered: "If only you will make us all beautiful like you, you can do whatever you want to us." Blackbird then told them: "Tomorrow I will give you all a potion, so that you will be black."

The next day, Blackbird rose early and went into the forest where he found Guinea Fowl eating termites out of the ground. He was offended that this bird was so unclean. "What are you eating?" he asked. Guinea Fowl answered: "Termites." Then Blackbird said: "You begged a potion from me, while you eat dirt insects. I can't help one such as you?" Then she cursed the bird: "Guinea Fowl, I will give you a speckled coat, so that you resemble a leopard, and when a leopard finds you, he will devour you—all because you do not eat properly, as I do. And you, Francolin, you shall be red about the mouth and on the head, and you shall always eat the grain belonging to others. You shall be trapped by people and they will bring you trouble. All the birds who begged from me, I give them in the same manner, things good for them or things not good for them."

Thereupon Ringdove, whose neck had been encircled, was also cursed, and told: "And you, too, Ringdove, you shall always eat the grain belonging to me, so that you may die. All the birds I condemn, because they begged for potions, saying, 'Let us be like Blackbird,' whereas in truth they do not resemble me at all, they do not act as I act, nor eat as I eat. To make you look like me is simply impossible. I refuse." So, although Ringdove has color around its neck where Blackbird's finger encircled it, in that alone they are alike. As for the rest of the birds, they are in trouble, they are killed, they are ensnared, they are persecuted. Some are caught in traps. And all because they were cursed by Blackbird.

—Ila

50
Saving the Rain

There was a great drought in the land, and Lion called together a number of animals so that they might devise a plan for gathering up water when the rains fell. The animals who attended at Lion's summons were Baboon, Leopard, Hyena, Jackal, Hare, and Mountain Tortoise.

It was agreed that they should scratch out a large hole to catch the rain, and so the next day they all set to work. Only Jackal didn't help; he hovered nearby, muttering that he was not going to scratch *his* nails off in making water holes.

When the hole was finished, the rains fell and soon filled it with water, to the great delight of those who had worked so hard. The first one to come and drink there, however, was Jackal, who not only drank, but filled his clay pot with water, and then went for a swim in the water hole, making it as muddy and dirty as he could.

This was made known to Lion, who was very angry. He ordered Baboon to guard the water the next day, armed with a huge fighting stick. Baboon concealed himself in a bush close to the water, but Jackal soon became aware of his presence there, and guessed the reason for it. Knowing the fondness of baboons for honey, Jackal immediately hit a plan. Marching back and forth, he every now and then, dipped his fingers into his clay pot, and licked them with an expression of intense relish, saying to himself in a low voice, "I don't want any of their dirty water when I have a pot full of delicious honey." This was too much for poor Baboon, whose mouth began to water. He begged Jackal to give him a little honey, as he had been guarding the water for several hours, and was incredibly hungry and tired.

At first, Jackal took no notice of Baboon. Then he looked around, and said, in a patronizing manner, that he pitied such an unfortunate creature, and would give him some honey on the condition that Baboon give up his fighting stick and allow himself to be bound by Jackal. Baboon foolishly agreed, and was soon tied in such a way that he couldn't move hand or foot.

Jackal now drank the water, filled his pot, and swam in front of Baboon. From time to time he chided him, pointing out how foolish he had been to be so easily duped, since he, Jackal, had no honey or anything else to give him, except a good blow on the head every now and then with his own fighting stick.

The animals soon appeared and found poor Baboon in this sorry way, looking the picture of misery. Lion was so exasperated that he had Baboon severely punished, and denounced him as a fool.

Then, Tortoise came forward, and offered to catch Jackal. They thought, at first, that he was merely joking, but when he explained his plan, it was considered so good that Lion told him to go ahead. Tortoise asked them to spread a thick coating of beeswax resin all over him. Then he went and placed himself across the path to the water hole, so that on his way to drink, Jackal would have to walk on him, and would stick fast.

The next day, when Jackal came, he approached very cautiously, wondering why no one was there. In order to get a better look around, he stepped on a large black stone—and, at once, he was stuck fast. Jackal saw that he had been tricked, for now the stone put out its head and began to move. Since Jackal's hind legs were still free, he threatened to smash Tortoise with them if he didn't let him go. Tortoise answered, "Do as you like." Jackal made a violent jump, and now found, to his horror, that his hind feet were also stuck fast. "Tortoise," he said, "I have still my mouth and teeth left, and will eat you alive if you don't let me go." "Do as you like," Tortoise again replied. Jackal made a desperate snap at Tortoise, and now found himself completely stuck, head and feet. Tortoise, feeling proud of his successful ruse, now marched quietly up to the top of the bank with Jackal on his back, so that he could be seen by the other animals as they came to the water.

They were indeed astonished to find how cleverly the crafty Jackal had been caught, and Tortoise was much praised for the capture.

Jackal was at once condemned to death by Lion, and Hyena was told to execute the sentence. Jackal pleaded hard for mercy, but finding this useless, he made a last request, asking that as Lion always was so fair and just in his dealings, he decree that Jackal not have to suffer a lingering death.

Lion inquired of him in what manner he wished to die. He asked that his tail be shaved and rubbed with a little fat, and that Hyena then swing him around twice and dash his brains out upon a stone. This was considered fair by Lion, and he ordered the sentence to be carried out in his presence.

When Jackal's tail had been shaved and greased, Hyena caught hold of him with great force, but before he could lift him from the ground, cunning Jackal had slipped away from his grasp, and was running for his life, pursued by all the animals, with Lion in the forefront.

After a long chase, Jackal got under an overhanging precipice, and, standing on his hind legs with his shoulders pressed against the rock, he called loudly to Lion to help him support it, as the rock was falling, and would crush them both. Lion put his shoulders to the rock, and exerted himself to the utmost. After some little time, Jackal proposed that he should creep out carefully and fetch a large pole to prop up the rock, so that Lion could escape and save his life. And so Lion—still believing the rock would fall on him—was left there by Jackal to starve and die.

—*Amalouw* or *Amakosa*

51
Stuffing the Hyena

A story. How does it go?

A hare and a small buck were friends and agreed to try and be as clever as they could. The hare said, "We'll go and smoke out the ant-hill holes, for ants are very good to eat," and the buck agreed. So the hare went inside the ant hill, and the small buck took grass and fire, and placed it in the mouth of the ant hill, and fanned it till he was tired. The hare said, "Are you tired?" and he said, "Yes." So the hare came out, and said "You go in." And the small buck went inside, and the hare took grass and stuffed up all the holes, and took fire and placed it, and cut thick grass and fanned it, and the smoke went inside and the small buck died, and the hare took his horns and blew them:

Pelu, pelu,
The little horn of the little buck,
The little horn,
He has been deceived,
The little horn of the little buck.

So the hare went on down the road and met an old woman guarding her field from elephants. He asked her, "Mother, what are you guarding?" She replied, "I am guarding against the elephants who eat the melons." The hare said, "Bring a large melon right now, and make a hole in it so that I can go inside. Stop up the hole, and then you can go away." The old woman followed his instructions, and the hare got into the melon with the horns of the small buck. When the elephants came, the mother-of-elephants swallowed the melon, swallowed it whole. Inside, the hare blew the horns:

Pelu, pelu,
The little horn of the little buck,
The little horn,
He has been deceived,
The little horn of the little buck, kapembee.

Then the elephants said, "The mother-of-elephants is crying." And they conferred with each other about it, asking, "You fellows, should we kill her?" and they all agreed that they should, and they did it. Then they asked the hare, "Now, you hare, can you eat the mother-of-elephants for us and finish her?" All that meat! He said "Yes." "Eat her now, then." The hare said "I must first roast the meat, of course, so tie me with rope. I'm going to the forest to cut firewood! Tie me with rope so I can't get away." They agreed, and tied him around the waist with a long rope, and he went to the forest, and was seen by a hyena. The hyena looked like he was going to bite. The hare said, "Do not bite me. Just let me tie you with the rope and I will take you where there is a lot of meat." The hyena consented because he was greedy. The hyena said, "Hare, now is this true?" The hare replied, "When have we ever joked together like we were pals? Of course it's true," and he tied him, saying, "Now you shut up, it is I who have the meat who shall speak." Then the hare shouted to the elephants, "Pull, use your strength." The elephants pulled, and when they saw the hyena, they said, "You, hyena, you, will you eat the meat for us and finish it?"

He said, "Yes." "Will you eat it raw or cooked?" He said, "I will eat it raw, the cooking is in the stomach." And he ate, and he was absolutely full, and he said, "Take me to the water." And he went and drank, and he vomited in the middle, and he returned and ate some more. The elephants said to each other, "Today again, let him drink as much as he wants." And he was taken to the water, and he drank at the side, and he became so full he could not find room even for breath. Then he was told, "Hyena." "What?" "Cry, as you cry, *U-u-u-wa-u.*" And he split and died.

The cunning of the hare.

—*Kiniramba*

52
Cutting the Elephant's Hips

One day, Hare gave a dance and Elephant came to it, and the two danced together, but Hare danced better than Elephant. Hare said to Elephant, "Your movements are too slow, owing to your size; if you would only let me cut off some of the flesh from your hips, you might dance better." Elephant caught at the suggestion, and said, "You come and cut off the flesh as you think best, so I can become a good dancer." Hare took a sharp knife and cut off a large quantity of flesh from Elephant, and then he left him.

This made Elephant very ill, and he called in Bushbuck to help him. He said, "Go to Hare and ask him to send back my flesh, because I shall die without it." So Bushbuck went to Hare and asked him for Elephant's flesh. Hare said, "Won't you eat first?" Bushbuck said he would, so Hare gave him some of the meat from Elephant to eat. Bushbuck said, "This is very good meat, where did you get it?" Hare said, "It comes from the hill, from a place frequented by this kind of animal." Bushbuck said, "Let us go and hunt them."

Hare agreed, and they went to a place in the bush. Hare said, "You stop and catch them here, and I will go further on. When you hear a little rumbling noise keep your head in, but when it is loud, put your head out." Bushbuck did so. When there was a little noise, he kept his head well in, but when it got louder, he looked out, and was struck by a rolling stone, which killed him.

Hare then came along, saying, "My friend, where are you?" Why do you hide?" When he reached the place, he saw that Bushbuck was dead, so he lifted up the body, took it home, cooked, and ate it.

In this very same way, Hare tricked all the messengers sent by Elephant, until the day Elephant sent Leopard. Hare made the same proposals to him as to the others, but Leopard was far too shrewd to be as easily caught, and when he heard the loud noise of the rolling stone, he kept his head well in, and it rolled past him. He then pretended to be dead. Hare came round and said, "My friend, what has killed you?" and thinking the leopard was dead, he took it up and carried it home.

When he was about to begin cutting it up, Leopard sprang to his feet, and said, "This is what you do every day, is it? You kill all the foolish animals?" Hare ran away as fast as he could and Leopard chased him, but couldn't catch him.

Hare crossed a river, and then turned back immediately and recrossed it. He met Leopard coming the other way. Leopard didn't recognize Hare, because he was so wet, and asked him, "Did you meet Hare on the other side?" He replied, "No, we have been hunting the King's leopards from early morning and have caught ten, and only you have escaped." When Leopard heard this he ran back to Elephant, but only to find him dead.

—*Baganda*

53

The Clever Wakasanke

A lioness and a cow lived near each other, though not in the same house; the lioness gave birth to a female lion, and the cow gave birth to a bull calf. When the two children grew up, the cow's son was a mischievous child, while the lioness's daughter was gentle and meek. After a time, the cow and the lioness dug a well, and got it into splendid shape. The lioness said to the cow: "We have an excellent well, but you know how full of mischief your son is, so please warn him lest he come and spoil our well, and cause us to quarrel and end our friendship." The cow readily agreed to do so.

Soon after this, the lioness went to buy food, and asked the cow to look after her child while she was away. The cow consented, and the two children played together near the house for some time, but after a while they wandered off and came to the well. First the calf knocked some dirt into it, and after more mischief, pushed the baby lioness into it, and she drowned.

The calf ran home to his mother, and said his companion had fallen into the well and died. The cow said: "The lioness will surely kill me for this. We better run away." So they packed hastily, and ran away to the bushbuck to hide with him. The bushbuck made them welcome, and promised to butt the lioness and drive her away if she should come.

When the lioness returned from her shopping, she found her house empty, and went on to the cow's house, but that was empty, too. She looked about and called, but got no reply. Eventually, after searching and searching, she discovered the body of her child in the well, and wept long and bitterly, bemoaning her loss. Then, she went hunting for the cow and at length came to the bushbuck, calling, "Whose, whose?" To this the bushbuck answered: "Yours, yours." And then he said to the cow: "You better run away, or I will get killed, too. You must run away to the antelope." So the cow and the calf did as he said, and hid with the antelope for a time. But when the lioness came to the antelope and asked for the cow, the antelope, too, said: "You better go away from here, or I will get into trouble and it will be my death."

Then the cow fled to the elephant and hid with him, but when the lioness came and discovered her and roared, the elephant said, "You better leave, or I'll have troubles because of you." So again she had to take flight.

It thus came about that the cow had constantly to run away from the lioness, and was always in fear. One day, as she was fleeing, she met a *wakasanke* bird who asked her why she was always running in this manner? The cow answered: "Because my child killed the lioness's child, and now she wants to kill me. So I am looking for a place where I can be safe from her anger." *Wakasanke* replied: "You can stay here with me. I will frighten the lioness and drive her away." The cow gladly agreed to remain.

Wakasanke made preparations for the lioness's onslaught. He first brought a flower of the plantain, which is shaped like the heart of an animal and is of a reddish-brown colour. Then he put some milk into a pot and placed it by the flower. Next he drew a pot of blood from the cow and put it near the other things. When all his preparations were made, he waited.

After a time, the lioness came, and cried: "Whose, whose?" *Wakasanke* answered: "Mine, mine." He took the pot of blood and dashed it on the lioness's breast, saying, "I have killed you. Isn't this your blood?" He struck the lioness with the flower, shouting, "Isn't that your heart? I have killed you." He then took the pot of milk and dashed it with all his might upon the lioness's head, saying, "Let me crush in your head and brains, and finish you off." In this way, he so terrified the lioness that she really thought it was her blood, heart and brains, and she rushed away leaving the cow in peace. Thus did *Wakasanke* prove too skillful for the lioness. Ever since that time, the *wakasanke* birds have lived near cows, and every herdsman, when he goes to his milking, first lets a few drops fall on the ground to commemorate the *wakansanke*'s action. And to this day whenever a lion meets a cow, it tries to kill it.

—*Baganda*

54
The Tricksters' Encounter

Hare and Spider were once great friends and used to pay alternate visits to each other. One day, Spider decided he wanted to marry. His fiancée lived in one of the heavenly bodies and he asked his friend Hare to accompany him on a trip to see his future parents-in-law. Hare accepted, without knowing that the journey was to the heavens.

At the appointed time, Hare dressed up and went to the home of Spider, who then revealed their destination. Hare told Spider that he could not go, after all, because he was unable to fly. It had always been Hare's habit to say that he could do whatever Spider did, and in many cases he succeeded by cunning. This time, however, he had to admit defeat, and Spider was very pleased to learn that at last his clever friend had to recognize his own great intelligence. He told Hare that he would devise a means for him to go, knowing that Hare would never rest until he found out how it was done. He, therefore, prepared food for Hare, and while Hare was eating, Spider said that he was going to take a bath. He then spun a web reaching to the heavenly body, and as soon as he had done this, he went into the bath so that Hare might not suspect him.

When Spider had bathed, and Hare had eaten, they set off. Spider tied Hare on his back and started climbing the narrow cobweb he had made. Hare was amazed and he greatly praised the cleverness of Spider, trying all the time to induce him to reveal his secret. This Spider refused to do. Hare then began to play his usual tricks. He told Spider that since they were respectable visitors, they ought to make a vow not to interfere with each other. When Spider asked him what he meant by this, Hare said that they should agree that whatever was given them in the name of the son-in-law should automatically belong to Spider—and Hare must not touch it—and whatever was given them in the name of the visitor should belong to Hare—and Spider must not touch it. Spider, not knowing that it was contrary to tradition on the heavenly body to use the name "son-in-law," accepted this quite happily. He thought that Hare was on the losing side.

When they arrived, they were welcomed warmly, and the mother-in-law of Spider called on her daughter to bring chairs for the visitors. Hare then said to Spider, "Have you not heard that the chairs are for the visitors? They must then be mine." Spider conceded. This went on for most of their stay—Spider didn't even get anything to eat. Finally, he became annoyed with his friend. He told Hare that he wanted to go outside to have a confidential talk with his girl friend. Hare accepted this and remained in the house. Outside, Spider told his girl friend that Hare was not a good person, and he told her, also, how he had been starving. She explained this to her parents, and from then on they only used "son-in-law." And so it went for a considerable time. Hare, however, couldn't keep up his end of the bargain and, broke his promise eventually, not to interfere. He made many unpleasant remarks about Spider. He remarked of his table manners, that it was the first time he had seen a greedy person who used his feet as well as his hands when eating. Hare said this in the presence of his fiancée in order to embarrass Spider, so Spider decided to punish his friend by leaving him behind. When, at last, his girl friend had become his wife, and was free to go with him, the three of them set off to the place where he and Hare had originally landed—but only Spider knew where it was. On the way, Spider asked Hare to go on ahead since he and his wife had family matters to discuss, and when Spider was out of sight, they went in the opposite direction, for that was where the web between earth and the heavenly body really lay.

Hare was now in a dilemma. He could neither live in that world nor leave it. He tried everything, but in vain. Then he decided to jump down. When he landed, he was unconscious. A woman and her son came by. Thinking he was dead, she picked him up and put him in her basket, in which she had some food for her son and the boy's shoes. As they walked, the boy, lagging behind, noticed that Hare was eating his food. But when he told his mother, she said not to be so silly for "How can a dead thing eat?" The boy kept quiet and so did Hare, who was pretending to be dead. But by and by, the boy saw Hare wearing his shoes, and again told his mother. The woman now grew suspicious and put the basket down in order to check. Hare immediately jumped out and ran away wearing the boy's shoes. The mother lamented this sorely.

Continuing on, Hare met Elephant, who asked him where he had bought the shoes. He said that he had made them. Elephant asked Hare to make some for him, but he refused, saying that as Elephant's feet were so big, the shoes would be very difficult to make, and it would take a long time. But Elephant was persistent, so Hare finally agreed, and asked him to go and dig four holes deep enough to stand in, and gather four piles of firewood. Elephant did this at once and then called Hare to start to make the shoes. Hare came and told Elephant to stand in the holes. He then arranged the firewood around Elephant's feet and set fire to it. Elephant endured the heat for a while and then started to complain that he was burning. Hare told him to have courage. "You are bigger and stronger than I am and yet you complain before one shoe is made. Your great size is useless. It is mere flesh without energy and resistance. You lack determination." Elephant persevered a little, but it was too late. His feet had burnt, and when Hare told him to come out, he simply fell down and died. Hare then rejoiced and said, "You pretend to be big and clever for nothing. I will now be able to enjoy your meat. Put on your shoes!" He then went into the dead animal and took out the fat part, which he took to his sister for making food.

—*Luo*

55
How Squirrel Robbed Rabbit of His Tail

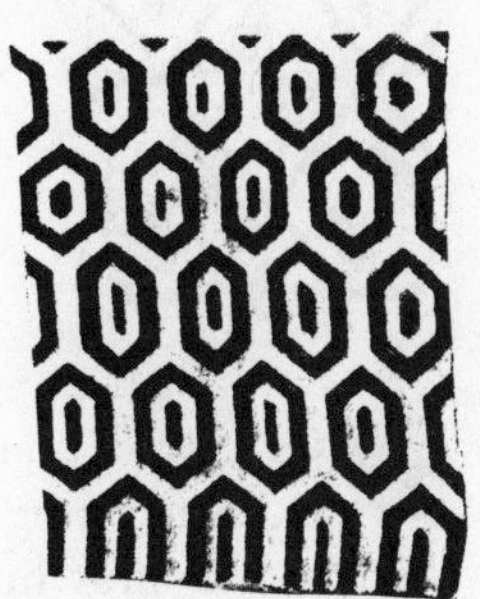

Rabbit and Squirrel were brothers-in-law and always had a harmonious relationship. One day Squirrel said: "Brother-in-law, let me have your tail to walk about with. I will return it." But Rabbit refused, saying he did not want to be left without a tail. Squirrel stopped asking, but after some days he started up again: "Truly, brother-in-law, I don't know why you refused me—I just wanted to walk about with your tail and said I would bring it back." So finally Rabbit consented, and Squirrel took his tail, saying he would return it in eight days' time.

Then Squirrel went home. On his arrival there, his people admired his fine tail and asked him where he had gotten it. Said he: "My brother-in-law gave it to me." They replied: "You are blessed indeed!"

When the eight days had passed, did Squirrel return the tail? Not he! Nine days passed, then ten days, and on the eleventh day, Rabbit followed his tail to Squirrel's place. On his arrival, he found Squirrel on the ground. "You have come!" said he, as soon as he saw him. Then Squirrel jumped into a tree, climbed up, and laughing heartily, said: "What have you come after, brother-in-law?" Rabbit didn't say a word. So Squirrel asked him a second time. Rabbit answered then, saying, "As for me I am angry. You have simply deceived me. You did not bring back my tail." Thereupon, he got very mad. Squirrel again laughed aloud, and said; "As you are so angry, perhaps you will climb up into the tree, and get your tail! If you do not climb the tree, you will never see your tail again."

Then Rabbit thought to himself: "What am I to do without a tail? How am I to stay among all the other animals? They have all got tails. I am the only one lacking a tail." Thereupon, he went to a hill, and to this day, he lives among the rocks.

—Ila

56
Victims of Vanity

Once upon a time, a hare went to seek work with a lion, and agreed to attend to the drying of the meat the lion killed. One day, when the lion was away hunting and the hare was busy attending to his task, some hyenas came by and seeing the meat, asked the hare to give them some. The hare refused, explaining that it belonged to the lion, his master. But the hyenas just ignored him, and took the meat and made off with it anyhow.

This went on every day, and the hare became so much distressed by it, that he decided to try to trap the hyenas. He dug a game pit, and after putting pointed stakes in the bottom, covered it up with grass. That afternoon he went out for the daily supply of firewood, and on his return, found to his distress, that the lion, not the hyenas, had fallen into the pit, and been killed.

Now he had not only to defeat the hyenas, but to avenge the death of his master, as well. He raised the lion out of the pit, carefully removed the skin, dried it, and stuffed it with grass. He lay the stuffed body down in the forest close by, and attached one end of a rope to its neck; then he went back to his work. Presently, the hyenas came along, as usual asking for meat. The hare this day invited them to come and take what they wanted. Pretending to be friendly, the hare remarked how well one of them would look with a necklace, and because the hyena's vanity was touched, he allowed the hare to fasten a rope around his neck. Now the other end of this rope was attached to the stuffed lion, so when, at the next moment, the hare called out that the lion was coming back, and the hyenas started to run away, they found that the lion followed them. Wherever they stopped to get breath, there he was, still on their tracks, so they decided to run for a hole they knew, where they could hide. After they had been there for some time, one of them gathered the courage to peep out, but there was the lion waiting for them. Day by day, they became hungrier and hungrier, but every time they looked out, they always saw the lion waiting. So the robbers grew weaker and weaker, and eventually they starved to death.

—*Wayao*

57

Death by Burning

Neither Hare nor *Mulala* Dragon had fire, so Hare suggested they steal some from the village, and Dragon agreed, but wondered how they could do it. Hare answered: "Let us be clever in our stealing." Dragon said: "Clever in what way?" Said Hare: "Come here, Dragon, and let me tie some grass around your head," and he did. Then Hare told him: "Go to the village. When you get there, stick your head into the fire and the grass will catch. Then run away and come back here."

So Dragon went to the village of men. When she got there, everyone said: "Here's a dragon," and ran away in fear. Dragon entered a house and found fire blazing. She put in her head, still tied round with grass, and it caught. She ran away, then, returning to Hare, calling out: "Hare! Hare!"

Hare answered, saying: "Well!"

"Here comes the fire!"

"Bring it here!"

So Dragon ran toward him. But Hare started running, too, and got far ahead, for he was much faster. Then the fire began to cover Dragon, and she died.

When Dragon's son saw what happened, he said: "As my mother has died from fire, I shall go and sleep in a hollow tree and in a burrow. I shall not again sit by a fire." Then he grew very fierce, and red wattles appeared around his neck—symbols of the fire which burned his mother long ago. To this day Dragon does not warm himself by the fire, though he is frequently burnt to death in the hollow of a tree and in the burrows where he sleeps. It is Hare that showed how to kill Dragon by fire.

—*Ila*

58
The Ant's Burden

K*weku Anansi* and *Kweku Tsin,* his son, were both very clever farmers. Generally, they had fine harvests from each of their farms. One year, however, they were very unfortunate. They had sown their seeds as usual, but no rain had fallen for more than a month after and it looked as if the seeds would never sprout.

Kweku Tsin was walking sadly through his fields one day, looking at the bare, dry ground, and wondering what he and his family would do for food, if nothing ever came up. To his surprise, there was a tiny dwarf seated by the roadside. The little hunchback asked why he was so sad, and *Kweku Tsin* told him. The dwarf promised to help him to bring rain to the farm. He had *Tsin* fetch two small sticks and tap him lightly on the hump, while singing:

O water, go up, O water, go up,
And let rain fall, and let rain fall.

To *Tsin*'s great joy it immediately began to rain, and it kept up until the ground was good and soaked. Then the seeds sprouted and the crops began to look very promising.

Anansi soon heard how well *Tsin*'s crops were growing—while his were still languishing in the earth. He went straightaway to his son and demanded to know the cause. *Kweku Tsin,* being an honest fellow, at once told him what had happened.

Anansi quickly decided to get his farm watered in the same way, and immediately set out for the place where *Tsin* had met the little dwarf. As he went, he cut two big, strong sticks, thinking, "My son made him work with little sticks. I will make him do twice as much with my big ones." He carefully hid the big sticks, however, when he saw the dwarf coming toward him. Again the hunchback asked what the trouble was, and *Anansi* told him. "Take two small sticks, and tap me lightly on the hump," said the dwarf. "I will get rain for you."

But *Anansi* took his big sticks and beat so hard that the dwarf fell down dead. The greedy fellow was now thoroughly frightened, for he knew that the dwarf was jester to the king of the country, and a big favorite of his. He wondered how he could fix the blame on someone else. He picked up the dwarf's body and carried it to a kola tree, climbed up, and laid it on one of the top branches. Then, he sat down under the tree to watch.

By and by, *Kweku Tsin* came along to see if his father had succeeded in getting rain for his crops. "Did you not see the dwarf, father?" he asked, as he saw the old man sitting alone. "Oh, yes!" replied *Anansi;* "but he climbed this tree to pick kola. I am now waiting for him." "I will go up and fetch him," said the young man—and immediately began to climb. As soon as his head touched the body, the dwarf, of course, fell to the ground. "Oh! what have you done, you wicked fellow?" cried his father. "You have killed the king's jester!" "That is all right," quietly replied the son (who saw that this was one of *Anansi*'s tricks). "The king is very angry with him, and has promised a bag of money to anyone who would kill him. Now I can go and get the reward." "No! No! No!" shouted *Anansi.* "The reward is mine. I killed him with two big sticks. I will take him to the king." "Very well!" was the son's reply. "You killed him, you may take him."

Off set *Anansi,* quite pleased with the prospect of getting a reward. But when he reached the king's court, it was only to find the king very angry at the death of his favorite. The body of the jester was shut up in a great box and *Anansi* was condemned—as a punishment—to carry it on his head forever. The king enchanted the box so that it could never be set down on the ground. The only way in which *Anansi* would ever be able to get rid of it was by getting some other man to put it on his head. This, of course, no one was willing to do.

At last, one day, when *Anansi* was almost worn out with his heavy burden, he met Ant. "Will you hold this box for me while I go to market and buy some things I need badly?" said *Anansi* to Mr. Ant. "I know your tricks, *Anansi,*" replied Ant. "You want to be rid of it." "Oh no, indeed, Mr. Ant," protested *Anansi.* "Indeed, I will come back for it, I promise."

Mr. Ant, who was an honest fellow, and always kept his own promises, believed him. He took the box on his head, and *Anansi* hurried off. Needless to say, the sly fellow had not the least intention of keeping his word. Mr. Ant waited in vain for his return—and was obliged to wander all the rest of his life with the box on his head. That is the reason we so often see ants carrying great bundles as they hurry along.

—*Hausa*

59
Their Soft Crowns Discovered

At one time, all the eagles and hawks used to be afraid of fowls, and especially of the cock; because of his crest of red horns they thought he must be very dangerous. One day, after talking it over, they decided to send their little brother, *Katotola,* smallest of the hawks, to see if their fears were warranted.

So *Katotola* flew down to the earth as an ambassador of peace. He found the cock strutting about with his family and explained to him that the eagle, *Kapungu,* their king, wished them to be on friendly terms with the cock, but they all were afraid of his crown of red horns. The cock answered that it was not made of horn, but was quite soft. "Come and feel it," said he, "it is nothing to be afraid of." *Katotola* was frightened, but when the cock repeated the invitation, *Katotola* did as he asked. He was surprised to find it soft and harmless, just as the cock had said.

The cock accepted the eagle's message of friendliness, so *Katotola* said goodbye and prepared to fly away. Just then, he spied one of the cock's daughters and no longer afraid, he darted down, picked her up, and flew with her back to the others, saying, "See here, I have carried off one of his daughters. The cock is nobody to be afraid of." And that is the reason that today, all the eagles and hawks know that the fowls are a weak tribe, and they easily make war on them and carry off their children.

—*Wayao*

60

The Pig's Nose and the Baboon's Rear

Long ago, the pig and the baboon used to live together on the hillsides. One day, it was very cold and a cutting wind was blowing. As the pig and the baboon sat in the sun trying to get warm, the baboon turned to the pig, and said, "This wind is enough to wear the end of one's nose to a blunt point." "Yes," answered the pig, "it's really enough to blow the hairs off one's buttocks and leave a bare, dry patch." "Look here," said the baboon, getting cross, "you are not to make personal remarks!" "I did nothing of the kind," retorted the pig, "but you were rude to me first." This started a quarrel, and they came to the conclusion that neither cared for the other's company. So they parted, and the baboon went up on to the rocky top of the hill, while the pig went down to the plains, and there they remain to this day.

—*Wayao*

61

One Trick Deserves Another

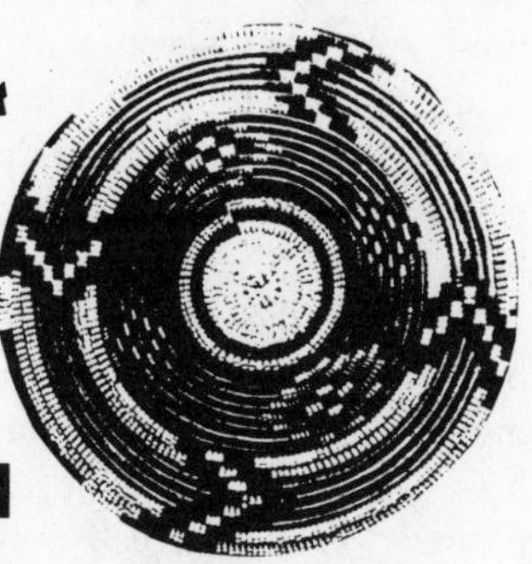

Not very long ago, perhaps sixty years, perhaps more, there was a man who possessed a beautiful calf, sleek and round and full of promise. He used to feed it with great care, because he knew it was of real value and a good asset to his home. He gave it a big bundle of sweet potato vines daily, plus some porridge made of crushed maize. It was his only consolation, because his wife had been childless for years and years.

One day, as always, he left his wife at home preparing food, saying that he was going to the field to collect the sweet potato vines and would be back soon.

But from the field he heard the beer drinkers carousing in a village nearby. The temptation was too much for him, for the sun was hot and he was thirsty. Without considering very much what he had told his wife, he hid the long string he used for tying up the sweet potato vines and went to the feast in the village, sure that he would enjoy a few horns of beer with his chums.

Meanwhile, at home, a cunning man, called *Wakahare,* approached the man's wife, and asked: "Good woman, where is your husband?" "He left just now and went to the garden in the valley to collect a bundle of sweet potato vines for the calf you see there." "What a beautiful calf," said *Wakahare,* "very fat, well shaped, but, but—" "But what?" asked the surprised woman. "Yes, it is very sad. I don't mean to be rude, my woman, but from what I hear everywhere this calf is the reason for your barrenness. You know, I am a medicine man, and I know something about it. But cheer up, for I think I can help you. If you like, I am ready to give you the medicines you need. Imagine your joy when you embrace your baby next year. We must kill the calf that is causing your problems, and I will tell you what to do with its blood and the contents of the stomach. After all, which means more to you, having a calf or a baby?"

The idea of having a baby of her own in her arms was simply too alluring for the woman. Without hesitating, she agreed to *Wakahare*'s plan, and the calf was slaughtered. They used a calabash to collect the blood, and the contents of the stomach were collected in one of those split gourds you find in every *Kikuyu* home. The make-believe medicine man told her what to do with the blood and how to use the contents of the stomach. But he insisted that she should not eat the meat, not a single morsel, lest she remain barren until the end of her life.

Later in the day, when her husband came home with the usual bundle of potato vines, he said to his wife: "Take this to the calf, for it must be hungry: I had some beer at *Kemani*'s and could not come before." "But there is no calf now," said the woman. "What do you mean?" "Well, the calf was slaughtered today at noon." "Shut your mouth," said the man, "and don't fool around. Besides, I have had some beer, so I am not fully responsible for my actions." "If you will quiet down," answered his wife, "I will tell you all about it. A man came here, named *Wakahare,* and told me that I would certainly give birth to a child if only I knew how to use the blood of the calf and the contents of its stomach. I know you are longing for a child just as I always have. And after all, what is a calf when we can have a child! So we killed the calf and here is the blood and the contents of its stomach." Her husband shouted: "You did this you fool? You must be the greatest fool on earth! I don't know whether to beat you or slaughter you like a goat? And where is the meat?" She answered: "*Wakahare* took the meat, for, as he said, it's taboo for me to eat it. If I did I could never give birth to a child." "I can't think of a stupider woman than you!" her husband told her. "My beautiful calf, which I had built all my fortunes on! I am leaving here. I will travel the whole world until I find another woman as stupid as you, and then I'll bring her back to be your husband."

The poor man took a staff in his right hand, threw an old blanket over his shoulders, and simply left. He went on and on for many days. At last he arrived at a large village. When he asked around, he found out that it was the homestead of a very rich man. Pretending to be an ordinary traveler, he begged for somewhere to stay in a place nearby. Meanwhile he asked around about the rich man, his habits, his wives, and his possessions. And, as always, he found that there was no lack of people who delighted in such talk. Now he thought that he would be able to play a good trick and try *his* luck.

One day the rich man went to see his herd where it was grazing. It was rather far from his home. The would-be tricker went to spy on what he was doing. Then, when he thought it was safe, he disguised himself, smearing mud and dirt all over his body and his head. Thus camouflaged, he went to the rich man's wife. He had been fasting for three days, and so looked very emaciated. He came by as the woman was cooking her food outside her home. She looked up and saw the miserable beggar. She was horrified, and cried out.

"Keep quiet, dear woman, keep quiet. There is nothing to fear, I won't hurt you" said the beggar. "Who are you?" "My name is *Kemando*" (which was the name of a man belonging to that family who had died about twelve years before). "What did you say?" she said in a scared voice. "I come to ask something from you, which I need desperately." "What is it?" "Money, a big pocket of money. I come in the name of *Wagaki* and *Kenyai* (two others who had recently died). They sent me to you because we have no money and we are starving." "I am sorry, spirit," said the woman. "We had better wait until my husband comes back. There is some porridge here if you like. Help yourself." "No, thanks. We of the other world do not eat the kind of food you eat. I must have money only for then we are able to buy our kind of food. If you refuse, I must take you with me to our land and you will feel the pinch of hunger as we often do." "Oh! no!" said the woman, "I don't want to die. I am still young. There is plenty of money in this house. I'll give it to you. You will leave immediately!" She went into her home and brought forth a big sack of money, very heavy, and threw it on the ground in front of the beggar, for she didn't want to touch him. "It's heavy," she said. "If you want, I will carry it for you." "No, no," said the man, "don't trouble yourself. Besides, you can't come along, for you could never come back." "Go away," said the woman, "and be quick about it."

A few hours later the rich man came home. "I am tired," he said, sitting on his stool in front of the house. "What sort of food have you made for me?" "There is some porridge in the calabash and the maize is just boiling. But I must tell you what happened this morning when you were away." "What is it?" "A man came here, a very ugly creature and very thin, he looked like a skeleton, with a body quite different from our own. He was painted in red and had very long hair. He brought me the greetings of *Keriha* and *Wagaki* and *Kanyai*. They sent him here to get money, as there is great famine in their place and they have absolutely nothing to eat. They want to buy food of the kind they eat there. I offered him some porridge but he refused it, saying that they do not eat our food. I was so scared of what he told me that I gave him the sack of money we had here and off he went."

The rich man was furious. He grabbed his wife by the throat and threw her to the ground. Then he came to his senses and realized it was useless to hit his wife for it wouldn't bring back the money. So he asked: "Which way did he go?" "That path across the brook." The man took a spear in his right hand and ran away down the path where his wife was pointing. He ran like a gazelle and finally sighted in the distance a man on the road, trudging slowly with a burden on his shoulders. But the rascal had been expecting him and had a trick in store. He had procured some banana leaves and a machete by scaring away an old farmer. He scared the old man into climbing a tree by telling him that a chief was after him.

Meanwhile, the rich man arrived, perspiring and gasping after his long run. He asked the deceiver: "Have you seen a man passing this way?" "A man? Is it the man who is up there in the tree?" The rich man went to the tree and looking up, said: "Yes, that is the man I want." The poor wretch was told to come down immediately, but he was afraid and couldn't bring himself to move. After a while, the rich man got mad and decided to climb the tree and throw him down. Meanwhile, the rascal placed the bag of money under his arm, took the beautiful blanket laid down by the rich man when he climbed the tree, and swiftly, like a leopard, he slid into the thick forest nearby, and disappeared. All trace of him was lost. He walked day and night and after seven days he arrived back at his home rich and safe.

Poor rich man. As soon as he discovered that he had had a bad trick played upon him, he resigned himself to returning home. Dejected and crestfallen, he had to think hard about how to save face. "What am I going to say to my wife?" he asked himself as he walked. "Oh yes, I will say this. I saw for myself that the man was really poor and needy, so I, too, consented to give him the money and even gave him my blanket." So that is what he said to her. And his wife added: "Didn't you say that I was a fool? I know only too well you never trust me, you are never kind to me."

—*Kikuyu*

62
The Pleasure of His Company

A man once hoed his garden and planted it with beans, but when the crop grew, the animals from the forest came and damaged it, so he set a snare to catch them.

One day, a leopard came that way and got his leg caught in the trap. He lay there unable to move, and, after a time, he spied a bushbuck with his mate and four young ones, whom he called to come and help him. The bushbuck, when he saw the leopard in the trap, took pity on him, and undoing the rope, set him free. Said the leopard, "I have been here three days and am famished. You have been very kind to me. Will you extend your kindness and take me to your home and give me food? I am very much indebted to you, and to show my gratitude, I will remain with you." So the bushbuck agreed and led him to his home, where beans were cooked and put before the leopard. But the leopard refused them, saying that he did not eat beans, and made his host kill and give him some fowls to eat.

Every day, after that, he was given fowls to eat, until none were left; soon the same thing happened with the goats. Finally, when there was no more meat to feed the leopard they offered him beans again, at which, the leopard repeated his indebtedness to his benefactor, the bushbuck, and said he would like to show his gratitude by staying with him, but he really could not eat beans. Then he asked the bushbuck to give him one of his children. Not wishing to offend his guest, he killed one of his little ones, and the leopard ate him. Next day, the leopard asked for and received another child, and so on, until all had been sacrificed and only the bushbuck and his wife remained. The leopard demanded the wife and the poor bushbuck, not knowing how to get out of it, had to give the leopard his own wife to be eaten. When the leopard again felt hunger, he said to the bushbuck, "Well now, you have been very kind to me and given me all you have, but *you* still remain. I think I will have to eat you, too." The bushbuck, now really frightened, made off into the forest, chased by the leopard.

After running for three days, the bushbuck met a buffalo who asked him what he was running from. The bushbuck told him and asked his advice, and the buffalo answered, "Well, I don't think that you can do anything except continue your kindness and give yourself up to the leopard." But the bushbuck ran on, and soon met an elephant who, when he heard the story, offered advice identical with the buffalo's.

All the animals of the forest said the same, except the hare who, after listening to the bushbuck's story, offered to act as judge in the case.

When the leopard came up, the hare told him he would like to see how the whole thing had come about, from the moment he got caught in the trap. All then repaired to the place where it had happened. "Now," said the hare, setting the trap, "will you just show me how you got caught? Of course if you are trapped, I will free you again." So the leopard stepped on the snare and was immediately caught by the leg. "Ah," said the hare, "that is the way it happened, is it?" saying which, he went off, taking the bushbuck with him. The man soon found the leopard in the snare and killed him.

—*Wayao*

63 The Dog Eats All the Ants

A leopard and his wife and a dog all lived together in a house that the leopard owned. Though they were friends, the dog was often treated more like a servant. When the rainy season came, the leopard said to the dog, "Let us go and look at our ant hill, and see whether the ants are about to swarm because the year is ended." They went, and soon caught a large quantity of ants, which they took home. The leopard's wife cooked them, and they had a sumptuous meal. Those which were left over, they fried, and then dried in the sun. The leopard afterwards said, "I will take four bundles of those dried ants to my wife's relations." The dog agreed to go with him, and they settled on a day for the journey.

Early on the morning of the appointed day, the leopard dressed in his best clothes, took his harp, because he was an expert player, and said to the dog, "You carry the ants." The dog made the bundles into a load, put them on his head, and started off after the leopard.

On the way, they met some people they knew, and greeted them. Their friends asked them where they were going, and the leopard replied, "I am going to see my wife's relations." They asked him to play a tune on his harp, which he did, and sang:

I have a load of white ants like the ones that the dog carries
I have a load of white ants like the ones that the dog carries.

Their friends thanked the leopard for the tune and song, took leave of him, and went on their way. The leopard and the dog, too, went on their way.

After a time, the dog said, "Sir, I don't feel well. I need to go out into the grass." The leopard said, "All right, go," and waited in the road for him. While in the grass, the dog ate all the ants, filled the packets with dry grass, and returned after tying them up as before. The leopard and dog continued on their way. After a time, the dog said to the leopard, "Sir, lend me the harp that I may play and sing as we walk." The leopard did so, and the dog played and sang:

A load of rubbish for my wife's relations
A load of rubbish for my wife's relations.

The leopard thanked the dog for his song, and said, "You played very well," to which the dog replied, "Thank you, sir."

When they reached their destination, the leopard greeted his wife's relations and asked how they were. They in turn, asked how the leopard and his wife and relations were, but they took no notice of the dog. The leopard's relatives then brought out their pipes and gave the leopard one to smoke, but still the ignored the dog. After a time, the dog walked away, and as soon as he got out of sight, he ran as fast as he could.

A while later, the leopard said he had brought them some ants to eat, and began to untie the parcels, but to his great surprise and annoyance he found nothing but dry grass. Realizing the trick that had been played on him, he called for the dog, but the dog had gone. Then, he went to his earth spirit and consulted him about what to do. The god answered, "When you beat the drums for twin dances, the dog will come." Some time later, the leopard's wife gave birth to twins, and the leopard's friends and relations came together and beat the drums for the twins, and they danced, too. The sheep, who was a friend of the dog, also came to the celebration. As they danced, they sang,

Who will show me the dog?
Who will show me the dog?

Others took up the refrain and waved their tails, saying,

There is no dog here, there is no dog here.

Late in the evening, although the dance was still going on, the sheep went home. He told the dog about the dance, and what a wonderful entertainment it was. The dog said: "I am sorry I was not there to see it." The sheep replied: "In the morning I will put you in my tail and take you." The next morning the sheep put the dog into his tail, and they went to the dance; when the drums beat they all sang:

Show me the dog.
Who will show me the dog?

Others answered:

Here there is no dog,
here there is no dog.

In the evening, when the drums were sounding loudly, the sheep became excited and danced and sang, and waved his tail so violently that the dog slipped out and fell to the ground; he immediately ran away and again escaped. The leopard was very angry and caught the sheep and killed him. The dog ran off to Mr. Man and lived with him. Now, whenever a leopard meets a dog, he kills it if he can. From that time, too, there has been enmity between the sheep and the leopard, because the sheep protected the dog.

—*Baganda*

64
No Longer Fear the Cock's Comb

At one time, the fowls used to be lords of the wild cats, for they had combs of fire that put fear into the cats. They made them their servants and used them to supply them with food. Whenever a cat caught flying ants, the fowls demanded four-fifths of them. This tax was paid in large packets of ants, which the cats had to bring before the fowls to let them see how great were the spoils they had taken, and exactly what share should be theirs. The cats did not like this arrangement, and once or twice they wished to rebel, but their fear of being burned by the fowls' combs, stopped them.

One day, the cat's fire had gone out and a mother cat sent one of the younger members of the family to the fowls to beg for fire. When the young cat arrived, he found the cock very drunk and fast asleep, and the others away from home. He tried to wake him, but couldn't, so he went back and told his mother. The mother said: "This time, take some dry grass with you and put it to his comb and bring the fire." He went back and touched the grass to the comb, but it didn't take fire.

The young cat returned to his mother and told her the grass would not catch; the mother was angry and said: "You have not really tried. Come along with me and do it again." When they arrived, the cock was still asleep. They approached him very slowly, touched the comb with the grass, and then blew on it to see if it was on fire, but there was never a spark. They felt the comb to see if it was hot, putting their hands gently on it, though they were afraid of being burnt. To their great surprise, they found that the comb was quite cold, even though it was red. After this discovery, they finally waked the fowl and told him they were not going to serve him any longer, they were tired of his rule. The fowl was angry and began to make a great noise, and tried to terrify the cats with threats, but they said: "We don't fear you. We tested your comb while you were asleep and know that it has no fire in it, and now we will kill you if you say anything more." The fowl saw that his empty boasting had been discovered, and from that time, fowls have had to escape cats because of the enmity between them. For this reason—to be safe from cats—fowls took refuge with man.

—*Buganda*

65 How Honey Guide Came to Have Power over Honey

Honey Guide, the silent one, and Wheatear, the songbird, at one time lived together in one place and ate out of one dish. Honey Guide was the elder, Wheatear the younger. One day, they decided to go after honey, and as they searched, Honey Guide said: "Smile, Wheatear, when you see where the honey is." Soon Wheatear smiled, although he did not really see the honey; but then Honey Guide smiled, and he really did see it. They returned home, leaving the honey behind, and planning to come back for it the next day. After a while, Wheatear quietly disappeared and went back to steal the honey Honey Guide had led him to by his smile.

The next morning, Honey Guide said: "Let us go to our honey." Of course, when they came to the honey place all they found there was a bit of bare honeycomb, mangled and thrown about, but when Honey Guide asked Wheatear about it, Wheatear replied: "My brother, I have seen neither it nor him who has stolen the honey, and as for me, I wouldn't eat any of this honey unless you had given it to me."

So then Honey Guide said no more, and they went out again looking for honey. When they found some, Honey Guide saw it before Wheatear did, and he tested Wheatear by saying: "Smile." Wheatear said: "I cannot see the honey, smile yourself, my brother." Honey Guide said: "No, child, smile." So Wheatear smiled and then he saw the honey. Honey Guide asked him: "What do you see?" Wheatear said: "It looks as if it might be flies fluttering in front of my eyes." Honey Guide said: "Haven't you seen it?" But Wheatear was deceiving him, for he saw the honey all the time. When Honey Guide was about to smile, he saw the honey, and said: "Let us cut down the tree to get it." Wheatear refused, saying: "No. As you accused me of stealing the honey, well, I am Wheatear! Let us bring some birdlime and set a trap beside the honey, then if it be I who steal the honey you will catch me." "A good thought," replied Honey Guide.

They went off to get some birdlime from the humans. Honey Guide said: "Tomorrow we'll come back to set the trap." But later that same day Honey Guide quietly disappeared and went off in secret to set the birdlime. Said Wheatear to himself: "Let me go quietly and eat the honey." But the birdlime was already set, although he did not notice it. When he sat down beside the honey, he sat on the birdlime. Said he, "I will strike it with my wing," but he stuck to it. And when he struck with his tail he stuck to it. When he wanted to draw back his right wing, it was stuck fast. He tried to strike it with his breast but he stuck. When he attempted to bite it with his beak, he bit the birdlime. Why, then he simply died for lack of breath.

When Honey Guide appeared on the scene, he found Wheatear already dead. Then he mocked him, saying: "Wheatear, smile!" As Wheatear was dried up, Honey Guide said that was the reward of thievery. "From today you will not steal any more. The chieftainship over honey is mine and to be extolled! As for you, from today your portion shall be birdlime already spread, and thus you will be killed by people."

While he spoke, Honey Guide was standing upon the corpse of Wheatear. Separated on account of thievery they became distinct in other ways, though their cries remained the same. And to this day, Wheatear's portion is to be trapped in birdlime.

—Ila

66

The Trapper Trapped

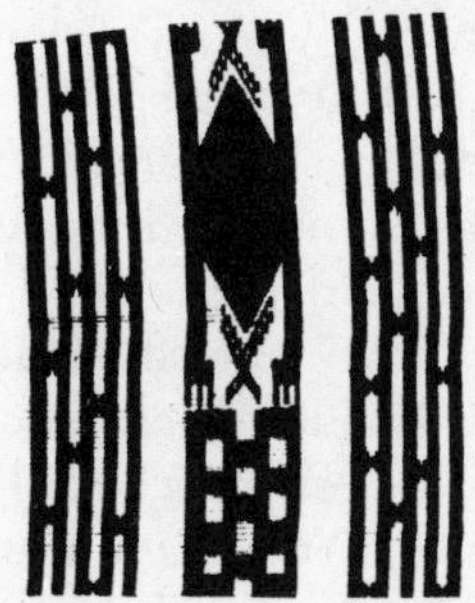

Goat and Fox were quarreling and Goat told Fox that he intended to get him into trouble so bad he would never be able to get out. Fox said, "All right; you do that, and I will return the favor to you."

Goat went for a walk and saw Leopard; being frightened, he asked, "Auntie, what you are doing here?" "My little one is sick," said Leopard. Then Goat, thinking quietly, said, "Fox has medicine that will make your little one well." Leopard said to call him, so Goat went to Fox and said, "They are calling you."

"Who is calling me?" replied Fox. "I don't know," said Goat; "I think it is your friend. Go this way and you will run into him." Fox went down the path and at length came upon Leopard. Fox was frightened, and inquired: "Did you call me?" "Yes, my son; your brother is sick. Goat came just a while ago and told me you had medicine that would make my little one well." "Yes," said Fox, "I have medicine that will cure your little one, but I must have a little goat horn to put it in. If you get me a goat horn I will let you have the medicine." "Which way did Goat go?" asked Leopard. "I left him up there," replied Fox. "You wait here with my little one, and I will bring you the horn," said Leopard, and away she ran. Soon after, Leopard killed Goat and returned with his horns to Fox. Beware, lest you fall into the trap you set for someone else.

—*Vai*

67

Medicine to Catch Him

Lion, Leopard, and Dog were living together. They heard the news that Goat had built a big town. Lion said to Leopard, "We had better make war on that town, as we have nothing to eat here." So the two joined forces and invaded Goat town. They fought a whole day, but were unable to capture it. They went to tell Dog of their bad luck, and asked him to join them in another attempt. The next morning, after fighting all day, the three took Goat town.

They entered it, and found only one Goat and one Cat. Lion caught Goat and Cat and said they were going to carry them away. Cat begged to be left untied so that he could dance, and Lion agreed. Then Goat said, "You should leave me untied as I am a doctor," and Lion agreed to that, too. "Let me see you dance now," said Lion. Cat began to dance and he danced well. Then he said, "I can jump." "Jump then," said Lion. Cat jumped over the barricade and ran into the bush.

Lion turned to Goat, and said, "You say you are a doctor. Well, Cat has run away. I want you to try your medicine, so that we can catch him." Then Lion, Leopard, and Dog all closed up around Goat to prevent his getting away, too. Goat told Lion to bring him a large pot. Then, Goat put his hand in his bag, and he took out a bottle filled with honey. He placed the honey in the pot. "You must put a cloth over me and the pot," said Goat. Lion did not know that Goat had honey; he thought it was water in the pot. Goat took a spoon and gave Lion some of the honey in the pot, saying, "This is some of the water my medicine gave me."

When Lion tasted the honey, he said: "Oh, you are really a doctor." Lion said: "I know you are a doctor now, so make me some medicine to wear around my neck." Goat told Lion that medicine worn around the neck is put up in leopard skin, and that he must kill Leopard to get some of his. "All right," said Lion. Lion started after Leopard, and Leopard ran, and Lion after him, and Dog followed. So Goat made his escape back the other way.

So Lion dislikes Leopard, Leopard dislikes Goat, and Goat dislikes Dog.

—Vai

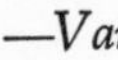

68
Friends for a Time

A certain hunter no longer wanted to live in his own village, but decided to make a little home for himself in the far bush. He searched for a nice place and there built a small house and made a little farm of yams and cassava. But he had lost his gun and was unable to get any meat.

One day he returned to his house and found there a young lion, who said to him: "My friend, I have come to see you. This is my country, but I like you and we two will share this house."

The man did not mind at all and agreed that the lion should live with him. Now, every day the man went out and looked at his farm and watched the crop growing, while the lion went away into the bush and killed meat, which he brought back and shared with the man. Thus they became fast friends.

But one day the lion said to his friend: "You told me you were a hunter, and yet all this time that we have been together it is I, not you, who have killed our meat." Then the man told the lion that men killed their meat with guns, and the lion said nothing.

However, he set forth and came near the dwelling places of Man. One day he saw a band of men come out to a farm, and all begin to hoe the field together. First, though, they had set their guns against a tree. So the lion rose up and went to the tree and took away one of the guns with all the little bags of powder and medicine attached to it. These he carried home and gave them to his friend, the man.

The hunter went out every day and killed meat until they were both tired of it. Then the man said that it was now time for him to leave the bush and return to the villages of men. The lion said he was sorry, but that the man knew best, and that he, the lion, would never forget him and would remain his friend so long as he never told other men that he had a lion as a friend. The man promised, and left the bush and settled in a village where he married and had many children.

One day the lion, remembering his friend, decided to visit him to find out if the man was still faithful to their friendship. He came down to the man's farm and hid himself near some rocks, pretending that he was asleep. When one of the man's youngest children found the lion, he told his father to come quick and kill it. Then the man went to see, and when he looked, he remembered, and said: "Maybe it is my friend. I will not take its skin." The lion got up and thanked his friend, and said that now he knew truly that the man was his friend and would go back to the bush happy.

Not long afterwards, the lion again wished to visit his friend, to show him his eldest son. So he took the cub with him to the farm and again hid himself, pretending to be asleep. But this time he did so in a different place. The cub was told to keep away, but to watch how his father's friend was a good man.

When the man and his children came to the farm, one of the boys saw the lion and told his father that there was meat lying there. The man then took his gun and went to the spot, and thinking that this lion was not his friend—since he had chosen a different place to hide himself in—shot the lion and killed it.

Then he saw that it was his friend and he began to weep. But the lion's child, who had watched his father killed, was angry. He swore that from that day onward, he and all other lions would never again look on the face of hunters with pleasure, and that they would kill them whenever they had the chance.

That is why, from that day to this, hunters and lions hate each other.

—*Krachi*

The Great Overland Trek

In the days when animals still could talk, Crocodile was the acknowledged leader of all water creatures—(if you judged from appearances, you'd say he still is)—and it was his special duty to look after them. One year, when it was exceedingly dry, and the water of the river where they had lived became scarce, he was forced to make a plan to walk overland to another river, a short distance from there.

He first sent Otter out to spy. Otter stayed away two days and brought back a report that there was still good water in the other river, real sea-cow holes, that not even a drought of several years could dry up.

After he had heard this, Crocodile called Tortoise and Alligator to his side. "Tonight I need you two to carry a report to Lion," he said. "Get ready. The field is dry, and you will probably have to travel for a few days without any water. We must make a peace treaty with Lion and his subjects, otherwise we will all perish this year. He must help us to travel to the other river, especially past the white man's farm that lies in between, and to get there unharmed by any of the animals of the field. A fish on land is sometimes a very helpless thing, as you all know." The two had it mighty hard in the burning sun and on the dry field, but eventually they reached Lion and handed him the treaty.

"What is going on now?" thought Lion to himself, when he had read it. "I must consult Jackal." But to Tortoise and Alligator, he said that the following evening he and his advisers would be at the appointed place, the big willow tree, at the farther end of the water hole where Crocodile had his headquarters.

When Tortoise and Alligator came back, Crocodile was exceedingly pleased with himself at the turn things had taken.

He invited Otter and a few others to join him on that evening, and ordered them to have plenty of fish and other good food lying under the willow, ready for their guests.

That evening as it grew dark, Lion appeared with Wolf, Jackal, Baboon, and a few other important animals, at the willow tree and they were received with the greatest cordiality by Crocodile and the other water creatures.

Crocodile was so overjoyed with the meeting of the animals that he now and then let fall a great tear of joy that disappeared into the sand. After the guests had done well by the fish, Crocodile laid the situation open to them and told them of his plan. He wanted peace among all animals, for not only did they destroy one another, but unless they banded together, the farmer would in time destroy them all.

To irrigate his land, the farmer had already stationed no less than three steam pumps at the source of the river, and water for the animals was becoming scarcer every day. Worse, because they had to stay in the shallow water, the farmer was able to kill them, one after the other. As Lion himself clearly saw the need to make peace, it was to his glory to give his hand to these peace-making water creatures. He agreed to escort them from the dried-up water, past the farmer's farm, and to the long sea-cow pools.

"And what benefit shall we receive from the peace?" asked Jackal.

"Well," answered Crocodile, "the peace made will benefit all of us. We won't kill each other off. If you want to come and drink water, you can do so with an easy mind, and not be the least bit nervous that I, or any one of us, will seize you by the nose; and so also with all the other animals. And on your side, we are to be safe from Elephant, who, whenever he gets the opportunity has the habit of tossing us with his trunk up into some narrow fork of a tree."

Lion and Jackal stepped aside to talk the whole thing over and while they did, Lion asked how he could be sure that Crocodile would keep to his part of the contract.

"My word of honor," was the prompt answer from Crocodile, and he let drop a few more long tears of honesty into the sand.

Baboon then said everything seemed honest and open as far as he could tell. He thought it was nonsense to attempt to dig pitfalls for one another, and he also well knew that his race would benefit, too, from this contract of peace and friendship. He would, however, like to suggest to Lion that it would be well to have everything put down in writing, so that there would be no problems in case there was disagreement.

Jackal did not want to listen to the terms of the treaty. He could not see that it would benefit the animals of the field. But Wolf, who had fully satisfied himself with the fish, was in an exceptionally peace-loving mood, and he advised Lion to close the agreement.

After Lion had listened to all his advisers, and also to the pleading tones of Crocodile's followers, he made a speech in which he said that he was inclined to enter into the agreement, seeing that it was clear that Crocodile and his subjects were in a very tight spot.

A document was drawn up immediately, and it was resolved to begin the move overland before midnight. Crocodile's messengers swam in all directions to summon together the water animals for the trek.

Frogs croaked and crickets chirped in the long water grass. Soon, all the animals had assembled at the willow. Lion had earlier sent out a few messengers to his subjects to raise an escort group, and long before midnight they, too, were at the willow in the moonlight.

The walk overland was regulated by Lion and Jackal. It was agreed that because Jackal was to act as spy, he would take the lead, but when he was able to draw Lion to one side, Jackal said to him:

"See here, I don't trust this affair one bit, and I want to tell you straight out, I am going to make tracks! I will spy for you until you reach the sea-cow pool, but I am not going to wait long for you there."

Elephant was to act as advance guard because he could walk so softly and could hear and smell so well. Then would come Lion with one division of the animals, then Crocodile's group with protection on both sides, and Wolf would bring up the rear.

While all this was being arranged, Crocodile was making his preparations as well. He called Yellow Snake to one side and said to him: "It would be good for us if these animals, who go among us every day, and who will continue to do so, fall into the hands of the farmer. Listen. You remain behind, out of sight, and when you hear me shout you will know that we have arrived safely at the sea-cow pool. Then you must stir up the farmer's dogs as much as you can, and everyone will have to look out for themselves."

Thereupon, the group moved out. They had to go very slowly since many of the water animals were not used to traveling on land; but they trekked past the farmer's property in safety, and toward break of day they were all safely at the sea-cow pool. At once, most of the water animals disappeared into the deep water, and Crocodile prepared to follow their example. With tearful eyes he said to Lion that he was very thankful for the help, that, out of pure relief, he must vent his feelings by screaming with joy, and this he did until even the mountains echoed with his cries. He thanked Lion on behalf of his subjects, and purposely made a long speech, dwelling on all the benefits both sides would derive from the peace agreement.

Lion was just about to say goodbye, when the first shot fell, and with it Elephant and a few other animals.

"I told you all so!" shouted Jackal from the other side of the sea-cow pool. "Why did you allow yourselves to be misled by a few Crocodile tears?"

Crocodile had long ago disappeared into the water. All one could see was a lot of bubbles.

On the banks of the sea-cow pool there was war against the animals. The air crackled as the farmer shot them. But most of them, fortunately, made it out alive.

They say, Crocodile received his well-earned reward, when, shortly after, he met a driver with a load of dynamite.

Even today when Elephant runs into Crocodile, he pitches him up into the highest forks of the trees.

—*Amalouw* or *Amakosa*

70

The Shundi and the Cock

There was once a *shundi,* a spurred cockatoo, who wanted to be friends with the cock. The cock said, "Very well, friendship is not to be refused. Where do you live?" The *shundi* said, "I live in *Sekitu,* near to *Mpapayu.*" The cock said, "I live in *Mneese,* a great country." The friendship was made.

After a few days, the *shundi* sent word to the cock that he would come to see him, and named the day after tomorrow. The cock said, "Very well." He said to his wives, "My friend is coming with his wives." The *shundi* brought as visitors his three wives and four children. The names of his wives were these—the first, *Makipitu,* the second, *Makibengu,* the third, *Kiongwe.* The cock asked the *shundi* the news, and then he was given a goat as a relish, and he killed it, and they fed on it every day till they returned home.

Now, sometime after that, the cock sent word to his friend that he also should prepare for a visit, for he would be there the day after tomorrow. The *shundi* told his wives that the cock was coming, so they made the corn ready for pounding. The cock came with his wife, who was named *Makivulu;* she had no children. The cock was asked the news, and was given twenty large maggots as a relish. He ate them, and by the time he finished it was evening, so they went to sleep till morning. He stayed for a long time, and then went home.

After many days the *shundi* again sent word that he was coming to greet the cock. The cock told his wife to go and get some bananas. The woman did not know that her husband liked bananas, but she went to cut them, and she returned and peeled them all. The cock said, "Put them in the pot." His wife put them in. He said, "Have you finished?" She said, "I have finished, I have not left out one. I will put them on the fire." The cock said, "Pour water all over my body, and put me near the hearth stones. When the *shundi* comes and asks for me, tell him I am in the pot." His wife said, "All right." The cock went to the stones and lay down.

Before long the cock heard, "Hello!" His wife said, "Welcome visitors." The *shundi* arrived, alone, and squatted down on a stool by the door. When he asked, where the cock was, he was told, "He is in the pot." There between them the pot was boiling. He did not ask again; he was dumbfounded. The cock's wife went and took off the lid and, immediately, the cock came from behind the pot, shook his feathers and crowed, *"Ko, koi, koo."* The *shundi* asked, "Friend, where are you?" The wily cock said, "I came out of the pot." They ate the bananas, and in the morning the *shundi* went home.

After some days, the cock sent word that he was coming to the *shundi's*. The day he was to come, the *shundi* sent his wife *Makipitu* for bananas; he wished to do what the cock had done, and he said to his wife, "Put in the bananas." She put them in. The *shundi* said, "And put me in also." She said, "You will die." But he said, "No." So she put him in. When the cock came he saluted them all, and sat down by the door. "Where is the *shundi?*" he asked. *Makiputi* answered, "He has gone into the pot." The cock said, "What do you say?" She said, "It is true." The cock knew his companion was dead. *Makipitu* went and took the pot off the fire; they looked at him. *Shundi* was of yesterday, he was dead, all his feathers were awry. His wives wept, and then every woman returned to her father with her children. The cock went home.

Many days passed, then there appeared a leopard who said, "Mate, I want you to be my friend." The cock replied, "Very good. Friendship is not to be refused." But the cock foresaw trouble; he was afraid of the leopard on account of his size and ferocity. The leopard lived at *Lunguza*. The leopard was ready to journey with his wife *Makinyula;* they had no children. They went to visit the cock. The leopard was asked the news, and then they ate the food that had been prepared for them. After two days, they went home.

Soon after, the cock then got ready to return the visit to the leopard. When he arrived he was asked the news, and when he had finished, the cock and his wife were given very nice food. They stayed three days, and then went home. The mother leopard sent word to the cock that he was coming to see him again, and the cock said, "Very well."

The cock owned many goats, as did the leopard. The cock said to his wife, "The leopard is coming today. Now, when he comes and asks for me, say to him, 'Your friend is outside, he is waiting for his head, which went with the shepherds to feed.' " And the cock killed a goat, and he gave its head to the shepherds along with some meat. The leopard went into the village and greeted the people, and then went to the cock's house and gave greeting there. Only the wife was home to welcome him. He asked her about the cock, and was told, "The cock is outside, waiting for his head." The leopard went to look for him. Now, the cock had put his head under his wings, so that it appeared to have been cut off. Then, as the goats came home, he popped his head out again and entered into their midst. He met with the leopard, and the leopard asked the cock, "Friend, where were you?" "I was waiting outside for my head, which I had cut off and sent with the shepherds. Now it has come back." The leopard in his heart thought, "Listen to this clever one. He cuts off his head and yet does not die, for look at him alive and smiling." The leopard stayed as was proper, and finally returned home.

Again the cock sent word to the leopard that he, his friend, was coming. The day of the visit, the leopard said to his wife, "The cock is coming today. So tell the people to kill me like a sheep, and give my head to the shepherds." His wife said, "But you will die." He said, "Not so." She said, "All right." The leopard told her, "Now, when the cock comes and asks for me, say to him, 'The leopard is waiting for his head which he sent with the shepherds; he is outside the village.' " Then the people came and laid him down, and one took an axe and cut off his head at the neck, and he died immediately.

The cock came into the village and greeted the people. When he arrived at the leopard's house, he said, "Anyone in?" They replied, "We are in." When he asked, "Where is the leopard?" he was told, "He is waiting for his head outside the village; it has gone with the shepherds." The cock knew that the leopard was dead. The shepherds returned, the people went and found him dead, and they buried him. His relations completed the mourning, and the cock returned home.

All the animals said to each other, "Do not make friends with the cock, for he is exceedingly wily." That is why fowls are not liked by leopards; when leopards find them they eat them.

—Bondei

71 Spider Outwits the Rich Woman

There was a woman who lived by herself; she had no husband, only her many dogs. Their names were *Bangbi, Banga, Nguabakinde, Karawandorkiri,* and still others. She crossed a great expanse of water and made her home beyond it, right in the wilderness, with her dogs. She was very rich, she had much of everything—sesame, millet, and also dried meat in a separate granary. She went hunting with her dogs for all kinds of animals, and they caught buffalo, waterbuck, hartebeest, elephant—what big dogs, bigger than lions! She ate meat from her catch all the time.

When *Ture* the spider heard about this woman, he came to the edge of this great water and asked himself how he could get to the other side. Then he decided he would twine some cord to set a snare. He went and twined a very long length, and set his snare at the edge of this great water. Then he decided he would try it out, and he put his foot in the noose and it acted as a catapult and threw him to the other side. He said, "That's fine! I will eat all this woman's things." Then, *Ture* set another snare on the far side and he put his foot in the noose and it threw him back over again. *Ture* said, "Everything's ready." He took his big elephant-hide bag and hung it over his shoulder, he put his foot in the snare and again it lifted him and threw him to the far side, and then he stole to this woman's home. But he didn't find her there as she was out hunting with her dogs. *Ture* went and looked in her granaries and found peanuts in two granaries, sesame in three granaries, dried meat in four granaries, and grain in five granaries—every sort of food, for she was rich. *Ture* climbed up one granary and gathered up some of her dried meat and crushed it to cook on the fire. He put water for porridge on the fire, and when the meat simmered, he went out and gathered up some of her sesame to cook with it, and when the water for the porridge simmered, he mixed in flour from the grain and then quickly scraped out the porridge from the pot and put it into a bowl, and when that was done he took the meat off the fire. Then he went to sound on that woman's grindstone, which rang out like a bell, telling her to come. While *Ture* sounded on it and it spoke, the woman was far away searching for her animals. When *Ture* sounded on it she heard it and stopped. She stopped and said, "Who sounds on *Nawonggowong*'s stone?" *Ture* then played out on the stone: "I am here, I *Ture,* I sound on *Nawongowongo*'s stone. It says '*Wongo Ture, wongo Ture.*' "

As soon as she heard what *Ture* told her on the stone, she sent out her dogs, saying, "O *Bangbi,* that man who sounds on my stone, you must kill him." She ran along with them as fast as she could go; they rushed towards the entrance to the courtyard. *Ture* took the porridge as well as the meat and emptied them into his elephant-hide bag. The dogs saw *Ture* and they sprinted after him. *Ture* took the bag and ran to the catapult and it threw him back over the water, and the dogs got to the edge of this great water only in time to see *Ture* on the other side. *Ture* stood there and taunted this woman and her dogs, saying, "Look at the food I have stolen from you! What are you going to do to me?" Then *Ture* departed and this woman collected her dogs and returned her home.

Ture ate some of the porridge and took some more and went and gave it to that animal, *Digdig.* When *Digdig* ate it, it tasted so good to him that he exclaimed, "Oh friend, *Ture,* where did you find this wonderful food?" *Ture* replied, "I got it from that woman who lives on the other side of that river over there." *Digdig* asked him, "Friend, *Ture,* the next time you go to eat, you must tell me. I will even go with you tomorrow morning." *Ture* agreed to what *Digdig* said, and replied, "All right, that's just what I would like to do, so we will go together." They left early the next morning, and went on and on until they arrived at the edge of this great water. *Ture* set his snare-catapult and *Digdig* set one also. And when all was ready, they put their feet in the nooses and were thrown to the other side. They immediately set the snares again so everything would be ready for them to get back over—but, *Ture* secretly went and loosened *Digdig*'s. Then they entered the woman's home and looked for her, but she was away again. They went to her granary and grabbed dried meat and jammed it into a big pot and put it on the fire. When it was simmering they collected grain and pounded it. And when that was done, they roasted it and ground it into flour. They cooked grain flour, and they cooked meats, and all was ready. She still hadn't come back for she had gone far. *Ture* went and sounded on her stone so that it would taunt her again, thinking that when she heard it she would come. He sounded on the stone and it called out her name: "*Nawongowongo.*" She asked, "Who is sounding *Nawongowongo*'s stone-o?" *Ture* said: "I am here, I *Ture,* I sound on it. It says '*Wongo Ture, wongo Ture!*' "

She sent forth her dogs and called out to them, saying, "Look for the one who sounds on my stone." The dogs rushed ahead towards *Ture* and *Digdig,* who quickly emptied the porridge and meat into their bags and ran away. *Ture* put his foot into his noose, and it threw him to the other side. But when *Digdig* put his foot into his—oh no! It didn't throw him to the other side, because *Ture* had loosened it. The dogs started to pursue *Digdig* and chased him hotly along the riverbank, and caught him and killed him. *Ture* stood on this side to watch them, how they treated *Digdig* on the other side. *Ture* taunted them, saying, "Since you are killing *Digdig* because of the lost food, just look at your food in my hands. What can you do to kill me, for there is all that water between me and you. What will you do to catch me?"

Ture took out some porridge and ate it, and the dogs could only sit there and watch him. He stuffed himself till he could eat no more. Then he put what was left back into the bag and went and showed it to another animal, the large antelope, Red Duiker. *Ture* gave some to him, and he took it, and when he ate it, it tasted fine to him, and he asked, "Where did you get it?" *Ture* said, "If you want to come with me and get some more like this, sleep, and just as it is light, come here and we will go to the place I found it."

So, Red Duiker slept, and early in the morning he went to *Ture*'s home, and said, "Let us go." They traveled till they arrived at the edge of the water, and then they set their snares. When they were ready, they put their feet in them and were thrown to the other side. Then they prepared the new snares to get them back over. *Ture* and his companion went then to the woman's homestead, but they did not see her; she was wandering. So they collected dried meat and put it on the fire, and they cooked porridge quickly and took it off the fire, and waited for the meat to be finished. *Ture* spoke to Red Duiker thus: "I am going to the bush to shit. Stay right here and watch over things." Ture did not go to the bush, but to spoil Red Duiker's snare just as he had done before to *Digdig*'s. *Ture* returned and once more sounded his taunt on the stone. The woman asked, "Who sounds on *Nawongowongo*'s stone?" *Ture* replied on it: "I am here, I *Ture,* I sound on it. It says *'Wongo Ture, wongo Ture.'* "

Again she sent her dogs, and quickly they came on and on. When they got near, *Ture* picked up the porridge and poured it into the bag. They saw *Ture* and they began to chase him and Red Duiker. The mistress of the dogs cried out to them, saying, "You must catch *Ture* this time!" But when they got near to *Ture,* he stepped on his snare and again it threw him to the other side. But Red Duiker cried out and trod on his snare in vain, for *Ture* had loosened it. The dogs chased Red Duiker hotly along the riverbank, on and on, until they caught him. Then the woman shouted out: "*Ture,* just wait till my dogs get you!" *Ture* replied from the other side: "Can you cross this great water to catch me?" *Ture* talked to her from the other side, stuffing himself and taunting her. Then the woman killed Red Duiker and went home with him.

When he was satisfied, *Ture* took what food remained and gave it to the small antelope, the Gray Duiker. It tasted good, and the antelope asked where he had found such a nice thing. *Ture* replied, "Would you like to go with me to get some more?" He said yes. *Ture* told him: "You sleep. Then very early tomorrow, you come and we will go together." At dawn, Gray Duiker appeared before *Ture,* and said, "I have come for that journey we arranged yesterday." They traveled to the edge of the great water and prepared their snares, and when they were ready, the snares took them to the other side. They went to the woman's home, but she was out wandering with her dogs. *Ture* showed Gray Duiker around, saying, "That is the granary for sesame, that is the peanut granary, that is for grain, and that is the one for dried meat." They gathered up some grain-flour to cook it, and as they were making porridge, *Ture* said that he was going to the bush, but, of course, it was not to the bush he was going. *Ture* thought he would be able to deceive Gray Duiker with this lie, but Gray Duiker was no fool. *Ture* went to loosen Gray Duiker's snare just as he had loosened *Digdig*'s and Red Duiker's. After loosening up the snare, he set his own in order, and then he went back.

Then Gray Duiker said to *Ture* that he too had to go to the bush, and Gray Duiker came and saw that *Ture*'s snare was in good order whereas his own was completely messed up. He left his as it was, though, thinking, "No matter that *Ture* has spoilt mine, because I will use his instead." He went back to the homestead, but he said nothing.

They cooked porridge. And when it was ready, *Ture* broke off a lump and dipped it into the broth and gave it to Gray Duiker to eat. Gray Duiker said, "Who is going to carry the bag with porridge in it?" *Ture* answered, "I'll carry it, of course." Gray Duiker said, "No you won't. It is for me to carry it who am a child." *Ture* went and sounded on the woman's stone for her to come. He sounded on it and it spoke as always. The woman asked: "Who sounds on *Nawongowongo*'s stone?" *Ture* replied: "I am here, I *Ture,* I sound on it. It says '*Wongo Ture, wongo Ture.*' "

She herself heard it before her dogs heard it. *Ture* sounded again and then her dogs heard it, too, and she spoke to her dogs each by name, "*Bangbi, Banga, Karawandokiri, Nguabakinde,* you run. That man *Ture* who has been such a thorn in our sides, catch him." They ran on and on. And as they approached *Ture* they began to chase Gray Duiker, and he fled right to the place of *Ture*'s snare, and *Ture* said, "No, no, that's not yours!" But Gray Duiker would not listen. He put his foot into *Ture*'s snare and was thrown to the other side, along with the porridge. *Ture* looked around in vain for something with which to catapult himself across the water, but there seemed to be no means of escape. When *Ture* saw Gray Duiker on the other side, he was very angry.

The dogs started to chase *Ture* hotly along the riverbank. To escape, he plucked the red fruits of the *Kaffir* apple, put them over his eyes, took a harp and climbed with it into a tree, and there he made music to enthrall the dogs and their mistress. He played beautifully, looking only upwards, and singing a song:

Looker-up, I look down,
All men die, shimmering.
Looker-up, I look down,
All men die.

The woman came with her dogs. She said to *Ture,* "That's fine! Man, have you seen here that man *Ture?*" But *Ture* did not answer her. She asked him again, "Hey, Man, have you seen *Ture?*" She did not know that he was *Ture,* on account of *Ture*'s deception. She asked *Ture* once more, and he said to her, "I do not look downwards, I only look up, for if I look down everybody will die." *Ture* said to her, "Tie up your huge dogs to a tree. If you don't tie them to a tree I will look down right now and you will die." When she heard *Ture*'s words, she said "Oh, don't do that. I will tie them to a tree, just don't look down at me." So she tied her dogs to a tree, and she went away. It was those huge dogs of hers which *Ture* feared and therefore he told her to tie them to a tree. *Ture* then came down from the tree and escaped safely away.

—*Zande*

72 Softly, Over the Head of the Great

Leopard and Cat were friends. Leopard gave birth to one child, and Cat to three. When Leopard saw that Cat had so many children, they were no longer on good terms.

Cat's three children were in the habit of going for firewood. They also brought her water, went to market, and hunted food for her. Cat herself stayed home and did nothing.

Leopard's child was still young. She could do very little for her mother. Leopard went to see Cat. She said, "Now I get up at cockcrow and I go for wood, for water. I work all the time. Lend me one of your children to watch over my daughter, so that I have more time to get food." Cat promised to send her one.

Then Cat called her three children together, and said, "Which of you can go to watch over Leopard's child, without being caught?" The mother asked her eldest son, "How many times must you be annoyed before you are on your guard?" The boy said, "Three times." She called the second and asked him the same thing. The second said, "Four times." She called the youngest, and she asked, "My child, how many times must you be annoyed before you are on your guard?" The child answered, "I am not sure, but I think if I am annoyed once, I will be on my guard."

When Little Cat said that, Cat said, "Good. You will go to watch over Leopard's daughter."

Little Cat came to Leopard. As they ate that night, Leopard said to him, "Now you are to sleep on the mat over there."

When she said that, Little Cat went to sleep high up in the rafters. He left his cloth, however, on the mat just as though he were lying down there. But he went to sleep up high.

Towards midnight, after they had gone to sleep, Leopard got up and seized the cloth on the mat. Little Cat said, "Mother, what is the trouble?" Leopard said, "Oh, nothing. I was dreaming." They went back to sleep.

The next day Leopard said, "Tonight you are to sleep on that stone there." That was the stone on which they crushed millet and ground nuts. Little Cat lay down beside the stone, but placed his cloth on the stone, just as though he were there himself.

During the night, Leopard threw herself on the stone, thinking that the cloth was Little Cat. Little Cat said, "What is the trouble, mother?" Leopard said, "I was dreaming again. Where are you sleeping?"

The following night Leopard said, "Now you are to sleep in my bed, because I am going to be away from home all night, and I will come back late tomorrow. You are to sleep with my child in my bed."

Before going out, Leopard gave one cloth to Little Cat, and one to her daughter. Then she went out, and hid near the house. When Little Cat went to sleep he exchanged his cloth for the cloth of Leopard's daughter, and he also changed places with Leopard's daughter.

At night, when Leopard came back softly, softly, she saw Little Cat's cloth and thought it was he sleeping on the outside, as she had told him. She threw herself at her daughter and devoured her.

Little Cat said nothing. He had hidden himself above, and watched Leopard. When she finished eating her daughter, Little Cat said, "Why did you eat your daughter? Me, I'm going home to my mother. You told me to come and watch your child. Now that you have eaten your child, I have nothing more to do in your house. I am going home."

When he came home, Cat took her children up into the Loko tree, and they took refuge there from Leopard's anger. They brought with them a cord that reached from the ground to the top of the tree, and with it the mother cat could go up and down whenever she wanted.

One day Cat left her family and went out. That day Leopard came. Now, whenever Cat went away, she left a gong near the tree, and when she came home, she tapped on it seven times, and the children knew it was their mother, and let down the cord. When Leopard came, she also tapped the gong, but she tapped it eight times, and Cat's children were not fooled.

That night Leopard hid behind a tree and waited for Cat to come home, so as to learn how many times to beat the gong. She heard the mother cat give seven strokes, and because Leopard could not count, she clawed marks on a tree, so that she would know the right number.

The next morning, Cat again went away to find food. Leopard waited a good while after she was gone, and then took up the gong and struck it seven times. The children threw down the cord, and she climbed up. She said, "I see your mother is not home. I came to visit you, what will you give me?"

Little Cat had cooked food for the children, and he gave it all to Leopard. After she ate, they asked Leopard, "Are you going?" She said, "No, I will stay a while." Little Cat said to the others, "To make her leave, do you know what we'll do?" The eldest answered, "Yes! We'll get sticks and beat her." The second said, "Yes! We'll insult her." But Little Cat said, "No."

Now on this tree there was a dead branch. If one stepped on it, one got down in a hurry. The little one said they would give her a mat to rest on. "We will lay the mat there, near the dead branch, and then we will heat some water."

The children put down the mat for Leopard and then they put some water on to heat. Now, they had Leopard in a good place! Now, they could throw boiling water on her head, and if she tried to hold on, she would have to reach the dead branch. Little Cat said, "All softly, over the head of the great," and he threw the boiling water over her. Leopard grabbed the branch, the branch broke, and she fell to the ground on her left side.

Before this, when Leopard saw you, she would turn sideways. Now, since she hurt her side, she must meet her enemy face to face.

—Dahomey

73

Treachery Repaid

Hare used to get on well with Jackal and they were firm friends. One day, when they were sitting around, Hare said to Jackal, "Let's kill our mothers," and Jackal agreed.

Jackal thereupon got hold of his mother and killed her, but crafty Hare had never intended to kill *his* mother. Jackal then began to suffer cruelly from hunger, while Hare went to his burrow and said, as follows:

Mother open the door-o,
I am not like that Jackal-o,
Who killed his mother-o,
He of the long tail-o!

When he had finished singing, his mother opened the door, and Hare had his food. When he had finished eating, he went to join Jackal. Jackal, meanwhile, had really shriveled up with starvation. One day, he followed Hare and heard him sing his song outside the door of the burrow:

Mother open the door-o,
I am not like that Jackal-o,
Who killed his mother-o,
He of the long tail-o!

He saw Hare's mother open the door. Hare went in and found his mother had cooked food. He ate, went out, and told his mother, "Make the door fast." Jackal saw all this and said to himself, "Well, now I know."

A day or two later, Jackal went up to the burrow and sang Hare's song:

Mother open the door-o,
I am not like that Jackal-o,
Who killed his mother-o,
He of the long tail-o!

Hare's mother opened the door and Jackal went in and ate the food. Then he took Hare's mother, killed her, and left, leaving the door shut behind him.

Soon, Hare came along and sang in the same way as always. When no sound came from inside he sang again, but all was silent. Then he opened the door and saw his mother lying there with bared teeth, and he said, "Hey mother, what are you laughing at?" When there was no response, he took hold of her and saw she was dead. "Who has done this?" he asked himself. "It must be Jackal. We'll see about that."

He went out and found Jackal eating some fruit. Hare said to him, "What have you done?" Jackal replied, "You told me, 'Let's kill our mothers,' and though I did so, you refused. You tricked me, and now you see what's happened."

From that time, friendship of Hare and Jackal came to an end.

—*Fipa*

74
The Great Dikithi

Once, in the old days, *Nthoo* the Leopard invited *Mbwawa* the Silver Fox into the forest with him to eat wild berries. When they were in the forest, *Nthoo* climbed up the *Thaa* tree. While *Nthoo* was in the tree, *Mbwawa* took *Nthoo*'s ladder and threw it on the ground. Then he went home and left *Nthoo* in the tree.

Now, while *Mbwawa* was home, he married *Nthoo*'s wife. *Nthoo,* who could not get down from the tree, made a little red bird called *Kavuramakhithi* from its fruits. He sent *Kavuramakhithi* to tell his wife that *Mbwawa* had left him there up in the *Thaa* tree. When *Kavuramakhithi* reached *Nthoo*'s home and told *Nthoo*'s wife what had happened to her husband, she did not answer him. *Kavuramakhithi* returned to *Nthoo* and told him this.

Nthoo again sent *Kavuramakhithi* the red bird to his wife. When it reached *Nthoo*'s home, he again gave the message, saying that *Nthoo* was up in the *Thaa* tree and could not get down. One of the small children of *Nthoo* heard this, and ran to his mother, and said: "Mother, listen to the bird in the tree."

Nthoo's wife now sent the children into the forest with the little red bird. He flew in front, and they followed him until they reached the tree where their father was sitting. When *Nthoo* saw his children, he was very pleased, and told them to take the ladder and put it up against the tree. When the children had done it, their father came down. He said, "Let's go home, children."

Now, when they reached their home, *Mbwawa* the silver fox ran away. *Nthoo* said, "One day I will catch *Mbwawa.* He thinks he is very clever, but I will kill him and give his meat to the vultures."

After a while, an old man called the Great *Dikithi,* who had only one eye, came along with his wife. He asked if *Nthoo* would like to take his wife and children and go with *Dikithi* across the river to live, because there were many cattle there. *Nthoo* agreed to go.

When they reached this new place one-eyed *Dikithi* left all the people in the new village and went to steal cattle. He brought the stolen cattle to the river and shouted to his wife, "Take the guinea fowl and beat the water with it, so that the cattle will cross the river." She did as *Dikithi* said, and all the cattle crossed the river to the new village, where they were slaughtered for a great feast.

The cattle were cooked all night long. In the night, old *Dikithi* awakened and ate all the meat from the pots and left only water. When the people awoke in the morning, they found that all the pots were empty.

In the afternoon, old one-eyed *Dikithi,* who also had only one leg and only one arm, went back to the place where he had stolen the cattle, and there he stole some more. He said to his wife, "Beat the water with the guinea fowl again, and I will give you ten cattle because you are so clever." Then old *Dikithi* started singing:

> Maenga Nyambi, *beat the water with the guinea fowl.*
> *The ten cattle are yours.*

Dikithi's wife beat the water with the guinea fowl and the cattle crossed the river. Now all these were killed for another feast. When they had been cooked, *Kadimba* the Hare said to himself, "*Dikithi* ate all the meat last night."

Kadimba said to himself, "I will take two small fireflies from the river and put them on my skin trousers tonight, set them on my clothes, so that *Dikithi* will see them when he comes to steal the meat from the pots, and will think that we see him."

That night when *Dikithi,* who was also a great giant and a cannibal, came to steal the meat, he saw two eyes looking at him. He became very angry with *Kadimba* and said, "Why don't you sleep in the night? *Thimba* the Genet, *Thinona* the Gray Wildcat, *Kangambe* the Polecat, *Dimbungu* the Hyena, and *Nthoo* are all asleep."

Dikithi came back a second time to steal the meat fro1 1 the pots, but he saw the same bright eyes looking at him. He was very angry at *Kadimba* and said, "Your balls!" Then *Dikithi* went back to his house.

Early in the morning, *Dikithi*'s sons cleaned up the big wooden basins to put in the meat from the pots. *Nthoo* called one of them to go and tell *Dikithi* to come and serve up some meat. *Dikithi* said, "I don't want to eat any meat that has been cooked for a long time." Then the boys ate the meat from the pots.

Dikithi took his hoe and went to the elephant's path and dug a big hole. After the hole was finished, he covered it with grass so the elephants couldn't see it. Then he took off his skin trousers, threw them up in a tree, and started singing over and over again, "Please elephants, take my trousers down from the tree." When the elephants came he said to them again,

Please elephants, take my trousers down from the tree.

But when the elephants tried to do it, they fell into the hole. Then *Dikithi* took his spear and killed them.

After that, *Dikithi* went to his children and told them to help him bring the elephants home. He said to them, "I am not going to give you any of the meat because you ate all my meat this morning."

When the boys had brought all the meat home, *Dikithi* sent *Thinona* and *Thimba* to go and call his mother-in-law to come and help him eat the elephants.

When *Dikithi*'s mother-in-law arrived, he told his children that they were all going back to the village where they used to live. The children started cutting wood for carrying the meat of the elephants. *Dikithi,* too, cut a long pole so he could help carry the meat. He put some of the meat on one end of the pole and some of the meat on the other end. He then started singing:

I want to try my load before I carry it.

After *Dikithi* sang his song, they began the journey. When they reached their old home, they started cooking the meat. In the evening, *Kadimba* went to the river and found some fireflies. During the night, he put two of them on his belt. When *Dikithi* awakened and came to the pots, he saw the eyes looking at him. He became very angry with *Kadimba* and cursed him. Then he went home to sleep.

In the morning, *Nthoo* sent a boy to ask *Dikithi* to give them some meat. *Dikithi* refused and said, "I will not give you any meat; and I will not eat meat that has been cooked for a long time."

That night *Dikithi* told his wife, *Thinona, Thimba,* and *Kadimba* to take all his things and leave *Nthoo*'s village. He said, "*Nthoo* is no good."

Dikithi's wife said, "I want to take my mother with us." *Dikithi* said, "No, you may not bring your mother with us." Then they left the old woman and went away. But when they made camp for the night, they saw an old woman, the mother-in-law of *Dikithi*. She was singing this song:

You took my daughter away. I will follow you.

Early in the morning, *Dikithi* killed the old woman and covered her with a pot. Then they continued their journey. On the way, the rain came, so they waited under a tree for it to stop. After the rain stopped, they continued on their journey. Then further along, they found a dead eland. When *Thimba, Kadimba,* and *Kangambe* saw it they began to complain because one pot had been left behind. They said to their chief, "Please let us return and get the pot," and *Dikithi* let them go.

When they reached the pot, *Kadimba* touched it. The pot said, "Who is touching me?" *Kadimba* said, "It is I, *Kadimba*." Then the old woman who had been left behind, said, "All right, you may take the pot because I will go with you to see my daughter." But *Kadimba* and the other boys ran off with the empty pot, and left the old woman behind.

The old woman came near to the camp of *Dikithi*, singing this song:

You took my daughter. I will follow you.

When *Dikithi* saw the old woman coming, he took some fire and burned the grass so that she could not cross to the camp. The old woman took off her leather skirt and started beating the fire. She sang this song:

I will quench this fire and come through to you.

The old woman could not put out the fire so she got into an ant-bear hole until the fire passed over her and away. At midnight she came out of the hole, and followed them again. When she reached the others she said to *Dikithi*, "I am going to kill you and cut off your balls because you lost me twice on the road."

When *Dikithi* saw that the old woman was still following him, he took his wife and ran away and climbed up a *Kakoma* tree. The old woman pursued them until she reached the tree.

She said to *Dikithi,* "I am going to cut off your balls." Then she started to cut down the *Kakoma* tree with her axe. She sang this song:

I am cutting down the tree.

Dikithi called locusts to come and bite his old mother-in-law. The locusts came and bit the old woman. She took off her skirt and started to beat the locusts with it. She sang:

I am fighting with locusts.

Then the locusts went away.

Dikithi now called *Nyemay* the Lion. When *Nyemay* came the old woman started singing:

I am fighting with Lion.

The old woman then got into a hole in a big tree and *Nyemay* went away. After *Nyemay* had gone, she got out of the hole in the tree, and shouted to *Dikithi,* "I am going to cut off your balls!"

Dikithi now called *Thitengo* the Bird. *Thitengo* built a fire around the old woman, whose name was *Kakaurukathi,* the Old Woman Giant, and burned her to death.

When *Dikithi* saw that she was burned to death, he and his wife got down from the *Kakoma* tree. He took the foreleg of old *Kakurukathi* and made a whistle of it. He then took the whistle up in the *Kakoma* tree and started whistling with it, and singing:

I am whistling with the foreleg of old Kakurukathi.

Then came the very old *Dikithi,* the father of the Great *Dikithi.* The very old *Dikithi,* who was a mighty head chief, said to the young *Dikithi,* "Throw that whistle to me!" The Great *Dikithi* said, "No, I will not; for the whistle is mine."

The Great *Dikithi* took out a long rope and said to Old *Dikithi,* "If you want to come and whistle up in the *Kakoma* tree, you must let me tie your neck with this rope and I will pull you up."

Old *Dikithi* agreed to the Great *Dikithi*'s plan. Old *Dikithi* put the rope around his own neck, and then his son began to pull him up into the tree, but Old *Dikithi* started crying, "You are hurting me, let me down!" After the Great *Dikithi* had loosened the rope from his old father's neck, he began to whistle again. When his father heard him he said, "Throw that whistle to me!" The Great *Dikithi* said, "I will not throw the whistle to you. If you wish to whistle, you must come up into the tree."

Once again, the Great *Dikithi* tied the rope around the neck of his old father and began to pull him up. When the old man was almost to the top of the tree, the Great *Dikithi* cut the rope. Old *Dikithi* fell down, broke his neck, and died.

The Great *Dikithi* and his wife got down from the *Kakoma* tree. He said to his wife, "I know the stomach of this old man is full of cattle, goats, and everything." *Dikithi* called *Dikwii* the Vulture to come and open the stomach, but *Dikwii* broke his beak trying. Then *Dikithi* called *Mombo* the Heron to open the stomach of the old man. *Mombo* tried hard but he, also, broke his beak. Then, *Dikithi* asked another bird called *Dipongo,* but he, too, broke his beak on the tough stomach of Old *Dikithi*. After *Dipongo, Ngonga* the Eagle tried, but he did not fare any better than the others.

Finally *Dikithi* called *Kavuramakhithi,* the small red bird. *Kavuramakhithi* told *Dikithi* to cook some mealy bugs for him. After he ate the cooked mealies he got inside the mouth of Old *Dikithi* and went straight through him until he came out of his anus. Then the stomach of the old father of *Dikithi* opened up and all the animals, many people, cattle, elephants, and goats walked out.

Dikithi then called these animals and people together and told them they could all live in his village.

—*Bantu*

75

The Work Done by Itself

The hyena had a little one, and it died: the bush cat also had a little one, and it died, too. The bush cat took a dislike to its country, and so did the hyena. Therefore, each went to seek for a better place.

When it arrived at a spot it liked, the hyena said, "This will do.

Tomorrow, at daybreak, I will come and pull up the grass." The bush cat chanced upon the same place and it pleased him too. He tore up the grass and went away to sleep.

Next morning the hyena returned. "Oh!" he cried, "what a good place! I was going to pull up the grass, and the grass has already pulled itself up." He took possession, swept the ground, and went away. The bush cat came back in his turn. "Oh!" he said, "what a good country! I was going to sweep, and the ground has swept itself." He cut down some trees to use as house poles, left them on the ground, and went away.

The hyena returned, fixed the poles in the ground, and went away to sleep. Then the bush cat came. "The poles," he said, "have planted themselves," and he cut some bamboos and put them on the ground. The hyena came and fastened the bamboos to the poles. Then the bush cat took the grass and thatched the house. "How is this?" said the hyena when he came again. "The roof is made."

He divided the house into two parts, keeping one room for himself and leaving the other for his wife. Then the bush cat returned. "Good!" he said. "The house has divided itself into two. This part I shall keep for myself, and that I shall give to my wife. In five days I will bring my property here, and settle down." The hyena, too, arranged to move in at that time.

When the fifth day arrived, the bush cat took his property and came with his wife. The hyena did the same. The hyena went into one room, and the bush cat into the other. Each believed that there was nobody else in the house. Then, at the same moment, each one broke something, and each one said, "Who is breaking something in the next room?" And each one ran away.

They ran as far as from *Keta* to *Amutino,* and then they met. "What are you doing, oh, Hyena?" asked the bush cat. "I had built a house," said the hyena, "and something drove me out. I don't know what." "The same thing happened to me," said the bush cat. "I cut down trees, and the poles planted themselves." The hyena said, "I found a place that I liked, and I was going to pull up the grass, but when I went to do it, the grass had pulled itself up!"

Then the bush cat and the hyena began running again. They have never been able to look at each other since.

—*Ewe*

76

Two Friends from Their Childhood

There were two men who from their childhood had been fast friends, and never were known to have quarreled with one another. So great was their friendship that they had built their homes close together. They were divided one from the other only by a native path.

Now there was a wicked wit in their town, who had determined, if possible, to make the friends quarrel. This man made a coat, one side or half of which was red in color, while the other was blue. And he walked past these two as they were busy on their farms, making enough noise to attract their attention. Each of the friends looked up to see who was going past, and then went on with his work.

"Ugh, say! Did you see that man?" said one.

"Yes," answered the other.

"Did you notice the bright coat he wore?"

"Yes."

"What color would you say it was?"

"Why, blue, of course."

"Blue, man! Why, it was a kind of red!"

"No, friend, I am sure it was blue."

"Nonsense! I know it was red, but—"

"Well! you are a fool!"

"A fool. How now, we have been friends all our lives, and yet you call me a fool! We must settle this thing at once. Our friendship is at an end."

And the friends began to fight it out. But their women screamed and interfered, and managed to separate them.

Then the wit walked quietly back, and saw the two friends seated, each on his own farm, with his elbows resting on his knees, and his head between his hands, and his eyes staring at the path. Then they saw the joke that had been played on them, and they were sorry. They ordered the wit never to come that way again, but the women cursed him and hoped that he would die.

—*Fjort*

77

Talking Drums Discovered

One story is coming!

The guinea fowl's best friend was the hawk. The hawk's name was *Setu* or Laughter, the fowl was called *Nmengu* (at that time, all animals were known by names like ours). But something came between these two. The hawk went to make talking drums for them so they could dance the *dogho,* and the fowl agreed to help. They got to the bush and cut down a big oak tree. They made the talking drums and they put them in the sun. The fowl asked the hawk to take care of them. But the hawk was hungry and wanted to go away, the distance from here to *Danko,* to go and eat and return. He told the fowl, "When the drums are dried, don't beat them until I have returned. If you beat the drums before I return, there will be trouble between us." The fowl said, "All right!" The hawk went to *Danko* and found food to eat. The talking drums dried. The fowl went to inspect them and see whether they were dry. He stroked the talking drums. He beat them "*gben-gben-gben.*" He liked the sound. Then the fowl really beat them hard and the sound was very nice:

Setu, Setu, Setu, Setu,
Setu yee Setu
Setu yee Setu
Setu yee Setu
Dzaan, dzaan, dzaan
Dzaan, dzaan, dzaan

The hawk was in *Danko,* but he heard the sound of the drums. He was annoyed and flew up very high to return. The fowl kept playing, not knowing that the more he beat the angrier the hawk grew. He beat again, and sang three times:

Setu, Setu, Setu, Setu,
Setu yee Setu
Setu yee Setu
Setu yee Setu
Dzaan, dzaan, dzaan
Dzaan, dzaan, dzaan

The hawk flew very fast past the fowl. The fowl thought that the hawk was happy, so he beat the drums again:

Setu, Setu, Setu, Setu,
Setu yee Setu
Setu yee Setu
Setu yee Setu
Dzaan, dzaan, dzaan
Dzaan, dzaan, dzaan

The hawk swooped down again to cut the fowl's head off. As the hawk was coming, the fowl began to run, *pi, pi, pi*. This is how the friendship between the hawk and the fowl was spoiled, and they are enemies to this day. Neither the fowl nor the hawk took the talking drums. But the people of the village took them and used them in dancing *dogho*.

My story is finished.

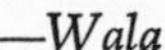
—*Wala*

Part IV
Tales in Praise of Great Doings

Introduction

There are a great many stories in Black Africa concerned with the origins of the people—not just creation stories and other mythical narratives of the way things were "in the beginning," but stories concerned with historical progenitors and their heroic accomplishments. To be sure, as we see in a great many of the tales in this section, these deeds involve such supernatural powers and abilities that even allegedly historical narrative reads like myth.

In the first story in this section, "Gassire's Lute," we see the hero of the title operating in response to the goddess Wagadu's loss. The almost epic-like telling of his great doings gives us what is virtually an allegorical discussion of morality and human frailty, combined with a dazzling recounting of Gassire's abilities to fight, endure, use his wits, and play and sing.

This ability to perform as well as fight is characteristic of most heroes in African stories. Not only do we see Gassire achieving identity as a bard, but it is often through song and dance that the heroes Mandu and, especially, Mwindo, are linked with powerful supernatural forces.

In all of these stories, the hero lives as the leader of men—indeed of his people. Again and again, his doings are associated with the genesis and flourishing of his people—and his feats are set against those of other great heroes and the welfare of their peoples. The deeds are the songs and the songs are the deeds in the purest sense. For as in other epic traditions, the heroes would not be known had their exploits not been sung. In African tales, the audience is reminded of this through actual singing of the deeds when a character—often the hero himself—retells the hero's story. Indeed, in the great Mwindo Epic, this is done twice: once when Mwindo recounts his deeds on returning to his aunt Iyangura's house from his journey to the underworld; and again, when he returns to his village with his father-enemy and asks for judgment from the assembly.

The major portion of this chapter is given over to *The Mwindo Epic,* as collected by Daniel Biebuyck and Kahombo C. Mateene from the Banyanga—the people of Nyanga—and appears as it was sung among them by the bard Shé-Kárisi Rureki in the early 1950s. I have attempted to maintain the sense of an imposing performance and an elevated, often ceremonial diction, while making the narrative somewhat easier to follow.

I have given the story in toto, with all the songs in place, as a way of underscoring the performance character of African narrations. But more than this, I wish to introduce the reader to one of the great bardic traditions of the world. Here is a text that demonstrates that the epic form is very much alive, and that the deeds of great warriors and culture heroes continue to be sung. Throughout Africa, one still finds bards who are engaged to sing one person's praises, to castigate another, or as in *Mwindo*, to chant the greatest stories of the people.

The reader will notice that many of the episodes are reminiscent of the Mediterranean epic traditions. The hero is cast off by his father, Shemwindo, who attempts to have him killed as an infant. But Mwindo is born, full-strength and more, and he is able to outwit his father. In a series of adventures, he confronts his father's allies and defeats them one by one. Shemwindo retreats to the underworld, and Mwindo pursues him there. They confront each other, and it is Mwindo's magic that prevails in the epic battle. They return to earth and, in the midst of a great ceremony and celebration, Mwindo is given the kingship by his father.

In the process, several other devices reminiscent of Homeric technique appear. For example, laudatory epithets are common, especially that used of Mwindo: "Little-One-Just-Born-He-Has-Walked." And in the recounting of deeds that are embedded in the ceremony, we are given a number of epic catalogues.[1]

[1] These are detailed in Biebuyck-Mateene (see Bibliography of References), and even more in Biebuyck's later book, *Hero and Chief* (Berkeley and Los Angeles: University of California Press, 1978), where he provides other texts of *The Mwindo Epic*, as well.

78

Gassire's Lute

Four times *Wagadu* stood there in all her splendor. Four times *Wagadu* disappeared and was lost to human sight: once through vanity, once through falsehood, once through greed, and once through dissension. Four times *Wagadu* changed her name. First she was called *Dierra,* then *Agada,* then *Ganna,* then *Silla.* Four times she turned her face. Once to the north, once to the west, once to the east, and once to the south. For *Wagadu,* whenever men have seen her, has always had four gates: one to the north, one to the west, one to the east, and one to the south. Those are the directions whence the strength of *Wagadu* comes, the strength in which she endures no matter whether she be built of stone, wood, or earth, or lives but as a shadow in the mind and longing of her children. For, really, *Wagadu* is the strength that lives in the hearts of men and is sometimes visible because eyes see her and ears hear the clash of swords and ring of shields, and is sometimes invisible because the indomitability of men has overtired her, so that she sleeps. Sleep came to *Wagadu* for the first time through vanity, for the second time through falsehood, for the third time through greed, and for the fourth time through dissension. Should *Wagadu* ever be found for the fifth time, then she will live so forcefully in the minds of men that she will never be lost again, so forcefully that vanity, falsehood, greed, and dissension will never be able to harm her.

Hoooh! Dierra, Agada, Ganna, Silla! Hoooh! Fasa!

Every time that the guilt of man caused *Wagadu* to disappear she won a new beauty which made the splendor of her next appearance still more glorious. Vanity brought the song of the bards that all peoples [of the Sudan] imitate and value today. Falsehood brought a rain of gold and pearls. Greed brought writing as the *Burdama* still practice it today, and which in *Wagadu* was the business of the women. Dissension will enable the fifth *Wagadu* to be as enduring as the rain of the south and as the rocks of the Sahara, for every man will then have *Wagadu* in his heart and every woman a *Wagadu* in her womb.

Hoooh! Dierra, Agada, Ganna, Silla! Hoooh! Fasa!

Wagadu was lost for the first time through vanity. At that time *Wagadu* faced north and was called *Dierra.* Her last king was called *Nganamba Fasa.* The *Fasa* were strong. But the *Fasa* were growing old. Daily they fought against the *Burdama* and the *Boroma.* They fought every day and every month. Never was there an end to the fighting. And out of the fighting the strength of the *Fasa* grew. All *Nganamba*'s men were hereos, all the women were lovely and proud of the strength and the heroism of the men of *Wagadu*.

All the *Fasa* who had not fallen in single combat with the *Burdama* were growing old. *Nganamba* was very old. *Nganamba* had a son, *Gassire,* and he was old enough, for he already had eight grown sons with children of their own. They were all living and *Nganamba* ruled in his family and reigned as a king over the *Fasa* and the dog-like *Boroma. Nganamba* grew so old that *Wagadu* was lost because of him and the *Boroma* became slaves again to the *Burdama,* who seized power with the sword. Had *Nganamba* died earlier would *Wagadu* then have disappeared for the first time?

Hoooh! Dierra, Agada, Ganna, Silla! Hoooh! Fasa!

Nganamba did not die. A jackal gnawed at *Gassire*'s heart. Daily *Gassire* asked his heart: "When will *Nganamba* die? When will *Gassire* be king?" Every day *Gassire* watched for the death of his father as a lover watches for the evening star to rise. By day, when *Gassire* fought as a hero against the *Burdama* and drove the false *Boroma* before him with a leather girth, he thought only of the fighting, of his sword, of his shield, of his horse. By night, when he rode with the evening into the city and sat in the circle of men and his sons, *Gassire* heard how the heroes praised his deeds. But his heart was not in the talking; his heart listened for the strains of *Nganamba*'s breathing; his heart full of misery and longing.

Gassire's heart was full of longing for the shield of his father, the shield that he could carry only when his father was dead, and also for the sword that he might draw only when he was king. Day by day *Gassire*'s rage and longing grew. Sleep passed him by. *Gassire* lay, and a jackal gnawed at his heart. *Gassire* felt the misery climbing into his throat. One night *Gassire* sprang out of bed, left the house, and went to an old wise man, a man who knew more than other people. He entered the wise man's house and said: "Ah, *Gassire, Nganamba* will die; but he will not leave you his sword and shield. You will carry a lute. Shield and sword shall others inherit. But your lute shall cause the loss of *Wagadu!* Ah, *Gassire!*" *Gassire* said: "*Kiekorro,* you lie! I see that you are not wise. How can *Wagadu* be lost when her heroes triumph daily? *Kiekorro,* you are a fool!" The old wise man said, "Ah, *Gassire,* you cannot believe me. But your path will lead you to the partridges in the fields, and you will understand what they say, and that will be your way and the way of *Wagadu*."

Hoooh! Dierra, Agada, Ganna, Silla! Hoooh! Fasa!

The next morning *Gassire* went with the heroes again to battle against the *Burdama. Gassire* was angry. *Gassire* called to the heroes: "Stay here behind. Today I will battle with the *Burdama* alone." The heroes stayed behind and *Gassire* went on alone to do battle with the

Burdama. Gassire hurled his spear. *Gassire* charged the *Burdama. Gassire* swung his sword. He struck home to the right, he struck home to the left. *Gassire*'s sword was as a sickle in the wheat. The *Burdama* were afraid. Shocked, they cried: "That is no *Fasa,* that is no hero, that is a Damo" [a being unknown to the singer himself]. The *Burdama* turned their horses. The *Burdama* threw away their spears, each man his two spears, and fled. *Gassire* called the knights. *Gassire* said: "Gather the spears." The knights gathered the spears. The knights sang: "The *Fasa* are heroes. *Gassire* has always been the *Fasa*'s greatest hero. *Gassire* has always done great deeds. But today *Gassire* was greater than *Gassire!*" *Gassire* rode into the city and the heroes rode behind him. The heroes sang: "Never before has *Wagadu* won so many spears as today."

Gassire let the women bathe him. The men gathered. But *Gassire* did not seat himself in their circle. *Gassire* went into the fields. *Gassire* heard the partridges. *Gassire* went close to them. A partridge sat under a bush and sang: "Hear the *Dausi!* Hear my deeds!" The partridge sang of its battle with the snake. The partridge sang: "All creatures must die, be buried and rot. Kings and heroes die, are buried and rot. I, too, shall die, shall be buried and rot. But the *Dausi,* the song of my battles, shall not die. It shall be sung again and again and shall outlive all kings and heroes. *Hoooh,* that I might do such deeds! *Hoooh,* that I may sing the *Dausi! Wagadu* will be lost. But the *Dausi* shall endure and shall live!"

Hoooh! Dierra, Agada, Ganna, Silla! Hoooh! Fasa!

Gassire went to the old wise man. *Gassire* said: "*Kiekorro!* I was in the fields. I understood the partridges. The partridge boasted that the song of its deeds would live longer than *Wagadu.* The partridge sang the *Dausi.* Tell me whether men also know the *Dausi* and whether the *Dausi* can outlive life and death?" The old wise man said: "*Gassire,* you are hastening to your end. No one can stop you. And since you cannot be a king you shall be a bard. Ah! *Gassire.* When the kings of the *Fasa* lived by the sea they were also great heroes and they fought with men who had lutes and sang the *Dausi.* Oft struck the enemy *Dausi* fear into the hearts of the *Fasa,* who were themselves heroes. But they never sang the *Dausi* because they were of the first rank, of the *Horro,* and because *Dausi* was only sung by those of the second rank, of the *Diare.* The *Diare* fought not so much as heroes, for the sport of the day, but as drinkers for the fame of the evening. But you, *Gassire,* now that you can no longer be the second of the first [i.e., king], shall be lost because of it." *Gassire* said: "*Wagadu* can go to hell!"

Hoooh! Dierra, Agada, Ganna, Silla! Hoooh! Fasa!

Gassire went to a smith. *Gassire* said: "Make me a lute." The smith said: "I will, but the lute will not sing." *Gassire* said: "Smith, do your work. The rest is my affair." The smith made the lute. The smith brought the lute to *Gassire. Gassire* struck the lute. The lute did not sing. *Gassire* said: "Look here, the lute does not sing." The smith said: "I told you it would not." *Gassire* said: "Well, make it sing." The smith said: "I cannot do anything more about it. The rest is your affair." *Gassire* said: "What can I do, then?" The smith said: "This is a piece of wood. It cannot sing if it has no heart. You must give it a heart. Carry this piece of wood on your back when you go into battle. The wood must ring with the stroke of your sword. The wood must absorb down-dripping blood, blood of your blood, breath of your breath. Your pain must be its pain, your fame its fame. The wood may no longer be like the wood of a tree, but must be penetrated by and be a part of your people. Therefore it must live not only with you but with your sons. Then will the tone that comes from your heart echo in the ear of your son and live on in the people, and your son's life's blood, oozing out of his heart, will run down your body and live on in this piece of wood. But *Wagadu* will be lost because of it." *Gassire* said: "*Wagadu* can go to hell!"

Hoooh! Dierra, Agada, Ganna, Silla! Hoooh! Fasa!

Gassire called his eight sons. *Gassire* said: "My sons, today we go to battle. But the strokes of our swords shall echo no longer in the *Sahel* alone, but shall retain their ring for the ages. You and I, my sons, will that we live on and endure before all other heroes in the *Dausi*. My eldest son, today we two, thou and I, will be the first in battle!"

Gassire and his eldest son went into the battle ahead of the heroes. *Gassire* had thrown the lute over his shoulder. The *Burdama* came closer. *Gassire* and his eldest son charged. *Gassire* and his eldest son fought as the first. *Gassire* and his eldest son left the other heroes far behind them. *Gassire* fought not like a human being, but rather like a *Damo*. His eldest son fought not like a human being, but like a *Damo*. *Gassire* came into a tussle with eight *Burdama*. The eight *Burdama* pressed him hard. His son came to help him and struck four of them down. But one of the *Burdama* thrust a spear through his heart. *Gassire*'s eldest son fell dead from his horse. *Gassire* was angry, and shouted. The *Burdama* fled. *Gassire* dismounted and took the body of his eldest son upon his back. Then he mounted and rode slowly back to the other heroes. The eldest son's heart's blood dropped on the lute, which was also hanging on *Gassire*'s back. And so *Gassire*, at the head of his heroes, rode into *Dierra*.

Hoooh! Dierra, Agada, Ganna, Silla! Hoooh! Fasa!

Gassire's eldest son was buried. *Dierra* mourned. The urn in which the body crouched was red with blood. That night *Gassire* took his lute and struck against the wood. The lute did not sing. *Gassire* was angry. He called his sons. *Gassire* said to his sons: "Tomorrow we ride against the *Burdama*."

For seven days *Gassire* rode with the heroes to battle. Every day one of his sons accompanied him to be the first in the fighting. And on every one of these days *Gassire* carried the body of one of his sons, over his shoulder and over the lute, back into the city. And thus, on every evening, the blood of one of his sons dripped on to the lute. After the seven days of fighting there was a great mourning in *Dierra*. All the heroes and all the women wore red and white clothes. The blood of the *Boroma* [apparently in sacrifice] flowed everywhere. All the women wailed. All the men were angry. Before the eighth day of the fighting all the heroes and the men of *Dierra* gathered and spoke to *Gassire:* "*Gassire,* this shall have an end. We are willing to fight when it is necessary. But you, in your rage, go on fighting without sense or limit. Now go forth from *Dierra!* A few will join you and accompany you. Take your *Boroma* and your cattle. The rest of us incline more to life than fame. And while we do not wish to die fameless we have no wish to die for fame alone."

The old wise man said: "Ah, *Gassire!* Thus will *Wagadu* be lost today for the first time."

Hoooh! Dierra, Agada, Ganna, Silla! Hoooh! Fasa!

Gassire and his last, his youngest, son, his wives, his friends, and his *Boroma* rode out into the desert. They rode through the *Sahel*. Many heroes rode with *Gassire* through the gates of the city. Many turned. A few accompanied *Gassire* and his youngest son into the Sahara.

They rode far: day and night. They came into the wilderness and in the loneliness they rested. All the heroes and all the women and all the *Boroma* slept. *Gassire*'s youngest son slept. *Gassire* was restive. He sat by the fire. He sat there long. Presently he slept. Suddenly he jumped up. *Gassire* listened. Close beside him *Gassire* heard a voice. It rang as though it came from himself. *Gassire* began to tremble. He heard the lute singing. The lute sang the story of the great deeds of *Dausi*.

When the lute had sung the *Dausi* for the first time, King *Nganamba* died in the city of *Dierra;* when the lute had sung the *Dausi* for the first time, *Gassire*'s rage melted; *Gassire* wept. When the lute had sung the *Dausi* for the first time, *Wagadu* disappeared—for the first time.

Hoooh! Dierra, Agada, Ganna, Silla! Hoooh! Fasa!

Four times *Wagadu* stood there in all her splendor. Four times *Wagadu* disappeared and was lost to human sight: once through vanity, once through falsehood, once through greed, and once through dissension. Four times *Wagadu* changed her name. First she was called *Dierra,* then *Agada,* then *Ganna,* then *Silla.* Four times she turned her face. Once to the north, once to the west, once to the east, and once to the south. For *Wagadu*, whenever men have seen her, has always had four gates: one to the north, one to the west, one to the east, and one to the south. Those are the directions whence the strength of *Wagadu* comes, the strength in which she endures no matter whether she be built of stone, wood, or earth, or lives but as a shadow in the mind and longing of her children. For, really, *Wagadu* is not of stone, not of wood, not of earth. *Wagadu* is the strength that lives in the hearts of men and is sometimes visible because eyes see her and ears hear the clash of swords and ring of shields, and is sometimes invisible because the indomitability of man has overtired her, so that she sleeps. Sleep came to *Wagadu* for the first time through vanity, for the second time through falsehood, for the third time through greed, and for the fourth time through dissension. Should *Wagadu* ever be found for the fifth time, then she will live so forecfully in the minds of men that she will never be lost again, so forcefully that vanity, falsehood, greed, and dissension will never be able to harm her.

Hoooh! Dierra, Agada, Ganna, Silla! Hoooh! Fasa!

Every time the guilt of man caused *Wagadu* to disappear she won a new beauty which made the splendor of her next appearance still more glorious. Vanity brought the song of the bards, which all peoples imitate and value today. Falsehood brought a rain of gold and pearls. Greed brought writing, as the *Burdama* still practice it today, and which in *Wagadu* was the business of the women. Dissension will enable the fifth *Wagadu* to be as enduring as the rain of the south and as the rocks of the Sahara, for every man will then have *Wagadu* in his heart and every woman *Wagadu* in her womb.

Hoooh! Dierra, Agada, Ganna, Silla! Hoooh! Fasa!

—*Soninke*

79 The Mwindo Epic

The Courtship of Mukiti and Iyangura

Long ago there was in a place a chief called *Shemwindo*. That chief built a village called *Tubondo,* in the state of *Ihimbi. Shemwindo* was born with a sister called Iyangura.

And in *Shemwindo*'s village there were seven meeting places of his people. When he became chief, *Shemwindo* married seven women. After *Shemwindo* had married those, his seven wives, he summoned his many people: the juniors and the seniors, the advisers, the counselors, and the nobles. All people, young and old, male and female, officeholder and commoner, were called to meet with him in council.

When they were together, *Shemwindo* sat down in the middle of them. He made a decree, saying: "You, my seven wives, the one who will bear a male child among you, I will kill; all of you must each give birth to girls only." Having made this interdiction, he threw himself hurriedly into the houses of the wives, and then launched the sperm where his wives were.

Among his wives there was one who was beloved and another who was despised. The despised one had her house built next to the garbage heap and his other wives lived in the clearing in the middle of the village. After a certain number of days had elapsed, those seven wives became with child, and all at the same time.

Close to the village of *Shemwindo* there was a river in which there was a pool, and in this pool there was a water serpent, master of the unfathomable. In his dwelling place in the pool, the serpent *Mukiti* heard that downstream from him there was a chief who had a sister called *Iyangura.* She glistened like dew reflecting the rays of the sun, she was so beautiful. *Mukiti* heard the news of the beauty of that young woman, *Iyangura,* and he went to court her.

Mukiti, the water serpent, reached *Tubondo; Shemwindo* accommodated him in a guest house. When they were already in twilight, after having eaten dinner and food, *Mukiti* said to *Shemwindo:* "You, my uncle, my mother's brother, I have come here where you are because of your sister *Iyangura." Shemwindo* gave *Mukiti* a black goat as a token of hospitality and, moreover, said to *Mukiti* that he would answer him tomorrow. *Mukiti* said: "Yes, my dear father, I am satisfied."

When night turned day, when it was morning, *Mukiti* dressed himself up like the anus of a snail, the very cleanest of the clean. He was clothed with bunches of raphia fronds on the arms and on the legs, and with a belt of bongo antelope, and he also wore the *isia* crest of elephant tail and whiskers of leopard fixed in a brass disk on his head. In their homestead, *Shemwindo* and his sister *Iyangura* also outdid themselves in dressing up. The moment *Mukiti* and *Shemwindo* saw each other, *Mukiti* said to his uncle: "I am astonished. Since I arrived, I have never met with my sister." Hearing that, *Shemwindo* assembled all his people, the counselors and the nobles; he went with them into secret council. *Shemwindo* said to his people: "Our sister's son has come to this village looking for my sister; and you then must answer him." The counselors and nobles, hearing that, agreed, saying: "It is befitting that you first present *Iyangura* to *Mukiti."* They passed with *Iyangura* before *Mukiti. Mukiti,* seeing the way in which *Iyangura* was bursting with mature beauty, said to himself in his heart: "Now, she is not the one I expected to see; she is like a *ntsembe* tree in her beauty and blood." *Iyangura*, indeed, was dressed in two pieces of bark cloth imbued with red powder and *mbea* oil. Seeing each other, *Mukiti* and *Iyangura* irresistibly darted against each other's chest in salutation. Having thus greeted each other, *Iyangura* said to *Mukiti*: "Do you really love me, *Mukiti?*" *Mukiti* told her: "Don't raise your voice anymore, my wife; see how I am dancing, my back shivering like the raphia-tree larvae, and my cheeks holding in my laughing."

After *Mukiti* and *Iyangura* looked on each other like this, the counselors and nobles of *Shemwindo* answered *Mukiti*, saying: "We are satisfied, *Mukiti*, because of your word. Now you will go forth to gain treasures and trophies. Whether you win many, whether you win few, from now on you win them for us." After *Mukiti* had been spoken to in such a manner, he returned home with soothed heart. During his absence, the villagers fixed him a seven-day feast in celebration of the valuables he would bring for his part of the marriage.

After *Mukiti* was home, he assembled his people and told them that he was just back from courting, that he had been asked for a great number of valuables, nine thousand, and a white goat, and a reddish one, and a black one, and one for sacrifice, and one for the sacred calabash, and one for the mother, and one for the young men. The counselors and the nobles, hearing that, clapped their hands, saying to their lord that they were satisfied, that they could not fail to find that payment of goods reasonable, because this maiden was not to be lost. After the seven days were up, in the morning, *Mukiti* took the marriage payments with him while his people remained behind.

On leaving his village the next morning, he went to spend the night in the village of the *Baniyana*. The *Baniyana* gave him a ram as a token of hospitality. *Mukiti* and his people slept in their village. In the morning, when *Mukiti* woke up, he propelled himself into the village of the *Banamitandi*, those kin of the spiders, those helpers of heroes. They gave *Mukiti* a goat as a token of hospitality. And so he spent the night there. In the morning, he and his people took a pathway out of the village, and at long last they came to the village of his wife's family, in *Tubondo*, at *Shemwindo*'s.

When they arrived in *Tubondo*, *Shemwindo* showed them a guest-house to sleep in, and also gave them a ram-goat as a present of hospitality. In the evening, *Iyangura* heated water for her husband and they went together to wash themselves (for it is the custom for a wife to wash her husband's feet before bed). Having finished, they anointed themselves with red powder and climbed into bed. *Iyangura* put a leg across her husband.

In the morning, there was a holiday. *Shemwindo* assembled all his people and they sat together in a group. Then, *Mukiti* came out with the marriage payments and placed them before the elders of the village, who were very satisfied with them. They told him: "Well, you are a man—one who cannot be stopped by anything, one who is able to overcome fear and doubt." After they had laid hold of the marriage payments, the people of *Shemwindo* told *Mukiti* to return to his village and they would bring his wife to him for the marriage. Hearing this, *Mukiti* said: "Absolutely all is well. What would be bad would be to be deceived." He returned to his village and had his people prepare much food to entertain the guests to come.

Shemwindo, who had remained in his village, waited until *Mukiti* had been gone a day. In the morning, he set out to follow him, taking *Iyangura* with him. The attendants carried *Iyangura,* without allowing her foot to touch the ground, as they went through mud or water. When the attendants and the bride arrived at *Mukiti*'s, *Mukiti* showed them to a guesthouse, where they sat down. A rooster was caught and cooked "to clean the teeth." In this guesthouse the elders had *Iyangura* sit on a stool to indicate how significant this wedding would be.

When she was seated, she took out the remainder of the banana paste from which she had had breakfast in her mother's house in their village. She and her husband, *Mukiti,* ate it. While they were eating, still more banana paste, with taro leaves, was being prepared for them. When the paste and the leaves were ready, the elders told *Mukiti* also to sit down on a stool, and they placed the paste between both of them. They told *Iyangura* to grasp a piece of paste in her right hand and have her husband eat it along with a portion of meat. *Iyangura* took a piece of paste from the dish, and fed it to her husband; and her husband took a piece of paste, and he, too, fed it to his wife. After both husband and wife had finished the ceremonial eating of the paste, the counselors of *Mukiti* gave *Shemwindo* and his people a strong young steer as a gift of hospitality.

After they had finished eating the steer, they spoke to *Mukiti,* saying: "Don't turn our child here, whom you have just married, into a woman in ragged, soiled clothing. Don't transform her into a servant who does nothing but work for you."

After they had said this, in the early morning, right after awakening, they went, having been given money as a going-away gift by *Mukiti.* When the bridal attendants arrived in *Tubondo,* they were very happy, along with their chief, *Shemwindo.* By the river, where *Mukiti* and his people and his wife, *Iyangura,* remained, he made a proclamation saying: "All my people, if one day you see a man walking downstream against the flow of the river, then you will tear out his spinal column. For it is forbidden, thus, to walk this way. You, all the various houses, all the people of *Maka,* the people of *Birurumba,* of *Ankomo, Tubusa,* and *Mpongo.* This other path here, the one that follows the flow of the river, this is the great path on which all people must pass." Now in his village there lived his headman called *Kasiyembe.* After *Mukiti* had voiced this interdiction regarding the two paths, he told his big headman, *Kasiyembe:* "Henceforth you must dwell with my wife, *Iyangura,* at the borders of the pool; and I, *Mukiti,* shall reside here where all the dry leaves collect, from now on, and always, here where all the fallen tree trunks are obstructed in the middle of the pool."

Mwindo's Unusual Birth and His Brief Early Years

Because of his power and virtues, *Shemwindo,* together with his wives and people, became very famous not only in *Tubondo,* but throughout the country. When many days had passed, his wives came into labor! They gave birth to female children only. One wife among them, the seventh and the Preferred One, lagged behind in her pregnancy. When the Preferred One saw that her companions had already given birth, whereas she was still heavy with child, she continually complained: "How terrible this is! It is only I who are still dragged down by this pregnancy. What then shall I do? My companions, with whom I became pregnant at the same time, have already gone through it all, and I alone remain with this burden. What will come out of this pregnancy?"

Just after she had finished these sad reflections, she found a bunch of firewood at her door. She did not know from where it had come. It was her child, the one that was inside her womb, who had just brought it.

After some time had passed, while looking around the house the Preferred One discovered a jar of water standing there. She did not know from whence it had come. It was as if it had brought itself into the house. And again, after some more time had passed, she found raw vegetables sitting in the house. Now, she was even more astonished. It was the child in her womb who was carrying out all these miraculous tasks for her.

When the inhabitants of the village saw that the Preferred One continued to drag on with her pregnancy, they started sneering at her: "When is this one going to give birth?" they would mock. The child, dwelling in the womb of its mother, meditated to itself, saying that it could not come out from the underpart of the body of its mother, because people might make fun saying that he was the child of a woman. He did not want to emerge from the mouth of his mother, for then they might make fun, saying that he had been vomited up like a bat.

The pregnancy had gone so far beyond its term that the old midwives, the wives of counselors, came. They arrived when the Preferred One was already being troubled with labor pains. The child, dwelling in the womb, climbed to her belly, wandered through her limbs and torso, and went on and came out through her middle. The old midwives were astonished when they saw him wailing on the ground. They pointed at him, asking: "What kind of child is that?" Some among them saw that it was a male child, and were worried and wanted to shout it about the village that a male child had been born. Others refused, saying that no one should say that the child was a boy, because when *Shemwindo* heard, he would kill him. The counselors sitting with *Shemwindo,* shouted, asking: "What sort of child is born there?" But the old midwives sitting in the house kept their silence, never giving an answer. Afterwards, the midwives gave him the name *Mwindo*—first-born male—for there had only been female children born in that family before him.

In the house where the birth took place that day, a cricket appeared on the wall carrying omens of great and dreadful things. After *Shemwindo* had asked what child was born and the midwives had refused to answer, the cricket had left the birthhouse and had carried the news to him: "Chief, a male child has been born to you. They call him *Mwindo,* the first boy child, and that is why those in the hut there have not answered you." When *Shemwindo* heard that his Preferred One had given birth to a boy, he took up his spear. He sharpened it on a whetstone, and he carried it to the house where the child had been born. The moment he prepared to throw it into the birth hut, the child shouted from inside, saying: "Each time this spear is thrown, may it hit the bottom of the house pole, where the household spirits reside. May it never end up where these old midwives are seated here. Neither may it arrive at the place where my mother is." *Shemwindo* threw the spear into the house six times, and each time it hit nothing but the pole. When the old midwives saw those extraordinary happenings they swarmed out of the house. They fled, saying to one another that they did not want to die in that place.

When *Shemwindo* had become exhausted in his anger, for he ran back and forth with his spear but completely failed to kill *Mwindo,* he spoke to his counselors, saying that they should dig a grave to throw *Mwindo* into, for he did not want to see a male child. When the counselors had heard the order of the lord of their village, they did not argue with him; rather they went ahead and dug the grave. When the grave was finished, they went to fetch the child, *Mwindo.* They carried him gently, as a baby should be handled, and went to bury him. *Mwindo* howled from within the grave, saying: "Oh, my father, this is the death that *you* will die, but first you will suffer many sorrows." When *Shemwindo* heard the remarkable curse of the little castaway, he scolded his people telling them to cover the grave right away. His people went to fetch the plantain and banana trees to lay on the grave, as is the custom. They placed them on top of him and above the plantains they heaped much soil. But at that very moment, it became evident that *Mwindo* had been born with a *conga* scepter, the royal fly swatter made of the buffalo tail, which he held in his right hand. He also carried an adze, which he held in his left hand. A little bag of the spirit of *Kahombo,* the carrier of good fortune, was slung across his back on the left side, and in that little bag there was a long magic rope. Most wondrously, *Mwindo* was born laughing and also speaking, already a man among men.

When the day was ending, those sitting outdoors looked to where *Mwindo* had been discarded earlier in the day, and saw that there was light coming forth, as though the sun were shining from within. They ran to tell the others in the village, and they came running. They saw the emanation, but they could not stand still there because the great heat, which was like fire, burned them. As one would pass by, he would attempt to cast his eyes on the light, but he would have to move on, it was so bright.

When everyone had fallen asleep for the night, *Mwindo* emerged from the grave and sneaked into his mother's house. There he began to wail. In his home, *Shemwindo* heard the child's wailing in the house of the Preferred One. He was totally astonished, saying: "This time what was never seen is seen for the first time. A child is crying again in that house. Has my wife given birth to another child?" *Shemwindo* was wracked with indecision, unsure whether or not he could even stand up because of his fear. But in his manliness, *Shemwindo* did stand up, going to the house of his wife, the Preferred One, slithering like a snake, without making a sound. He arrived at the hut, peeked through the open door, and cast his eye on to the child sleeping on the floor. He entered the hut and questioned his wife, saying: "Where does this child come from? Did you leave another one in the womb to whom you have given another birth?" His wife replied to him: "This is *Mwindo* here." Where *Mwindo* was sitting on the ground, he kept silent. *Shemwindo* witnessing this marvelous event, his mouth itched to speak, but he left the house without being able to speak another word.

He went to wake up his counselors. Arriving there, he told them: "I was not deceived. He has returned. It is astounding." He told them also: "Tomorrow, when the sky will have become day, then you will go to cut a piece from the trunk of a tree. You will carve in it a husk for a drum. You will then put the hide of an antelope in the river to soften."

When the sky had become day, all the people called one another and assembled. Then, together they went to see *Mwindo* in his mother's house. *Mwindo* was devoured by the many longing eyes. After they had looked at him, the counselors went to the forest to cut a piece of wood for the husk of the drum. They cut it, the piece of wood, and returned with it to the village. Then they carved the wood, they hollowed it out so that it became a husk.

When the husk was finished, they went again to fetch *Mwindo.* They carried him gently and put him within the husk of the drum. *Mwindo* said: "This time, my father has no mercy. What! A small baby is being mistreated!" The people of *Shemwindo* went to get the hide for the drum. They attached it on top of the drum. They covered the drum with it. When *Shemwindo* had seen his son placed within the drum, he declared to all his people that he wanted two expert swimmers, divers, to go the next day to throw the drum into the pool where nothing moves. After the swimmers, divers, had been found, they picked up the drum. Then, all the people left the village to throw *Mwindo* into the water.

When they arrived at the pool where nothing moves, the divers dove into it with the drum, swimming in the river. When they arrived in the middle of the pool, they asked in a loud voice: "Shall we drop him here?" Those sitting on the edge of the river answered: "Yes." All said together: "Drop it there, so that you can't be accused of his return." They released the drum in the middle of the pool and it sank into the depths. The waves made rings above the place where the drum had entered.

After the swimmers had thrown him into the pool, they returned to the shore. *Shemwindo* was very pleased with them: "You have performed good work!" He awarded each swimmer a maiden. That day, when *Mwindo* was thrown away, earth and heaven joined together because of the heavy rain. It rained for seven days and that rain brought much famine in *Tubondo.*

After they had thrown *Mwindo* away, they returned to the village. When they arrived in *Tubondo, Shemwindo* threatened his wife *Nyamwindo,* the Preferred One, saying: "Don't shed tears weeping for your son. If you weep, I shall send you to the same place your son has been thrown." That very day, *Nyamwindo, Mwindo*'s mother, turned into the Despised One. Unable to weep, *Nyamwindo* went on merely sobbing—but not one little tear did she shed.

Where *Mwindo* dwelt in the pool where he had been thrown away, when he was in the water on the sand, he moaned within the drum. He stuck his head on the side of the drum. He listened closely to its sound, and said: "I must not wash downstream in the river. I cannot leave without warning my father and all his people who have cast me away of the consequences of throwing me here. They must be able to hear the sound of my voice. If I wash away, then I am not *Mwindo.*"

From where the drum was beneath the water, it arose all alone to the surface of the pool—in its middle—and it remained there. It did not go down the river, neither did it go up the river.

From *Tubondo,* from the village where the people dwelt, came a row of maidens. They went to draw water from the river, at the wading place. Arriving at the river, as soon as they cast their eyes toward the middle of the pool, they saw the drum on the surface of the water, turning around and around. They inquired of each other: "Companions, we have dazzling apparitions. Lo, the drum that was thrown with *Mwindo* in it—there it is!" *Mwindo* living inside that drum in the midst of the pool, said: "If I don't sing while these maidens are still here drawing water from the river, then I shall not have anyone who will bring the news to where my father is in *Tubondo.*"

While the maidens were in the act of drawing water and still had their attention fixed toward the drum, *Mwindo,* where he dwelt in the drum in the pool, threw sweet words into his mouth. He sang:

I am saying farewell to Shemwindo!
I am saying farewell to Shemwindo!
I shall die, O Bira!
My little father threw me into the drum!
I shall die, Mwindo!
The counselors abandoned Shemwindo;
The counselors will become dried leaves.
The counselors of Shemwindo,
The counselors of Shemwindo,
The counselors have failed in their counseling!
My little father, little Shemwindo,
My little father threw me into the drum!
I shall not die, while that little one survives!
The little one is joining Iyangura,
The little one is joining Iyangura,
Iyangura, *the sister of* Shemwindo.

When the girls heard the way in which *Mwindo* was singing in the drum in the pool, they climbed up to the village, running and rushing, leaving the water jars behind them in disarray. The men, seeing them appear, running and rushing, at the outskirts of the living area, took their spears and went out, believing that they were being chased by a wild beast. Seeing the spears, the maidens beseeched their fathers: "Hold it! We are going to bring the news to you of how the drum that you threw into the pool has remained there. In fact it is singing: 'The counselors of *Shemwindo,* the counselors have failed in their counseling. The counselors will become dried leaves.' " When he heard that, *Shemwindo* accused the girls of lying: "What? The drum that we threw yesterday into the depths of the pool has come to the surface again!" The maidens averred this was true: "*Mwindo* is still alive. When *Shemwindo* heard that, again he assembled his people. Everybody went down to the river carrying spears, arrows, and torches. The village remained empty.

From where *Mwindo* was floating in the river, he was able to see the way in which the maidens had run from the river toward the village. So he stopped singing for a while, saying to himself that he would sing again when the people arrived, following the girls who had just witnessed his astonishing deed. All the people of the village, children and youngsters, old men and young men, old woman and young women, when they arrived at the river, seeing the drum in the middle of the pool, were joined together in staring at it. When *Mwindo* saw them standing in a group on the shore, he threw sweet words into his mouth. He sang:

I am saying farewell to Shemwindo;
I shall die, O Bira!
The counselors abandoned Shemwindo.
The counselors will turn into dried leaves.
What will die and what will be safe
Are going to encounter Iyangura.

When *Mwindo* had finished singing like that, bidding farewell to his father and to all the people of *Shemwindo,* the drum sank into the pool. The waves made rings at the surface. Where *Shemwindo* and his people were standing on the shore, they were very perplexed. They shook their heads, saying: "How terrible it is! Will some day there be born what has never been born?" After they had witnessed this extraordinary event, they returned to the village, *Tubondo.*

Mwindo headed upstream. He went to the river's source, at *Kinkunduri*'s, to begin his journey. When he arrived at *Kinkunduri*'s, he lodged there. He said he was going to join *Iyangura,* his paternal aunt, there where *Kahungu* had told him she had gone. He met up with his aunt *Iyangura* downstream, and he sang:

Mungai *fish, get out of my way!*
For Ikukuhi, *should I go out of my way for you?*
You are impotent against Mwindo,
Mwindo *is the Little One Just Born He Walked.*
I am going to meet Iyangura.

For kabusa *fish, should I go out of my way for you?*
You are helpless against Mwindo,
For Mwindo *is the Little One Just Born He Walked.*
Canta *fish, get out of my way!*
Canta, *you are impotent against* Mwindo.
I am going to encounter Iyangura, *my aunt.*
For mutaka *fish, should I go out of my way for you?*
You are helpless against Mwindo!
I am going to meet Iyangura, *my aunt.*
For kitoru *fish, should I go out of my way for you?*
You see, I am going to encounter Iyangura, *my aunt.*
For crabs, should I go out of my way for you?
You are impotent against Mwindo!
See, I am going to encounter Iyangura, *my aunt,*
Iyangura, *sister of* Shemwindo.
For nyarui *fish, should I go out of my way for you?*
Whereas Mwindo *is the Little One Just Born He Walked.*
I am going to encounter Iyangura, *my aunt,*
Sister of Shemwindo.
For cayo *fish, should I go out of my way for you?*
You see, I am going to encounter Iyangura, *my aunt,*
Sister of Shemwindo.
Look! You are impotent against Mwindo.
Mwindo, *the Little One Just Born He Walked.*
He who will go up against me, it is he who will die on the way.

Each time *Mwindo* arrived in a place where there was a swimming animal, he said that it should get out of the way for him, that they were powerless against him, that he was going to his aunt, Iyangura. When *Mwindo* arrived at *Cayo*'s, he spent the night there; in the morning he traveled on right after awakening. Again he sang:

For ntsuka *fish, should I go out of my way for you?*
You see that I am going to encounter Iyangura.
You see that you are powerless against Mwindo.
Mwindo *is the Little One Just Born He Walked.*
For kirurumba *fish, should I get out of the way?*
You see that I am going to encounter Aunt Iyangura.
You see that you are powerless against Mwindo,
For Mwindo *is the Little One Just Born He Walked.*
For mushomwa *fish, should I go out of the way?*
You see I am going to encounter Aunt Iyangura.
You see that you are powerless against Mwindo.
For Mwindo *is the Little One Just Born He Walked.*

The Encounter with the Dreaded Mukiti

Musoka, the junior sister of the evil *Mukiti,* had gone to live upstream from hated *Mukiti:*

> *For* Musoka, *should I go out of my way for you?*
> *You are powerless against* Mwindo,
> Mwindo *is the Little One Just Born He Walked.*

When *Musoka* saw *Mwindo* arriving at her place, she sent an envoy to *Mukiti* to say that there was a person there where she was, at *Musoka*'s, who was about to join *Iyangura.* The envoy ran quickly to *Mukiti.* Arriving, he gave the news: "There is a person back there who is joining *Iyangura.*" *Mukiti* replied that the envoy should tell *Musoka* that the man must not pass beyond her place—"If not, why would I have placed her there?" That envoy arrived at *Musoka*'s. He told how he had been spoken to by *Mukiti.* Then *Musoka* blocked *Mwindo*'s passage, although she did not know that he was a child of *Mukiti*'s wife, *Iyangura. Musoka* spoke to *Mwindo,* saying: "*Mukiti* refuses to let you by. So it is only by proving your manhood that you will be able to pass. I, *Musoka,* I am placing barriers here. You will not find a trail to pass on." *Mwindo* answered her, softening his voice: "I am *Mwindo.* Never will I be forbidden to pass on any trail. I will break through exactly at the place where you would prevent me from going by." *Mwindo,* saying this, pulled himself together. He left the water above him, he dug inside the sand, and he burrowed to a place somewhere between *Musoka* and *Mukiti.*

After *Mwindo* had passed *Musoka* in this way, having broken through *Musoka*'s dam, he boasted: "Here I am, the Little One Just Born He Walked. No one ever points a finger at me." When *Musoka* saw him anew downstream, she touched her chin, saying: "How then has this tough one here gotten through? If he had passed above me, I would have seen his shadow; if he had passed below me, I would have heard the sound of his feet." *Musoka* railed at his escape, saying that she would be scolded by *Mukiti.*

After *Mwindo* had passed *Musoka,* he began to journey to *Mukiti*'s. He sang:

> *In* Mukiti's, *in* Mariba's *dwelling place!*
> *For* Mukiti, *should I go out of the way for you?*
> *You see I am going to encounter* Iyangura,
> Iyangura, *sister of* Shemwindo.
> Mukiti, *you are powerless against* Mwindo.
> Mwindo *is the Little One Just Born He Walked.*

When *Mukiti* in his dwelling place heard this, he asked who was talking about his wife. He moved and shook heaven and earth. The whole pool moved. *Mwindo* on his part said: "This time we shall really get to know each other, for I, *Mwindo,* never fear one who is nothing so much as a boasting and pampered child easily angered. I won't be worried about such a one until I have myself against him."

Mwindo, organizing himself, went to appear at the spot where the monster *Mukiti* was coiled up. When *Mukiti* saw him, he said: "This time it is not the one whom I expected to see. He surpasses all expectation!" He asked: "Who are you?" *Mwindo* responded, saying that he was *Mwindo,* the Little One Just Born He Walked, child of *Iyangura. Mukiti* said to *Mwindo*: "What do you want, then?" *Mwindo* answered saying that he was going to be with his paternal aunt, *Iyangura.* Hearing that, *Mukiti* said to *Mwindo*: "You are lying. No one ever passes over these logs and dried leaves. Are you alone the man who in spite of all will be able to pass through the forbidden spot!"

While *Mukiti* and *Mwindo* were still boasting and arguing with each other, maidens went from *Iyangura*'s place to draw water at *Mukiti*'s place, because there is where the water hole was. As soon as the maidens heard the way in which *Mwindo* always referred to *Iyangura* as his aunt, they ran to tell her. "Over there, where your husband *Mukiti* is, a little man has come who says that *Mukiti* should let him pass, for he is *Mwindo,* that he is going to meet with *Iyangura,* his paternal aunt." When *Iyangura* heard that news, she said: "Lo! That is my child. I will go to where he is." *Iyangura* climbed up the slope. She went to the water hole. She looked to the river that she first might see the man who was calling her his aunt. As soon as *Mwindo* saw *Iyangura* coming to him, he sang:

I am suffering much, Mwindo.
I will die, Mwindo.

While his aunt *Iyangura* was descending the slope, he went on singing, looking in the direction from which his aunt was coming.

Aunt Iyangura,
Mukiti *has blocked the road to me.*
I am going to meet Aunt Iyangura,
I am going to encounter Iyangura,
Sister of Shemwindo.
For Mukiti, *shall I go out of the way?*
I am joining Iyangura,
Sister of Shemwindo.
For Mukiti, *my father, shall I go out of my way for him?*
You are powerless against Mwindo.

Iyangura said: "If my sister's son, the nephew of the people of *Mitandi*, is in this drum, let him come here so that I can see him before me." But though his aunt cited the people of *Mitandi* in this way, *Mwindo* refused to move in her direction. From inside the drum, *Mwindo* complained that his aunt had missed the mark. His aunt spoke again: "If you drum, if you are the nephew of the One Who Hears Secrets, come here. Draw near me." Though his aunt mentioned the One Who Hears Secrets, the drum still refused to draw near. His aunt said anew: "If you really are the nephew of the people of *Yana*, come before me." When *Mwindo* heard this, he went forth from the pool singing:

> *I am going to my Aunt* Iyangura,
> Iyangura, *sister of* Shemwindo.
> Kabarebare *and* Ntabare *mountain,*
> *Where the husband of my senior sister sets fish traps.*
> *And a girl who is nice is a lady,*
> *And a nice young man is a house pole.*
> *We are telling the story*
> *That the* Babuya *have told long ago.*
> *We are telling the story.*
> Kasengeri *is dancing, wagging his tail;*
> *And you see his tail of* nderema *fibers.*
> Nkurongo *bird had gone to court* mususu *bird;*
> Muhasha *bird has contracted asthma, is gasping for breath.*
> *If I am at a loss for words in the great song,*
> *If it dies out, may it not die out for me there.*
> *They are accustomed to speak to* Mukiti *with bells.*
> *The tunes that we are singing.*
> *The uninitiated ones cannot know them.*
> *I would like to be as perfect in body as the*
> Mburu *monkey and still eat a lot,*
> *I would remain satisfied with my flat belly. . . .*

Mwindo was still flowing with the river, and as he floated by his aunt, she seized the drum. Her people gave her a knife and she slashed the drum open. Removing the hide, she saw the multiple rays of the rising sun and the moon—such was the beauty of the child, *Mwindo*. *Mwindo* rose out of the drum, still holding his *conga* scepter and his adze, together with his little bag that contained the magical rope. When Hawk saw *Mwindo* meeting with his aunt, he went to bring the news to the elder who had been sent to *Iyangura* to keep watch over her continually. He arrived there, and told him: "You, you who are here, it is not merely a little man who appears over there; he carries with him stories of his many attributes and feats. He is going to kill you." Hearing this news,

Kasiyembe said: "You bearer of news, go! When you have arrived at *Mwindo*'s, tell him he must not attempt to pass by this side, for if he tries, I will tear out his backbone. I am setting up traps here, pits and pointed sticks and razors in the ground, so that whenever he tries, I will catch him in his attempts."

Seeing all this going on, *Mukei* the Hedgehog, acting as a messenger going the other way, went to *Mwindo,* and told him: "*Mwindo,* our enemies are holding secret council against you. They are even preparing pit traps against you, and pointed sticks and razors. I say this, I, *Mukei* the Hedgehog, who is a master of going underground, into the depth of the earth." *Mwindo* answered: "Yes, I always see you burrowing; it is within the earth that you live, so you must know well of such things." After warning *Mwindo, Mukei* also told him: "I am going to build a road which bypasses him, so that it goes where you are, inside the house of your aunt, at the base of the house pole." *Mwindo* approved of this plan gladly. *Mukei* the Hedgehog began to dig in the ground, inside it. *Mwindo* told his aunt *Iyangura*: "You, Aunt, go on ahead, get going on your way home, and I shall meet you there. *Kasiyembe,* who threatened me over there, I shall first meet up with him. If he really is powerful, I shall deal with him." He also said to his aunt: "Tell the one who is threatening me there, that he should get ready for me." Then Master Spider came out of the pit traps and began to build bridges. He built them out over the pits. Indeed, the pits became merely bridges. He said to himself that it was there that *Mwindo* was going to play. "As far as I, Master Spider, am concerned, *Mwindo* cannot be beaten as long as we are there."

After *Mwindo* had told his aunt to go along, she did not attempt to fool him—she went home. Back where *Mwindo* had stayed, he took the road made by *Mukei.* Thanks to his helpers, he came out in the house of his aunt, at *Iyangura*'s. When *Kasiyembe* saw where he was, he said: "*Mwindo* is already over here. Now, from where has he come?" The people of his village said that they did not know how he had gotten there.

When *Iyangura* saw that her son *Mwindo* had already arrived, she said to him: "My boy, don't eat yet. First come to my side, so that we may dance to the rhythm of the drum." After *Mwindo* had heard his aunt's words, he came outdoors to where his aunt was. He agreed to dance with her without having eaten food, but said that he was going to faint with responding to the calls of the drum. His aunt replied to him: "Not at all! Dance away, my son. You must know I am ordered to have you do this by *Kasiyembe,* my protector, but your enemy. He says that you must dance to tire you out. What then shall we do? You must dance all the same!" Hearing the word of his aunt, *Mwindo* said: "Oh! Right you are. Let me first dance, for hunger never kills a man." *Mwindo* sang and the dance became a source of his strength. He howled, he inveighed against *Kasiyembe,* saying:

> Kasiyemba, *you are powerless against* Mwindo,
> *For* Mwindo *is the Little One Just Born He Walked.*
> Kasiyembe *said: "Let us dance together."*
> Shirungu, *give us a morsel!*
> *If we die, we will die for you.*
> Kasengeri *is dancing with his* conga *scepter,*
> Conga *scepter of* nderema *fibers.*
> *I am saying farewell to* Mpumba,
> *My* Mpumba *with many raphia bunches.*

Mwindo danced round about in the midst of the pits. He danced with his body bent over the pits, without being injured by the razors. He went back and forth everywhere that *Kasiyembe* had placed traps for him, without injuring himself.

Iyangura told her son to have some food, saying that since the time he arrived he had not once rinsed his mouth in preparation for eating. *Iyangura* gave her son a head of cattle as a token of hospitality. Then she killed it and prepared it for him. Those on the side, the maidens, ate from it for several days.

After *Mwindo* had received this hospitality gift (but did not eat of it), *Kasiyembe,* the man filled with hatred, persisted in trying to kill him. He said: "Is this the boy against whom I shall be impotent, whereas I heard that he came from the inside of a drum?" *Kasiyembe* implored Hedgehog, *Nkuba* the lightning hurler, saying: "*Nkuba,* you must go and cut *Mwindo* in two. Come to the house where he is staying with all these young women and take care of this problem."

When *Mwindo* heard the way in which *Kasiyembe* repeatedly threatened him, he told the ladies to sit down near him because *Kasiyembe* wanted to strike him with lightning. Then *Mwindo* turned threateningly to Master *Nkumba* saying: "*Nkumba,* since you insist on attacking me, you must strike on one side of the house. You must not strike the side where *Mwindo* is sitting." Master *Nkuba,* on hearing the voice of *Kasiyembe,* ignored the warning and descended on the house. *Mwindo* pointed at him, saying: "You, too, will die the same death; you are climbing a hard tree." Master *Nkuba* then struck seven times on *Mwindo*'s side of the house, but try as he might, he could not come close to the place where *Mwindo* was sitting: The fire burnt only on the side where there was no one, and that side of the house was turned into ashes.

Where *Iyangura, Mwindo*'s aunt, was sitting, so many tears rolled from her eyes that they reached her legs. She feared that the boy was dying and wept that she had not even seen him yet. *Mwindo* then came out of the house along with the young women. Setting himself boldly in front of the crowd of people, he announced to all that he had arrived and was well, and remained the Little One Just Born He Walked. He told his aunt to approach him so that he might speak to her. She came close and *Mwindo* spoke: "No more crying. You, my aunt, are the reason *Kasiyembe* tested me in such an evil fashion. Tomorrow, if you see me no more, it means that you are not worthy of *Mwindo*." All this he told his aunt within the twinkling of an eye. Then, by his great powers, he made *Kasiyemba*'s foolish mop of hair catch on fire. Where *Kasiyembe* was, people could see, all at once, that his foolish mop of hair was already aflame. Indeed, the tongues of flame rose into the air in such a way that all the lice and all the vermin that were nestled on his head were entirely consumed.

When they saw that *Kasiyembe*'s mop of hair was burning, the people of *Kasiyembe* went to fetch water in jars to put out the fire. But by the time they arrived with the jars, there was no water in them. All the water had dried up in the jars, there was not a drop left. They went straight to the water-carrying plantain stalks, but these, too, were already dried up. They said: "What is this? I guess we will have to spit on his head!" But even that was impossible, for their mouths, too, were so dry that no one had any spit left.

As they were going through all of this, they said: "This *Kasiyembe* is about to die. Go to his master, go to *Mukiti*'s place, and see if there is any help there, for there is a pool at *Mukiti*'s." But when they arrived, they found *Mukiti* with butterflies and flies flitting about him, for there, too, all water had evaporated. In fact the whole pool had dried up, so much so that you couldn't find a drop in it. When his aunt saw what was happening, she went to beg before the boy: "Widen your heart, you my son 'of the body,' my nephew who is such a unique creature. Did you come here just to attack us? Widen your heart for us, and take the spell off my husband. Stretch your heart that you may heal the afflicted without harboring further resentment against them." After the aunt had finished humbly imploring the boy, *Mwindo* cooled the anger of his heart. He awoke *Kasiyembe,* waving his *conga* scepter above him, and singing:

> *He who went to sleep wakes up.*
> *You have no power against* Mwindo,
> Mwindo *is the Little One Just Born He Walked.*
> *He who went to sleep wakes up.*
> *Look, I am playing with my* conga *scepter.*

Suddenly, *Kasiyembe* was saved. And in the storage jars water again appeared. And the green stalks of the plantains, again there was water in them. And where *Mukiti* was staying, there, too, the water came back and the river flowed on beneath. When the people saw this feat, they were much astonished, saying: "*Mwindo* must be a great man." *Kasiyembe* saluted *Mwindo,* saying "Hail! Hail! *Mwindo.*" And *Mwindo* answered, "Yes."

After he had accomplished that deed, *Mwindo* informed his aunt that he would be going to *Tubondo* the next day to fight his father, for twice his father had thrown him away, and so he would, in his turn, go to stand up against him. The aunt said to him: "O powerful one, you won't be able to overpower your father. For you are only yesterday's child, born just a little while ago. Will you be worthy of ruling *Tubondo,* village of seven meeting places? I, who had you taken out from within the drum, must strongly say no to such a question. No one should even try to go alone, for the lonely path is never a pleasant one to travel."

When *Mwindo* heard the way in which his aunt was speaking, he refused to listen; he blocked out his aunt's words by humming to himself. The aunt told him: "Do not go to fight with your father. But if you do go, then I shall go with you to watch as your father cuts you into pieces."

She instructed the maidens to pack up her household objects so she could accompany *Mwindo,* for the lonely path is never pleasant—without fail, something comes along with the power to kill. When the sky had become daylight, they breakfasted before the journey back to *Tubondo.* And *Mwindo* sang of deeds of glory to give him strength and attractiveness. *Mwindo* sang:

I am going with the aunt.
The Little One has slept, all prepared for the journey.
O my father, the Little One set out right after awakening .
I warn you, we are already underway.

The evening of this journey that *Mwindo* was making with his aunt, in spite of everything, found him at his maternal uncles, among the people of *Yana.* They had killed a goat of hospitality for him, and he rested there. After they all had eaten of the goat, *Mwindo* said to his maternal uncles: "I am going to fight *Shemwindo* in *Tubondo.* You who are the blacksmiths of large light spears, my uncles, make me strong and resistant." The people of *Yana* said that they were going to remake him by the forge. They dressed him in shoes made entirely of iron and pants all of iron too, they also made him an iron shirt and a hat of iron. They told him: "As you are going to fight your father, may the spears that they will unceasingly hurl at you stroke only this iron that is on your body." After his uncles had finished forging, they said they would no longer stay where they were, but would go with him so that they might see the battle to come. In the morning, *Mwindo* set out with his uncles, and his aunt *Iyangura,* accompanied by all of her servants. *Mwindo* sang out angrily, boasting:

I shall fight over there at Shemwindo's
The cattle that Shemwindo *possesses,*
May they join Mwindo.

When they had the village in sight, *Mwindo*'s aunt said to *Mwindo:* "O our leader, let's get out of here. Just looking up at your father's village makes us dizzy with fear. *Tubondo* over there is a village of seven gates. There are too many people there. They will destroy us." *Mwindo* answered his aunt: "I, *Mwindo,* I am never afraid of anyone with whom I have not yet fought, much less that overgrown child. I want to try this *Shemwindo.* He is too much spoiled by pride." *Mwindo* went on singing:

We are going over there to Tubondo,
Where Shemwindo *lives.*

When they arrived in the glen, he said: "Let us spend tonight in this village." His aunt howled, she said: "Where will we sleep, here there is no house, and *Kiruka-nuambura* has arrived, bearer of rain that never ceases." The aunt shouted, she said: "Oh! my father, where shall we sleep? The rain has just rumbled, the young woman is destitute." *Mwindo* looked around, and said that he wanted to have houses—and houses assembled themselves in two rows! *Mwindo* indicated that his uncles should take one row of houses, and his aunt the other row. And *Mwindo*'s house arose by itself in the middle of them all. His aunt shouted saying: "Yes, our leader *Mwindo,* hail for these our houses. *Shemwindo* has fathered a hero. *Kahombo,* my father, I shall give you some children, my father's grandchildren. Let us go with our prestigious man. May our prestigious man escape thunder and lightning! In spite of himself, *Shemwindo* brought forth a son who is never afraid. And *Mwindo* is making himself into a hero already through his great doings." There in the glen, the houses put themselves together. *Mwindo*'s aunt said to him: "O *Mwindo,* my leader, let us escape, for you are powerless in the face of this mass of people who are in *Tubondo.*" *Mwindo* said that he must first test himself. *Iyangura, Mwindo*'s aunt, said to him: "O *Mwindo*, what shall we eat then? Look, the great number of your uncles here, and I, too, *Iyangura*, have an entourage with me, and you, *Mwindo*, you have drummers and singers with you. What will this whole group eat?" *Mwindo* saw that his aunt was telling him something important, and had to agree: "I see that the whole group that is with us is already hungry." He lifted his eyes to the sky. He said to himself that he must begin with the food that was over there in *Tubondo,* in the village of his enemies, that this must be magically captured—and so great were his powers that it happened. The food came to him, so that he might go to fight. *Mwindo* sang while carrying back the food from his father's camp. His aunt was still shouting out in hunger, "O my leader, what shall we eat today?" *Mwindo* howled back, singing:

> *The foods that are in* Tubondo,
> *May the foods come to* Mwindo,
> Mwindo, *the Little One Just Born He Walked.*
> *The animals that are in* Tubondo,
> *May the animals come to* Mwindo.
> *The meats that* Shemwindo *stores,*
> *May the meats come to* Mwindo Mboru,
> Mwindo, *the Little One Just Born He Walked.*
> *The wood that* Shemwindo *keeps,*
> *O leader, may it come to* Mwindo Mboru!
> *For* Mwindo *is the Little One Just Born He Walked.*
> *And the fire that* Shemwindo *possesses,*
> *May the fire also come to* Mwindo.
> *And the water that* Shemwindo *possesses,*
> *May the water also come to* Mwindo Mboru.
> *The jars that are at* Shemwindo's,
> *May the jars come to* Mwindo,
> Mwindo, *the Little One Just Born He Walked.*
> *The clothes that are at* Shemwindo's,
> *May the clothes come to* Mwindo,
> *Mwindo* is going to fight!
> *The wooden dishes that are in* Tubondo,
> *May the wooden dishes also come to* Mwindo,
> *O father, Little One Just Born He Walked.*
> *Hopes to be victorious.*
> *The beds that* Shemwindo *possesses,*
> *May the beds come to* Mwindo.
> *And the wicker plates that* Shemwindo *possesses,*
> *May the wicker plates also come to* Mwindo.

And the salt that Shemwindo *possesses,*
May the salt also come to Mwindo,
The Little One Just Born He Walked.

It was in this way that *Mwindo* was speaking!

And the chickens that Shemwindo *possesses,*
May the chickens also come to Mwindo.
The praise-singers of cheer sing together;
They began their praising together long ago,
The singers of praise sing as one voice;
They have achieved harmony in the middle of the village.
That which-will-die and that which-will-be-saved,
May it come to Iyangura *here,*
Iyangura, *sister of* Shemwindo.
The goats that are at Shemwindo's,
May the goats come to Mwindo.
The cattle bellowed, saying,
"O father, let us go to Mwindo!"
The dogs that are in Tubondo,
May the dogs come to Mwindo.
The dogs barked, saying,
"O father, let us go to Mwindo!"
We are seated, stretching out our voices
Like the diggers of traps.
The banana groves that are in Tubondo,
May the banana groves come to Mwindo.
And the tobacco that Shemwindo *possesses,*
May the tobacco also come to Mwindo.
The mukusa *asp swallowed froth;*
Auger is in the heart.
And the pipes that Shemwindo *possesses,*
May the pipes also come to Mwindo.
The spears that are at Shemwindo's,
May the spears come to Mwindo.
The adzes that are at Shemwindo's,
May the adzes come to Mwindo.
The billhooks that are at Shemwindo's,
O father, may the billhooks join Mwindo!
May there be none left to go gardening.
The pruning knives that are at Shemwindo's,
May the pruning knives come to Mwindo.
Little pruning knife, little scraper of mbubi lianas.

May the little pruning knife come to Mwindo.
The little dog bells that Shemwindo *possesses,*
May the little dog bells come to Mwindo.
May there be nobody left to go hunting.
The bags that Shemwindo *possesses,*
May the bags also come to Mwindo.
The razors that Shemwindo *possesses,*
May the razors also come to Mwindo;
May there be nobody left who is shaved.
The butea *rings that* Shemwindo *possesses,*
O father, the butea *rings,*
May they be ready to come to Mwindo;
May there be nobody left who wears them.
The necklaces that Shemwindo *possesses,*
May the necklaces also come to Mwindo;
May there be nobody left who wears these.
The needles that Shemwindo *possesses,*
May the needles also come to Mwindo;
May there be nobody left to do hook work.
The fire drill that Shemwindo *possesses,*
May the fire drill also come to Mwindo;
May there be nobody left who makes fire.
The hoes that Shemwindo *possesses,*
O father, the hoes,
May they come to Mwindo;
May there be nobody left who hoes.
The pots that Shemwindo *possesses,*
May the pots also come to Mwindo;
May there be nobody left who cooks.
The baskets that Shemwindo *possesses,*
May the baskets also come to Mwindo.
May there be nobody left who goes to work.
The mumanga *piercer that* Shemwindo *possesses,*
May the mumanga *piercer come to* Mwindo;
May there be nobody who bores shafts.
Let us recite from the story
That the Babuya *are used to reciting.*
The bisara *billhooks that* Shemwindo *possesses,*
May the bisara *billhooks come to* Mwindo;
May there be nobody who prunes banana trees.
And the bellows that Shemwindo *possesses,*
May the bellows also come to Mwindo;
May there be nobody left who smiths.
And the hammers that are at Shemwindo's,

May the hammers also come to Mwindo;
May there be nobody who smiths.
And the blacksmiths at Shemwindo's,
May the blacksmiths also come to Mwindo;
May there be nobody who smiths.
The nkendo *knives that are in* Tubondo,
The nkendo *knives that* Shemwindo *possesses,*
May the nkendo *knives come to* Mwindo;
May there be nobody who plaits.
The raphia palm trees that are at Shemwindo's,
May the raphia palm trees come to Mwindo;
May there be nobody who plaits
Or who traps.
And the drums that are in Tubondo,
O father the drums!
May they join Mwindo;
May there be nobody who dances.

Thus did *Mwindo* invoke and call to him magically all of his father's possessions.

Mwindo and his uncles and his aunt and the servants who had arrived with them, the singers and the drummers, when the latter opened their eyes—all the things that were in *Tubondo* and at *Shemwindo*'s had come to them. When *Mwindo*'s aunt saw all these things, she said to her son *Mwindo*: "You will suffer because of those things belonging to other people that you brought together here." And it was true, for all those with *Mwindo* got sick, gorging themselves with food. They were not cold any more, they found their warmth again. They said: "Lo! *Mwindo* is a man who does not lie when he says that he is the Little One Just Born He Walked. He always has something to rely upon. The one who will try to climb over him will be the first to die alone and abandoned—he is not a man to provoke."

When *Mwindo* had seen that all the important things of his father had come to him, he said that now his father remained there, drunk and abandoned. He said to his aunt that he wanted his uncles to start the fight, and that he, *Mwindo,* would remain there with her for awhile so that he might see how his uncles handled themselves in battle. His uncles fought on the land and in the air, but the people of *Tubondo* said: "You will not win out today."

After a time, *Mwindo*'s uncles were completely wiped out. They died. The people of *Tubondo* finished them. One of *Mwindo*'s uncles escaped from the midst of the battle, but he was seriously injured. He ran to *Mwindo* to tell him the news. "The people of *Tubondo* have overcome us. All the people, all your uncles, are lying there in their own congealed blood." When *Mwindo*'s aunt saw this messenger—blood had covered his whole body—and also heard the news of how the people had completely dried up like water into the soil, she exclaimed: "O leader, *Mwindo,* I warned you of this. I said that you were going to be helpless against the people of *Shemwindo*. But you said, 'Not at all.' Now just pick up this useless tooth here, the fruit of your victory. Just look how your uncles have been wiped out." *Mwindo* said to his aunt: "First, I'm going to find out why my uncles were all defeated. And if *Shemwindo* does not meet me face to face, then I am not *Mwindo*." His aunt said to him: "Oh, *Mwindo,* don't! You will be responsible for all of us getting killed. If you enrage the people in *Tubondo,* then we are all going to die." *Mwindo* did not listen to the mouth of his aunt, and said that he was going to fight: "You, aunt, stay here with my axe and my little bag in which there is a rope. And I will carry my scepter with me."

Mwindo went climbing up to *Tubondo*. As soon as the people saw *Mwindo* arriving, they pointed to him, saying to *Shemwindo*: "See the little man who just appeared at the village entrance alone." *Shemwindo* answered his people: "What can one little man do all by himself? Even if he comes, we shall cut his throat and he will die." His people answered him: "There, from where *bisibisi* insects emerge, one day red ants will come out of it. This little man will be able to make us run away from the village and we won't be able to do anything against him." *Shemwindo* answered his people: "Let this little fool go swaggering into the garbage heap."

Mwindo came through the village entrance singing and swinging his scepter around. When *Mwindo* arrived in *Tubondo,* he came to the middle of the village. He talked to the people. He demanded to dance to the rhythm of their drums. The people of that village taunted him, seeing his size: "You are helpless against our drums here, you are a little fool." *Mwindo* answered them that this was an insult. Before he even had time to rest, they began the challenges and slanders. The people of that village told him that there was no drum there. To that *Mwindo* said that the drums would be coming. *Mwindo* went on speaking to them in that way while his father was in his compound. *Mwindo* sang his boast about himself:

> *He is climbing up here in* Tubondo,
> *He is going to fight with* Shemwindo.

While he was singing, he declaimed: "May whoever dies and whoever is saved join *Iyangura*." He raised his voice to the sky, singing:

What will never die but will be saved,
May it, O father, join Iyangura,
Iyangura, sister of Shemwindo,
The most exalted mother of my cradling string.
O father, whoever will die and whoever will be saved,
May they join their aunt,
Sister of Shemwindo!
My junior and my senior sisters,
Be ready to join me.
What will never die but will be saved,
May they join Iyangura,
Aunt, sister of Shemwindo.
My senior brother, come,
Who will die and will be saved,
May they join Aunt Iyangura.
May you, O my mothers, come!
What will not die but be saved,
May they join Aunt Iyangura.
I die, O Bira!
What has been said will be said again.
Let me fight here in Tubondo,
Even though Tubondo *has seven entrances.*
Rightly have the counselors feared to advise Shemwindo.
Whoever will die and whoever will be saved,
May they join Aunt Iyangura.
The counselors retreated before Shemwindo.
Who will die and who will be saved,
May they join Aunt Iyangura.
Hatred is in the heart.
When I have a bridge built for myself,
He who crosses it will be cut in two.
I prayed for Aunt Iyangura,
Aunt Iyangura, *may you be blessed with the favor of the spirits.*

Mwindo shouted, saying:

Hatred is in the heart,
My friend Nkuba, *god of lightning, may you be on my side*
And make me victorious.
I shall fight here in Tubondo,
Even if Tubondo *has seven entrances.*
Here, in Tubondo, *send seven lightning flashes to close them off.*
I shall fight here in Tubondo.

I send seven lightning flashes now!
Mwindo *thought back over his grievances.*
The counselors ran away leaving Shemwindo.
For the counselors were not worthy of their office.
It's you who will die, and turn into dried leaves.
My father threw me into the drum.
I shall fight here in Tubondo;
May Tubondo *turn into dried leaves, merely.*
The counselors ran away leaving Shemwindo;
The counselors were not worthy of that office.
May the counselors turn into dried leaves.
My friend Nkuba, *may you strike in victory.*
Hatred is in the heart.
I implored Aunt Iyangura,
Whoever will die or be saved,
May they join Iyangura,
Aunt, sister of Shemwindo,
My little fiery father.
My insignificant father threw me into the grave.
My insignificant father believed that I would die.

Mwindo raised his eyes into heaven and said:

My friend Nkuba,
Here in Tubondo *send seven lightning flashes!*

While *Mwindo* was looking up into the sky, he pointed his scepter there as well. From the sky where *Nkuba* dwells, seven lightning flashes came, descending on *Tubondo,* on the village. *Tubondo* turned into dust, and the dust rose up. All who lived there turned into mere dust.

Where *Shemwindo* was sitting in his compound, he exclaimed: "There is no time for lingering here." Having spoken, he went down behind the house without looking back. Where he fled, he arrived at a place in which there was a *kikoka* plant. Tearing it out, he went into the ground at the base of its root.

After his victory at *Tubondo, Mwindo* boasted in the middle of the village. He said: "This time the one who climbs on me, the one who digs into me while fighting with me, will be wearing himself out in vain." He spoke like this when the corpses of the first of his uncles to die had already begun to decay. *Mwindo* went down to where his aunt still stayed in the glen in order that they should walk together to the crest of the hill at *Tubondo.* The aunt asked him: "Is it good news that you carry from where you are coming?" *Mwindo* answered her that *Tubondo* was ablaze. He also said to her and the others gathered: "Let's go to *Tubondo* now, for it is higher up. Let's get away from here in the lowlands." When the aunt began to gather her belongings, *Mwindo* stopped her from doing so. He said to her: "Leave all of these things, for they will bring themselves to *Tubondo*." Having spoken, he went on up the hill, and his aunt followed him, together with the group of servants who had come with them. They climbed up to *Tubondo*. When they got there, all those things they had left in the low ground came to them. *Mwindo* said he could not chase his father so long as he had not resuscitated his uncles. Then he brought them back to life, smiting them with his scepter, and singing:

He who went to sleep, awake!
My uncles, brothers of my mother, wake up.
I have been testing the people of Yana.
My uncles, brothers of my mother, forge me!
You who are powerful blacksmiths and followers of Nkuba,
forge me.
Shemwindo, *you are powerless against* Mwindo,
Mwindo *is the Little One Just Born He Walked.*
My uncles, brothers of my mother, forge me,
You who are blacksmiths of light spears.

The Visit to the Underground

Mwindo finished waking up all of his maternal uncles. They came back to life. Where *Shemwindo* had fled, he went bumping into everything, and hurting himself in the process. Finally, he got to the place of the god *Muisa,* who lives where no one ever clusters around the fire, for fire is unknown there in that dark place.

In *Tubondo,* where *Mwindo* settled with his aunt, with his uncles, and with his servants, singers, and drummers, he told them: "Let's search out *Shemwindo* where he headed to *Muisa*'s. Let us go to find him." His aunt gave him his bag in which there was the rope. She also handed him his axe, whereas he still clasped his scepter in his hand, he the owner of its great powers. *Mwindo* said to his aunt: "My aunt, stay here in the village of your birth, in *Tubondo*. Here is the rope. Stay here holding one end of it in your hand. I'll follow my father to *Muisa*'s dark and desolate realms. If you feel that this rope has stopped moving, then wait for me no longer, for lo, the fire will have dwindled and I will be dead then."

After he had spoken, Master Sparrow alit where *Mwindo* was sitting, and told him: "Come here, for I will show you the path your father took to the bush, and where he entered at the base of the root of the kikoka plant. Indeed, when your father fled, I, Sparrow, was on the roof of the world and saw him fleeing and stumbling." After Sparrow had given him this news, *Mwindo* said farewell to his aunt. Holding one end of the rope, *Mwindo* rushed hurriedly toward the village gate. When he arrived at the *kikoka* plant, where his father had entered, he too pulled it up. Then he went into the earth, passing through. He went to the well at *Muisa*'s place. Arriving there, he met *Kahindo,* the spirit of good fortune and daughter of *Muisa. Kahindo* embraced him, saying: "This is my welcome, *Mwindo*." *Kahindo* was sick with yaws. The yaws started from her tooth and went up to the crotch, they descended down her legs and went to the toes of her feet. When *Mwindo* tried to get by, *Kahindo* prevented him. She said: "Where are you going?" *Mwindo* answered that he was going to *Muisa*'s to look for his father, because he knew it was there that he would be found. She told him again: "First stop here where I am. In *Muisa*'s village one can never get through. Will you succeed in getting by, when all others have not?" *Kahindo* said to *Mwindo*: "If you are going to *Muisa*'s, when you arrive there, when you enter the meeting place, you will see a very big man and tall, too, curled up in the ashes near the hearth. He is *Muisa.* If he greets you, if he says: 'Blessing be with you, my leader,' you, too, will answer, 'Yes my leader.' When he offers you a stool, you will refuse it. You will tell him: 'No, my leader. Will the head of a man's father become a stool?' When he hands you a little gourd of banana beer for you to drink, you will refuse, answering: 'No, my father, even though a person is one's child, is that any reason why he should drink the urine of his father?' After *Muisa* has recognized you that way, he will say to you: 'Blessing, blessing, *Mwindo*.' And you will answer him: 'And to you blessing, blessing also, leader.' When he gives you paste to eat, you will answer him: 'Even though a person is one's child, is that a reason why he should eat the excrement of his father?' "

After *Mwindo* had heard *Kahindo* speaking these words of wisdom, he said to himself that he must not leave without washing *Kahindo*'s yaws. *Mwindo* began washing, smoothing them, taking away all the scabs. After *Mwindo* had washed them like that for some time, they were healed entirely.

Now *Mwindo* went on ahead of *Kahindo*. He went and climbed up to *Muisa*'s. He arrived there and headed for the meeting place. *Muisa,* seeing him, greeted him with "Blessing." *Mwindo* answered, "Yes, my father." *Muisa* recollected: "Bring a chair for *Mwindo* to sit on." *Mwindo* answered him: "Not at all, don't bother, for even though a man is a guest, is that a reason for him to sit on the head of his father?" *Muisa* also said that he had a gourd of beer left there: "Let me pour you a bit." *Mwindo* said: "No, I would not do that. For even though a man is a guest, is that a reason for him to drink the urine of his father?" *Muisa* said: "Let them prepare some paste for you, O *Mwindo!*" *Mwindo* answered him: "No, for even though a man is a guest, is that a reason for him to eat the excrement of his father?" Hearing that, *Muisa* said to him: "Twice blessings, *Mwindo.*"

Seeing *Mwindo* pass those tests, *Muisa* said to *Mwindo:* "Go and take a rest in *Kahindo*'s house." *Mwindo* went inside, he looked around in it. He saw *Kahindo* inside the house, cleansing herself, dressing up and rubbing herself with red powder and castor oil. *Mwindo,* seeing her, was stunned for she appeared as a sunbeam inside the house. *Kahindo* noticed, and greeted him: "Come in, O *Mwindo!*" *Mwindo* said: "May the one who remains behind hurt himself, O my sister!" When she saw that *Mwindo* had come into the house, she said to herself: "Lo, *Mwindo* is hungry." She got up, she went to make some paste of ashes, the mythical food of *Muisa.* After she stirred it, she brought it there to *Mwindo* in her sacred hut. When *Muisa* saw *Kahindo* bringing the paste to *Mwindo,* he dashed quickly toward the house of his daughter where he might see where *Mwindo* was sitting. He said to *Mwindo:* "Oh, *Mwindo,* I see you are eating this food. Tomorrow, as soon as you are up and about, you must begin cultivating a new banana grove for me. You must first cut leaves, then plant the banana trees, then fell the trees. You must then cut the newly grown weeds, then prune the banana trees, then prop them up, then bring the rope bananas to me. After you have performed all those works I shall know to return your father to you." After *Muisa* had spoken like that to *Mwindo,* he also said to him: "When you leave for the fields, I will send a man with you to make sure you are doing the farming correctly." After he had thus spoken, he left the doorway, returning to his meeting place. *Mwindo,* sitting in the house, started eating the paste.

In the morning, when the sky had become daylight, *Mwindo* took up his billhook and went to cultivate the bananas as he had been instructed. *Muisa* picked out a man to go with *Mwindo* to the fields. As they traveled, the man showed *Mwindo* a mountain with mango trees all over it. *Mwindo,* seeing that mountain, placed the billhooks on the ground, so that they might, by themselves, lay out fresh trails for them to get through the bush. When they finished cutting the trails, the billhooks mowed the grasses. Having cut the grasses, the banana trees planted themselves. *Mwindo* placed a number of axes there along with the billhooks. The axes felled the trees. Having finished there, the billhooks went across the banana grove, cutting the newly grown weeds. *Mwindo*'s companion returned to *Muisa.* When he arrived there, he brought *Muisa* the news, saying: "This time he there is not just a cultivator. He is fast, a cultivator of marvelous things.

He has not touched one iron tool. The iron tools themselves are hoeing, and sawing and felling trees, and cutting weeds."

Having given the news, he returned again to where *Mwindo* was in the field of fresh bananas. The billhooks had finished cutting the weeds there, and now cut poles. The poles, by themselves, were propping up the banana trees. The poles completed the propping of the trees, and the banana stems were ripened. The observer ran back with this news to *Muisa.* "I have observed more than a man in the fields cultivating today. The banana trees already have stems and the bananas already are ripe." And *Mwindo,* he also exclaimed, was already on his way carrying a stem of bananas. Hearing this, *Muisa* said: "Lo, this boy is going to manage to pass all of these tests there in the forest. I slept having set traps for him last evening, but he freed himself by his wits and escaped those dangers. Today I have again tested him, but here he is about to escape again." Having thus been astonished because of *Mwindo, Muisa* sent his powerful belt of cowries over to where *Mwindo* was, saying to it: "My belt, you are going to *Mwindo.* When you have seen him, you must break him in two and smash his mouth against the ground." The belt, obeying the instructions of its master, went to the banana grove. When it saw *Mwindo* in the banana grove cutting up the banana stems on which there were ripe bananas and carrying them away, it fell upon him and lashed at him, making *Mwindo* scream. It crushed him, smacking his mouth against the ground until froth came out. He couldn't breathe. Urine and excrement flowed out of him, so little could he control himself. Seeing its master unable to find means to escape, *Mwindo*'s scepter recalled its duty. It drew itself up above the head of *Mwindo. Mwindo,* in sneezing, lifted his head. He opened his eyes and gazed about.

During the time *Mwindo* had been pinned down by *Muisa*'s belt, the rope that he was attached to was stilled. It did not move any more. His aunt, back in *Tubondo,* had held on to the other end of the rope. When it was still, she threw herself down, saying that her son was dead. She uttered a cry, low and high, imploring the gods, and she said: "However he returns, I will take care of him." Back where *Mwindo* was, he lifted up his eyes, and sang:

Though Muisa *slay* Mwindo
And I shall die,
Muisa, *you are really helpless against* Mwindo,
Against Mwindo, *the Little One Just Born He Walked.*

Mwindo, while singing, remembered his aunt: "You there in *Tubondo,* I felt that my rope did not move, that it had become still because *Muisa* had pinned me to the ground. He wrapped me up like a bunch of bananas. But don't worry any more, there where you are, because I am saved. It is my scepter that brought me back to life."

Mwindo now sent his scepter to *Muisa* in the village, saying: "You, my scepter, when you have arrived where *Muisa* is in the village, you must smash him powerfully. You must force his mouth to the ground so that his tongue will cut the earth like a hoe. For as long as I stay away from the village, you must not let him loose again."

The scepter went whirling around. When it arrived at *Muisa*'s meeting place, it smashed him. It shoved his mouth to the ground. His tongue dug into the earth. He could not control his bowels and he messed himself badly. He couldn't breathe.

Mwindo stayed in the banana grove preparing a load of bananas, both green ones and ripe ones. When he returned to the village, he glanced over at the meeting place and he saw *Muisa*. Foam spewed out of his mouth and nose, he was so enraged. *Kahindo, Muisa*'s daughter, seeing *Mwindo,* hurried to him. She told him: "You are just coming here, while my father's body has already cooled in death." *Mwindo* answered *Kahindo* that he had come looking for his father: "Now bring my father here, so that I may go home with him." *Kahindo* answered: "First you must heal my father. Then I will show you your father, and deliver him to you." *Mwindo* sang while awakening *Muisa:*

He who sleeps shall wake up.
Muisa, *you are powerless against* Mwindo
Because Mwindo *is the Little One Just Born He Walked.*
Kahombo, *whom* Muisa *brought forth,*
He-who-is-accustomed-to-mocking-himself.
Muisa, *you are helpless against* Mwindo.
A bit of food, thanks, puts an end to a song.

Mwindo went on singing like that while incessantly beating *Muisa*'s head with his scepter to bring him back to life. When *Muisa* had awakened and saw that he was safe, he said: "You, *Mwindo,* lo, you are a powerful man."

Muisa again tested *Mwindo*. "You, child, must go as soon as it is light and gather for me the honey that is in that tree there." After *Mwindo* had been shown that honey by *Muisa* so he could set out in the early morning to extract it, sky became night. *Kahindo* stirred paste for *Mwindo*. Having eaten the paste, they went to sleep.

When the sky had turned to day, *Mwindo* took up his axe and went straight into the forest to gather the honey. He took coals with him to start a fire. When he arrived at the base of the tree, he climbed up into it, arriving at the hive where the honey was. *Mwindo* made the fire, and used it to smoke out the bees. When it was ready, he struck his axe against the trunk, singing:

> *I am extracting honey in* Muisa's *country;*
> *My friend* Nkuba, *may you be victorious.*
> *Hatred is in the heart.*
> *My little father threw me into the drum into the river;*
> *My father believed that I would drift away.*

Muisa, back in the village, said: "I think this man will finally gather this honey!" *Muisa* sent his magical belt. It flew and smashed *Mwindo* against the tree trunk. Again he couldn't breathe and he couldn't control his bowels. Urine and excrement ran down his legs.

His aunt *Iyangura* saw that the rope was still, and again she feared that he was dead. Where *Mwindo* had left it, his scepter realized that its master was dying. It climbed up to where he was, pressed against the tree trunk, and it beat and beat on the head of *Mwindo. Mwindo* sneezed. He lifted his eyes and gasped. *Mwindo* said: "Lo, while I was perched here, I was on the verge of death." When he had opened his eyes, he implored his friend *Nkuba,* singing:

> *My friend* Nkuba, *be victorious.*
> *Hatred is in the heart.*

In climbing down, he gazed into the sky, saying: "My friend *Nkuba,* I am suffering." When *Nkuba* heard the cry of his friend *Mwindo,* he descended to the tree. He cleaved it into pieces. On the ground, his friend *Mwindo* did not have a single wound.

Mwindo had come down with the basket of honey. He carried it to *Muisa*'s. He laid the honey basket at his feet. Then *Muisa* sent a boy to look for the place where he had hidden *Shemwindo*. The boy arrived there, but *Shemwindo* was gone. Having seen no one there, the boy returned to *Muisa* and *Mwindo*. He told them: "While you were sitting here, *Shemwindo* has fled. He is not where he has been." Just then *Kahungu* came in and told *Mwindo*: "Your companion *Muisa* lies, for he has warned your father to flee to *Ntumba*'s, the sacred aardvark, saying that you are too powerful." After *Kahungu* had told *Mwindo* the news in that manner, he flew away into the sky.

Mwindo then told *Muisa* the truth bluntly. "Bring me my father right now! Have him emerge from where you have hidden him so that

I may take him with me. You scoundrel, you said that when I plowed a field for you, and when I gathered honey for you, you would then give me my father. I want you to produce him right now." When *Muisa* heard how *Mwindo* was criticizing him, he twitched his eyes. He said: "This time, this boy is really getting annoying, and right here in my own village."

Having seen that *Muisa* did not produce his father, *Mwindo* began to beat *Muisa* on the head with his scepter. *Muisa* then couldn't control himself and excrement stuck to his buttocks. He fainted away. His urine ran all over the ground, and froth came out of his nose and eyes and covered his face. He tossed his hooves up into the air and he stiffened like a viper. *Mwindo* said, "Stay like that, you dog." He would not heal him until he came back. *Mwindo* was going in pursuit of his father, where he had gone to the aardvark, *Ntumba*'s. *Mwindo* went on singing:

I am searching for Shemwindo
In the place where Shemwindo *went.*
Shemwindo *fled into* Ntumba's *dwelling.*
I am searching for Ntumba's *dwelling*
Ntumba, *open for me.*
Shemwindo *is in flight inside* Ntumba's *dwelling.*
I am searching for my father Shemwindo
In Ntumba's *dwelling.*
The sun begins to set.
I am searching for Shemwindo.
Shemwindo *is in flight inside* Ntumba's *dwelling.*
My little father threw me into the drum.

Mwindo implored lightning-bringing *Nkuba,* saying:

My friend Nkuba, *may you be victorious.*
Hatred is in the heart.
My little father, the dearest one,
I am searching for my father in Ntumba's *dwelling,*
My friend Nkuba, *may you be victorious,*
Hatred is in the heart.
I am looking for my little father.
My little father threw me into the drum,
My little father, eternal malefactor among people.
My little father shot me into the river.
Ntumba, *open for me.*

Mwindo paced around *Ntumba*'s cave where his father was, but inside *Ntumba* paid no attention to him. Then the aardvark, *Ntumba,* made a sign to *Shemwindo,* saying: "You be ready to go. The little man at the door is strong, and you see the way he is threatening at the entrance of the cave." When *Shemwindo* heard how his son was toughening himself (like a hide drying in the sun) at the entrance of the cave, he said: "The little boy comes to us looking severe." Then he told his friend *Ntumba* that he was going to continue to run away. *Shemwindo* then escaped to *Sheburungu*'s—the god of creation, known too as *Onfo*.

Where *Nkuba* was in the sky, when he heard the voice of *Mwindo,* he said: "My friend is already too tired of praying to me." *Nkuba* sent down seven bolts of lightning. They struck inside the cave, cleaving it into a million pieces. The cave turned into dust. Realizing that his friend *Nkuba* had struck the cave, *Mwindo* opened the door, and walked inside. He searched for his father there in the cave but did not find him. Then he met *Ntumba* and told him: "*Ntumba,* where did you let my father go, where have you hidden him?" The aardvark kept silent as though he had not heard. *Mwindo* spat at him, saying: "Get out, you scoundrel! While I was spending all my energy at the door asking you to open up for me, you refused. May you die of scrotal elephantiasis!"

When *Ntumba* saw the way in which *Mwindo* proceeded to blame him, he said to *Mwindo*: "You see how my house was just destroyed and all my crop. What am I going to do now?" Where *Kahungu* dwelt in the sky, he came down. He went to bring the news to *Mwindo*. He arrived, saying: "You know, *Mwindo,* that *Ntumba* has allowed your father to escape. Your father ran away to *Sheburungu*'s." *Kahungu,* having brought *Mwindo* the information, again flew away into the sky. *Mwindo* remained at *Ntumba*'s. Because of anger and weariness, he cursed the aardvark: "*Ntumba,* this is how you will die—may you never again find food in this country of yours." Where his aunt *Iyangura* dwelt in *Tubondo,* she went on pondering sadly, saying: "My heart will return to normal only when *Mwindo* is safely back from where he has gone." She looked at the rope that she was holding. She said: "Lo, *Mwindo* is still searching for the place to which his father has escaped."

Mwindo followed his father, going in search of him all wrapped up in hatred. He arrived at the entrance of the creation god, *Sheburungu*'s, village. He encountered a group of little children there. They greeted him, saying: "*Mwindo,* don't run ahead of us. We are hungry and we need you to give us food." *Mwindo* implored his aunt *Iyangura* to send him food, telling her that the children of *Sheburungu* were hungry. While asking for food from his aunt, *Mwindo* sang. *Mwindo* howled. He said:

Oh, you there, where Iyangura *has stayed,*
Sister of Shemwindo,
I must have seven portions of food.
You see where Mwindo *passed,*
I am suffering from hunger.
Aunt Iyangura,
I am claiming meat.

Having said to his aunt that he needed seven portions of meat and paste to come to him there where he was with the children of *Sheburungu, Mwindo* looked up, and the pastes had already arrived. *Mwindo* gave them to the youngsters. The children of *Sheburungu* began eating the paste, while *Mwindo* kept them company. When the children had finished eating, *Mwindo* returned the wicker plates to his aunt *Iyangura,* telling her to line them up so that they might be used as steps to climb up to *Sheburungu*'s. *Mwindo* sent back the wicker plates, singing:

I send back the wicker and wooden plates.
O Aunt Iyangura, *(I pay you honor),*
I send back the wicker and wooden plates.

After he had sent back the wicker and wooden plates, he climbed up to *Sheburungu*'s, and the youngsters followed him (as they always do when a visitor arrives). He went up to *Sheburungu*'s, singing:

Sheburungu, *you,*
I am looking for Shemwindo.
Shemwindo *gave birth to a hero*
In giving birth to the Little One Just Born He Walked.
Sheburungu,
I am looking for Shemwindo.

Sheburungu shouted and said:

O Mwindo, *let us gamble together!*

And *Mwindo* shouted and said:

O *my father* Sheburungu,
I am looking for Shemwindo.

And he—

O Mwindo, *let us gamble together!*

And *Mwindo* shouted, he said:

O my father, give me Shemwindo!
My little father threw me into the drum,
My little father threw me into the river.
The youngsters asked me to gamble with them,
The youngsters—I do not gamble with them.

After *Mwindo* had entreated *Sheburungu* to return his father, *Sheburungu* said to him: "I cannot just give your father to you. First we must gamble. Then I will deliver your father to you, and then you may go home with him." Thus *Sheburungu* spoke to *Mwindo. Mwindo* answered him: "Go ahead and spread the seed shells out on the ground that I may guess at how many there are (for that was how they gambled). I will not run away from you for you know the dangers that I have already escaped from." After *Sheburungu* had heard *Mwindo*'s response, he brought a mat and spread it out on the ground. He brought out the very old seed shells of the *isea* tree. *Sheburungu* wagered: "*Mwindo,* if you beat me, you will carry your father off with you. Here are three sums of money. If you beat me, you will carry them off, too." *Mwindo* wagered three sums of money. *Sheburungu* was the first to take a handful of seeds. With the first take-up, he won all of *Mwindo*'s money. *Mwindo* wagered the goats that remained in *Tubondo. Sheburungu* took the seeds and he won all the goats from *Mwindo. Mwindo* wagered everything, even his aunt—*Sheburungu* won all his goods and his followers and his aunt. *Mwindo* simply sat there all alone with his scepter. And then *Mwindo* wagered his scepter. When *Sheburungu* tried to take the seeds, he failed. *Mwindo* took the seeds. He won back from *Sheburungu* all the money that he had wagered. *Sheburungu* wagered again and *Mwindo* again took the seeds. All that *Sheburungu* had bet, *Mwindo* won it back. *Sheburungu* wagered all his objects, together with his cattle. *Mwindo* took the seeds up again, and again he won. Finally he won all the things of *Sheburungu*—people, goats, cattle. *Mwindo* piled up everything and *Sheburungu* was left all alone.

Kantori and *Kahungu* ran to where *Mwindo* was, warning him: "You, *Mwindo,* come quickly, your father is trying to run away again." After he had heard that news, *Mwindo* abandoned the game: he sped away to encounter his father in the banana grove of *Sheburungu.*

Seeing his father, *Mwindo* inquired of him: "O my father, are you here?" (Now he was able to pay the respect due to a father, for he had defeated him properly.) *Shemwindo* answered: "Here I am." *Mwindo* again inquired of his father: "O *Shemwindo*, is it really you?" *Shemwindo* again answered: "Here I am, my son."

After *Mwindo* had seized his father, he returned with him to *Sheburungu's*. *Mwindo* said: "*Sheburungu*, you have been hiding my father. This is my father, is he not?" *Mwindo* said further to *Sheburungu*: "*Sheburungu*, I don't want any of your things that I have won. Just keep all those things that I have won, for I am leaving here with my father." *Mwindo* gave his respectful farewell to *Sheburungu* and to all his people: "O father *Sheburungu*, farewell!" *Sheburungu* answered: "Yes, you, too, *Mwindo*, go and be strong, along with your father *Shemwindo*." After *Mwindo* had said farewell to *Sheburungu*, he returned singing:

Listen, Ntumba,
He who went away comes back.

Mwindo shook the rope, reminding his aunt, and telling her of his return. And where his aunt remained, she had bells attached to the rope. *Mwindo* sang:

He who went away comes back,
You see I am carrying Shemwindo.

Mwindo rushed headlong to the cave, which *Ntumba* had already finished rebuilding. *Mwindo* said to *Ntumba*: "Why did you hide my father away? Here I am with my father." *Mwindo* sang:

Ntumba, *even you are powerless against* Mwindo,
For Mwindo *is the Little One Just Born He Walked.*
I am on my way home from this point on in Ntumba's *house.*
Look, I am carrying Shemwindo,
My father, the dearest one,
Shemwindo, *senior brother of* Iyangura.
It is Shemwindo, *the one who gave birth to a hero.*
Aunt Iyangura, *I am on my way back.*
Mwindo *is the Little One Just Born He Walked.*
I am carrying my father, Shemwindo.

When *Mwindo* arrived at *Ntumba's*, he told *Ntumba* the whole story. He said to him: "You, *Ntumba*, you were wrong to offend me in vain." But he gave back all of *Ntumba*'s things, his land, and the banana groves, and his followers, everything. And *Mwindo* and his father *Shemwindo* spent the night there. Then, the next day, *Ntumba* said to *Mwindo*: "Go, I will never utter slander against you. I have no dispute with you." When *Mwindo* left *Ntumba*'s, together with his father, he went singing, reminding his aunt in *Tubondo*:

> *He who has gone away is back.*
> Muisa!
> *The sky has become day.*
> *The rooster crowed.*
> Mwindo *will arrive in the house of* Muisa,
> *I come from* Ntumba's.
> Muisa, *you are helpless against* Mwindo,
> *Since* Mwindo *is the Little One Just Born He Walked.*
> *It is you who are wrong for offending me in vain.*
> *Look! I am carrying* Shemwindo.
> Muisa, *you are helpless against* Mwindo,
> *Since* Mwindo *is the Little One Just Born He Walked.*
> *Look! I am carrying* Shemwindo.
> *I am returning to* Tubondo,
> *Where remained my aunt* Iyangura,
> Iyangura, *sister of* Shemwindo,
> *Aunt, birth-giver,* Iyangura.

When *Mwindo* left *Ntumba*'s village with his father *Shemwindo*, he went straightaway to *Muisa*'s house. When he was there, *Kahindo* came to *Mwindo*, saying: "You see my father here, his bones fill a basket. What shall I do then? It is fitting that you should heal my father. Don't leave him like that but wake him up. May my father wake up, because he is the chief of all the people." After *Kahindo* had spoken to *Mwindo* in that way, *Mwindo* woke up *Muisa*, singing:

> *He who went to sleep wakes up,*
> *Father* Muisa,
> *He who went to sleep wakes up.*
> *Look!*
> *You,*
> *It is you who have offended me in vain.*
> *Look! I am carrying my father* Shemwindo.
> Muisa, *he who went to sleep wakes up.*
> Muisa, *you are helpless against* Mwindo,
> Mwindo *is the Little One Just Born He Walked.*
> Shemwindo *brought forth a hero.*

I am going to Aunt Iyangura*'s village,*
Iyangura, *sister of* Shemwindo.

While *Mwindo* was awakening *Muisa,* he kept on striking him all the time with his scepter, saying: "You have offended me in vain. You have tried to be equal to *Mwindo,* whereas *Mwindo* is the Little One Just Born He Walked, the little one who does not eat earthly foods. The day he was born, he did not drink at the breasts of his mother." When *Mwindo* had finished awakening *Muisa, Muisa* was brought back to life. *Mwindo* revealed to him his great secret, that he had been forged by his uncles, the people of *Yana.* "My body is covered with iron only, and you, *Muisa,* don't you see me?" *Muisa* asked *Mwindo*: "You, *Mwindo,* how were you born? Do you have a medicine that makes you able to do these things?" *Mwindo* unwound for him the thread of his story. He told him: "*Muisa,* have you never heard that I came out of the middle of my mother? I was not born in the same way that other children are born, but I was born speaking and even walking! You, *Muisa,* have you never heard that I was thrown into a grave, one that they had even put banana stems on, but I came back to life. My father threw me once more into the drum, which he threw into the river, but I emerged from the water once more. Have you not heard all these marvelous things, *Muisa*? That is why you dared to make a fool of me."

When *Mwindo* was at *Muisa*'s, he shook the rope to remind his aunt there in *Tubondo* that he would return. *Iyangura* said to *Mwindo*'s uncles, the people of *Yana,* that where *Mwindo* had gone, he had long ago captured his father, and that he was now on his way home with him. While returning to *Tubondo, Mwindo* said farewell to *Muisa;* he sang:

You, Muisa,
You see me already leaving,
You Muisa, *taker of other's things.*
Where Aunt Iyangura *remains*
In Tubondo,
He who went away is back.

When *Muisa* saw *Mwindo* going, he said to him: "Oh, *Mwindo,* my son, it's befitting that you marry my *Kahindo* here." *Mwindo* answered him: "I cannot marry here, I shall marry later in *Tubondo.*"

The Return of the Hero

Mwindo set forth. He and his father went home, emerging where they had entered, at the root of the *kikoka* fern. When *Mwindo* and *Shemwindo* arrived at the entrance of *Tubondo,* those who were in the village, *Iyangura* and the uncles of *Mwindo,* swarmed there like bees. They went to greet *Mwindo* and his father at the entrance, where they met them. Seeing *Mwindo, Iyangura* and the uncles of *Mwindo* lifted him up into the air carrying him on their fingertips. When they had walked around the village of *Tubondo, Mwindo* told them to let him down. They put him down in the center of the village. They gathered many spear heads and put him on top of them. His maternal uncles put him to the test so they might know if their nephew had remained as he was when they had forged him. After *Mwindo* was seated in the middle of the village, he told his aunt the story of where he had been and how he had fought while searching for his father. He sang:

When I descended with the rope,
Aunt, I met with Kahindo.
Kahindo *shouted and said:*
"Mwindo, *let me charge you with these words:*
If you see Muisa, *what* Muisa *will say,*
You should refuse it."
Mwindo *said: "I go to the village, the village place*
Where Muisa *lives,*
If I am not victorious there Muisa *remains."*
When I arrived in the village of Muisa,
Muisa *shouted, and said:*
"Mwindo, *sit down here."*
Mwindo *shouted, complaining,*
Saying, "This is your head, Muisa."
Muisa *shouted, and said:*
"Counselors, give me some little beer
So that I may give it to Mwindo."
And Mwindo *shouted, complaining:*
"A father's urine a child never drinks."
Muisa *said: "Let us fight together."*
I kneaded Muisa *with my own hands,*
Quickly on my way.
I arrived in Ntumba*'s cave,*
In the cave of Ntumba,
Ntumba *said: "Let's fight together."*
I kneaded Ntumba *with my own hands,*
I, who had kneaded Muisa.

You too, Ntumba, *are powerless against* Mwindo,
Mwindo, *the Little One Just Born He Walked.*
I kneaded Ntumba *so that I got tired.*
Already I was hurrying to Sheburungu's *house.*
When I arrived there at the entrance of Sheburungu's,
One of the gods,
The youngsters howled, saying:
"*Oh,* Mwindo, *we are hungry.*"
I sent pastes over there.
The youngsters ate the pastes.
Already I was on my way to Sheburungu's,
Together with the youngsters.
Sheburungu *said: "Let us gamble."*
I said: "You Sheburungu,
You are powerless against Mwindo,
The Little One Just Born He Walked.
Who made Muisa *and* Ntumba *fail.*"
I shouted, complaining,
I, saying: "Give me my father here."
Sheburungu shouted, saying:
"Mwindo, *you are helpless in the game against* Sheburungu,
Which has beaten Heaven and Earth."
We took a handful of seeds.
Mwindo *shouted, and said:*
"Sheburungu, *you are helpless against* Mwindo.
Give me Shemwindo.
You see, I have already beaten you."
Kahungu *notified* Mwindo,
Kahungu *showed me* Shemwindo.
It is I who seized Shemwindo,
My father, the dearest one.
We were already on the return trip.
"Shemwindo, *let us go home,*
Let us go up to Tubondo
Where remained Aunt Iyangura."
What Shemwindo *accomplished!*
I arrive at the peak in Tubondo.
You see, I am carrying Shemwindo,
I am carrying my dear father.

Iyangura gave her son this order: "Since you have arrived with your father, bring him first into the shrine of good fortune to let him rest there." They carried *Shemwindo* into the shrine hut. He settled down in it. In giving due hospitality to his father, *Mwindo* killed the goat that never defecates and never urinates. They cooked it, along with the rarest of rice, for his father. He said to his father: "Here are your goats! It is you who were wrong in vain. You set yourself against *Mwindo,* the Little One Just Born He Walked, when you said that you did not want any boys, that you wanted only girls. You did a deliberate wrong in the way you wished things to be. You did not know the strength of the blessing of *Mwindo.*"

After *Mwindo* had given food to his father as a hospitality gift, *Iyangura* said to him: "My son, shall we go on living always in this desolate village, we alone, without other people? I, *Iyangura,* I want you to save all the people who lived here in this village. When you have brought them back to life it is then only that I shall be able to know how great you are in beating *Shemwindo.* Only then can I tell others the story of the ways in which he acted, and the evil that he did against you." *Mwindo* listened to the order of his aunt to heal those who had died. His uncles, the people of *Yana,* beat the drum for him while he, *Mwindo,* was dancing with the joy of seeing his father. They sang. His aunt shouted, and said:

My father, eternal savior of people.

Mwindo said:

Oh, father, they tell me to save the people.
I say: "He who went to sleep wakes up."
Little Mwindo *is the Little One Just Born He Walked.*
My little father threw me into the drum.
Shemwindo, *you do not know how to lead people.*
The habits of people are difficult.
My little father, eternal malefactor among people,
Made bees fall down on me,
Bees of day and sun.
I lacked all means of protection against them.

While *Mwindo* was healing those who died in *Tubondo,* he went on in the following way: when we arrived at the bone of a man, he beat it with his scepter so that the man would then wake up. The resuscitation was as follows:

Each one who died in pregnancy will come back to life
in her pregnancy.
Each one who died in labor revives while still in labor.
Each one who was preparing paste resuscitated stirring paste.

Each one who died defecating reborn defecating.
Each one who died setting traps comes to life trapping.
Each one who died copulating comes alive copulating.
Each one who died forging brought alive forging.
Each one who died cultivating comes to life cultivating.
Each one who died making pots and jars is reborn shaping.
Each one who died carving dishes comes to life carving.
Each one who died quarreling with a partner is brought back still quarreling.

Mwindo stayed in the village for three days bringing people back to life. He was bone weary. Each person he revived, arose straight up like a tree. *Tubondo* was lively once again with the people and the goats, the dogs, the cattle, the poultry, the male rams, and the female ewes, the teenage boys and girls, the children and the youngsters, the old males and females. In the middle of all those people were the nobles and counselors and the Pygmies and all the royal initiators. All those also were planted back in their own places. All the groups that formerly dwelt in *Tubondo* came back to life and became as they were before. Each person who died having things of a certain quantity, came back to life still having his things. *Tubondo* again became the big village with seven entrances.

When the people were revived, *Iyangura* began to speak in the middle of the crowd of people, saying: "You, *Shemwindo,* my brother, have your followers prepare quantities of beer and kill cows and goats for a feast. Let all the people meet here in *Tubondo*. Then we shall be able to examine in detail our deep concerns and to resolve them in our assembly." After *Shemwindo* had heard the voice of his sister *Iyangura,* he uttered a cry, high and low, to all his people, saying that they should have beer together so they might meet together, discuss important things together.

The Royal Presentation

After a week had passed, all groups within his domain swarmed into *Tubondo,* bringing beer and different kinds of meat. On the morning of the eighth day, all the people of the villages of *Shemwindo*'s kingdom pressed together in the assembly. After all the people, the children and the youngsters, the adults and the elders, had gathered about, *Mwindo* cleaned and dressed. His aunt *Iyangura,* she too wrapped herself in her clothes, those famous ones of *Mukiti.* His father *Shemwindo,* he too dressed himself from top to bottom: bark cloths on which were red color and castor oil, fringes, hair ornaments. He too became something to behold. After the people had grouped themselves in the assembly, servants stretched mats out on the ground in the place where *Mwindo* and his father and his aunt would pass. Everyone kept silent, a sacred total silence. Those three radiant stars, *Mwindo* and his father and his aunt, appeared from inside the house. They came out into the open to the assembly, marching solemnly. Those who were in the gathering of the assembly gave them the gift of their eyes: There where the powerful ones appeared, that is where their attention was focused. Some among them asked who the marvelous boy was, saying: "I wonder, has *Shemwindo* been reborn in the form of another young man?" Some answered: "*Shemwindo* is there with the chief of *Shekwabahinga,* together with his wife." Some said: "No, *Shemwindo* is there with his sister, *Mukiti*'s wife, and with *Mukiti* himself." The remainder knew that *Shemwindo* was with his sister *Iyangura, Mukiti*'s wife, together with his son *Mwindo,* the Little One Just Born He Walked, the man of many wonders, the one who was formerly slain and cast off by his father.

Shemwindo and *Mwindo* and *Iyangura* went in a line, while appearing in the middle of the gathering of the assembly. *Mwindo* begged his friend, lightning-bringing *Nkuba,* for three copper chairs. *Nkuba* sent them down. When they were close to the earth, they remained suspended in the air about five meters from the ground. *Mwindo* and his father and his aunt climbed up onto the chairs. *Iyangura* sat down in the middle of both, *Shemwindo* on the right side and *Mwindo* on the left side. When all the men had grouped themselves within the assembly and had entered fully into the silence, *Mwindo* stood up from his chair. He raised his eyes into the air, imploring *Nkuba,* saying: "Oh, my friend *Nkuba,* prevent the sky from falling!" Having spoken like that, he lowered his eyes toward the ground, down upon the mass of people. He said, he lauded them, saying: "Be strong, you chiefs." They approved of it. He said: "You counselors be strong." They approved of it. Then he said: "You seniors, be strong." They approved. *Mwindo* praised the council, holding all the powerful things with which he had been born: the scepter, the axe, the little bag in which the rope was. He also held an ancient stick so that he might respectfully praise the council. After *Mwindo* had finished praising the council, he made a proclamation: "Among the seven groups that are here in *Tubondo,* may each group be seated together in a cluster, and the chiefs and the seniors of the other villages, may they also be seated in their own group."

After he had finished speaking, the people gathered themselves in an orderly manner, each group in its own cluster: *Mwindo* also ordered that all his father's wives, his seven mothers, be seated in one group but the *Nyamwindo,* the mother who gave birth to him, should separate herself somewhat from his other mothers, called "the little mothers." After he had spoken like that, the little mothers moved to form their own cluster. His mother who gave birth to him moved a short distance away, all the while remaining near her co-spouses so they might not spite her.

Mwindo now ordered *Shemwindo* to speak: "My father, it is your turn. Explain to the chiefs why you have had a grudge against me. If I have taken a portion larger than yours, if I have borne ill will against you because of your goods, if I have snatched them away from you, tell the chiefs the story of what has happened so that they may understand." *Shemwindo* was flabbergasted. Sweat arose from his big toe, climbed up to his testicles, arrived at the hair on his head. In a manly move, *Shemwindo* got up. Because of the great shame in his eyes, *Shemwindo* no longer praised the chiefs. Quivering, he spoke, choking a bit as he did so: all this brought about by the great evil that caused him to destroy *Mwindo. Shemwindo* said: "All you chiefs who are here, I don't deny the harm that I have committed against this, my offspring, my son. Indeed, I had passed a law upon my wives, in the middle of the group of counselors and nobles, stating that I would kill, together with her child, any among my wives who would give birth to a son. Among all the wives, six gave birth only to girls, but it was my beloved one who gave birth to a boy. After my beloved one had given birth to a boy, I came to despise her. My preferred wife became my despised one. In the middle of all this anger, I armed myself with a spear. I threw it into the birth hut six times. I wanted to kill the child with its mother. When I saw that the child was not dead, I made an agreement with the counselors and the nobles—they threw this child away into a grave. When we woke up in the morning, upon awakening, we saw the child already wailing again in its mother's house. When I heard that, I asked myself in my heart: *If I continue to fail to kill this child, then it will usurp my royal chair. Now I have seen all these amazing things that he is doing here, so this child will cause me a big problem.* It's only then that I put him into the drum and threw him into the river. Where this child went, I believed that I was doing away with him, but I was only making him stronger. It is from these acts that the child's anger stems. When he came out of the river, he marched right against me, attacking me right here in *Tubondo.*

"From that point on I began to flee, all my people having been wiped out. Where I fled, I rejoiced, saying I was safe, thinking that where I was going, there was salvation, whereas I was casting myself into the thorns of rambling around throughout the country, counting tree roots, sleeping in filthy places, eating terrible foods. From that moment on, my son set out in search of me. He went to deliver me from the abyss of evil in which I was involved. I was at that time withered like dried bananas. And it is like that, that I arrive here in the village of *Tubondo*. So may the male offspring be spared for he has shown me the way in which the sky becomes daylight and has given me the joy of witnessing again the warmth of the people and of all the things here in *Tubondo*."

Then *Iyangura* spoke to the men who were sitting in the assembly, reproaching *Shemwindo* openly. "Here I am, aunt of *Mwindo,* you chiefs. Our young man here, *Shemwindo,* has married me to *Mukiti*. I got accustomed to it thanks to the confidence of my husband. Thanks to my labor and to getting along with him, my husband raised me high up, so that he loved me above all the wives he had married. So then, you chiefs, so that I may not bore you, let me not carry you far off in a long line of many words. Suddenly, this child appeared where I was living. *Mukiti* was then on the verge of killing him because he did not know of our relationship. But his intelligence and his anger saved him. From then on I followed him to show him the way to *Shemwindo*'s. It's there that *Mwindo*'s fights with his father began, because of the anger caused by all the evils that his father perpetrated against him. He subdued this village, *Tubondo,* and his father fled. Where he fled, *Mwindo* went in search of him, saying that his father should not go to die in the leaves like an animal. When he found him, he seized him. Then *Mwindo* made his father return again to this village, *Tubondo*. So it is that we are in this meeting of the assembly of the chiefs.

"You, *Shemwindo,* acted badly, together with your counselors and nobles. If this plan of torment had emanated from a counselor against *Mwindo,* then his throat would be cut, here in the council. But you are safe, it being you from whom this plan sprang. You acted badly, you, *Shemwindo,* when you discriminated against the children, saying that some were bad and others good, whereas you did not know what was in the womb of your wife. What you were given by the creator god, you saw it to be bad. The good was turned into the bad in your eyes. But nevertheless, we are satisfied, you notables, because of the way in which we are up on our feet again here in *Tubondo,* but this *Shemwindo* has committed an iniquitous deed. If the people had been exterminated here, it is *Shemwindo* who would have been guilty of exterminating them. I, *Iyangura,* I am finished."

After *Iyangura* had spoken, *Mwindo* also stood up: he praised the assembly, he said: "As for me, I, *Mwindo,* man of many feats, the Little One Just Born He Walked, I will not hold a grudge against my father. May my father here not be frightened, believing that I am still angry with him. No, I am not angry with my father. What my father did against me and what I did against my father, all that is already over. Now let us examine what is to come, the evil and the good. The one of us who will start an argument, it is he who will be in the wrong—

and all those seniors here will be the witness of it. Now, let us live in harmony in our country, let us care for our people well."

Shemwindo declared that as far as he was concerned, the act of giving birth was not repugnant in itself. He said that where he was here, no longer was he chief. Now it was *Mwindo* who would succeed him, and if anyone insulted *Mwindo,* the seniors would denounce him. When *Mwindo* heard his father's voice, he answered him: "Father, sit down on your royal chair. I cannot be chief as long as you are alive, otherwise I would die suddenly." The counselors and nobles agreed with *Mwindo.* They said to *Shemwindo:* "Your son did not speak wrongly. Divide the country into two parts and give your son one part and you keep a part. If you were to give away all authority, you would again be immensely jealous of him, and this jealously could trouble this country in the long run." *Shemwindo* said: "No, you counselors and nobles, I cannot agree, for I want my son to become chief. From now on, I shall always work behind him." The counselors told him: "You, *Shemwindo,* divide your country into two parts, you take a part and your son a part. You always used to say that you alone were a man surpassing all others but that you feared what was to come. That is why we witnessed all these deep discussions—we had no way of disagreeing with you because you inspired fear. If the chief cannot be disagreed with, then the talking is too great a foolishness." *Shemwindo* said: "Since you, my counselors and my nobles, come to give me this advice, so I am ready to divide the country into two parts—for *Mwindo* a part and for myself, *Shemwindo,* a part, because of the fear you inspire. But in my own name, I had wanted to leave the country to *Mwindo,* and from then on, out of respect, always have eaten the food after my son for I have felt and do feel much shame in the face of my son and of all the people."

After *Shemwindo* had spoken thus, he conferred the kingship upon his son: He stripped himself of all the things of kingship that he bore. He gave *Mwindo* a dress dyed red and two red belts; he also gave him the expensive bracelets made of raphia string to wear on his arms; he gave him a boar skin belt and gave him a raphia and hair belt as well; he gave him a powerful fur hat; he also gave him the hide of a white goat. *Shemwindo* dressed *Mwindo* in all those things while *Mwindo* was standing up, because a chief is always dressed in such things while he is standing. The counselors went to fetch the chair imbued with powerful powder and oil. They gave it to *Shemwindo. Shemwindo* made *Mwindo* sit on it. *Shemwindo* handed over to *Mwindo* the scepter of copper on which there were incisions imbued with the powerful powder and oil. *Shemwindo* handed these things over to him when he was already seated on the chair. When he stood up, his father also handed over to him the wrist protector and the bow. He also gave him the quiver in which there were arrows, with royal emblems on all of them. They dressed him in all these things in the guesthouse.

After *Shemwindo* had thus enthroned his son, *Mwindo* shouted that he now had become famous, but he would not act as his father had, causing his own name only to be perpetuated by having only one group remain on earth, named after him and honoring his deeds. "May all the various families and groups be celebrated here. May many boys and girls be born and our people increase. May there be born also deaf and cripples, because a country is never without some handicapped." After *Shemwindo* had dressed his son in the chiefly paraphernalia, he distributed beer and meat for the chiefs who were there. Each group took a goat and a cow. They also gave *Iyangura* one cow to bring back to her husband *Mukiti*. Then the chiefs and the counselors who were there, said: "Let *Mwindo* remain here in *Tubondo* and let *Shemwindo* go to dwell on another mountain." Hearing this, *Shemwindo* clapped his hands—he was very satisfied. During *Mwindo*'s enthronement, his uncles, the people of *Yana*, gave him a maiden. *Mwindo*'s father, he, too, gave him a maiden called *Katobororo* and the Pygmies gave him one as well. During *Mwindo*'s enthronement, he was given, altogether, four women—he went on getting himself married while he was crossing the country. After *Mwindo* had been enthroned, the assembly dispersed. All those who came from somewhere, returned there. *Shemwindo* also took possession of his mountain. He left *Tubondo* to his son.

When *Iyangura*, aunt of *Mwindo*, returned to her husband, she anointed *Mwindo* in the middle of the group, saying:

> O, Mwindo, *hail!*
> *Blessing, here, hail!*
> *If your father throws you into the grave, hail!*
> *Don't harbor resentment, hail!*
> *May you stand up and make your first step, hail!*
> *May you be safe, may you be blessed, hail!*
> *And your father and your mother, hail!*
> *May you bring forth tall children, boys and girls.*
> *Be strong, my father. As for me, there is nothing*
> *ominous left, hail!*

When *Mwindo* took leave of his father, his father also gave him a blessing. *Mwindo* handed over to his aunt two counselors to accompany her. He also gave her four goats and a return gift of twenty baskets of rice and five little chicken baskets.

Confronting the Dragon, and Being Punished for His Deeds

After a fixed number of days had elapsed since he had been enthroned, *Mwindo* said that he had a terrible craving to eat some wild pig meat. He sent his Pygmies forth, for they were his hunters, out into the forest. Where the Pygmies went in the forest, when they had already been hither and yon, they felt tired, they slept halfway. In the morning they set out right after waking up. They found the trail of wild pigs, followed them, met them. They sent the dogs after them, seeing that they were fleeing. The dogs hurled themselves after them. Crossing two plateaus, they met a red-haired pig who was old and fat. They hurled a sharp spear at it. The pig hadn't the strength to resist, turned its hooves up and died. They cut it into pieces on the spot.

There where they were, in the very dense forest, when they were cutting the pig to pieces, Dragon heard their mumbling. Dragon said: "What now, people here again? I thought that I was the only one living here, whereas there are still others." Dragon went after them, snakelike. When he came close to them, he threw himself onto them. He took away three Pygmies from there—he swallowed them. One among the Pygmies, called *Nkurongo,* wrestled himself loose. He fled and the dogs followed him—they fled with him. Dragon said to himself: "Let this wild pork remain here, for I will trap the dogs and the Pygmy who fled." Dragon nestled down beside the corpse of the pig. *Nkurongo* fled. When he arrived, he looked back, saying: "Lo, my companions have been overtaken by night. They are already dead." At the time when he fixed his eyes on the Dragon, he saw that he had seven heads and seven horns and seven eyes. When that little Pygmy there was already on the crest, he shouted: "I flee, eh!" He fled and the dogs followed him.

He appeared in the village of *Tubondo.* Nearly bursting with breath, he arrived in *Mwindo*'s house. After he had rested awhile—"for as long as it takes a pot of paste to be cooked"—*Mwindo* asked him: "Is there peace there, from where you are coming?" He answered him: "There is no peace there, chief! We went to the forest, four of us, and Dragon has swallowed three of us, and I, *Nkurongo,* escaped, together with the dogs. This Dragon, he is as large as the sky." Hearing that, *Mwindo* said: "Well, now, this time it's tough. My Pygmies in their very first hunt are already exterminated in the forest." He looked up to the sky, lowered his eyes to the ground, and said: "O, my scepter, be victorious tomorrow." That day his father, *Shemwindo,* was in the village. *Mwindo* said to his father: "I shall be gone when the rooster crows, long gone. Right after awakening I shall go with this Pygmy to fight with Dragon." When *Shemwindo* heard this, he forbade his son: "Oh, no, don't go there. Dragon has always been a destroyer. He eats man's bones. If you provoke this Dragon, then you cause great disaster in this country."

Mwindo said to his father: "I do not care. At any rate, I will be gone at dawn. You stay behind to tell the counselors that I have gone to fight with Dragon."

When it was very early in the morning, *Mwindo* took up his scepter and the Pygmy went before him. Thus they proceeded in the forest. When they appeared at the place where they had cut the pig into pieces, the Pygmy pointed at Dragon, saying: "There he is." *Mwindo* said to the Pygmy: "Stop first. Let me take a look at him." *Mwindo* said to the Pygmy: "You stay here. When Dragon swallows me, it is you who will announce the news in the village." *Mwindo* took in hand his subduer of a scepter. He went snakelike after Dragon. When he was eye-to-eye with him, *Mwindo* said: "You will not be my measure today." Dragon was overcome with surprise. He stood up. When he was about to fly against *Mwindo, Mwindo* put sweet words into his mouth. He sang:

Dragon, you are helpless against Mwindo,
For Mwindo *is the Little One Just Born He Walked.*
Dragon, you have challenged Mwindo.
Dragon, you are powerless against Mwindo,
For Mwindo *is the Little One Just Born He Walked.*
Shemwindo *gave birth to a hero.*
Comrade, you are powerless against Mwindo.

When Dragon attempted to swallow *Mwindo, Mwindo* exclaimed: "This time he is finished." *Mwindo* came to where he was, and *Mwindo* beat him with his scepter. Dragon fell upside down and died. *Mwindo* called, shouting to his Pygmy to come to cut up Dragon. The Pygmy came. When he was about to touch Dragon with his great knife, *Mwindo* forbade him, saying: "First, leave him like that. Let us call people in the village to carry him back there so that *Shemwindo* may see the wonders I perform." *Mwindo* implored those who were in the village. *Mwindo* sent his scepter to fetch the people so that they could bring back this god of a dragon. He sang:

O, my scepter, go for me.
Those who have remained in Tubondo *over there,*
Those who have remained in Tubondo *over there,*
At Shemwindo*'s,*
May Shemwindo *send people to me.*

Where the scepter went, it arrived in front of *Shemwindo*. It wagged itself in front of him, and all the people of the village ran out of their homes, they went to see the way in which the scepter was wagging itself in front of *Shemwindo. Shemwindo* said that the scepter was bearing the news: "If *Mwindo* is not dead, it is Dragon who is dead." *Shemwindo* sent a group of people there, saying:

Be ready to leave the village!
Go and join Mwindo!
In the dense forest there are many things—
There are snakes that bite.
Go and join Mwindo,
Where Mwindo *has gone.*
Shemwindo *has given birth to a hero.*

Having wagged itself in front of *Shemwindo,* the scepter flew away together with the people whom *Shemwindo* had provided. When *Mwindo* saw his scepter with the people, the scepter came into *Mwindo*'s hands. *Mwindo* said to the men to lift up Dragon. They made a stretcher and put Dragon on top of it. But that stretcher broke because of Dragon's weight. They made another and put Dragon on it again, they lifted him up and carried it to the village. When he appeared, the whole village crowded together—so many young, so many old people! They let Dragon down in the middle of the village. When the people saw him, they were astonished. They whooped, they said: "Now, things will be coming out of the forest!" But some of them were worried, saying, "Whoever has killed the Dragon cannot fail to kill one of us, perhaps even all of us." *Mwindo* said to his people to cut up Dragon, and he, *Mwindo,* sang:

Dragon is being skinned and cut up on the
little raphia palms.
Shemwindo *howled, saying:*
"Dragon is being skinned and cut up on the
little raphia palms."
Dragon always devours people;
Dragon has exterminated people.
Shemwindwo, *my father, be afraid of me.*

When they opened the belly, there came out a man who leaped up, being alive. There came out another man. He, too, was alive. When they opened the belly, there came out yet another who leaped up, being alive. After Dragon had been cut up and the three Pygmies had come out alive, *Mwindo* gave an order: "When you begin to eat this Dragon, you will eat him with bones and all. Don't throw any of them away."

After Dragon had been cut up, *Mwindo* distributed to his people all the meat with the mass of bones. He told them also that if he saw even a little bone behind somebody's house, he would make him pay for it for Dragon must be roasted in public. When Dragon had been divided up and divided again into many parts, they seized his eyes. They roasted them hot on a piece of potsherd. Each time that there appeared a splatter and the eye burst open, there came out a man. When all the eyes of Dragon had been roasted, there had appeared one thousand people. *Mwindo* said: "These are my people." Then *Mwindo* said farewell to the people one by one.

My mother who carried me,
You are seeing that I am already going.
Nyamwindo *howled, complaining:*
"What shall I do with my child?"
Nyamwindo *howled, saying:*
"I die, I die, along with my child."
Shemwindo *howled, saying:*
"I die, I die, along with my child."

Now, it so happened that *Nkuba* had made a blood pact with Dragon. And there, where *Nkuba* resided in the sky, he breathed in the smell of his friend Dragon that came from his friend *Mwindo* in *Tubondo*. *Nkuba* descended on the spot to take *Mwindo*. He arrived in *Mwindo*'s village. *Nkuba* said to *Mwindo*: "I come to take you, you my friend. I want to teach you because I am very vexed with you, you my friend, since you dared to kill Dragon, for Dragon, too, was my friend. So know that you are doing wrong." Hearing this, *Mwindo* was not afraid of going away with *Nkuba,* but his people were stricken with anxiety, thinking that their chief was going forever. *Mwindo* sang:

Let us go up to Bisherya *over there,*
For Nkuba *has come to take* Mwindo.
I am about to climb up to Bisherya *over there,*
For Nkuba *has come to take* Mwindo.
O, Nkuba, *you are powerless against* Mwindo,
For Mwindo *is the Little One Just Born He Walked.*
Shemwindo *gave birth to a hero.*
My friend, you are powerless against Mwindo.

Mwindo went on singing like that while *Nkuba* was climbing with him slowly into the air, and the people of *Mwindo* had their attention diverted by the spectacle. *Nkuba* disappeared into the clouds, together with *Mwindo*.

They arrived at *Nkuba*'s. *Nkuba* asked him: "My friend *Mwindo*, you acted wrongly when you dared to kill my friend Dragon, when you roasted his eyes so that the odor drifted up to me, so that I smelled it in the air. If only you had made the odor descend to earth, then I would not have been angry." *Nkuba* still said to *Mwindo*: "I have rescued you many times from many dangers, so now you show that you are equal to me."

Mwindo arrived there at *Nkuba*'s. He felt there much cold, and the icy wind there was strong. No house! They lived there in wandering, no settling in one spot. *Nkuba* seized *Mwindo*, he climbed up with him to Rain. When Rain saw *Mwindo*, he told him: "You, *Mwindo*, never accept being criticized. Word of your toughness, your heroism, we surely have heard those stories. But here there is no room for your heroism." Rain fell upon *Mwindo* seven and seven times more. He made hail fall upon him, and he soaked him thoroughly. *Mwindo* said: "This time I am in trouble in every way." *Nkuba* lifted *Mwindo* up again. He had him ramble across Moon's territory. When Moon saw *Mwindo*, he pointed at him: "We heard you were tough, but here in the sky there is no room for your pride." Moon burned *Mwindo*'s hair. *Mwindo* complained: "O, father *Shemwindo*, bless me, and may my scepter not get out of my hands." *Nkuba* lifted *Mwindo* up again. He went and climbed up with him to the domain of Sun. When Sun saw *Mwindo*, he harassed him with heat. *Mwindo* lacked all means of defense against Sun—his throat became dry, his thirst strangulated him. He asked for water. They said to him: "No, there is never any water. Now we advise you to grit your teeth and take it." After Sun had made *Mwindo* sustain these pains, *Nkuba* lifted *Mwindo* up. He went and and made him arrive in the domain of Star. When Star saw him, he pointed him out. He told him: "We have heard that surely you are very tough, but here there is no room for your heroism." Star ordered Rain and Sun to come.

All—*Nkuba*, Rain, Sun, Star—all those gave *Mwindo* but one message: "We have respect for you, just that much. Otherwise, you would vanish right here. You, *Mwindo*, you are ordered to go back. Never a day should you kill an animal of the forest or of the village or even an insect like a centipede. If one day we learn the news that you begin to kill anything of these forbidden things, then you will die, then your people will never see you again." They pulled his ears seven times and seven more, saying: "Do you understand?" And he: "Yes, I have understood." They also said to *Mwindo*: "It is *Nkuba* here who is your guardian. If you have done wrong, it is *Nkuba* who will give us the news, and that day he will seize you all at once, without any chance to say goodbye to your people."

After *Nkuba* had made *Mwindo* ramble everywhere through the sky, they gave him the right to return home. On his return, *Mwindo* had by then spent one year in the sky, seeing all the good and all the bad things that are there. *Nkuba* raised *Mwindo* up. He returned with him home to *Tubondo*. *Mwindo* threw sweet words into his mouth. He sang:

> Mwindo *was already arriving*
> *Where* Shemwindo *had remained.*
> *Where* Shemwindo *had remained*
> Mwindo *was already arriving.*
> *He who went away returns.*
> Shemwindo *brought forth a hero.*
> *What will die and what will be safe,*
> *O my senior sister, may it join* Mwindo!
> *My friend* Nkuba, *be victorious.*
> *Let me go to* Tubondo,
> *To* Tubondo, *village of my mothers.*
> *May I see my mother,*
> *I descend here in* Tubondo,
> *In father's village, my dearest one.*

The will says: "*Mwindo,* if you kill an animal, then you die."

> O Mwindo, *never try again!*
> *From now on may you refuse meat.*
> Nkuba *said:*
> *"Never try again."*

When *Nkuba* was returning with *Mwindo,* he went on slowly descending with him. He went and let him down in the very middle of the village place of *Tubondo*. When his father, *Shemwindo,* saw his son being brought back by *Nkuba,* he rewarded *Nkuba* with a maiden dressed with a bracelet of copper, *Nkuba*'s metal. They also gave him the prescribed white fowl. It is there that the custom of celebrating the cult of *Nkuba* originated. From then on they always dedicated to him a maiden wearing a copper bracelet. After *Nkuba* had received his gift, he returned to his domain in the sky.

When *Mwindo* had rested, he assembled all his people. He told them: "I, *Mwindo,* the Little One Just Born He Walked, performer of many wonderful things, I tell you the news of the place from where I have come in the sky. When I arrived in the sky, I met with Rain and Moon and Sun and *Kubikubi* Star and Lightning. These five personages forbade me to kill the animals of the forest, of the rivers, and of the village, saying that the day I would dare touch a thing in order to kill it, that day the fire would be extinguished. Then *Nkuba* would come to take me without saying farewell to my people, then the return would be lost forever." He also told them: "I have seen in the sky things unseen which I cannot divulge." When they had finished listening to *Mwindo*'s words, those who were there dispersed. *Shemwindo*'s and *Nyamwindo*'s many hairs had gone "high as that," as the long hairs of the ghost of the forest, and in *Tubondo,* the drums had not sounded anymore, the rooster had not crowed anymore. On the day that *Mwindo* appeared there, his father's and his mother's long hairs were shaved, and the roosters crowed, and that day all the drums were being beaten all around, throughout the earth and in the sky.

When *Mwindo* was in his village, his fame grew and traveled widely. He passed laws for all his people, saying:

May you grow many foods and many crops.
May you live in good houses, may you moreover live in a beautiful village.
Don't quarrel with one another.
Don't pursue another's spouse.
Don't mock the invalid passing in the village.
And he who seduces another's wife will be killed!
Accept the chief. Fear him. May he also fear you.
May you agree with one another, all together, no enmity in the land nor too much hate.
May you bring forth tall and short children—in so doing you will bring them forth for the chief.

After *Mwindo* had spoken like that, he went from then on to remain always in his village. He had much fame, and his father and his mother, and his wives and his people! His great fame went throughout his country, it spread into other countries, and other people from other countries came to pay allegiance to him.

Part V
Making a Way Through Life

Introduction

Looking at these stories only in terms of the types of narrative that are unique to Africa, may leave the impression that the courtship-quest sort of tale, so common in the West, is seldom found there. In fact, however, a very great part of the repertoire of the subcontinent is given over to such stories. But because they draw upon the complex cultural institutions of courtship, marriage, and the correct manner of keeping a household, such tales are often extremely difficult to understand for an outsider—even another African. Too much esoteric information is required. Nevertheless, there are a few tales sufficiently accessible to at least illustrate the type here.

Many of the stories in this chapter employ the same language and situations we have seen in the wonder tales. And like them, they are told both for purposes of entertainment, and to impart practical and moral instruction about correct behavior. Some, like the first tale, "Salt, Sauce and Spice, Onion Leaves, Pepper, and Drippings," are fanciful in theme and spirit, and directly concerned with courtship tests. "The Cloth of Pembe Mirui," on the other hand, focuses on the question of how to keep a wife, whom you love, happy.

A number of these stories are directly concerned with the fortunes of women successfully making their way through life by means of marriage and otherwise. For instance, both "The Child in the Reeds" and "A Woman's Quest," are unusual in that a woman plays the active role. The former concerns a child hidden away in the reeds, a similar situation to that in "Mandu," but this time the child is a girl. She goes through initiation, and after a short period emerges fully grown. In the latter story, there is also a turnabout. A handsome man is pursued by women, and it is they who must journey, undergo trials, and obtain a magical helper.

"The Three Sisters" is also concerned with the role of women. This story is an African *King Lear,* a pointed tale of what happens when a man's favoritism towards one of his three daughters-in-law results in jealousy on the part of the other two and the subsequent death of the first.

Some of the stories in this section are, like those in section three, concerned with the doings of Trickster, but this time when he's courting. Tales like "Chameleon into Needle," maintain the comical style of the earlier stories, but they are included here not for their humor, but for the insight they provide into the details and intense feelings of the courtship process. The similar tale, "The Wooing Battle," treats the same themes and uses some of the same characters, but does it in a more serious tone.

Finally, "The Old Woman with Sores" and "How it Pays Sometimes to be Small," illustrate some of the problems of establishing understanding across cultural lines. These stories, which come not from a village setting, but from the forest Pygmies of the Ituri, relate familiar kinds of tales of wooing and winning. The first story, however, also concerns itself with problems these small hunting and foraging people have in dealing with their larger neighbors, especially those who constantly try to take advantage of them. The second concerns the getting of honey as the basis of a bride-price payment. This is especially significant because the Ituri are the honey gatherers for their sedentary gardening and cattle-keeping neighbors, and, as a result, are involved in complicated exchange-relationships with them. Thus, in both stories, an intricate social drama is reenacted for us, but one which is fully comprehensible only when we recognize that the Pygmies must constantly overcome the stereotypical view of them held by their neighbors.

80

Salt, Sauce, and Spice, Onion Leaves, Pepper, and Drippings

This story is about Salt, and Sauce and Spice, and Onion Leaves, and Pepper and Drippings. A story, a story! Let it go, let it come. Salt and Sauce and Spice and Onion Leaves and Pepper and Drippings heard a report of a certain youth who was very handsome, but the son of the evil spirit. They all rose up, turned into beautiful maidens, and then they set off.

As they were going along, Drippings lagged behind the others, who drove her still further off, telling her she stank. But she crouched down and hid until they had gone on, and then she kept following them. When they had reached a certain stream, where they came across an old woman who was bathing, Drippings thought they would rub down her back for her if she asked, but one said, "May Allah save me that I should lift my hand to touch an old woman's back." The old woman did not say anything more, and the five passed on.

Soon Drippings came along, encountered the old woman washing, and greeted her. She answered, and said, "Maiden, where are you going?" Drippings replied, "I am going to find a certain youth." And the old woman asked her, too, to rub her back, but unlike the others, Drippings agreed. After she had rubbed her back well for her, the old woman said, "May Allah bless you." And she said, too, "This young man to whom you are all going, do you know his name?" Drippings said, "No, we do not know his name." Then the old woman told her, "He is my son, his name is *Daskandarini*, but you must not tell the others," then she fell silent.

Drippings continued to follow far behind the others till they got to the place where the young man dwelled. They were about to go in when he called out to them, "Go back, and enter one at a time," which they did.

Salt came forward first and was about to enter, when the voice asked, "Who is there?" "It is I," she replied, "I, Salt, who make the soup tasty." He said, "What is my name?" She said, "I do not know your name, little boy, I do not know your name." Then he told her, "Go back, young lady, go back," and she did.

Next Sauce came forward. When she was about to enter, she, too, was asked, "Who are you?" She answered, "My name is Sauce and I make the soup sweet." And he said, "What is my name?" But she did not know, either, and so he said, "Turn back, little girl, turn back."

Then Spice rose up and came forward, and she was about to enter when she was asked, "Who is this, young lady, who is this?" She said, "It is I who greet you, young man, it is I who greet you." "What is your name, young girl, what is your name?" "My name is Spice, who makes the soup savory." "I have heard your name, young woman, I have heard your name. Speak mine." She said, "I do not know your name, little boy, I do not know your name." "Turn back, young lady, turn back." So she turned back, and sat down.

Then Onion Leaves came and stuck her head into the room. "Who is this, young girl, who is this?" asked the voice. "It is I who salute you, young man, it is I who salute you." "What is your name, little girl, what is your name?" "My name is Onion Leaves, who makes the soup smell nicely." He said, "I heard your name, little girl. What is my name?" But she didn't know it and so she also had to turn back.

Now Pepper came along. She said, "Your pardon, young man, your pardon." She was asked who was there. She said, "It is I, Pepper, young man, it is I, Pepper, who make the soup hot." "I have heard your name, young lady. Tell me my name." "I do not know your name, young man, I do not know your name." He said, "Turn back, young maid, turn back."

Now only Drippings was left. When the others asked her if she was going in she said, "Can I enter the house where such good people as you have gone and been driven away? Would not they the sooner drive out one who stinks?" They said, "Rise up and go in," for they wanted Drippings, too, to fail.

So she got up and went in there. When the voice asked her who she was, she said "My name is Drippings, little boy, my name is *Batso,* which makes the soup smell." He said, "I have heard your name. There remains my name to be told." She said, "*Daskandarini,* young man, *Daskandarini.*" And he said, "Enter." A rug was spread for her, clothes were given to her, and slippers of gold. And then of Salt, Sauce, Spice, Onion Leaves, and Pepper, who before had despised her, one said, "I will always sweep for you," another, "I will pound for you," another, "I will draw water for you." another, "I will pound the ingredients of the soup for you," and another, "I will stir the food for you." They all became her handmaidens. And the moral of all this is that it is from such common things that our most blessed foods are made. So just as such common stuff may be transformed under the right circumstance, if you see a man is poor, do not despise him. You do not know but that someday he may be better than you. That is all.

—*Hausa*

81

The Old Woman with Sores

One day a young Pygmy decided to go and look for a wife. He heard that there was a beautiful girl of marriageable age only two villages away, so he set off in that direction. As he passed the first village, an old woman called out to him. "Come here young man!" she cried. The young Pygmy turned around to see who was calling him, and he saw an old, old woman, sitting on the ground, hugging her knees. Horrible to look at, she was readied unto sickness and all covered with sores. He answered her: "You are very ill, Mother, and I don't want to get sick. I am passing through on my way to get married and I won't go near you!" "Very well then, go ahead," said the old woman, and the young man went to the next village.

When he reached the next village, he saw a kind-looking elder sitting outside his house, singing. The young Pygmy greeted him and sat down. The elder went on singing for a while, then said: "There's a young girl here, looking for a young man just like you!" The Pygmy was delighted at his good fortune, and said: "Fine I'll sleep here, then." Then, the two of them made songs together for that is what Pygmies are known for. When evening came, the young Pygmy went in and slept with the girl. When he was fast asleep, the elder crept into the room and killed him.

The next morning, one of the young Pygmy brothers said: "Our brother went down the road and hasn't come back. I'll go and follow him." And he left by the same path. As he passed the first village, the diseased old woman was still sitting on the ground, hugging her knees. "Come here, young man!" she called. The Pygmy looked around to see who was summoning him, and then he hurried on all the more quickly, saying: "You are all covered with sores, old woman, and I don't want to get sick. I won't come near you!" "Very well then, go ahead," croaked the woman.

The Pygmy went on until he reached the next village, where he saw the kind-looking elder sitting outside his house, singing. "Have you seen my brother?" asked the young Pygmy after they had exchanged greetings. "Oh yes!" answered the man. "He came yesterday and passed the night here. He is out walking in the village just now. Why don't you sit down awhile?"

So the young Pygmy sat down, and the elder told him that there was a fine young girl in the house, looking for a husband just like him. The Pygmy was delighted. "Fine!" he said, "I'll sleep here then." And the two of them started singing away together. Night fell, and the Pygmy went into the young girl's room and slept with her, as his brother had done. While he was sleeping, the elder crept in and killed him, too.

The third Pygmy was very worried when neither of his two brothers returned, and the next morning he set off to find them. As he passed the first village, the old woman with sores was sitting on the ground, hugging her knees. She looked up and called out: "Come here, young man!" The young Pygmy turned to see who was speaking to him, and went up to the old woman. "Well, mother, what can I do for you?" he asked. "There is a wicked old man in the next village," said the woman. "He sits outside his house and sings. He traps young Pygmies like you by telling them of his beautiful daughter. He has killed your two brothers, and when you go in to sleep with his daughter, he will try to kill you."

The young Pygmy was very upset, and could not think what to do. "Here is a bird," said the old woman with sores. "Take it with you and it will protect you."

The Pygmy took the bird, thanked the old woman for her kindness, and went on his way. He traveled on to the next village, and there was the elder, sitting outside his house, singing. He greeted the Pygmy and invited him to sit down. "Have you seen my two brothers?" asked the Pygmy. "Oh, yes!" replied the elder. "They are visiting friends in the village. Why don't you rest here awhile before going to look for them?" So the Pygmy sat down. Then after a little time had passed the old man said: "There's a pretty young girl here, looking for a young man just like you!" "Fine!" said the Pygmy, "I'll sleep here then." The elder sang, and the Pygmy sang.

Night came, and the Pygmy went into the young girl's room. He lay down to sleep with her. Outside, the old man sat in the darkness and sang. The Pygmy sang. And when the Pygmy fell asleep, the bird that he had been given by the old woman with sores sang. The bird went on singing, and the old man outside listened, and said, "I cannot go in and kill him yet, he is still awake. I shall wait." But the bird sang even louder, and before long the old man himself was asleep. Then the singing bird woke up the Pygmy, and he came out and killed the old man.

Then, the Pygmy took the girl back to his village, and on the way he passed the old woman with sores. He greeted her and told her what had happened. "Good," she said. Then he went on to his village, where he told all his friends and relations how he had killed the bad old man who had killed his two brothers, and how he himself had been saved by the talking bird given to him by the old woman with sores.

And he lived happily then with his young wife.

—Ituri

82

How It Pays Sometimes to Be Small

There was once a fine young girl who was much sought after in marriage. *Sundu* the Red Antelope came to her village and announced that he was looking for a wife. Everyone thought what a good husband this handsome *sundu* would make, and they said: "We have just the wife for you!" "Good!" said *Sundu,* "I will sleep here."

That night he slept with his wife-to-be, and the next morning she said to him: "Go and get me some honey!"

Off he went. He found a honey tree, cut a long liana and tied it to the tree. He started to climb up to where the honey was, but it was a long, long way, and as big and as strong as he was, the handsome red antelope was unable to reach it. When he gave up and returned without the honey, all the villagers said: "What sort of animal are you, that you can't even get your wife-to-be some honey? You are no husband for her. Be off with you!"

So off he went, back to his camp, where he told his sad story. *Boloko* the Ape listened and said: "Now, I need a wife, and I am strong and handsome. I will surely win this girl." And he went straight to the village. "I hear that you have a fine young girl here," he said. "I will sleep with her and I will take her for my wife." He was very sure of himself. That night he slept with his wife-to-be and in the morning she said to him: "I want some honey—go and find some for me!"

So off to the woods went *Boloko,* and found himself a fine *Nbanda* tree. He, too, cut himself a great big liana and fixed it to the tree where the honey was. But when he started to climb up towards the honey he found that it was much further than he had thought, and the limbs would bend and crack and he stepped on them, and try as he might he could not reach it. At last he was forced to come down without the honey. The villagers said to him: "What sort of animal are you, that you can't even bring your wife-to-be some honey? You are no husband for her. Be off with you!" And off he went, back to his camp.

Now, a little mouse lived in that same camp, and he had heard all about the girl. He had thought how much he would like someone like that for his wife. But when he saw *Sundu* go off he felt sure that the girl would marry him, he was such a fine red antelope. And when Sundu failed and Boloko went off, the mouse said to himself: "Such a handsome animal will surely win his bride!" But now the ape had returned, and little *Makatuwa* the Mouse got up, and said: "I am only a mouse, but I will go and ask this girl to be my wife." Everyone laughed at him, but off he went.

The villagers received him as they had received the antelope and the ape, and that night the mouse slept with his wife-to-be. In the morning he said to her: "I will go and fetch you some honey," and he went to the forest and found a tall tree filled with it. He, too, cut himself a liana and tied it to the tree. Then he climbed up as quickly and as easily as could be. Working very hard, he dug out all the honey there was, brought it down, and took it back to the village. "Ah!" said the villagers, "here at last is someone who can fetch honey for his wife-to-be. *Makatuwa* is the husband we want for our daughter!"

And so it was not the fine red antelope, nor the handsome ape, but the little mouse who won for himself the fine young bride.

—Ituri

83
The Cloth of Pembe Mirui

Now *Amadi* loved his wife *Fatima* with such passionate devotion that he could refuse her nothing. She had only to ask and her request was gratified immediately: silks, muslins, gold, and jewels, all were heaped at her feet by her infatuated husband. *Fatima* was content, counted herself fortunate to have such a husband, and was lavish in praise of him when she spoke with her neighbors. But after a while the women of the village became jealous of *Fatima*'s beauty and good fortune, and they went to her one by one and belittled *Amadi* before her. "These silks," they said, "are nothing, those jewels are but glass, and that gold is but imitation. If your husband really loved you he would bring you the Cloth of the serpent *Pembe Mirui,* which is the rarest thing in the world."

At first *Fatima* took no notice of these attempts to poison her mind against *Amadi,* but the same story was poured daily into her ears until it produced its intended effect, and she became gloomy and discontended. *Amadi,* whose love for *Fatima* made him observant of all her moods, observed this, and said, "What is ailing you, *Fatima?*" *Fatima* pouted and cast down her eyes, and replied, "Alas, my husband! You don't love me anymore." *Amadi* said, "How can you say that I no longer love you? You are surrounded with proofs of my passion. But tell me what you need, and if it is in my power I will get it for you." *Fatima* said, "It is true that you don't love me anymore. If you loved me you would get me the Cloth of the serpent *Pembe Miuri,* for there is no other like it, and I want it very much." Then *Amadi* answered, "What you say is not true. I love you and no one else. Nevertheless, to prove my love, I will get this cloth, though what it is and how I may gain possession of it, I don't know."

On the next day, *Amadi* made ready food for a journey, and, placing fifty rupees in his belt, he set out. He traveled for many days, asking on all sides where the serpent *Pembe Mirui* might be found, but without success. At last he came upon an old woman, wrinkled and bent, and he asked, "Tell me where I can find the serpent *Pembe Mirui,* and obtain the Cloth that he guards." The old woman said, "Give me money, and I will help you." So *Amadi* gave the crone thirty rupees. Then the old woman called out, and a cat came from the house carrying under his arm a bag. The old woman told this cat to go with *Amadi* and show him the road. Then, *Amadi* went out again upon his journey, and the cat went with him, carrying the bag under his arm.

So they traveled until they came upon a serpent lying asleep. *Amadi* asked, "Are you *Pembe Mirui?*" This question he asked three times, and three times the serpent replied, "I am not *Pembe Mirui.*" A little further on they came upon a serpent having two heads and two tails, and of him *Amadi* thrice asked, "Are you *Pembe Mirui?*" Three times the serpent replied, "I am not *Pembe Mirui.*" Proceeding again upon their way they met with a serpent having three heads and three tails, and, further on, another having four heads and four tails, and then, in succession, one having five heads and five tails, and one having six heads and six tails. To each of these serpents *Amadi* three times put the question, "Are you *Pembe Mirui?*" and each serpent thrice replied, "I am not *Pembe Mirui.*"

After many days they came to a sunless thicket, dark because of the thick foliage overhead. In the midst of it, they saw a great snake, with seven heads and seven tails, coiled and sleeping. *Amadi* asked him three times, "Are you *Pembe Mirui.*" The serpent reared up upon its seven tails, and three times answered, "I am *Pembe Mirui.*" Having spoken, *Pembe Mirui* rushed into the thicket, where he concealed himself and lay in wait for *Amadi.* Then the cat said to *Amadi,* "Be on your guard. Do not move or he will strike you." So *Amadi* drew his sword and waited, and presently *Pembe Mirui* rushed upon *Amadi,* hissing and spitting venom. But *Amadi* evaded his attack, and with his sword, cut off one of the seven heads of the serpent. The cat immediately sprang forward and picked up the head and placed it in the bag he carried. Seven times in all *Pembe Mirui* rushed *Amadi,* seeking to destroy him, and each time *Amadi* cut off one head, which the cat gathered up and placed in his bag. But at the last rush, some of the venom that *Pembe*

Mirui spat forth, hit *Amadi* in the face, and he, at the completion of his task, fell senseless beside the writhing body of the serpent. Then the cat kindled a fire, and, taking a razor from his bag, he cut open *Pembe Mirui* and took fat from underneath his skin. He also took a metal bowl from the bag, and in it he heated the fat over the fire. When the fat was melted, the cat went to the bag again and got a small box of medicine, which he added to the melted fat. Taking the mixture, he smeared *Amadi*'s ears and his nose and his mouth with it, whereupon *Amadi* recovered his senses and got up.

When *Amadi* had regained his strength, he approached the body of *Pembe Mirui,* and cut open his belly. Reaching inside the serpent, he drew forth the Cloth, which was like silk, but more beautiful, and, which, though large enough to cover a man from head to foot, yet, folded, was small enough to lie in his hand.

Placing the Cloth carefully in his wallet, he returned, followed by the cat. When they reached the place where the old woman lived, she came out to meet them, and the cat handed her the bag containing the seven heads of *Pembe Mirui. Amadi* also gave to her the twenty rupees which he had left. As he went his way, she said to him, "Tell your wife to be content with what she has, and not to seek for that which she doesn't have."

When he reached his home, he gave to *Fatima* the cloth of *Pembe Mirui,* and told her everything that had happened. *Fatima* received him with joy, and, hearing of all the dangers through which he had passed, and of what the old woman had said, listened no more to the idle talk of the women, but devoted herself to the care of her husband. The story is finished.

—*Swahili*

84
The Wooing Battle

One day a frog emerged from the surface of a little pond and looking around with its two big eyes, discovered a large stone in the warm sunshine. "The water is so cold today," it said, "I think it is better to bask in the sun for a little while." So it left the water and crouched on the tepid stone.

After some time a girl by the name of *Ngema* came to the pond to fetch some water. The frog remained on the stone, quite unconcerned, till he heard the girl wonder aloud if he were sick. The frog then spoke: "Do you think I am a lazy creature? Why did you say I am sick? Don't you see how strong I am?" and in saying so, he stretched up on his four legs like a spring. "I am a young man with plenty of cattle and goats enough to buy a beautiful girl."

The eyes of the girl grew big, and she said: "The other frogs usually plunge quickly into the water at the approach of people, but you don't even seem scared. That's why I thought you must be sick." The frog said: "Listen to me. I was born here in this very place, and a dying curse rests on me. When my father was on his death bed, he told me: 'You will spend most of your time in this place until the day comes when you will meet a girl here and ask her to marry you. If she accepts, it will mean happiness for both of you, but if she refuses, she will die.' Now it is up to you to live or to die." The girl set to thinking hard and after a while, she answered: "If that curse rests on you, it rests on me as well. I don't want to die while I am still so young." So the girl agreed to marry the frog. The frog asked to see her home and parents, and so off they went.

While on the road, the girl looked at the frog with surprise, and said: "I am puzzled about the way you walk." "Well, what is the difference? What do you see wrong in me?" he asked. "Why do you bend so much forward in your walking?" "Quite natural. My country is very hilly and so we must keep out buttocks very close together, so that they do not shake too much." While still chatting about one thing and another, they arrived at the girl's home. She took him inside to speak to her parents, so that things could be arranged.

In the courtyard of the homestead there was a beautiful tree. Among the leaves of its branches stood a chameleon looking at these strange happenings. The girl waited near him for the frog to return, and he saw his chance. Moving slowly and cautiously, descending from branch to branch, turning his round little eyes forward and backward, he finally succeeded in approaching the girl. He ventured to speak to her so that he could get closer. The girl said: "Since you began to move from the upper branch, I was looking at how slowly you walked down. Do you know how long you took to reach me?" The chameleon said: "Don't you know that I am a stranger here? Had I rushed into this house, people would have been alarmed, and asked: 'Who is there?' Instead I didn't disturb anyone and now we can talk quietly without anyone interfering with us. Listen, I came early this morning and I was anxious to meet you. I feel a great attraction for you. Let me tell you the whole truth. I love you from the bottom of my heart, and I am asking you if you will become my wife." The girl remained silent for a little while, and said: "I cannot become the wife of anyone who moves so slowly." The chameleon said: "Clever people do not make a great noise when absorbed in their business. Our elders say: 'Empty gourds make a great noise.' But you have not yet answered my question. Tell me, my dear, won't you become my wife and be happy ever after?" The girl looked indifferently at the tree for a moment, and said: "Well, frog is inside talking with my family and asking to marry me. Whichever of you can satisfy my father, he will be my husband." So the chameleon went inside and had a long talk with the girl's father. Believing they agreed, and leaving the frog still arguing his case, the chameleon returned home very pleased.

A few days after, he returned to the girl's home and to his disgust found the frog still pleading his cause with her parents. The chameleon interrupted in a challenging tone: "You call me a panting animal, you destitute, naked creature, slippery, boneless, and buttockless, you with glazy skin which resembles a piece of wood polished with sandpaper. I am going to shut you up." They went on insulting each other for some time, because neither of the two wanted to be defeated in front of the one they loved.

At last the girl persuaded them to stop such abuse and behave. When both were ready to listen, she said: "As I told you before, I do not refuse your proposals: He who satisfies the requests of my father, will be my husband." Both asked the father of the girl the bride-price he wanted for his daughter. The father told them the desired amount of food and cattle, and gave them an appointment for six days hence. The suitor who arrived first with the promised goods would have the girl for his wife. Both agreed to the proposal and without further discussion returned home.

The frog invited a great number of she-frogs to help him and prepared a great quantity of beer and food of every kind: sweet potatoes, dove peas, yams, and so on. The chameleon did the same with she-chameleons, preparing in addition a good quantity of porridge.

At last the appointed day arrived. The frog called the she-frogs and distributed the loads of food to carry. The caravan began to move out, led by the would-be bridegroom. They marched very fast in order not to be beaten by the chameleon. It was a comical spectacle to see the long row of frogs hopping down the road, but especially funny, because at every hop of the carrier, the beer spilt from the gourd, the bananas dropped from the basket, and the food crumbled in pieces in the open bags and scattered on the ground.

When they arrived at the girl's house, they were received with prolonged cheers and songs of praise by the women of the village. They exchanged greetings and were offered congratulations. But when they came to unfasten the loads, they were horrified to see that all the bowls were empty. The women of the household called the father of the girl, and told him: "Come and see the kind of presents these people have brought you. They gave only empty bowls."

The old man looked at the frog with a serious countenance, and said: "What do you mean by this farce? Do you think that I would give you my daughter for a few empty receptacles? I am not yet so needy. How can I trust you if you start with a trick like this? Go and seek a wife elsewhere!" The frog was ashamed and silently slunk away with the gang of she-frogs, hopping slowly along the roadside.

In the meantime, the chameleon arrived triumphantly with his caravan of carriers. He also was received with prolonged cheers and songs of praise and greetings. This time when the women went to inspect the loads, they found them to be numerous and full of every kind of food and beer.

There was great rejoicing and offering of congratulations. They made merry for two days, and the satisfied father gave his daughter to the victorious chameleon, who took her for his wife.

—Kikuyu

85

The Orphan with the Cloak of Skin

This story is about orphans. A story, a story. Let it go, let it come. A certain man died and left two sons, and their mothers, two women. Then one of the mothers fell sick. She was taking medicine, but her illness refused to go away. When she saw she was going to die, she said to her sister-in-marriage, "I know I am going to die. When Allah, the Exalted One, has taken my life from me, behold I will put my young son in your charge, for the sake of Allah and the prophets." The other said, "This is only fitting. I will care for him as my own." But, in truth, that can never be.

Some time passed after the woman died. Now, the two boys each had a fowl, and they were rearing them together. One day, when the orphan was not at home, the remaining mother lifted a stick and hit his bird and killed it. When he returned and found his hen dead, he said only, "Alas, Allah, the Powerful One, today my hen has died." Then he picked it up, plucked it, prepared it well, placed a pot on the fire, cooked the hen thoroughly, and took it to the market. Whoever came saying he wanted to buy it, he would answer that he would not sell it, except for a horse.

Then the chief's favorite son came. He, too, was quite a little boy, and he was mounted on a powerful horse. He said the flesh of this hen was what he wanted most and it must be sold to him. But the orphan said, if he did not trade him his horse, he could not eat this meat. So he was given the horse, and the chief's son the meat, and the boy took his horse home. But his stepmother said, "Take your horse and put it in this house, and close up the door with earth. In about seven days, if you open it, you will see it has become fat enough to burst its house." She thought if he did so, the horse would die, of course. Now, the boy believed his stepmother, so he put the horse in the house, and plastered up the door. When about ten days had gone by, he opened the door, and he saw his horse had become fat. And his stepmother's heart grew black with anger.

Well, things went on, and one day she said, "Today there is nothing to cook and eat. You must sell your horse and buy some stalks of grain." When he objected and asked why, she told him, "Just because I am not your real mother, do you think you can argue with me?" He said, "I am not arguing, I'll do as you say." So he sold the horse for grain stalks, and brought them to her. But instead of cooking them she threw them in the fire, burned them all, leaving only three very small pieces. He picked these up, sewed a little bag, and tied them inside.

Another day, he went for a walk, and coming to a village, he thought he would worship there. But when he climbed up on the altar, some people saw him, seized him, and said they would cut his throat. Then he said: "I have heard the news that your chief is blind, and for that reason I came to make medicine for him. If you don't want me to try, then kill me." But they said they would let him try, so he was brought to the chief's compound and given a hut. When night came, he carried with him his grain stalks, those three that the fire had not burnt. He set fire to one stalk and walked around the back of the chief's house till it died out. And the chief began to see a very little. Then he lit another, and when it was burned up, then both the chief's eyes opened. Thereupon they did the boy honor.

At dawn, the chief assembled the people, and said, "You have seen that the boy has made medicine for me. My eyes are healed, and I shall give him half of the town to rule over." But the boy answered, "I am only a trader, passing through, and I do not rule." They said, "If you will not rule, take whatever you wish and go." So he took slaves and cattle and everything beautiful, and went off with them and returned to his own town. The people were astonished. But his stepmother said,

"Come, let us go to the road by the stream. I have seen a rat enter a hole. You dig it out for me to make soup." And he said, "Come now, my mother, what kind of meat is a rat's? Look, I have brought you guinea fowls, and hens, and rams." And she said, "We all know you have wealth, but for me, rat's meat is what I want." So he said, "There is no harm in that. Let us go, you show me." Now she had seen it was really a snake's hole, but she told him a rat so that she might bring him trouble. A big slave of his rose up to come along with him, but she said, "I know you are the owner of slaves, but you only must go with me." So he told his slave to sit down, and the two set off together, alone.

The stepmother took him to the hole, and told him to dig. As he was about to start, she said, "Put down your hoe and reach in with your hand." So he put in his hand and drew out a magnificent bracelet. She said, "That is not it! A rat, I said, was there." So he put in his hand again and drew out a golden bangle. Growing angry, she went back home and called her own son. He came, to the hole, but when he put his hand inside, the snake bit it and they had to carry him home. He died before they got there, and the stepmother died three days later, leaving the orphan with the house and property. So goes the saying, "The orphan with the cloak of skin is hated, but when it is a metal one he is looked on favorably." That is all.

—*Hausa*

86

Tungululi and the Masters

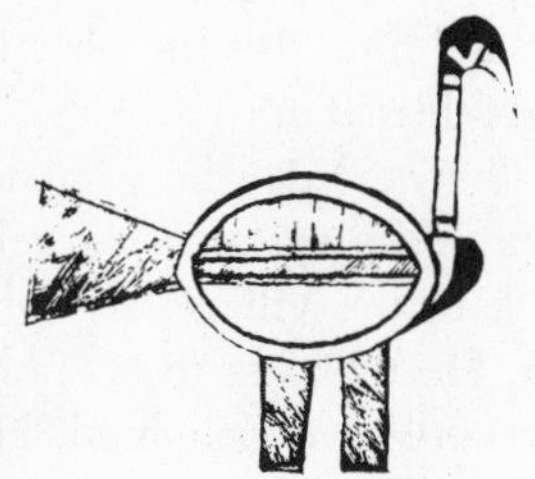

There was a certain man who liked to hunt very much, and he used to go out every morning to inspect his game and bird traps. But after his marriage he sent his wife instead. They had game and birds to eat every day.

Then the wife became pregnant. When the man saw that his wife was big, he sent his brothers to look after the traps. Before the year was out the woman produced a baby son, and they called him *Tungululi*. A week after his birth, the mother returned to minding the traps. She went on in this way, while *Tungululi* grew up and began to herd cattle.

Then one day the lady told her husband, "I'm not going to see to the traps today, because I've had some very bad dreams." But her husband scolded her, saying, "If you don't go, you can get out of here altogether!" So in the end the lady went, much afraid. She came to the first trap and found a small animal in it. She went on and checked all the other traps, except for one that was in a cave. Then, as she approached the last trap, she suddenly saw a lion. Trembling violently, she realized that unless she was very careful she would die. So, stealthily, she approached the trap and began to move the log holding it, but it slipped out of her hands and struck the lion. Then she saw that it was dead. While she was looking at the body, another beast came out of the cave and, gripping her by the neck, it killed her and began to eat her.

Meanwhile, the man began to search for his wife, seeing it was past midday. He took the path to his traps, and when he got there, he found the clothes of his wife all stained with blood and smelling of a lion. Forthwith he returned to the village and arranged for a mourning ceremony. Three days after the mourning was over, he began to send his son *Tungululi* to see to the traps.

The first day, *Tungululi* found a mole. When he brought it to his father, this man scolded him severely, saying, "You are an incompetent good-for-nothing who will never know how to trap. You are an idiot!" Without replying, *Tungululi* went out and ran off. He took the mole back and released it, and went on to the next trap, where he found a partridge. He took it to his father, who scolded him as before. So he took the partridge back, too, and released it. The next day he returned and found a pigeon. When he took it to his father, and his father again scolded him, this time beating him repeatedly. He took the pigeon back and released it.

The next day he went to the traps and found a young girl. At first *Tungululi* was afraid to release her, but at length he did, and took her back to the village, though all the time exchanging not a word with her. He took her to his father as he had the other things, but this time the latter was delighted. He told his son, "Yes, my child, and what is this you have brought me? Before you brought me nothing of any value, but at last I see you have learned sense. I have nothing with which to reward you except this girl, so take her as your wife."

The son asked the girl what she thought of this, and she said, "Good." Straightaway they set about brewing millet beer for a wedding ceremony such as had never been seen in the village. The father went back to looking after his own traps, hoping to obtain something similar for himself. While these things were going on, the girl said to her future father-in-law, "Father, give me leave to go with my future husband to greet the ladies of my own village." The father agreed.

So on the day of the final preparation of the wedding beer, she went off with her husband-to-be, *Tungululi*. When they were far from his village, she said to him, "I must leave you for a moment to tell my people to make millet porridge for our visit." So she went away. Now, this girl was in fact not a human being but a monster. When she reached home she told her father, "I am bringing you some unusually tender meat." Then she returned to *Tungululi.*

When *Tungululi* and his wife-to-be arrived in the village, they were well received and given plenty of good food. For six whole weeks they ate well. Then the monsters said to *Tungululi*: "When tomorrow comes, you are going to dig a field of compost mounds so big that if a person stands at one edge of it he will be unable to see the other side. If you refuse to do this we shall eat you."

Then *Tungululi* saw that he was indeed in a desperate situation. The next morning he took a hoe and went out into the bush, but he knew that the task was impossible. Nevertheless, he raised the hoe and completed one mound, then began another. Then he saw a multitude of moles around him, all working to make compost mounds, and as they worked, they sang:

> Tungululi, Tungululi, Tungululi!
> *We are digging compost mounds,* Tungululi!
> Tungululi, Tungululi!

They told him that they were helping him because he had helped their friend to escape from the trap. *Tungululi* thanked them very much.

By the time it was just past midday, the work he had been commanded to do was completed. He returned to the village, and told the monsters the field was ready. They went out to look, and saw that he had done as he was told, and more. That evening the monsters came again, and said, "Tomorrow you are going to spread out all those mounds, and if you fail to complete the job we shall eat you."

Tungululi was exhausted, and the prospect of still more hard work the next day dismayed him. However, the next morning he took a hoe and went to the field and began to spread the mounds. He had hardly finished one when a flock of partridges and pigeons arrived, and began to demolish the mounds, singing as they did so:

> Tungululi, Tungululi, Tungululi!
> *We are spreading the mounds,* Tungululi!
> Tungululi, Tungululi, Tungululi!

They worked together with *Tungululi* until the field was finished, and *Tungululi* returned to the village. He told the monsters he had done the job, and they were very angry. That evening they had only cassava to eat. They told *Tungululi*: "Tomorrow you will go out and harvest the millet, and if you fail, we'll eat you."

When *Tungululi* got to the millet field the next day, he found the same birds there, and they pecked at the millet, singing as they did so:

Tungululi, Tungululi, Tungululi!
We are harvesting the millet, Tungululi!
Tungululi, Tungululi, Tungululi!

When they had finished the field, they told *Tungululi*: "We've helped you because you released our friends from the traps."

Tungululi returned to the monsters' village. They were furious when they saw he had completed the task, and they began plotting to go and eat him in the night, when he was sleeping. They made all preparations, salting the water in the cooking pot, and so on. After that, they went stealthily to *Tungululi*'s hut, trying to see what was happening inside.

Tungululi was lying on his bed, tossing and turning in fear. In a corner of the hut was a wooden effigy of a god, and he prayed to it for help. Then he happened to glance down and saw a mole, who said to him, "Put that wooden effigy under the blanket so the monsters think it is you on the bed, but don't go out of the door because they are waiting for you there. Instead, go out of that hole you see there. Do it at once, because the monsters are coming."

Tungululi did as the mole told him. Meanwhile, the monsters were saying to one another: "This meat of ours is quite small—it'll be each for himself when we get him!" Then they all gathered at *Tungululi*'s hut and broke down the door. They seized the effigy and, supposing it to be *Tungululi,* they each bit into the wood until their teeth broke, while those outside burst in determined to have their share.

Tungululi, meanwhile, had escaped through the hole and returned to his village. His father welcomed him back with celebrations surpassing those of any wedding. In a few days, the monsters were all dead—the wood had given them a fatal stomach sickness. Thus there was an end of monsters in that country.

And so ends my story.

—Fipa

87

Chameleon into Needle

A story, a story. Let it go, let it come. A chief had a beautiful daughter. Indeed, she was so beautiful that she had no equal in the town. And he said, "Whoever hoes on the community hoeing-day and hoes the most and best, he will marry the chief's daughter. So on the day the chief calls hoeing-day with his neighbors, let all the eligible young men come and hoe. But the one who hoes and does so better than everyone else, I will give my daughter to him as wife."

Now the chameleon had heard about this a long time before, and had been studying magic and eating medicine to make him strong. When the day of the contest came round, the chameleon did not emerge until those hoeing were at work and far away. Then he came, struck one blow on the ground with the hoe, and climbed on the hoe and sat down; and then the hoe itself started to hoe, and fairly flew until it had done as much as the hoers. It passed them and reached the boundary of the furrow. The chameleon got off, sat down, and rested, and only later did the other hoers get to where he was.

But the chief would not consent to let the lizard have his daughter, and now said that he who ran and passed everyone should marry her instead. And so they had a race. The hartebeest said he would win because he could run fastest of all, but the chameleon turned into a needle; and leaped up and stuck himself to the tail of the hartebeest. There he stayed as the hartebeest ran, passing everyone, until they came to the entrance of the chief's house. As they passed it, the chameleon let go of the hartebeest's tail.

When the hartebeest came back he found the chameleon embracing the beautiful maiden, for he had won the match in everyone's eyes and she was his. Thereupon the hartebeest began to cry, and that is why, even today, you can see what look like tears in a hartebeest's eyes. From that time he has wept and not dried his tears.

—*Hausa*

88

Mother Come Back

This is what one woman did. She was then living in the bush and never showed herself to anyone except her daughter, who lived with her and used to pass the time sitting in the fork of a tree, making baskets.

One day, a man appeared there just after the mother had gone to kill game. He found the girl making baskets, as usual. He said, "Here now! There are people in the bush! And that girl, what a beauty! Yet she is all alone. If the king were to marry her, would not all the other queens leave the palace?"

Going back to the town, he went straight to the king's house, and said: "I have found a woman so beautiful that if you brought her here she would put all your wives so much to shame, that they would have to go away."

The following morning, the king called many of the people together, and set them to grind their axes. Then they went into the bush. As they came in view of the place where the man had seen the girl, they discovered the mother had once again gone to hunt. Before going, she had cooked porridge for her daughter and hung meat out for her to eat. Only then had she started on her expedition.

The people said: "Let's cut down the tree where the girl sits." So they put their axes to it. At once the girl began singing:

Mother, come back!
Mother, a man is cutting down our shade tree.
Mother come back!
Mother, a man is cutting down our shade tree.
Cut! The tree in which I eat is falling.
Here it is falling.

Suddenly, the mother dropped down, as if from the sky, saying:

Many as you are, I shall stitch you with this big needle.
Stitch! Stitch!

The people at once fell to the ground and were killed. The woman allowed only one to get away, so he could report. "Go," she said, "and tell the news." There at the town, when he arrived, the villagers asked: "What has happened?" He said: "There where we have been, I say, things are rather bad."

Likewise, when he stood before the king, the king asked: "What has happened?" He said: "We have met great misfortune. I am the only one to come back."

"Good heavens! The rest are all dead! If that is so, tomorrow go to So-and-So's compound over there, and bring other people. Tomorrow morning let them go and bring to me the woman."

They slept their fill.

Next morning early, the men ground their axes and went to the place. They, too, found the mother gone, the porridge already made, and the meat hanging on the shade tree. "Bring the axes." But the song had already started:

Mother, come back!
Mother, a man's cutting down our shade tree.
Mother, come back!
Mother, a man's cutting down our shade tree.
Cut! The tree in which I eat is falling.
Here it is falling.

The mother dropped down among them, singing in her turn:

Many as you are, I shall stitch you with this big needle.
Stitch! Stitch!

They all fell down dead. The woman and her daughter picked up the axes.

"What is this, then?" asked the king. "Today let all those that are pregnant give birth to their children." So one woman after another straightaway brought forth her child. Soon there was a whole row of them, a whole band, making a confused noise. They marched into the bush to get the girl.

When the girl saw them, she said: "There is no joke about it now. Here comes an army of red infants with the umbilical cords still hanging on."

They discovered her in the fork of the shade tree. "Let me give them some porridge," the girl thought. The babies just plastered the porridge on their heads. They did not eat it. The last-born then climbed into the shade tree, picked up the baskets that the girl was weaving, and said: "Now, bring me an axe." The girl shouted out once more:

Mother, come back!
Mother, a man is cutting down our shade tree.
Mother, come back!
Mother, a man is cutting down our shade tree.
Cut! The tree in which I eat is falling.
Here it is falling.

Again the mother dropped into the crowd:

Many as you are, I shall stitch you with this big needle.
Stitch! Stitch!

But her magic did not work with these babies, and the tree was chopped down.

The troop began dragging the girl to the king. They tied her with their umbilical cords, yes, with their umbilical cords. The mother went on with her song, trying to stop them:

Many as you are, I shall stitch you with this big needle.
Stitch! Stitch!

But it was in vain. The troop was already in the fields and out of the bush. The mothers of the babies sang a song of triumph into the heavens as the babies marched into the town.

When they got there, the maiden's mother said: "Since you have carried away my child, I must tell you something. She is forbidden to pound grain in the mortar, neither can she fetch water at night. If you send her to do one of these things, mind you, I will know where to find you." With this, the mother returned to her home in the bush.

The following day, the king said: "Let us go hunting." And to his mother, he said: "My wife does not pound in the mortar. All she can do is stitch baskets."

While the husband was away, the other wives, as well as the mother-in-law, said: "Why should she not help us prepare food and pound in the mortar?" When the girl was told she must help them pound, she refused, but a basket of corn was brought to her anyway. When she had pounded it, the mother-in-law herself took the meal from the mortar, and then the other women, in their turn, brought some more corn and forced it on her.

So the little girl pounded away, singing at the same time:

Pound! At home I do not pound,
Here I pound to celebrate my wedding.
If I pound I go to heaven.

The little maiden began to sink into the ground. She went on singing:

Pound! At home I do not pound,
Here I pound to celebrate my wedding.
If I pound I go to heaven.

She sank into the ground as far as her hips, and then as far as her chest.

Pound! At home I do not pound,
Here I pound to celebrate my wedding.
If I pound I go to heaven.

Soon, she sank down as far as the neck. Now the mortar began to pound by itself, pounding the grain on the ground, not in the mortar. Finally the girl disappeared altogether.

Although nothing more of her was to be seen, the mortar still pounded as before. The women then said: "Now what shall we do?" They called a crane, and told it: "Go and break the news to her mother, but first let us know what you will say." The crane answered: *"Wawani! Wawani!"* They said: "That has no meaning. Go back." Then the women told each other: "Let us send for the crow." "Now what will you say?" they asked it when it came. The crow replied: *"Kwá! Kwá! Kwá!"* "The crow, too, does not know how to call," they said. "We must have the quail instead." But when they asked the quail: "What will you do?" it answered: *"Kwalulu! Kwalulu!"* "The quail does not know how to do it either. Let us listen to the dove." They said: "Let us hear, doves, what will you call her mother?" The dove sang:

Kuku! Ku!
She-who-nurses-the-sun is gone,
She-who-nurses-the-sun.
You who dig,
She-who-nurses-the-sun is gone,
She-who-nurses-the-sun.

They said, "Go, you know how to do it."

The mother went towards the town. She carried medicines in a pot, as well as tails of animals with which she beat the air. When she reached the town there, she sang:

Let me gather, let me gather
The herd of my mother.
Mwinsa, *get up.*
Let me gather the herd.
Let me gather, let me gather
The herd of my father.
Mwinsa, *get up.*
Let me gather the herd.

She then heard the mortar still sounding right above the child. So she got out her medicine and prayed on it. Slowly, the girl began to emerge, from the ground, still pounding. Little by little, her head appeared, and then her neck. Soon her song was heard again:

Pound! At home I do not pound,
Here I pound to celebrate my wedding.
If I pound I go to heaven.

The child was now in full view, completely out of the earth. And so she was brought back to the king, and stayed there as a reminder of how one must always observe the prohibitions given us. I have finished.

—*Berre-MuKuni*

89
The Three Sisters

There was a certain woman who had many daughters. Among them were three of exceptional beauty, and of these, one was more beautiful than all the rest.

Now, it happened that three young men from a neighboring country arrived at the village where these girls lived, and when they saw them, they fell in love at once. That very day, they decided to marry, and the next day the men brought the hoes that symbolize engagement. When formal greetings had been exchanged, the young men went home until the end of the year, after which they would return for the marriage ceremonies.

When the appropriate time came, they went to the village headman to obtain his agreement. The future father-in-law of the most beautiful of all the girls, whose name was *Cuulu,* gave his prospective daughter-in-law ten head of cattle and many fine things, better than the marriage gifts made to the other two sisters. When these two girls realized this they were very jealous. From then on they sought every day to kill *Cuulu.* Meanwhile, *Cuulu*'s father-in-law continued to love her best and to lavish presents on her.

One day, everyone in the village went off to work except *Cuulu,* who remained behind because she had a headache. Seeing this, the two sisters also stayed behind, hoping for an opportunity to kill her. But when they reached her hut they found no one there. Then they noticed the water pot was missing and realized *Cuulu* had gone down to the river. "Well," they said, "let's follow her."

So they did, but on approaching the river they met *Cuulu* already on her way back. Very courteously, as if they had no evil intentions, they greeted *Cuulu,* saying, "My dear, how have you slept? We have just been to visit you and found you not at home. We know you've just gone to the river, but won't you go back there with us now?" *Cuulu* replied, "No, I am too tired. But why don't we return to my hut where we can talk with each other more easily than standing here."

So they all went back to *Cuulu*'s hut, where she gave them some nice stools to sit on and cooked some food so that they might eat together.

After a while, when *Cuulu* was clearing the things away, one sister said to the other, "Here's our chance—let's go home and get some knives, then come back and kill her here." But the other replied: "No, you go alone. I'll say you have just gone home to cook some millet porridge." So the other left to get the knives.

In the meantime, *Cuulu*'s husband had finished his work in the fields, and was hurrying home because he loved his wife very much. As he arrived, *Cuulu* was putting a pot on the fire to bake some flour.

When the sister who had gone for the knives returned, the sister who had remained with *Cuulu* quickly went outside to her. She told her that *Cuulu*'s husband had come, so they hid the knives in the grass because they could not kill her then. When they went back into the hut, *Cuulu* gave them millet porridge and the three sisters sat down together and ate. Afterwards, *Cuulu* and her husband walked the sisters home, and all the while, the two women were planning some other way to kill *Cuulu.*

Some while later, it happened that each of the three sisters gave birth to a baby son. At this, *Cuulu*'s father-in-law was delighted, and he said to *Cuulu*: "Help yourself to all the animals in my cattle corral." But *Cuulu* declined to accept more than five beasts. Even so, the other two sisters felt more jealous than ever, seeing that all they got on this occasion was one sheep apiece for having given birth to sons, for their fathers-in-law were not so openhanded.

Three days later, everyone in the village went out to the fields to work, with the exception of the three sisters who were still resting after childbirth. When the two jealous women saw that everyone had left the village, they put their children to sleep and went to visit *Cuulu.* They said to her, "Our sister, let us go to the river, because when the people come back from the fields they will need a lot of water." *Cuulu* replied, "No, my sisters, I have just been there." But they cajoled her until at last she agreed to return with them. At this the two jealous women were delighted.

When they got to the riverbank, they said to *Cuulu,* "Now you start filling the pots." She refused. Then they said, "All right, if you won't begin, then we won't draw any water either. But we'll take the water you've drawn already and tell the father-in-law who loves you so much that you're neglecting his grandson."

Then *Cuulu* was afraid, and said, "Well, I'll get water, only keep our children out of it." But as she was drawing the water from the river, the two sisters threw her into it, together with the water pot and the ring she used to balance the pot while she carried it on her head. Then they drew water and returned to the village, rejoicing.

When the people came back from the fields, they began to wonder where *Cuulu* was, asking, "But where can she have gone, and left her small child behind?" Her husband, her father-in-law, and mother-in-law were furious that she should have done this. They inquired of the two sisters, who said they did not know where she was (all the while, they were rejoicing in themselves). Every path around the village was searched. *Cuulu*'s despairing husband grew thin, thinking of his wife. Other people began to forget her.

Then one day, a little old lady was going to the river when she heard a voice coming from it, saying:

Cuulu *draws water,* Cuulu,
Goes to the village, Cuulu,
Now Cuulu *is forgotten.*
Don't you forget me, Kaleekaminisya,
Yes, I am Cuulu.

The old lady gave a start. She thought at first it was a bird, then perhaps a frog. But, as she was drawing water from the well, she heard the voice again:

Cuulu *draws water,* Cuulu,
Goes to the village, Cuulu,
Now Cuulu *is forgotten.*
Don't you forget me, Kaleekaminisya,
Yes, I am Cuulu.

The old lady lost no time in collecting her water pot and her carrying ring and returning to the village. Once there, she said: "You elders, when I was drawing water from the river just now I heard a voice coming from it." Some people thought that the old lady had been dreaming, or else that she was a liar. But there were others who believed her, and the two sisters who had thrown *Cuulu* in the river began to tremble. In the end, everyone went down to the river and listened, but no voice was heard. Then many people were angry and wanted to beat the little old lady, but a number of elders forbade it, saying, "Let all those who don't believe her story return to the village. Then we shall see."

When the people had gone, the old lady approached the river and began to draw water. Then a voice was heard, saying:

Cuulu *draws water,* Cuulu,
Goes to the village, Cuulu,
Now Cuulu *is forgotten.*
Don't you forget me, Kaleekaminisya,
Yes, I am Cuulu.

Then, singing, *Cuulu* emerged from the river. The people around rejoiced and took her back to the village. Then everyone came to see her, and one of the olders got up, and said, "*Cuulu,* we are most glad to see you again here, but how did you come to be in the river? Let us hear just what happened to make you disappear."

At this *Cuulu* got up and stood in the midst of them, her two sisters included, and said: "As you see, I am delighted to be back in this village once more. You know well that I am the mother of this child *Kaleekaminisya,* and also that I was married on the same day as these, my sisters. One day, everyone went to work in the fields, except we three sisters. They put their babies to sleep, and came to my home. They said: 'Let us go and get water.' When we got to the river they persuaded me to draw water first, and while I was doing so, they threw me in, along with my water pot and carrying ring.

"When I reached the bottom of the river I met a crocodile, who was very pleased to encounter such good food as myself. But when he saw that I was a woman, he told me he would not eat me, but would marry me instead. Now, I don't know how I could believe the words of a crocodile. Anyway, after some time had passed in such a way as you may imagine, the crocodile saw that I was getting thin and drove me away, saying, 'I cannot bring myself to sleep with a woman as thin as you.' So I returned, you elders, and now I am here! Those who threw me into the river are my sisters here, who were jealous because my father-in-law loved me."

At this *Cuulu*'s father-in-law got up with spear in hand and stabbed those two women. Then everyone got sticks and stones and beat them until they died. They took their corpses and threw them in the river. *Cuulu* recovered and lived with her husband from then on.

So my story ends.

—Fipa

The Messenger Bird

A man named *Zili* married a woman and then found he did not like her. One day, he said to her: "It has been a long time since we went to visit your parents. Make a pot of beer and we will go." So she put the pot on her head, and they set out. He led her by a path that she didn't know—one that no one used. When she asked why they went that way, he answered, "Never mind, it is another way." They came to a tree and stopped to rest beneath it. The woman objected, saying, "There is no room to sit down." "Just put down your pot of beer, so I may drink," said he. She set it down and he drank. Then he grabbed her and killed her. He cut off her head, her arms, her legs—everything that had human shape. These he wrapped in a bundle of grass, and then climbed up and hung them at the top of the tree. Then, he took the remainder of the body, skinned it, cut the flesh into strips, which he also wrapped up in grass, and took them with him.

As he left, a bird began to sing:

Zili! Amasesendini, amasendi, *old man!*
You are a witch, sesendini!
What's that kind of meat! Sesendin!
It has got no tail! It has no horn! Sesendin!

He asked, "What bird is this that sings and calls me by name?" He threw his stick at the bird and killed it. Then he lifted his burden and went on his way. But the bird rose again. It followed him, passed close to him flapping its wings, *pfu pfu,* perched on another tree, and sang its song once more. *Zili,* astonished, exclaimed: "How can the bird follow me like this? Is it possible that I did not kill it?" He gave chase to it, knocked it down, tore it limb from limb, and threw the mangled remains to the winds. Once more, he picked up his load, and continued on his way.

But look, the bird again gathered together its scattered limbs, and came back to life. Once more, *Zili* pursued it a long way, and killed it yet a third time. He lighted a fire with a wooden flint, laid the dead bird on the wood, and watched it slowly burn to ashes. Then, grinding the ashes to powder, he scattered them far and wide. He stayed sitting at this place for a long time. As the bird did not return, he said to himself, "This time it is quite dead." He then resumed his journey and duly arrived with his load at the village of his parents-in-law.

They hastened to meet him. "Here is *Zili.* Good day, *Zili!*" They took from his hands the bundle of grass filled with flesh, they bade him enter the hut, and before untying the bundle, they asked for news of his home. Then his mother-in-law took up the bundle and said, "Today you are treating us as princes!" And she began to open it. But, lo, swiftly and silently the bird arrived, and, perching on the top of the hut in which they were sitting, it began its song:

Zili! Amasesendini, amaesendi, *old man!*
You are a witch, sesendini!
What's that kind of meat! Sesendin!
It has got no tail! It has no horn! Sesendin!

Zili kept quiet. "What a curious bird that is!" said his parents-in-law, listening to its song, but others said it was just ordinary. And the bird sang on.

"How was our daughter when you left home?" inquired the parents. "Quite well," *Zili* answered. "She will soon come herself." And the bird continued its song:

Zili! Amasesendini, amasendi, *old man!*
You are a witch, sesendini!
What's that kind of meat! Sesendin!
It has got no tail! It has no horn! Sesendin!

Then the bird flew into the hut. They drove it out, but it would not keep silent. Slowly, the parents began to understand a little of the real meaning of its words. *Zili* trembled, but spoke not at all. Then the mother began to roast the flesh *Zili* had brought, and the bird went to sing in her ears. Finally, she understood, and she fainted.

Then the men of the village went to *Zili* and asked him to explain, saying, "What bird is this that follows you and calls you by name?" But *Zili* declared: "The bird came not with me. I heard it here for the first time in this hut." "If that is so, come and let us see our child," the people said.

They set off, the bird flying before them and guiding them. It led them to the big tree in the bush and then began to sing loudly close to the bundle of grass that *Zili* had hung up. Someone climbed up the tree and untied the bundle. They opened it, and, at once, the men recognized the girl's face and the bracelets she wore on her wrists and ankles. They seized *Zili* and bound him. Then, some of them went on to *Zili*'s village to gather all his relations into one hut. When the others arrived, they threw *Zili,* still bound, into the hut, and then set fire to it.

So died *Zili* and his relations.

—*Thanga*

91
The Child in the Reeds

There was a boy called *Hlabakoane,* his sister was *Thakane,* their mother *Mahlabakoane,* and their father *Rahlabakoane*. The father and mother looked after the gardens, *Thakane* stayed at home, and her brother herded cattle.

One day *Hlabakoane* said, "*Thakane,* give me some *kumonngoe.*" That was the name of the incredible tree that gave both parents food in plenty, for when it was chopped by an axe, milk spurted out of it. But the children never ate of it, for it was forbidden them. The boy again said to his sister, "*Thakane,* give me *kumonngoe.*" *Thakane* said, "My brother, it is a tree of which we must not eat, only father and mother eat of it." He answered: "If that be so, I will not herd. The cattle shall remain in the corral." *Thakane* thought about it while her brother stayed in the reed enclosure. Presently she said, "When will you be taking the cattle out?" He said, "I shall not go to herd."

Now she took an axe and chopped at the *kumonngoe.* But only a little piece broke off, and when she gave it to him, he refused it. He said it was too small and not enough for an appetite like his. She went back and cut much more from it. Now thick milk poured out in a flood, like a river flowing into the hut. She cried for help, saying, "*Hlabakoane,* my brother, help me, for *kumonngoe* is coming out in a flood. It is filling the hut." In vain they tried to stop the thick milk. Still it poured out, still it flowed.

Presently, the milk ran outside the hut and down the path to the gardens. It was seen there by the father, who said to his wife: "Look, *Mahlabakoane,* there is *kumonngoe* coming to the gardens. The children must have done some mischief at home." The father took the milk in his hand and ate it, the woman took it in her hand and ate it. Then they gathered what was left, threw their hoes away, and ran home to see what had happened.

When they arrived, they said: "*Thakane*, what have you done that the tree from which your father and mother eat is making its milk flow so to the gardens?" She said, "It is my brother's fault, not mine. He left the cattle in the corral, refusing to herd, because he said he wanted *kumonngoe.* He made me give him some of it."

The father said that now they must go and bring back the sheep from the field. After, he slaughtered and cooked two of the sheep, while the mother ground grain and made bread. Then, the father went to fetch a smith to fasten beautiful rings on his daughter. The smith fastened them on her legs, her arms, and round her neck. When that work was finished, the father took clothes and clothed her, made her a fine petticoat and put it on her.

Now, he called together the men of the court to explain what he intended to do. "I am going to cast *Thakane* off," he said. "But how can you do this?" they asked him. "She is your only daughter." "She has eaten of the forbidden tree," he answered.

Then the father set out to take *Thakane* to an ogre to be eaten. When they were just outside their own gardens, there came a steenbok antelope. It asked *Rahlabakoane,* "Where are you taking this beautiful daughter of yours?" He answered, "You may ask her, she's old enough." *Thakane* said:

I have given to Hlabakoane kumonngoe,
To the herder of our cattle kumonngoe.
I thought our cattle were going to stay in the corral,
kumonngoe,
And so I gave him my father's kumonngoe.

Then the steenbok said, "I hope it is you that gets eaten, *Rahlabakoane,* and that the ogre leaves this child."

A little later they met with eland antelopes, who also asked: "Where are you taking this beautiful child of yours?" *Rahlabakoane* said, "You may ask her, she is old enough. She has done me much hurt back at home." Then the maiden said:

I have given to Hlabakoane kumonngoe,
To the herder of our cattle kumonngoe.
I thought our cattle were going to stay in the corral,
kumonngoe,
And so I gave him my father's kumonngoe.

Then the eland said, "I hope it it you who will die, *Rahlabakoane.*"

They passed on, sleeping in the open country. Soon they were approached by springbok gazelles, who inquired: "*Rahlabakoane,* where are you taking this beautiful child of yours?" He said, "You may ask her, she is old enough. She has harmed me much back at home." Now his daughter said:

I have given to Hlabakoane kumonngoe,
To the herder of our cattle kumonngoe.
I thought our cattle were going to stay in the corral,
kumonngoe,
And so I gave him my father's kumonngoe.

The springbok said, "I hope it is you who gets eaten, *Rahlabakoane.*"

At last they arrived at the ogre's village. There, *Rahlabakoane* saw that the court of *Masilo,* the ogre's son, was full of people. It was his father who ate people—as for him, he did not eat them. *Rahlabakoane* sat down in the court with *Thakane.* They took a skin and spread it out. The maiden sat on it and her father sat on the ground. The chief, *Masilo,* asked him, "*Rahlabakoane,* where are you taking this beautiful child of yours?" He said, "You may ask her, she is old enough." His daughter said:

I have given to Hlabakoane kumonngoe,
To the herder of our cattle kumonngoe.
I thought our cattle were going to stay in the corral,
kumonngoe,
And so I gave him my father's kumonngoe.

She told her tale in the men's court where they held their palavers.

Then *Masilo,* the chief of this tribe of ogres, sent for his court messenger, and pointing at *Rahlabakoane* and *Thakane* he said to him: "Take these two to my mother's courtyard, and tell her to bring the man to my father, for he must pay his respects to him, but to keep the maiden safe." And so, the mother brought *Rahlabakoane* to her husband, the cannibal on the mountain. She sent the court messenger ahead to say, "*Masilo* has told me that I must bring you this man that he may pay his respects to you." The father of *Masilo* took *Rahlabakoane,* put a piece of broken pot on the fire, and threw him down into it. The man was burned, was well roasted, and became meat. The ogre ate him. Then the mother and court messenger went down the mountain and returned to the village.

Soon after that, *Masilo* took the beautiful *Thakane* as his wife. He had not yet married, refusing all available maidens, but now he wedded this daughter of *Rahlabakoane*. After a while she became pregnant and gave birth to a girl. Her mother-in-law said, "Alas, my child, you have suffered to no purpose." *Thakane* was silent, for she had heard that when girls were born they were taken to the ogre to be eaten by him. That ogre was as hungry as a grave.

Then they told *Masilo* that a girl child had been born. He said, "Oo! You must bring her to my father at once. He will take care of her." *Thakane* said, "Oh! oh! With us people are never eaten. When they die they are buried. I refuse to give my child." Her mother-in-law said, "Here no girls are to be born. Only boys are to be born, girls are taken away." *Masilo,* her husband, came, and said, "Well, my wife, you must give up this child to my father that he may take care of it." Again she refused, saying, "If she must die, I'll drown her myself. I will not allow my child to be eaten by your father, the ogre who ate my father."

She took her child, went to the river, and sat down near a pool where reeds were growing. She cried, she was afraid to destroy her child. Presently, an old woman came out of the reeds, she came out of the pool, and said, "Why do you cry, woman?" *Thakane* answered, "I cry on account of my child, because I have to throw it into the water." The old woman said, "Yes, at your place no girls are to be born, only boys. Give her to me and I'll take care of her for you. Name the days when you will come to see your child here in the pool." The mother gratefully consented, and gave the old woman her child.

Thakane went home, remained there some days, and then went to see her daughter. When she arrived at the pool, she said:

> *Give me* Lilahloane, *that I may see her,*
> Lilahloane *who has been cast off by* Masilo.

Now, when the old woman brought the child out, the mother saw how much she had grown, and she rejoiced. She stayed with that old woman for a very long time. She stayed and stayed. Then the old woman took the child and went back with her into the water, and the mother returned home.

After many days, *Thakane* came again to see her child. She visited *Lilahloane* very often and, in only one year, the girl grew up and became a maiden. Then, the old woman made her go through the initiation ceremony to make her a woman, and so it happened that on a certain day, when *Thakane* went to the river, she saw that her daughter was now a girl who had just passed through initiation.

Now, a man of the village had come to cut some branches near the river and he saw that maiden. As he looked at her he saw that her style of beauty was like *Masilo*'s. The man arose and went home. The wife of *Masilo* also went home. The man told *Masilo* in secret, saying, "I have seen your child with her mother by the river. It was the child she said she was going to kill." *Masilo* said, "It wasn't drowned in the water?" He said, "No, and now she is a maiden just initiated." *Masilo* said, "What can I do?" The man answered, "On the day that your wife says she is going to bathe in the river, go there before her. It is her habit, is it not, to tell you she is going?" *Masilo* said, "She usually tells me." The man said, "Go there before her and sit down in the bush, so that when your wife arrives you are already hidden."

Now, when that day came, *Thakane* told *Masilo,* saying, "I am going to bathe." He let her go, but he went quickly there before her, and sat down in the undergrowth and hid himself. When his wife arrived, she stood by the pool, and said:

> *Give me* Lilahloane, *that I may see her,*
> Lilahloane *who has been cast off by* Masilo.

The old woman brought the maiden out of the water. When *Masilo* looked at her, he saw that she must be the child whom her mother had said she was going to drown. He wondered, he wept when he saw that his child was already fullgrown. Presently the old woman said, "I am afraid. It is as if somebody was here spying." She took the maiden and went back into the water with her. *Masilo* sneaked away before *Thakane* and went home by another route.

When *Masilo* arrived, he went into his hut when it was still noon. He could not stop crying. At dusk he finally spoke to his wife, saying, "I have seen my child where you said you were going to drown her. I have seen that she is already a maiden." The wife insisted that she did not know what he was talking about. He implored her, saying, "Oh, let me see my child." She said, "You will tell me to take her to your father to be eaten by him." He said, "No more will I say that she must be eaten, because she is now grown up."

Next morning, *Thakane* went to the old woman, saying: "*Masilo* saw us. He says that I must come and beg you to give him his daughter that he may see her." Then the old woman said, "You must give me a thousand head of cattle." She went home to her husband, and said, "The old woman asks for a thousand head of cattle." He said, "It is a small matter if it is only a thousand head of cattle. If it were two thousand I would still give them to her, because without her my child would be dead."

The next day, he sent one of the men of his court with the order that messengers should go to all the people and tell them to bring cattle—a thousand head of cattle came. The cattle went to the water, to that pool with reeds. They came and stood near it. Then *Thakane* stood up, and said:

> *Give me* Lilahloane, *that I may see her,*
> Lilahloane *who has been cast off by* Masilo.

Presently, the old woman brought out the maiden. As she began to emerge from the water, the sun ceased to shine, it was darkened, but when she stood completely out of the water, the sun shone again. *Masilo* saw his child. All the people saw the child of *Masilo,* already a maiden, where her mother had left her. Then the cattle were thrown into the water, but it was water on the surface only, underneath it was where the tribe of that old woman lived.

They went back to the village. *Masilo*'s mother said that *Thakane* should be permitted to go home so that her mother and brother might see her again—as for her father, he was dead. A court messenger was sent to give orders to the people to come with all their cattle to see *Thakane* off.

Everyone went to escort *Thakane.* As they were still going on, and were nearing the place on the highroad through which she and her father had passed, they saw that a rock had grown in the middle of the place, blocking it. This rock was her father, *Rahlabakoane,* whose heart had become a stone. *Thakane* said to *Masilo,* "What does that rock mean there in the way, in this place?" *Masilo* said, "Perhaps you did not notice it when you came through here with your father." She said, "No, that rock was not there." They were still walking with the people and the cattle—*Thakane* was going in front, as it was she who knew the way to her village.

When they arrived at that place near that rock, the rock began to speak, saying:

> Rue le, le rue, *I shall eat you,* Thakane, *my child,*
> *You who lead the way. I shall eat the people afterwards.*

Now his daughter, realizing what was happening, said, "All right, you may eat the cattle." She said to *Masilo,* "It is my father, he has come to lie in ambush for me." They took many cattle, they gave them to that rock. The rock swallowed all these cattle, opening its huge mouth.

Presently, *Rahlabakoane* spoke again, saying:

> Rue le, le rue, *I shall eat you,* Thakane, *my child,*
> *You who lead the way. I shall eat the people afterwards.*

Now they took the rest of the cattle and gave them to him. He swallowed them, too. Then that rock said again:

> Rue le, le rue, *I shall eat you,* Thakane, *my child,*
> *You who lead the way. I shall eat the people afterwards.*

The daughter said, "You may eat the people too." She gave him some and her father ate them.

They tried then to pass on, but he stopped them again, saying:

> Rue le, le rue, *I shall eat you,* Thakane, *my child,*
> *You who lead the way. I shall eat the people afterwards.*

So she took the rest of these unfortunate people and gave them to her father, and all were eaten. There remained only *Thakane* and *Masilo* and their two children, *Lilahloane* and a younger one. As they were trying to pass, the rock blocked the way. It said again:

Rue le, le rue, *I shall eat you,* Thakane, *my child,*
You who lead the way. I shall eat the people afterwards.

She gave herself up to her father with her husband and her children. All of them were eaten, they went into her father's belly. Inside it there was a cavern made of flesh. They found there a young man who was making a hole in the wall of that belly. The other people in there were telling him, "You will bring harm on us," but he went on hacking out pieces of flesh. He cut and he cut until he finally opened a door out of the belly. And then it died, that rock, it fell down.

Now, people came out of it, many people—the only ones who stayed were the decayed ones the rock had eaten long ago. The people who had just entered it went out as well as many others, and also the cattle still living and walking in the belly of that rock. All these people could now return home.

Then *Thakane* and *Masilo* went to her mother's village. When they arrived it was like a miracle, because her mother and brother had heard nothing about *Thakane* for such a long time. They sat down, they were happy, they wept for joy. Cattle were slaughtered for a feast. That woman and her husband were well received.

It is the end of the tale.

—*Basuto*

92

A Woman's Quest

Another story is coming. Stop talking and listen.

There was a very handsome young man, very handsome, and he was called *Dzerikpana*—his public name. Every young lady liked *Dzerikpana,* wanted him, and fell in love with him, but he was fed up with them all. They did not know *Dzerikpana*'s birthname, the private one, which was *Dzerikpoli.* Nor did they know where he came from. One day he told his father, *Na,* that there were so many girls who loved him that he did not know which one of them to marry. So he devised a trick. He would lie down and Father *Na* would cover him with a funerary cloth, and tell all the girls that if any of them knew his name, he would marry her. So *Na* covered him and all the girls in this district were told that their future husband was dead, and if any one of them could weep and call *Dze*'s private name, then he would wake up from death and marry that girl. Girls from *Zongo* came, but did not know the right name. Girls from *Saa* also came, but could not succeed. Girls from *Kpagru* came to try, but they failed too. Women from *Tshere* came, but they did not know *Dze*'s real name either. Good-time girls from *Wa* also came, but failed. Then one woman, on her way from *Kpongu* to *Busa,* said she would go and say *Dze*'s name and marry him because of his handsomeness.

From *Kpongo,* she passed by *Sukpayiri* and walked toward *Nayiri.* On the way, she saw an old woman taking her bath. The old woman said, "My granddaughter," and the young woman greeted her in return. And the old woman said, "Come and wash my back for me before you go." The young woman agreed and went to wash her back, and when she had finished, she said that she had finished. Then the old woman said, "Granddaughter, it is all right! But at *Busa,* there is a man whose name is *Dzerikpoli.*" The young woman thanked her for telling her the name of the handsome young man. From there, she started for *Busa* and took the road that passes by the old police station and the chief's farms. On the way to *Busa,* she started her song:

O Dzerikpoli,
I will marry Dzerikpoli-*o!*
O Dzerikpoli, *I will marry* Dzerikpoli.

Dze's father and mother had built a long compound with seven rooms, and kept his corpse in the last, the seventh room, well barred with large doors. As the girl sang *Dze*'s private name, the first door swung open. *Dze* could hear her song when she was still at the chief's farm, so he also started his song:

Oh, oh, oh, my mother,
Open the doors for me.
Wo, wo, wo, *my mother,*
Open the doors and let me out.

Another door opened. On nearing *Kampaha,* the girl sang again:

O Dzerikpoli,
I will marry Dzerikpoli-*o!*
O Dzerikpoli, *I will marry* Dzerikpoli.

The third door opened. The young man heard her, and also repeated his song:

Oh, oh, oh, my mother,
Open the doors for me.
Wo, wo, wo, *my mother,*
Open the doors and let me out.

And another door was opened, leaving three.

The girl then went some few yards from *Tokoro* hill, and started her song again. *Dze* heard her and again he sang his song. Another door was opened. Now the young woman could see the walls of *Vaara* and started singing again. The good-time girls, on hearing this woman sing *Dze*'s name, were all surprised and stood watching her as she approached. Then they stood up and started weeping: "*Wolu, wolu, wolu, wolu*—who is this strange woman from another place who has been able to find out this man's name though we *gentras,* good-time girls, and *tutuhi,* prostitutes, have not been able to know it?" While they were saying all this, the girl sang again, this time louder:

O Dzerikpoli,
I will marry Dzerikpoli-*o!*
O Dzerikpoli, *I will marry* Dzerikpoli.

The young man, now left with two doors to pass through, also sang his song:

Oh, oh, oh, my mother,
Open the doors for me.
Wo, wo, wo, *my mother,*
Open the doors and let me out.

At this, another door was opened and he was left with one door to pass through. Still, the *Zongo* women, the *Nantiri* women, and the *Wa* prostitutes stood wondering how this woman, who was a stranger, got to know *Dze*'s name, and would thus now have the chance of marrying him.

When the woman was a few steps from where *Dze* was, she started her song again:

O Dzerikpoli,
I will marry Dzerikpoli-*o!*
O Dzerikpoli, *I will marry* Dzerikpoli.

After this, the last door opened and *Dze* came out, and said, "This woman, who has found out my name, she shall be my wife." *Dze* then went and embraced the woman and they started, *kiri, kiri, kiri,* fast toward *Wa*.

On the way, as they were nearing *Kampaha* village, they saw the old woman bathing again. She asked the young woman to come and wash her back, but the young woman, hearing this, turned sharply, and said, "Stop that nonsense! How can I be marrying such a nice young man and come and wash the back of an old woman?"

After this, the two passed by *Kampaha* and, while there, the woman was turned into a leper. At that moment, the young man said, "Why should there be so many beautiful girls and I marry you, a leper?" And then he ran away as fast as he could. Immediately, the leper started, *kpidu, kpidu, kpidu,* running after him. They chased each other until they were in the middle of a thick bush. The man turned into a reed, the type used for making mats lain on by women who have just given birth. The leper turned into a *daangu*, the fiber used to weave the reeds together to make the mats.

A weaver then went to cut the reed and the fiber to weave a mat. After the mat was made, a woman who had just given birth bought it, and while she lay on it, it made some noise, *miu, miu, miu.* This sound shows that the leper has not stopped running after the young man and the young man has also not stopped running.

—*Wala*

93

Never Ask Me About My Family

Long, long ago when the *Ndemi* and the *Ngumba* were ruling our country there was a young man called *Mwenendega*. He was a handsome youngster, but his father was very poor. They had neither cattle nor food enough for their sustenance.

One day *Mwenendega* went down to a small river not far from his home. When approaching the left bank of the river, he saw a beautiful girl, very attractive, fair as the moon and bright as the stars in the sky, with a halo on her head like a rainbow. She was timid and silent like the sun.

The youngster greeted her with hesitation and fear, and asked: "Kind and beautiful girl, how are you?"

"I am very well, perhaps better than you."

"Gracious girl, where is your home?"

"Why do you put a question like that to me? I have no father, no mother, and nowhere to stay."

"If that is the truth, would you agree to come with me and become my beloved wife?"

The girl looked pleased and, smiling graciously, answered with a sweet voice: "With great pleasure I consent, but on one essential condition, which is this: During all our companionship, in fact, during all our life, you must never ask me about my father, my mother, or my country of origin." *Mwenendega* answered that he found the condition very reasonable, and accepted it entirely. "I will never ask about your father or mother or your country during all our life."

And so she gave him her hand and cheerfully both climbed the riverbank, making for the boy's village. *Mwenendega* built a large and beautiful hut for his bride-to-be, and in a few days they married. They arranged for a great celebration to solemnize the event. The relations were invited and they came in great number. There was a family dance and after that, there was a great feast with singing, drinking, and merrymaking. People were greatly surprised at the beauty of the girl.

Many years passed in peace and love and mutual understanding. During those happy years, seven children were born to *Mwenendega* and he was very pleased with each new addition to his family. The children grew and the time arrived when the first-born had to go through the rites of circumcision. I am going to tell you now what happened at that event. When the solemn rites were near the end, just before each of the initiates shaved the hair of his head, *Mwenendega* said to his beloved wife: "Darling, from the day of our marriage until now, I have never seen your father or your mother. What has prevented them from coming today to see their grandchildren, how fine and strong they are? Don't you think that they should have taken part in this family feast?"

Good heavens! That was the start of a disaster! At the sound of those words the gentle lady suddenly grew frantic. She rose from the ground like a bouncing ball, and fell down heavily on the earth, making a hole seven miles deep, all the while shooting in the air stones, trees, rubble, and mud, like a blast of gunpowder. Meanwhile, she shouted with an awful cry, "My father, my mother, and all my kinfolk, where are they? Children of *Mboto,* come out." After that cry, the old spirits came down in great number from the top of Mount Kenya carrying beer, goats, cattle, and food. They went straight to *Mwenendega*'s house to play havoc. A long blast from a horn was heard in the valley and a heavy roar of drum beating followed. There was a great noise in the air and on earth. A frightful storm of hail soon covered the ground with iced stones. The thunder was rumbling in the sky with a terrific noise and the lightning was flashing from one end of the country to the other, like a great conflagaration. Terrified, the inhabitants took refuge in the huts and in the caverns nearby. Then the old spirits started to pour beer on the earth, and in a few instants the country was flooded and looked like Lake *Naivasha.* Shall I tell you what the old spirits made of the poor *Mwenendega?* They surrounded him, and in the twinkling of an eye they carried him and his wife and his children to the top of Mount Kenya, and buried them in a big hole under the stones.

So when you look at Mount Kenya, remember this story. It is the reason why our people, when they make a sacrifice or slaughter a goat, turn themselves toward Mount Kenya to glance at the white spot, lest some misfortune happen to them as it did to those others. This sad event occurred in this, our *Kikuyu* country, long, long ago.

—*Kikuyu*

94
A Man Marries a Lioness

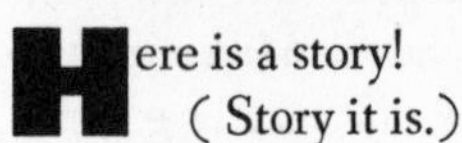

Here is a story!
(Story it is.)

The goats of Kimona-ngombe *are asleep;*
The slave of Kimona-ngombe *is asleep;*
The hen of Kimona-ngombe *is asleep;*
The pig of Kimona-ngombe *is asleep;*
The sheep of Kimona-ngombe *is asleep;*
Kimona-ngombe *himself is asleep,*
Kimona-ngombe *himself is asleep.*

I will tell you all a story of lions, who are, as all know, second only to elephants in strength and power. One time there were no lions here on the land, but then they came and settled here. One year there was a terrible famine that came upon the earth. There was no place anyone could go to eat for there was no food, and the lions began to wander around, looking everywhere for something to feed themselves and their families.

So they got together and spoke among themselves, wondering where they could try next. "What are we going to do? We are all so hungry." One of them said, "Well, Man always has his cattle. So we must go out and find Man." One of them asked, "But how do we get there? We have always shied away from Man, and I don't even know where he lives!" The first one said, "They don't live so far away. I'm sure maybe as close as one day's walk. We just have to go looking."

They started out, and before they knew it, they found themselves on the outskirts of one of the villages. One of the young lionesses, then, was turned into a human being so they could have someone go in and find out what was going on in the village, how many cattle were left, and where they might find other food if they needed it. The others dressed her and trimmed her hair, so she was beautiful to look at. Then they told her what she must look for and what she must say to the headman of the village: "You will pass through the village of a man who is well known for having many head of cattle, by the name of *Ngana Kimona-ngombe kia na Mbua*, 'The Owner of Mr. Dog's cattle.' When you pass this man, he'll stop you, and you must pay him proper respect by saying, 'Good sir, I am going to see my brother who lives in the next village.' *Kimona-ngombe* sees you, he is certain to want to talk with you and have you for his wife, for you have been made to look like such a beautiful young woman. You must agree to marry him, and then you can kill him and we can catch all of his cattle to eat." She agreed to all of this, and took to the road.

She arrived at *Kimona-ngombe*'s gate and saw him there sitting at the entrance to his house. He asked, "You, young woman! Where are you going?" just as they said he would. And she replied, "I'm going to visit my brother who lives in the next village. But I'm so tired and thirsty, may I sit and have a little water to drink?" He sent his servants right away to bring her some water and he welcomed her into his yard. He began talking with her right away, he was so struck with her beauty. *Ngana Kimona-ngombe* asked her, "Young woman, are you married already?" and she replied, "Not yet." He proposed to her immediately and she accepted, saying, "You have a fine house, many servants and cattle here." She said, "I must go home first to tell my parents. I'll return in two days."

She went back to where the lions were staying and told everyone what had happened: "It worked. *Kimona-ngombe* has talked to me and asked me to marry him." The others, when they heard, were overjoyed. The woman slept for two days and then went back to the man's house and found him there. He was so glad to see her again, he had a goat killed for her, and she had her fill. Then they built her a house in preparation for the marriage, and she went into it.

That night, *Ngana Kimona-ngombe* said, "I am going to sleep in the house of my new bride." His son from his first wife clung to his father, begging to be allowed to sleep wherever he slept. His mother said to him, "Your father is going to sleep in his new bride's house. You must let go." But he kept on crying. Finally his father said, "Well, the child is hanging on and crying so, let him come along with me."

So they came to his bride's house and went in and sat on the bed. She said, "The chief has come with a child. How did this happen?" And he said, "Well, he was hanging on to me and crying so hard, and just wouldn't stay with his mother." So they lay down on the ground to go to sleep, the woman and the man and his child.

In the middle of the night, the woman got up and turned back into a lioness and went to catch the man to kill him. The son, who was lying behind the man, saw her and woke his father up, saying, "Father, there is an animal here in the house who is going to bite you." So the man got up, and the lioness quickly changed herself back to a woman.

Day came and went, and the next evening arrived. Again the man brought his crying son with him. The woman said, "Oh, Chief, last night the child kept waking you up so that you couldn't get a good night's rest. Why did you bring him along again?" The chief said, "Well, he was crying and carrying on so much I just brought him along." So again they went to sleep.

In the middle of the night, the woman heard the other lions calling to her: "You were going to kill *Kimona-ngombe kia na Mbua,* so why don't you do it?" The woman answered:

The goat of Kimona-ngombe *is asleep;*
The slave of Kimona-ngombe *is asleep;*
The hen of Kimona-ngombe *is asleep;*
The pig of Kimona-ngombe *is asleep;*
The sheep of Kimona-ngombe *is asleep;*
Kimona-ngombe *himself is asleep;*
But his son never seems to sleep;
His son never seems to sleep!

After singing this, the woman turned into a lioness; again she wanted to catch the man. The son, who was lying behind the man, woke him up, saying, "Father, there is an animal here who is going to bite you." His father replied, "The house is brand-new; what animal can get in to bite me?" The son said, "Roaches and maggots on the ground." His father answered him, "Child, you're lying. I'm not going to listen." They slept again a little while longer.

The woman heard the others calling to her: "You went to kill *Kimona-ngomba kia na Mbua,* are you coming back to us or not?" Again she sang:

The goat of Kimona-ngombe *is asleep;*
The slave of Kimona-ngombe *is asleep;*
The hen of Kimona-ngombe *is asleep;*
The pig of Kimona-ngombe *is asleep;*
Kimona-ngombe *himself is asleep;*
But his son never seems to sleep;
His son never seems to sleep!

The child *Ndala* stood up and said, "Father, get up! there is a wild beast in here." Now his father got angry and said, "Let's go. I'm taking you back to your mother. You are disturbing my sleep!"

They went outside in the middle of the night. The son then told his father, "Your new wife has been turning into a wild beast." His father said, "My son, you're lying to me." The son said, "I'm telling you the truth, Father. Let's go back into the house and you will see what I mean." They went back and lay down.

The wife said, "You were going to take the child back to his mother. Why did you bring him back?" The man said, "The child would not stop crying." They lay down again, and the man covered himself with his cloth over his head; but he was looking.

The woman heard the other lions calling again: "You went to kill *Kimona-ngombe kia na Mbua*, are you ever coming back? She answered, saying:

The goat of Kimona-ngombe *is asleep;*
The slave of Kimona-ngombe *is asleep;*
The hen of Kimona-ngombe *is asleep;*
The pig of Kimona-ngombe *is asleep;*
The sheep of Kimona-ngombe *is asleep;*
Kimona-ngombe *himself is asleep, falsely;*
But his son never seems to sleep;
His son never seems to sleep!

The woman then turned into a lioness again. She went to the man, but *Kimona-ngombe* saw her. Now he believed what *Ndala* had been telling him: "*Ndala* spoke the truth." He got up and said, "My child, let's get out of here. I'll take you back to your mother!" They went outside, and he put him into the house of his mother. *Ngana Kimona-ngombe* told the village and his slaves that same night that they must set the house on fire. "The woman that I just married keeps turning into a lioness." They surrounded the house and set it on fire. The woman was roasted in the house. The day breaks.

And so it will always be: having children leads you on the way of truth. A woman was going to kill *Ngana Kimona-ngombe*, but his child, *Ndala*, saved his life.

So the story ends.

Bibliography

Parenthetical references indicate the specific group or country from which tales were collected.

Alland, Alexander, Jr. *When the Spider Danced.* Garden City, N.Y.: Anchor Press/Doubleday, 1975. (*Abron*)

Beidelman, T.O. "Eleven Kaguru Texts." *African Studies* 26. Johannesburg: Witwatersrand University Press, 1967. (*Kaguru*)

Bender, C.J. *African Jungle Tales.* Girard, Kan., 1919. (*Kpe*)

Biebuyck, Daniel, and Mateene, Kahombo C. *The Mwindo Epic.* Berkeley and Los Angeles: University of California Press, 1969. (*Nyanga*)

Bomeisler, Brian. "Legends Told by the Ituri Pigmies." Unpublished manuscript. (*Ituri*)

Bowen, Elinore Smith. *Return to Laughter.* Garden City, N.Y.: Anchor Press/ Doubleday, 1964.

Cagnolo, C. "Kikuyu Tales." *African Studies* 11, nos. 1 and 3. Johannesburg: Witwatersrand University Press, 1952. (*Kikuyu*)

Camara, Sony. "Tales in the Night: Toward an Anthropology of the Imaginary." In *Varia Folklorica,* ed. Alan Dundes. The Hague: Mouton and Co., 1978.

Camphor, A.P. *Missionary Story Sketches.* Cincinnati: Jennings and Graham, 1909. (*Liberia*)

Cardinall, A.W. *Tales Told in Togoland.* Oxford: Oxford University Press, 1931. (*Ashanti, Dagomba, Grumshi, Krachi, Togo*)

Cosentino, Donald. *Defiant Maids and Stubborn Farmers: Tradition and Invention in Mende Story Performance.* London and New York: Cambridge University Press, 1982. (*Mende*)

Dennet, R.E. *Notes on the Folklore of the Fjort.* London: The Folklore Society, 1894. (*Fjort*)

Edgar, Frank. *Hausa Tales and Traditions*, trans. Neil Skinner. New York: Africana Publishing Corp., 1973. (*Hausa*)

Egudu, Romanus N. *The Calabash of Wisdom and Other Igbo Stories*. New York: Nok Publishers International, 1973. (*Igbo*)

Ellis, A.B. *The Ewe-Speaking Peoples*. London: Chapman & Hall, 1890. (*Ewe, Vai*)

Ellis, George W. *Negro Culture in West Africa*. New York: Neale Publishing Co., 1914.

Evans-Pritchard, E.E. *The Zande Trickster*. Oxford: Oxford University Press, 1967. (*Zande*)

Fikry, Mona. *Wa: A Case Study of Social Tensions as Reflected in the Oral Traditions of the Wala of Northern Ghana*. Ann Arbor, Mich.: University Microfilms International, 1969. (*Wala*)

Finnegan, Ruth. *Limba Stories and Storytelling*. Oxford: Oxford University Press, 1967. (*Limba*)

Fox, D.C., and Frobenius, Leo. *African Genesis*. New York: Stackpole Sons, 1937. (*Soninke*)

Frobenius, Leo. *Atlantis*, vols. 7 and 9. Veröffentlichung d. Forschungs-Institut für Kulturmorphologie. Jena: Eugen Diederichs Verlag, 1921–28. (*Hausa, Karekare*)

Gecau, Rose N. *Kikuyu Folktales*. Nairobi: East African Literature Bureau, 1970. (*Kikuyu*)

Hauge, Hans-Egil. *Luo Religion and Folklore*. Oslo: Universitetsforlaget, 1974. (*Luo*)

Herskovits, Frances S., and Herskovits, Melville J. *Dahomean Narrative*. Evanston, Ill.: Northwestern University Press, 1958. (*Dahomey*)

Honëy, James A. *South-African Folk-Tales*. New York: Baker & Taylor, 1910. (*Amalouw, Amakosa*)

Jacottet, E. *The Treasury of Basuto Lore*. London: Kegan Paul, French, Trübner, 1908. (*Basuto*)

Johnson, Frederick. "Kiniramba Folk Tales." *Bantu Studies* 5, no. 4. Johannesburg: Witwatersrand University Press, 1931. (*Kiniramba*)

Johnston, H.A.S. *A Selection of Hausa Stories.* Oxford: Oxford University Press, 1966. (*Hausa*)

Junot, H.A. *The Life of a South African Tribe.* New York: University Books, 1962. (*Thanga*)

LaPin, Deirdre. *Story, Medium and Masque: The Idea and Art of Yoruba Storytelling.* Ann Arbor, Mich.: University Microfilms International, 1977. (*Yoruba*)

Larson, Thomas J. "Epic Tales of the Mbukushu." *African Studies* 22, no. 4. Johannesburg: Witwatersrand University Press, 1963. (*Bantu*)

Lindblom, Gerhard. "Kumba Folklore." *Archives d'Etudes Orientales* 20, no. 1 (1928); no. 2 (1935). (*Kumba*)

Mbiti, John S. *Akamba Stories.* Oxford: Oxford University Press, 1966. (*Akamba*)

Metelerkamp, Samm. *Outa Karel's Stories.* London: Macmillan & Co., 1914. (*S. Africa*)

Noss, Philip A. "Gbaya Tales Collected." In *African Folklore,* ed. Richard M. Dorson. Garden City. N.Y.: Anchor Press/Doubleday, 1972. (*Gbaya*)

Rattray, R. Sutherland. *Hausa Folklore, Customs, Proverbs.* Oxford: Oxford University Press, 1913. (*Hausa*)

Roscoe, John. *The Baganda.* London: Frank Cass & Co., Ltd., 1911. (*Baganda*)

Smith, Edwin W. *The Ila-Speaking Peoples.* London: Macmillan & Co., 1920. (*Ila*)

Stannus, H.S. "The Wayao of Nyssaland." *Harvard African Studies* 3 (1922). (*Wayao*)

Theal, George McCall. *Kaffir Folk-Lore.* London, 1882. (*Kaffir*)

Torday, E. *On the Trail of the Bushongo.* London: Seeley Service & Co., 1925. (*Luba*)

Torrend, J. *Specimens of Bantu Folklore*. London: Kegan Paul, French, Trübner, 1921. (*Bantu, Berre-MuKuni*)

Willis, Roy. *There Was a Certain Man: Spoken Art of the Fipa*. Oxford: Oxford University Press, 1978. (*Fipa*)

Woodward, H.W. "Bondei Folktales." *Folklore* 36 (1925). (*Bondei*)

Permissions Acknowledgments

Grateful acknowledgment is made to the following for permission to reprint or adapt from previously published material. In the case of adaptation, the author may have retitled some of the tales:

"The Contest of Riddles" from *When the Spider Danced* by Alexander Alland, Jr. Copyright © 1975 by Alexander Alland, Jr. By permission of Doubleday & Co., Inc.

"The Boy and the Bird" from "Eleven Kaguru Texts" (in *African Studies* 26, pp. 34–35) by T.O. Beidelman. Copyright © 1967 by Witwatersrand University Press. By permission of Witwatersrand University Press.

The Mwindo Epic by Daniel Biebuyck and Kahombo C. Mateene. Copyright © 1969 by The Regents of the University of California. By permission of the University of California Press.

Excerpt from *Return to Laughter* by Elinore Smith Bowen. Copyright © 1954 by Laura Bohannan. By permission of Doubleday & Co., Inc.

"The Frog and the Chameleon" and "Mwenendega and the Daughter of Wagothe" from "Kikuyu Tales" (in *African Studies* 11, pp. 125–127 and 3–4, respectively) by C. Cagnolo. Copyright © 1952 by Witwatersrand University Press. By permission of Witwatersrand University Press.

"The Five Helpers"; "Friends for a Time"; "Friendship True and False"; "Three Wives"; and "Wondrous Powers: Mirror, Sandals, and a Medicine Bag" from *Tales Told in Togoland* by A.W. Cardinall. By permission of the International African Institute, London, and Ada Cardinall.

"A Competition of Lies" from *Defiant Maids and Stubborn Farmers: Tradition and Invention in Mende Story Performance* by Donald Cosentino. Copyright © 1982 by Cambridge University Press. By permission of the author and Cambridge University Press.

"Rabbit and Carnivores" from *African Folklore* by Richard M. Dorson. Copyright © 1972 by Richard M. Dorson, collected and translated by Philip A. Noss from the narration of Daniel Ndanga. By permission of Doubleday & Company, Inc.

"The Chief's Daughter and Her Husband and the Chief's Son"; "The Chief's Son, the Poor Man's Son, and the Chief's Daughter"; "The Devil, the Girl, and Her Young Man"; "The Digger-Out of Ground Squirrels and His Son and the Arab"; "The Four Champions"; "The Maiden, the Two Young Men, and the Lion"; "The Man, His Womenfolk, the Well, and the Soldier" from *Hausa Tales and Traditions* by Frank Edgar. Translated by Neil Skinner. Copyright © 1973 by Africana Publishing Corp. By permission of Africana Publishing Corp., 30 Irving Pl., New York, NY 10003, and Frank Cass & Co., Ltd., London.

"The Two Sisters" and "Working for the Tiger" from *The Calabash of Wisdom and Other Igbo Stories* by Romanus N. Egudu. Copyright © 1973 by Romanus N. Egudu. By permission of Nok Publishers International.

"Ture and the Woman's Dogs" from *The Zande Trickster* (pp. 217–223), edited by E.E. Evans-Pritchard. Copyright © Oxford University Press 1967. By permission of Oxford University Press.

Excerpts from *Wa: A Case Study of Social Tensions as Reflected in the Oral Traditions of the Wala of Northern Ghana* by Mona Fikry. Copyright © 1969 by Mona Fikry. By permission of the author.

"Four Wives" from *Limba Stories and Story-Telling* (pp. 152–155) by Ruth Finnegan. Copyright © Oxford University Press 1967. By permission of Oxford University Press.

"The Hare and the Spider" from *Luo Religion and Folklore* by Hans-Egil Hauge. Copyright © 1974 by Universitetsforlaget. By permission of Universitetsforlaget.

"Leopard and Cat," "Outwitting Thieves," and "Profitable Amends: A Wife for One Cowry" from *Dahomean Narrative* by Frances S. Herskovits and Melville J. Herskovits. Copyright © 1958 by Northwestern University Press. By permission of Northwestern University Press.

"The Story of the Hare and the Small Buck" from "Kiniramba Folktales" (in *Bantu Studies* 5, pp. 347–348) by Frederick Johnson. Copyright © 1931 by Witwatersrand University Press. By permission of Witwatersrand University Press.

"The Snake, the Farmer, and the Heron" from *A Selection of Hausa Stories* (pp. 48–49), compiled and translated by H.A.S. Johnston. Copyright © Oxford University Press 1966. By permission of Oxford University Press.

"Monkey Steals a Drum" from *Story, Medium and Masque: The Idea and Art of Yoruba Storytelling* by Deirdre LaPin. Copyright © 1977 by Deirdre LaPin. By permission of the author.

"The Epic of the Great Dikithi" from "Epic Tales of the Mbukushu" (in *African Studies* 22, pp. 179–182) by Thomas J. Larson. Copyright © 1963 by Witwatersrand University Press. By permission of Witwatersrand University Press.

"A Man Who Could Transform Himself," "A Rich Man and a Poor Man," and "The King's Daughter Who Lost Her Hair" from *Akamba Stories* (pp. 133–135, 129–131, and 120–126) by John S. Mbiti. Copyright © Oxford University Press 1966. By permission of Oxford University Press.

"How the Friendship of Hare and Jackal Came to an End," "The Jealous Women," "The Man and the Muskrat," and "Tungululi and the Monsters" from *There Was a Certain Man: Spoken Art of the Fipa* (pp. 46–47, 62–66, 56–59, and 87–90), translated and edited by Roy Willis. Copyright © Roy Willis 1978. By permission of Oxford University Press.

Index of Tales

ABOUT THE AUTHOR

Roger D. Abrahams is Professor of Folklore and Folklife at the University of Pennsylvania in Philadelphia. He holds a B.A. from Swarthmore College, an M.A. from Columbia University, and a Ph.D. from the University of Pennsylvania. He is a past president of the American Folklore Society, a former chairman of the English Department at the University of Texas, and a Phi Beta Kappa Visiting Scholar.

Professor Abrahams has done fieldwork in a range of Afro-American communities, from a ghetto neighborhood in Philadelphia to the Caribbean. He has also studied and written about Anglo-American folk songs and children's lore. He has contributed widely to academic folklore journals as well as to such magazines as *Smithsonian*, and his most recent books include *The Man-of-Words in the West Indies, After Africa* (with John Szwed), and *Afro-American Folktales*, the companion volume to this book.

The Pantheon Fairy Tale and Folklore Library

African Folktales: Traditional Stories of the Black World
selected and retold by Roger D. Abrahams
0-394-72117-9

"A rousing good read....I suspect Mr. Abrahams' book will be read a generation hence." —*New York Times Book Review*

Afro-American Folktales: Stories from Black Traditions in the New World
selected and edited by Roger D. Abrahams
0-394-72885-8

"Wonderful...very human and often very funny." —*Booklist*

America in Legend: Folklore from the Colonial Period to the Present
by Richard M. Dorson
0-394-70926-8

"A scholarly book and a popular one....It all comes together joyously, grandly....It will rightly find a large reading audience."
— *Chronicle of Higher Education*

American Indian Myths and Legends
edited by Richard Erdoes and Alfonso Ortiz
0-394-74018-1

"Probably the most comprehensive and diverse collection of American Indian legends ever compiled. It is a worthy and welcome addition to the literature of our native peoples." — Dee Brown

Arab Folktales
translated and edited by Inea Bushnaq
0-394-75186-8

"A marvelous hoard of popular recited tales, witty and earthy, fanciful and mundane in equal measure. Rarely has a people's authentic spirit been so close at hand." — Edward W. Said

Chinese Fairy Tales and Fantasies
translated and edited by Moss Roberts
0-394-73994-9

"An enthralling collection." —*Los Angeles Times*

The Complete Grimm's Fairy Tales
introduction by Padraic Colum
folkloristic commentary by Joseph Campbell
translated by Margaret Hunt and James Stern
0-394-70930-6

"Everyone should possess and know *Grimm's Fairy Tales*—one of the great books of the world—and no English-speaking person could do better than this edition." —*New York Times Book Review*

Eighty Fairy Tales
by Hans Christian Andersen
translated by R. P. Keigwin
0-394-71055-X

"The stories shine." —*Philadelphia Inquirer*

An Encyclopedia of Fairies: Hobgoblins, Brownies, Bogies, and Other Supernatural Creatures
by Katharine Briggs
0-394-73467-X

"*An Encyclopedia* offers a supernatural host of legends, ballads, folk tales—and more than enough hobgoblins and dragons to fill minds little or large." —*Times* (London)

Favorite Folktales from Around the World
edited by Jane Yolen
0-394-75188-4

"A much-needed treasure...Here is a book which returns us all, child and adult, to our true roots." —Madeleine L'Engle

Folk-Tales of the British Isles
edited by Kevin Crossley-Holland
0-394-75553-7

"A marvelous introduction to the rich and varied storytelling traditions of the British Isles."
—*Time Literary Supplement*

French Folktales
by Henri Pourrat
selected by C. G. Bjurström and translated by Royall Tyler
0-394-54451-X (hardcover)

"Pourrat developed a unique style that captures the vigorous spirit of French folklore, and his diverse stories will enchant readers young and old." —Jack Zipes

Gods and Heroes: Myths and Epics of Ancient Greece
by Gustav Schwab
0-394-73402-5

"A superb volume—keystone for the home library—full of the magic that should be part of our young citizens' inheritance."
—*New Yorker*

Irish Folktales
edited by Henry Glassie
0-394-74637-6

"*Irish Folktales* contains plenty of what Joyce called 'laughtears,' a lot of mysteriousness, and even a bit of splendor." —Richard Ellmann

Italian Folktales
selected and retold by Italo Calvino
translated by George Martin
0-394-74909-X

"This book is impossible to recommended too highly."
—John Gardner, *New York Times Book Review*

Japanese Tales
edited and translated by Royall Tyler
0-394-75656-8

"Enchanting...the stories are variously witty, allegorical, mystical, gross, funny, and enigmatic....Tyler's poised translations are something of a masterpiece." —*Publishers Weekly*

The Norse Myths
introduced and retold by Kevin Crossley-Holland
0-394-74846-8

"Cheers for Kevin Crossley-Holland....He is a poet as well as a scholar, and it is in the myths themselves that his passions are most eloquent." —*Village Voice*

Northern Tales
selected and edited by Howard Norman
0-394-54060-3 (hardcover)

"[An] extraordinary, wide-ranging collection of northern tales which are, in turn, serious, funny, harsh, romantic, ribald, mournful—and wise."—Jane Yolen

Norwegian Folk Tales
Peter Christen Asbjørnsen and Jørgen Moe, compilers
translated by Pat Shaw Iversen and Carl Norman
0-394-71054-1
"A distinguished book of lasting value."—*Commonweal*

The Old Wives' Fairy Tale Book
edited by Angela Carter
0-394-58764-2 (hardcover)

"A reminder of how wise, clever, perceptive, occasionally lyrical, eccentric, sometimes downright crazy our great-grandmothers were, and their great-grandmothers."
—From the Introduction

Russian Fairy Tales
Aleksandr Afanas'ev
translated by Norbert Guterman
folkoristic commentary by Roman Jakobson
0-394-73090-9

"A beautiful book. I recommended it for all readers, young and old, who are interested in the folktale and its unique qualities."
—Isaac Bashevis Singer, *New York Times Book Review*

The Victorian Fairy Tale Book
edited by Michael Patrick Hearn
0-679-73258-6

"A superb new anthology...pure enchantment."
—*Washington Post Book World*

Yiddish Folktales
edited by Beatrice Silverman Weinreich
translated by Leonard Wolf
0-679-73097-4

"This gem of a collection opens a breathtaking vista upon a vibrant world now lost to us."—Barbara Kirshenblatt-Gimblett